# THE
# MAINLAND

## SARA FRANCIS

**Book 2 of *The Terra Testimonies***

**PUBLISHING**

I dedicate this book to Mom, Dad,
Mary Grace, Therese, and Catherine.

They're my inspirations, my biggest fans, my book helpers,
and more. Without them, these books would've
never been brought to life. Love you all.

# IT HAS BEGUN.

# PROLOGUE
## Alison

If you are reading this now, it is safe to assume that my—Alison Alexus of the Biomechatronics Isle—and my siblings' record logs have fallen into your hands prior to this transcript.

You are aware of our testimonies and what happened at the Isles. You also must be wondering and aching to know how things came to be. Now, you will. During our long haul to the RRPR (Resist, Rescue, Protect, Retake) base, our friend Mark and his siblings Shane and Aymie have agreed to tell us their story. We can finally hear this "tale for another time" Mark always mentioned.

A note before you read their testimonies:

Understand that these are being recorded in real time. No side commentary has been removed from the final transcription. The storytellers are communicating with me and the other members as the tales are being told.

Also, do not worry if you lose track of individuals. Their stories span 25 years and many have come and gone. A list has been made for your convenience.

Their stories are important. Those who don't know our history are doomed to repeat it. That's what happened in our world. Our future

# THE MAINLAND

has been damaged enough, and we deserve to know why.

Now, we will.

# Chapter 1
## Shane: I

It was a crisp winter night and the wind howled its bittersweet song.

What do you mean wait? Hello? Is this thing on? Oh, it is? Awesome.

Wait, Aaron, tell me. This thing is recording my voice and writing it on paper at the same time? How does it do that? Okay fine I will begin, but you better show me later.

So I will explain a few facts about myself, as I was instructed, before going into my life story…like I was trying to do but was so rudely interrupted.

My name is Shane Hodgins, and I am a leading officer for Project Resist Rescue Protect Retake (RRPR). I am 25 years old and sibling of Mark and Aymie. I am tall and have brown hair and green eyes. I also have Aquaphobia, but we won't get into that now. I am a skilled and limber fighter and am also incredibly fast. Not to brag, but I am faster than any of the world champion Olympic runners.

Now, I will tell you everything from the beginning, and maybe some questions you have will be answered.

When my siblings and I were born, the world seemed at peace.

Nations were content, leaders were satisfied, and no one crossed each other. Well, that is what we thought anyway. There are always hidden secrets. You just have to go and find them. In the end, I feel like that's what my siblings and I were born to do.

On June 23rd, 25 years ago, my mother brought triplets into the world: two boys and one girl. These babies were her and her husband's pride and joy.

A few months later, their happiness became sorrow and things took a turn for the worst.

I'll be honest; I don't remember anything from that night because I was so young. However, my foster father told me the story he knew when I got older, but it was never the full picture. I learned the truth later on. But for right now, I will tell you exactly what he told me.

It was a crisp winter night and the wind howled its bittersweet song.

Man, I'm poetic…sorry, anyway:

We were behind locked doors, fast asleep, when unexpected visitors came. Their plan was to take and destroy everything my father loved before his very eyes, including us. I never understood what their motive was but I knew this for certain: their throats were parched and revenge was their only satisfaction.

It was around 2:00 AM when they arrived. *BANG!* They knocked down our door, barging in like madmen and scaring us awake.

Hearing the commotion, our father jumped to his feet and pulled a gun out of his dresser drawer. He was afraid this would happen... no, he knew this would happen. Kissing his wife for the last time, he dashed downstairs in an attempt to fight off the intruders.

Our mother was prepared for that day. Like our father, she knew it was coming. Scooping us up, she made her way out the back door and into the dark streets. She clutched us ever so tightly as she ran. She felt as if she was still being watched and followed, no matter how far away she was. She never felt safe. Tears streamed down her face as she realized what needed to be done. Wrapping her arms around the three of us, she performed her heartbreaking duty.

The first stop she made was to an older couples' house. They lived on a narrow city road next to an old alleyway. The location was one of the most dangerous in the entire state, but it was a perfect hiding spot… for one child.

Lovingly, she kissed her little boy goodbye as she placed him on the step, rang the doorbell, and rushed off. She had no time to even look back and see if her crying baby was taken inside. While she ran, she pressed her other two children to her chest and sobbed.

At dawn, she reached her second destination.

Further into the city was a large and beautiful white mansion, guarded by a tall black fence. The windows were dark and the place seemed lifeless. Determined, my mother somehow slipped through the gate and to the front door. She carefully put my sister down and knocked loudly.

While she was hastily leaving, she heard voices calling and dogs barking. A piece of her was relieved knowing that her little girl was safe.

With one baby left, she kept going for hours without stopping and dared not to look back.

It was late afternoon of the next day when she reached her final destination in the countryside. She was exhausted but never stopped. Walking up to the door, she held me and looked at me for the last time. She gently placed me, rang the bell, and left quickly without a trace.

Twenty minutes later, a middle aged couple returned from an evening drive when they found me crying on their front porch. Baffled, they went up to the step, knelt down, and caringly looked at me.

Around my neck they found a single dog tag. On one side was my full name, Shane Thomas Hodgins, and birthdate, June 23rd. On the back was a beautifully unique illuminated letter H. No one had ever seen anything like it. Underneath me was a handwritten note, relaying everything my mother just did and begging whoever had her baby to protect him and keep him safe.

The wife, Monika, picked me up and brought me inside to be fed. Meanwhile, her husband, Charles, searched all over for my mother, but she was nowhere to be found.

That day, they swore to raise me as their own and, when the time was right, help me find my family…even though they didn't know they'd never get the chance.

So, all that I've just told you was documented on that little piece of paper I was found with, but told in my mother's distressed words. She never mentioned the names of my siblings, their locations, who she was, or any other dangerous information. For my own good, the couple burned the letter after memorizing every last detail, destroying any evidence that my mother even existed. They feared that if someone were to come after me that letter could prove to be more of a detriment than a help. They only told me what the letter had said when I had just about reached the age of reason.

I had a peaceful and quiet life growing up with Charles—well, Chuck—and Monika Baldwin. They were simple farmers who always wanted a child of their own. Their prayers were answered and they raised me as their son. However, they insisted I call them Uncle and Aunt just in case my mother came back for me. They loved me enough to tell me the truth and to let me go when the time was right.

Growing up on the farm was a blast. When I was first able to walk, I would help Aunt Monika with house chores, shopping, and all the things that mothers would do. As I got a little older, I was allowed to work with Uncle Chuck in the fields. He taught me how to farm, care for animals, build, swim, play guitar, and everything else he knew.

At five, I started going to school, which wasn't too far away. The first month or so my uncle would drive me, but one day the car wouldn't start. Instead of skipping school while he fixed it, I asked if I could walk there. I knew exactly where it was and how to get there, so I told them I wouldn't get lost.

Uncle Chuck had no problem and thought it was a great idea. Aunt Monika, however, was hesitant and didn't want me to go. Finally, she succumbed to the childish pleas of her husband, and I walked to school on my own.

I loved it so much; I decided to do it every day no matter what the weather. As the weeks went by, I began timing myself with an old stopwatch I found in the garage. I wanted to get there faster every day; so I worked up to it slowly, increasing my speed a little at a time. At school, I could outrun all the older students. I had a gift for running.

Little did I know it was the only thing that would save my life.

When I was seven, I went on my first hiking trip.  My uncle always told me stories of how he and his wife would go up the mountain every month and have a picnic. Finally, they decided I could handle it. I enjoyed every moment racing up the side of that mountain.

Reaching the top, little me ran right to the edge. The view was breathtaking, and I could never forget it. The orange sun was just beginning to set behind the purple mountains, casting a shadow on the valleys below. The fluffy clouds reflected the pinkish sky and slowly covered whatever was left of the sun. As I looked out, I couldn't help but think about my real mother. Uncle Chuck and Aunt Monika had only told me a few weeks before what had happened…

However, my little mind was easily distracted. Aunt Monika called me for dinner and I hastily returned to them. As we sat on the grass and ate our sandwiches, I felt an uneasy feeling inside of me. I asked my aunt what was wrong. Looking at me with her caring blue eyes, she told me that I may just be dehydrated or tired. My uncle joked by saying that there may be something wrong with her cooking.

We stayed up there until the sun set. Uncle Chuck brought his guitar and played us old folk songs as my aunt and I caught lightning bugs. Finally, the night had ended and it was time to head back.

Climbing down the mountain, I felt my uneasiness worsening. I kept telling myself it was nothing and continued with a smile on my face. It was dark when we finally reached the bottom, and we were about to head in for the night.

Suddenly, we heard a crash in the chicken coop.

My uncle ran over with a pitch fork. Sometimes foxes would try to get in and eat the animals, so we thought it was no big deal.

Then the car alarm went off, followed by the sound of breaking glass.

Worried, my aunt grabbed me and pulled me inside. She instructed me to run upstairs and pack anything I thought I would need. By the tone of her voice, I knew we weren't coming back. I took as much as I could carry in my large knapsack, and went to meet my aunt.

There was no one outside. The only thing I found was Uncle Chuck's brown coat lying strewn across the muddy ground. Throwing on the jacket that hung past my knees, I searched for them desperately. After twenty minutes, I finally heard them calling my name.

Following the sound of their voices, I ran through the fields and out into the dark, eerie forest.  I darted through and found them kneeling on the other side of a river, banged up and bleeding with two strange men in black behind them. In the dark I could barely make out their appearance.

The first man had many odd tattoos on his chest going up his brown neck and onto his bald head. The inked image I could identify the clearest was a double edged sword going from behind his left ear and down his chest, disappearing beneath his black leather jacket. The second man had a lighter skin tone and clean cut dark hair. He appeared more "normal" than his larger companion but his demeanor was more sinister. Their menacing eyes glowed as they stared at me.

"Stay there son, we are okay," my uncle said. The fear in his face told me otherwise.

"Shane, we don't have all night so I will make this quick," the bald man said. The sound of my name coming out of a stranger's mouth terrified me beyond belief. "Come help us," he continued, "and we will let them go."

My aunt began to protest but the second figure clamped his hand over her mouth. Keeping her quiet, he looked to me as if waiting for an answer. I wasn't sure what to do, so I just stood there in shock.

It wasn't very long before the man with the dark hair got impatient. "We tried your way," he growled to his companion, "now let's do it my way." He grabbed my aunt's long white hair and plunged her head into the water. She struggled and tried to get free, but it was no use. He was too strong.

My uncle screamed, and I froze. I stood there helpless, watching her drown. Finally, she stopped flailing and was still. Her murderer kicked her body into the water and she floated downstream.

With tears dripping down his face, my uncle looked me in the eyes and whispered, "We love you, Shane. So please, run."

Those were his last words before the bald man slammed his face into the river.

My uncle put up a fight and nearly stood up, despite his injuries. He would've succeeded if the second man hadn't come to his comrade's aid. Together they drowned the only other family I had.

I began sobbing in hysterics watching my uncle's corpse float away. Then, they trudged through the water and went after me.

Once I saw them step into the river, I bolted. I was so frightened that I never looked back, and I never stopped going until dawn.

[Yes, I agree with you, Sami, it was awful. Please stop crying it'll make me cry.

[Thank you, Shannon; I am trying to be more poetic and descriptive like you said. Am I doing it well enough? Okay good, satisfactory is better than I thought.

[I'll go on for a few more minutes. Once we are ashore, we'll have to stop and get moving.]

The next day I was exhausted and didn't know where to go. I was lost. I was scared. I had run so far that I was in a completely different part of the state.

Walking through the small, unfamiliar town, I searched desperately for help. No one listened. I was brushed aside, yelled at, and insulted. They all thought I was just another pesky child from the foster care a town away. Apparently children escaped from there a lot.

Finally, I went to the police, but it was worse than just wandering. Instead of hearing me out, they threw me in the car and brought me to the foster care everyone complained about.

A tall dark fence surrounded the huge brick building. Children played about on the front lawn and in the playground around back.

The policeman dragged me through the wooden front doors and up to the owner. "Another one escaped," he said complaining. "You have to either fix those gates or hire more staff, because this is getting ridiculous."

Apologizing, the owner replied, "Yes I know, and I am sorry. Rooms have been filling up like crazy, and the kids are getting restless.

New ones come in every month, which is more than ever before. I don't know what's going on, but I'm starting to think something isn't right."

This must have happened often because the man in charge didn't realize I never belonged. They chatted for a few minutes, forgetting about me completely. The man just pushed me away to go with the other kids while he continued speaking with the officer. With nowhere to go, I obeyed and made myself at home.

At first I didn't mind it so much. I got fresh food, shelter, and a clean bathroom. I refused to bathe, however. Watching my only family drown took its toll on me. I never wanted to see water or come in contact with it ever. Hydration was a real challenge. I only drank out of dark bottles so I couldn't see what was inside. It helped a bit, but whenever the cold liquid went down my throat I began to feel as if I couldn't breathe like it was consuming me. I would drink it only as a means of survival and nothing more.

I stayed for a few months. After the first week, the boys knew I didn't belong and never let me into any of the bedrooms. So, I ended up sleeping outside. There was a small shed outback that I slept in if it was raining; otherwise I was on its roof underneath the stars. Every night I would look up and hope to be reunited with my family one day. With this hope, I would let myself drift to sleep… only to be greeted by nightmares.

Oh, we are here. All ashore that's going ashore! This is the west coast of America. From here we take automobiles to reach our first stop. Once we are all buckled up and ready to go again, I can continue if you would like. Yes? Okay; it seems like Aymie is procrastinating anyway. Yeah, you are!

# Chapter 2
## Shane: II

Welcome to the Mainland! This area is mostly in ruin and the grass is yellow but, as they say, the grass is greener on the other side. In this case it's miles away, but nonetheless the grass is nicer over there. We just have to be careful because the Xeno—I mean, the Invaders are everywhere. Right now we don't want to start a fight.

So, back to my story.

After a few months of sleeping outside the foster home, I decided to run away. My plan was that if I wasn't chosen by a family on adoption day I would run away and find my own… and that's as far as seven year-old-me planned. I felt like I didn't have a choice; so that day, I lined up with the kids same as always and hoped for the best.

A larger crowd than normal came in. I began to get excited. *One of them has to adopt me*, I hoped. Scanning the faces, I noticed two of the men that came in looked strangely familiar. Then I took a closer look and my hopes disappeared.

They were the men that killed my aunt and uncle.

My heart fell to my shoes as they walked about the room. I kept my head down, trying not to be spotted, but it was no use. To them I stuck out like a sore thumb. I looked up and was frozen with fear when the man with the dark hair looked into my eyes. A sinister smile crept across his narrow, tan face. He called to one of the workers, pointed to me, and whispered something to her.

I couldn't bear to stay and see what was to happen next. I rushed out of the room and to the backyard. Grabbing my things, I jumped on the shed and over the fence. I heard angry voices calling after me as I darted away. I wasn't sure where I was going, but I knew I had to get there.

I ran without ceasing for about an hour.  I thought I was finally far enough away until I heard the hum of engines and caught a whiff of gasoline. I knew in an instant it was them. I couldn't believe how desperate they were; there were no roads, only dirt paths. I was in the middle of nowhere and they found me. With no time to rest, I kept running.

It was dark when I came across people who weren't trying to kill me. There were a few trailers and a large tour bus parked in an old lot. Wanting refuge, I darted to the bus and banged on the door in hysterics.

A stout man wearing pajamas abruptly opened the door. He didn't see me at first, but when he did he stared, confused. He was unsure what to say, but let me in once he heard cars screeching to a halt. He locked the door and sent me to the back of the bus where some other people were sleeping.

"Huh? Who goes there?" a drowsy man asked. Sluggishly he turned on the light and stared at me.  He looked up at the round man, who nodded. Without waking the others, he told me to climb into a chest he had next to his dresser and stay perfectly still.

With no choice, I obeyed and was locked inside. From within, I could hear the box spring of his bed as he tucked himself back in and pretended to be asleep. There was nothing left to do but wait and listen.

"Open up! State police!" the men called as they banged on the bus door.

I couldn't clearly hear the conversation between them and the man who let me in, but I knew it wasn't going well. I heard angry grunts and footsteps as they stormed to the back and woke everyone up on the bus.

"Everybody, listen up," the first fake cop yelled. "There is a dangerous child on the loose and we saw him enter here. There is no use hiding him. You will only put yourselves in danger, so just hand him over."

No one said anything.

"Fine, now let's do things my way," the second one said. I didn't need to see his face to know it was the sinister skinny man.

I immediately heard them rummaging through things, looking in and under beds, and violently questioning the drowsy bystanders.

Then, I heard footsteps coming my way. My heart raced. After a few seconds of awful suspense, I heard the man walk away. I wondered if he had even opened the chest. Afraid, I held my breath until I knew they were gone.

There was some final shouting and then footsteps stomping away. A car engine started outside and then the sound faded as it became further away.

*Click.* The chest lid opened.

I almost shouted, but held my tongue once I saw that it was the stout man in pajamas with the one who hid me right behind him.

"Are you okay?" the bigger man asked, lifting me out of the chest. "You seem quite shaken."

"I'm okay," I replied weakly as he put me down. "No one got hurt did they?"

The thin man said, "Everyone is fine. Those men seemed very serious and violent, I am glad you came to us. They could have hurt you."

"Yes, undoubtedly," the other man said stroking his curly mustache. Kindly, he asked, "What's your name, boy?"

"Sh-shane Hodgins," I stammered.

With a smile, he replied, "It's a pleasure, Shane. My name is Duke Rogers, and I am the founder and ring leader of the Regal Circus."

[Yes, yes, Yared, I guess you can say that I ran away to join the circus. No, Nic, for the billionth time this one did not have a bearded lady.]

"And I am Edwin the Extravagant," the other man said bowing. He was a tall, lanky man with short blond hair. His eyes sparkled and were full of life even at that late hour. "I see my magic chest fooled that one imposter. He peeked inside once and left it alone."

I was perplexed. Young me was astounded that the chest was magic. "Really? He opened it and didn't see me?"

Smiling, the magic man replied, "Yes, he sure did! But I mustn't reveal my secrets. Besides, you are probably exhausted."

To be honest, I was ready to drop to the floor. I had been running nonstop for almost an entire day with no food or water. I thank God I have great stamina. It was a miracle I made it for that long.

Once Duke calmed the rest of the folks down he found some blankets for me to sleep on. "I hope you don't mind sleeping on the floor," he said fluffing a pillow. "Nonetheless, get some rest. You can explain everything tomorrow."

I took it and placed it on my blanket mattress. The moment my head hit the pillow I fell asleep, but my nightmares kept me from enjoying the night's rest. I dreamt of my pursuers drowning my aunt and uncle again, and then I watched them drown Duke and Edwin the only ones to show compassion towards me since I lost my family.

I woke up with a start at five in the morning. Only a few people were awake and the bus seemed to have stopped.

"Ah, good morning!" a man whispered from behind me. It was Edwin. "Did you sleep okay? I heard you muttering some things in your sleep. Were you having bad dreams?"

Slowly, I nodded.

"I could tell. You seem to have a lot going on." Quickly changing the subject, he added, "We have just arrived at our next destination, but everyone still needs to get ready. While they're going through their daily routine, allow me to introduce you to everyone.

"First off, please excuse our messy bus. I know we have a ton of costumes, props, and such lying around." Leaning close to me, he whispered, "I blame the clowns." I heard a scoff from the farthest bunk. Chuckling, Edwin sat at the edge of his bed and pointed out all the performers to me. There were trapeze artists, sword swallowers, clowns, and two angry show dogs that had their own bed. It was a small circus, but I was still enthralled.

I wanted to go up and personally meet each one of them. I went up to the first bed where a boy sat pulling on his socks. He was a few years older than myself and was the son of the trapeze performers.

I cleared my throat and said, "Hello, Robert. I think it's really cool how you do flips and stuff. I would love if you could teach me."

He shot me a look with dark eyes as cold as ice. Uncomfortable and embarrassed, I walked back to Edwin and sat down next to him. From that moment, I knew Robert had something against me... I just wasn't sure how deep the rivalry would get.

Putting his hand on my shoulder, Edwin leaned so close that I could smell the oatmeal he ate for breakfast. "Ignore Robert," he whispered. "It's tough for him to make friends."

"He's not the only one here," a man said grumpily as he hopped off his bed, clearly hearing the comment. It was one of the clowns Edwin had pointed out. At that age I thought clowns looked like clowns even when they were sleeping. I had no idea they were actually normal people. He had scraggly brown hair and tired eyes. His face was unshaven and he seemed like he needed more sleep.

He flung a towel over his back and walked towards me. Scanning me up and down, the tall man tried to make sense of what I was doing there. "Welcome to the Regal Circus, kid," he grumbled, "'entertainment fit for a king'." Smirking, the clown ruffled my hair and left to take his morning shower.

"Please don't mind James," Edwin said as he left. "He is not the best at first impressions."

"I on the other hand," a voice said from the farthest bunk, "have slightly better people skills." A shorter man jumped down and marched right over to me. "Out of character, the name's Daniel," he greeted while holding out his hand. "My more well-known name is Shocky, and you've met my partner Boggles."

Shaking his smooth hand, I already took a liking to this clown more than the other. His attitude was not only friendlier, but he seemed like a big teddy bear.

"So, I see you met everyone, Shane," Duke called from behind me. "Why don't you come here and I can learn where you came from and how we can help."

I went over, sat down with him, and told him everything. While I relayed my past, I began crying halfway through…um, sort of crying. Not really.

When I finished my tale, the ringleader sat there dumbfounded. The other performers who overheard my story also stopped shuffling about.

Rubbing his bald head, Duke apologized for my misfortune. "I can't believe all this is happening to a child like you. I am so sorry." Thinking for a moment, he added, "Tell you what. We are a little shorthanded around here and we could use the help. If you want we can offer you a job and the pay is housing, food, and protection. Who knows, we may even let you be in some of the acts. What do you say?"

I was so grateful. "Thank you, thank you, thank you so much!" I exclaimed. "I promise I won't let you down. Just tell me what to do and I will do it."

The man chuckled. "Of course my boy. It is the least we can do after everything that you've been through. Before I give you any tasks, why don't you take a shower and get something to eat."

I hesitantly nodded and went to the bathrooms. Edwin gave me toiletries and new clothes. Mine were so ripped and stained that I had to throw them out, but I kept my uncle's brown work jacket.

Locking the door behind me, I undressed myself in the tiny bathroom. Slowly, I entered the running shower… I still hated everything about water, but forced myself to suffer through it. I tried not to think about what water had done to my aunt and uncle, but it was hard. Every time the thought came back I felt like I was suffocating.

Finally, I couldn't take it anymore. I jumped out and tried to breathe. With the towel draped around my naked body, I sank to the floor and tried to stop hyperventilating. I couldn't believe myself. *I'm afraid of water,* I thought, feeling my racing heartbeat. It took me a few tries, but I finally calmed myself down. I shook my head, stood up, and thought again, *I'm afraid of water.* Trying not to dwell on it, I dried myself off, threw my clothes on, and left.

"That was fast, little man," Daniel said as I walked out of the bathroom.

I forced a smile. "I didn't want to take up too much time."

"Don't worry about that," he told me. "Although, I guess it was good you were fast, because it's time to set up."

Looking out the window, I saw we were parked at an empty fairground where they would put on their next performance.

The moment I stepped foot off the bus, everything seemed to be thrown up into an organized chaos. Everyone rushed about, began unpacking, and setting up.

I thought they would have a huge tent with all kinds of equipment and show animals. To my surprise, they had only a small booth with a tarp as an awning, no tent, and those two pampered show dogs. They were set up within two hours. All their things were separated in front of the booth by acts, and everyone had their own little signs.

"Don't look so disappointed," Edwin told me as we carried out the last of his things, one of the small fluffy dogs following close behind. "We do bigger shows than this. We think of these more as promotional performances to get people to come to our larger ones. Besides," he said in the middle of shooing away the pooch that was rummaging through his duffle bag, "these are easier to prepare for and it is good pocket money."

Booths of other vendors set up around us as we finished. The performers of Regal Circus were all in costume and reciting their acts.

I stuck with my magician friend. "What should I do while you are all working?" I asked Edwin.

Placing a top hat over his trimmed blond hair, he smiled and said, "I am going to need an assistant. You already know what to do for my chest, so I figured why not have you help me with everything? Unless you have something else you would like to do."

"I would love to help," I exclaimed. "Besides, I don't know what else I'd be good at."

The magic man bent over to meet me at eye level. His blue eyes looked at me kindly. "I know for a fact that you have many talents. Everyone has a little magic inside of them. You just have to look for it." As he said that, he pulled a bouquet of flowers out of his sleeve and waved it before my eyes. With a smile, he stood up, went to his wardrobe, and pulled out a sparkly blue tuxedo. Holding it by the shoulder pads, he waved it in front of me.

Ecstatic, I snatched it and ran back to the bus to change; it was a perfect fit. Returning, I saw that we already had a few spectators. I quietly made my way to Edwin to receive further instructions.

"You look marvelous," he complimented when I got his attention. "Now, it is show time. I won't be performing all of my magic tricks today, so for now just stick by me and I will instruct you on the fly." Giving me a wink, Edwin walked out to the crowd of people and I followed close behind.

To my surprise, I wasn't afraid. I did as I was told and everything went well. The other performers did their stuff and we did ours. Everyone was amazed and bewildered at their acts. I wished I could have watched, but I felt proud to be a part of the action. For the first time in months, I actually felt happy. I wanted to keep it that way.

At the end of the day, when the crowd had left, we packed up our things and went into the bus for a good night's rest.

"You did wonderful today, Shane," Edwin said as he rubbed my head. "I think you will stick with me for quite some time. Maybe I can teach you a few of my tricks."

"If you find something you are good at, we can add that act to our show," Duke chimed in as he entered the bus. "But for now, you should get some rest. You must still be exhausted."

To be honest, I really was, but I didn't want to sleep. I was a very impatient boy, in fact I still am. I wanted to learn it all now. Patience is a virtue they always used to tell me. So I heeded the ring leader's advice. Once I was in my new pajamas, I lay on the floor of the bus and let sleep take me over.

# SHANE: II

Speaking of patience, it's my turn to drive so I'll have to wait to continue. It's time to let my sister begin her story.

# THE MAINLAND

# CHAPTER 3
## Aymie: I

Okay, so do I have to do that whole introductions thing? All right, fine. I just think it's stupid. No, Blake, I do not think everything is stupid.

Hello, everyone (and to those that are listening to this later), my name is Aymie Margaret Hodgins and you know my age, family, and job at the RRPR. I am tall for a girl and have gray eyes. As for my hair, it can be whatever color I think matches my outfit. Usually brown though. I have alopecia, which is a disease that causes your hair to fall out. I know… our whole family has problems.

As Shane told you before, I was left on the doorstep of a mansion in the city. Nice place. Good people, high education, always had a roof over my head. These people were the upper class, thank goodness. They were the only ones to survive the ridiculous taxes we had and they barely had to do anything. The middle class were the people to put our bread on the table. They were the worker bees. Yet, for some reason, the limitless government sought to destroy them.

So anyway, that's where I lived. Even with everything I could ever want, I was still lonely. The owners of the household—Adrian and Camilla Quartermane—only had one child. Her name was Abigail, and she was a few years older than me. Abigail loved me as a sister, but she grew up and left all too quickly.

Thankfully, there was always one person to be there for me whenever I needed him and that was—well is—Blake Bain. We had known each other since we were babies. His father was the head butler in our household and his mother was the head maid. They were old family friends, but when Mr. Bain lost his job, Mr. Quartermane offered him a position. They lived next door to the mansion and always did their tasks with a smile. When Blake was old enough, he would help them.

I wanted to do chores too but Mrs. Quartermane never let me… she wanted to raise me as a proper lady. By the age of five, I was playing piano and learning proper etiquette. I was training to be a princess some may say, but I believe that is just what they wanted me to think. Unfortunately, it backfired on them a few times. I felt like a princess from television and demanded they bend to my every whim. However, I was put back in my place.

"Now, Aymie, you may be a princess, but a true princess does not treat others like slaves," Abigail reminded me one day as she was brushing my long brown hair (back when I had it). "A true princess puts others before herself, is obedient, and virtuous in all things. Will you promise to always remember that?"

I looked up and smiled. "Anything for you, Mama, and Papa," I said just happy to be with her. At that moment, I didn't realize her words would resonate with me for life.

Abigail and her parents never told me I was adopted. I found out on the last day I would ever see them.

That final day, we were throwing a goodbye party for Abigail before she went off to college. I was about nine years old and I wasn't too thrilled; not only because she was leaving me, but because I would be the only kid at the party. Mr. Bain told me Blake would not be attending because he had extra schoolwork to do. I was going to be the only kid among a group of adults.

At the time, I abhorred the thought, but I never said that to anyone. Nonetheless, I did as my foster parents asked and got ready.

I dressed myself in my favorite pink ball gown adorned with white Rhinestones going across the chest. My sister curled my hair and decorated it with shiny butterfly clips.

"There," she exclaimed as she put in the last clip, "prettier than a princess."

I admired myself in the mirror as I twirled in my gown. "I love it, I love it!"

She smiled her beautiful smile. I always thought she was flawless. Everything about her illuminated perfection: her red hair, her brown eyes, her happy smile, everything.

Before we went out to see everyone, Abigail waltzed with me for a few moments. We always danced, whether it was at parties or in our bedrooms, we always were light on our feet.

"Are you going to perform a song on the piano for everyone tonight?" she asked as we danced.

I shrugged my shoulders. I loved to play—and I still do—but at that age I was never comfortable playing in front of people, not even Abigail.

"I think I will try," I said hesitantly, "but only because I am sure that is what a princess would do."

She picked me up, spun me, and kissed my forehead. "That's my girl. Now run along and see if Mrs. Bain needs any help."

I dashed to the kitchen which was filled with delicious aromas. I stood on my tip toes to peer over the high counters and catch a glimpse of that night's courses. I reached out to grab a cookie, but unfortunately our head maid caught me.

"Oh, no you don't," Mrs. Bain said as she pulled my hand away, "you will spoil your appetite. You know how your mother doesn't like you eating before the food is served."

"I am sorry, ma'am. I only wanted one," I said, ashamed.

Putting her hands on her hips, Mrs. Bain replied, "I know they are tempting, but don't do that again." She sighed, picked a cookie off the plate, bent over and handed it to me. "Don't tell your mother and don't grab again."

Ecstatic, I gave her a hug and ran off. As I ate my cookie, our first guest rang the doorbell. "I'll get it, Mr. Bain!" I shouted as I ran to the door. I quickly fixed my appearance, swallowed the rest of the cookie, and opened the door for our guest. To my surprise, it was my best friend, Blake.

He was handsomely dressed in a tuxedo and his prematurely gray hair was covered by a black top hat. His pale eyes shone brighter when he saw me. My poor friend had an odd case of what is called Waardenburg Syndrome. His whole head began to turn from brown to gray, and his eyes were a shocking light blue. I was happy he hadn't lost his hearing or got blotches on his skin...yet.

"What are you doing here?" I asked as I closed the door behind him.

"I was just going to ask the same thing," his father said coming up to us.

"Dad, I finished all my homework. May I please stay for the party? You promised I could if I finished," Blake begged.

Thinking it over, Mr. Bain finally replied, "Fine, you may stay, but under one condition." He held up a finger and pointed it to the silk top hat on his son's head. "You remove that and keep it off for the whole night."

Blake's face began to turn bright red and he played with the silver ring on his finger, which he always did when he was nervous. He was insecure about his condition.

I still feel bad for teasing him. A few times I compared my hair to his, saying how mine was much better. Be careful what you say. What goes around comes around.

"Okay, it's a deal," Blake said, shaking his father's hand.

"Yay!" I exclaimed as I tackled my friend. "Now tonight won't be boring!"

He held his arms out to catch me, exhaling sharply as he struggled not to collapse.

[Hey, I wasn't a fat kid, all right? He was just scrawny.]

"Okay, okay," he said, putting me down. "But later can I tell you about the dream I had? I can't stop thinking about it and I am getting nervous," he asked timidly.

# AYMIE: I

This "dream" he was referring to was one of his many lifelike nightmares. A few times he had sworn they came true. One dream he had was about the destruction of two skyscrapers in a city on the east coast. The following fall, it happened. At times he was so petrified, he never left his home. His parents tried to get him help, but it was no use. They thought it was a mental issue… no one believed him but me.

However, I wasn't going to let this dream ruin his night. "Of course, but let's have fun first, okay?" I replied elbowing him.

He seemed desperate to tell me immediately, but he trusted me… which ended up being a mistake.

Not too long after that, a pool of guests flooded in. It was mostly Abigail's friends and her friend's friends and her friends' friends' friends and so forth. Not to mention all the relatives that attended.

"Whoa… your sister sure knows a lot of people," Blake said as we slipped through the crowd to the back of the room.

"Yeah, she sure does. I didn't even think she had friends," I confessed. At that age, everyone seemed so tall and intimidating. No one bothered us. In fact, no one seemed to notice we were there. A few people complimented me and told me how much I grew, but that was about it.

"I am happy no one has said anything about my hair," Blake said relieved.

Rubbing his head, I replied, "No one would. Now let's go eat." After we helped ourselves to the dozens of different foods, Mrs. Quartermane stood up and addressed the crowd. She stood beneath an archway of pink and white balloons that matched the rest of the ballroom's décor.

"Good evening ladies and gentlemen," she began, "Thank you all for coming to our darling daughter's farewell party. We all know life is going to be sad and different without her, but we have to let her go so she can bring joy to others just as she has brought us joy."

Everyone applauded before Abigail stood up. "Thank you everyone," she began, "I can't thank you all enough for being here and supporting me. You all mean so much to me and I thank you for being a part of my life."

After she sat down and the cheers ceased, it was time for me to perform her favorite song on the piano. Nervous, I slowly went to the grand piano against the back wall and sat down.  I felt the eyes of about a hundred people watching my every move. There wasn't much to set up since I memorized all my music. I was blessed with a photographic memory.

I took a deep breath and did my best to perform Moonlight Sonata by Beethoven. My fingers moved with care up and down the smooth ivory keys. After the first few measures, I closed my eyes and let my hands do the rest. My body swayed to the beat and my hair bounced in rhythm.

Hitting the final note, my moved onlookers stood up and applauded. My sister ran up to me and gave me a big hug. "That was incredible," she said wiping the tears from her eyes.  "I have never actually seen you play."

I hopped off the platform and walked over to Blake who was staring in shock. "Why don't you ever play for me?" he said jokingly.

Before dessert was served, the orchestra played some slow songs. All of the adult couples stood up and danced. To my surprise, little Blake held out his pale hand. "Would you like to dance, princess?" Blushing, I agreed. I put my hand in his and he held me close to him.

[Of course I have to tell them that, Blake! It was so cute. Quiet, Shane, we were nine years old. It's a little too late for you to tell him to keep his hands to himself. Now, focus on driving the bus and not crashing.]

It was during the last song that things began to go wrong. The power went out and we heard some shouting from the kitchen.

The crowd began to panic and everything turned into insensible chaos. Tables flipped over, people were being trampled, and many were screaming.

Suddenly, Blake grabbed my arm and dragged me through the crowd. "No, no, no, please don't let this be happening. It was just a dream, it was just a dream."

"Where are we going? What are you talking about?" I shouted.

Before he could answer, Mr. Bain found us and led the way. He met up with his wife and the Quartermanes.

"What's going on?" Abigail cried.

"I am not so sure," Mrs. Quartermane said. "Adrian, what do we do?"

Mr. Quartermane said nothing, but sniffed the air. Doing the same, I smelled smoke of some kind. The man's face fell. "Fire" he said quietly. After a few moments he shouted, "Fire!"

Running, Mr. Quartermane brought us to the back door, but it was blocked. Someone had shoved an enormous cabinet in front of it along with a few tables, couches, and chairs.

*Who would do this?* I thought, horrified.

"Let's try the side door," Mrs. Bain suggested covering her mouth with her apron.

The same result. Someone had blocked all the exits and no one was able to escape through the high windows. The people were in a panic.

"Head for the second floor," Mr. Bain said finally. "The fire department should be able to reach us there."

Hastily, we dashed up the stairs.

# CHAPTER 4
## Aymie: II

I think someone else who won't give us flat tires should drive now, Shane. Oh boy, you are so stubborn.

Anyways… allow me to continue after I was so rudely interrupted.

We finally reached the top of the winding staircase and headed into the master bedroom.

"Do you think the fire department is on its way?" Mr. Bain questioned, gently pushing Blake and me into the room.

"To be honest, I don't know," Mr. Quartermane confessed. "They cut our phone lines and no one's cell phones work."

"The neighbors are bound to have called!" the head servant cried.

"I hope you are right," Mr. Quartermane said solemnly.

We all stood there hopeless for a second until Abigail rushed to the bed. "Can we tie the sheets together like they do in the movies?" she asked panting.

"It's worth a shot," Mrs. Quartermane said. "Quickly, now."

In a flash we had all the sheets tied. We fastened it to the bed and threw the opposite end out the window. Mr. Quartermane stuck his head out and looked down. "It isn't too far of a drop. I think we can—"

We heard a gunshot. He stopped midsentence and fell headfirst out the window.

"Dad!" I screamed. Everyone gasped in horror. Someone didn't want us to leave.

"What do we do?" Mrs. Bain panicked, shielding her only son.

"I…I don't know," Mrs. Quartermane whispered, staggering backwards.

The room got hotter and hotter and began to shake. The flames had engulfed the entire downstairs and were finally reaching us.

Feebly, Mrs. Quartermane went to her dresser, pulled out a dusty wooden box, and gave it to me. "Aymie, I think there is something you should know before—," her voice cracked and she couldn't finish.

Taking the box, I hugged her tightly. I didn't care what she was going to say. Everyone else wrapped their arms around us. We wanted to die together as a family.

But then, there was a glimpse of hope. We heard sirens coming closer. Bravely, Mr. Bain stuck his head out the window and waved. No one shot him so we thought it to be safe.

"We can go down the sheets now," Mr. Bain said. "They have a trampoline waiting underneath."

"Aymie and Blake first," Abigail insisted.

"No, we can't go without you!" I cried.

"It can't hold that many at a time," she argued. "No fighting and go."

Before I could say goodbye, Mr. and Mrs. Bain had us out the window. Clutching the box, I slid down the sheets after Blake.

Suddenly, I didn't feel the silk in my grasp anymore. I was falling. Plummeting, I watched a blast of fire consume the second floor. I felt the unbearable heat as the hot flames roared out the window.

I closed my eyes as my body hit the trampoline. I bounced a few times and rolled off. It took me a moment to come to my senses and realize that my hair and dress caught fire. I panicked and forgot all about the "Stop, Drop, and Roll" rule. Jumping to my feet, I ran around, frantically smacking the flames.

Finally, a fireman put out the fire with a bucket of water. Before I knew it, a blanket was draped around my shoulders and I was being dragged with Blake to a police car.

The moment they slammed the doors, the driver hit the gas, and we sped away. We watched through the back window as the Quartermane mansion collapsed with our families in it.

We couldn't believe our eyes. After sitting in shock for a few moments, we cried. Blake and I sobbed together for what seemed like an eternity. We were still in hysterics when we reached the police station. Somberly, we exited the car, went inside, and sat in the waiting room.

A kind policewoman calmed us down and brought us some fresh clothes and a head scarf for me. I was confused until I went into the bathroom and looked in the mirror.

My dress was tattered and burnt and my face was covered in soot. All but one of the butterfly clips were lost; the smallest one managed to get snagged on my shoulder. The worst was when I looked up. There were only a few small patches of hair on my head.  It was all gone. The hair I loved so much was gone. I felt like the ugliest princess in all the land. I stared at myself in horror and began to cry again.

After some time, the same officer came into the restroom and tried to comfort me. She dressed me and wrapped the scarf on my head. "You are still beautiful, my dear," she whispered.

At that moment, her words meant nothing to me.

She brought me out of the bathroom to where Blake was waiting. He was mostly cleaned up despite a few scratches and burns on his skin. He sat on the edge of the chair, his arms folded across his lap. "I knew this would happen," he said softly, his eyes to the ground. "I should have said something. I am sorry."

I ran to him and wrapped my arms around him. He held me as I sobbed. Finally, I had no tears left and we both sat in the waiting room, wondering what would happen next.

"Aymie, do you want to see what's in the box your mother gave you?" he asked, taking the small wooden container from the chair next to him. He had salvaged it from our fall for me. "Maybe it's a keepsake so we can never forget them."

He tried to help, but it was no use. Nonetheless, I was also curious so I opened the box; inside were a dog tag and a letter written by Mr. and Mrs. Quartermane:

*Dearest Aymie,*

*We have been meaning to tell you since we found you, but could never find the right time. The moment we laid eyes on you we loved you. We adopted you when you were a few months old. Your mother left you on our doorstep with nothing but a blanket and this dog tag with your full name, birthdate, and family emblem engraved in it. Your real name is Aymie Margaret Hodgins. We hope you can forgive us for not telling you sooner and we pray you still love us.*

*We love you, princess.*

*Love – Adrien, Camilla, and Abigail Quartermane.*

Instead of crying, I stared at the letter in shock. *What does it all mean? Is it all true?* I took out the dog tag and held it to the light. Everything was on there just as the letter described.

I sighed and shook my head. *I don't understand...*

Kindly, Blake took the necklace from my fragile hands and put it around my neck. "Don't lose this," he whispered. Unsure of what to say, I nodded. Before we could discuss it further, the policewoman came back in. I put the letter back in the box, along with the single butterfly hairpin that escaped a fiery fate.

"I have some news," she started, "It may be good, it may be bad." It took her a moment to think of how to put it nicely so we children could understand. "First, we have men on the crime scene now to figure out what really happened. So far, it seems like it was done on purpose. Not to mention what happened to your dad, Aymie. We will continue our investigation and catch the criminals behind this."

She took a deep breath. "Next, neither of you have any relatives left. So, we found some homes for you to live in, but they are quite far away from each other. We tried to keep you two together, but it was no use. All but these two are either filled or unwilling to take you two in considering the circumstance." Looking at my best friend, she said, "Blake, you will be taken to Saint John Bosco's Boys' Home in Michigan and Aymie you will be sent to a home for girls called Saint Maria Goretti's in Tennessee. Again, I'm sorry about the distance apart, but these were the only homes willing to help."

I didn't want help. I didn't want to leave Blake. I couldn't. He was my only friend. No one else would understand. "Please. There has to be some other way," I pleaded.

"Can we stay here at the station? We can live off of scraps. We will do anything," Blake begged.

"I am sorry," the woman apologized. "You should be grateful that these places are so willing to take you two in. They are filling up rapidly."

Saying nothing else, the woman brought us back to an empty holding cell. It was cold, damp and smelled like body odor. There we slept under her watch and waited for the next dreadful day.

When we woke up, we were quickly instructed to follow the policewoman where we were taken to the airport against our will. They were kind enough to pack us some food and extra clothing, but we were unable to feel grateful. We were going to be separated; most likely never to see each other again.

For hours, I sat with Blake and the policewoman in the airport. I kept my eyes locked on the white tile floor and barely spoke until they finally announced my flight.

The policewoman stood from her seat, stretched, and said with a yawn, "All right dear, time to say goodbye."

Jumping to my feet, I looked up at the woman with tears in my eyes. "Please, don't make me go," I pleaded.

Sympathetically, the woman bent down and put her hand on my cheek. "I am sorry. Maybe someday you two will be reunited. But for now it is time to say goodbye."

When she took her hand away, I turned and looked at Blake. I shook my head and muttered, "No, I won't say goodbye. This isn't fair."

Being braver than I, Blake took a deep breath and whispered,

"It'll be okay." He took off my new dog tag necklace, slid his silver ring onto it, and put it back around my neck. "So you won't forget me."

I choked back tears. That was his father's ring… and he was entrusting it to me. Shakily, I pulled the small knapsack off my shoulder, unzipped it, and rummaged through. Finding the wooden box from the Quartermane's, I opened it, took out my last butterfly hairpin, and clipped it to his shirt. "Take this," I said, my voice cracking, "so you won't forget me either."

With his frail hands, he rubbed the head of the butterfly. He held back his tears and threw his arms around me, hugging me close. I didn't want him to let go. The policewoman had to tear me from him and command the flight attendant to get me settled. The man grabbed me by the hand and tugged me along.

I wanted to throw a fit and demand that I stay with Blake, but the words of Abigail came flooding back: "*A true princess is obedient…*" I promised Abigail I would behave like a princess… so that was what I was going to do. Taking a deep breath, I held the man's hand and walked with him.

As we approached the jet bridge, I looked over my shoulder to see Blake one final time. My final memory of him before the doors closed was his big smile and his bright eyes. He clutched onto the butterfly pin with one hand and gently waved goodbye with the other. The kindness and love in his face gave me comfort as I was taken away from all I knew.

The flight attendant brought me to my seat where I settled in and waited for the plane to take off. Clutching onto the little knapsack, I curled myself up in a ball and cried myself to sleep. I was a small girl in a big world. Any second something could happen and I would be entirely unprepared for it and no one would be there to help me.

Hours later, I was awoken by a young man's voice: "You're here, kiddo. It's time to get up." He gently shook my soft shoulder.

My eyes fluttered open and I looked around. The blue seats were all vacant. Everyone had left. The flight attendant kindly took my bag from me and helped me up. Getting to my feet, my legs buckled from having fallen asleep. Once I was steady, he escorted me off and left me in the airport lobby.

I was alone in a crowd of people who scurried about, desperately trying to get to their destinations. None of them noticed a nine year old girl alone in an airport. If they did, they didn't care.

Seeing no point in waiting, I ventured off to find the ladies who were picking me up. I felt as if I was walking in circles until finally I saw a sign with my name on it. Taking a deep breath, I gripped the straps of my tattered backpack and walked up to the two women holding it.

I noticed their kind features. The first woman was dressed in a long brown skirt and milky white top. Her blonde hair fell loosely over her shoulders. Her eyes were kind and her smile big. The second woman had a peculiar taste in fashion. She wore a black long sleeved dress with a rope belt tied around her waist. Her round collar was white and ginormous; it covered her entire chest and seemed to wrap around her head as well. Draped on top of that was a long black veil that reached her belt in the back. Her skin was brown and her eyes were a soft hazel.

"Hello, child," the woman in black said kindly. "Are ya ready to go to your new home?"

I think that's all I can handle for now. I apologize for crying a few times while telling you all that. Okay, Nic, it isn't my fault that you cried with me! You big softie…

# Chapter 5
## Mark: 1

Okay, now's the moment you've all been waiting for. My "tale for another time" will finally be told. Hopefully mine won't be as tear jerking as my siblings. My past is just…odd. But can you promise me you won't all think differently about me because of it? I had no control over what happened, but I do have control over what *will* happen.

So I don't think I have to introduce myself. You all know I have blue eyes, brown hair, am a master hacker and thief, yada yada yada. You've known me for quite a while. However, there is a lot you don't know about me…like, a lot.

When my mother left me on the doorstep of those old folk's house, I cried for I don't know how long. The couple never answered the door. I was a lone little baby on the streets of a dangerous city. It was almost dawn when someone found me. Unfortunately, it was not someone my mom had in mind.

He was a homeless man, tattered and filthy. No one wanted to be near him. Those who passed by threw him scraps and scurried away as if he were an infectious disease. Yet, he was the only one to show me kindness. He brought me to his cardboard box and fed me whatever food he had. He kept me warm and alive.

That relationship only lasted a couple of hours (so I was told). I don't know if it was for better or for worse. After the homeless man rocked himself and me to sleep, a man infamous for taking children snatched me in the night.  As you can see, I'm popular among those kinds of people. This man, however, didn't bring me to a cardboard box. He took me for a train ride…to New York City.

When we got there, he brought me to an old abandoned bomb shelter where he and many other males lived together as a gang called Fallout.

Fallout was notorious for theft, cyber-attacks, and drug dealing. The police had been after them for years, but they were too good. Scratch that. They were invincible.

The man who took me in was their leader, Big Daddy, who wasn't always homeless. Long story short, he lived a normal life and had a family. He was CEO of a big computer company until it became bankrupt and hundreds lost their jobs… including him.

The truth was the government was quarreling with a neighboring country and they were too much in debt to fix it. So, they stole millions of dollars from his and many other companies. They left thousands of hard working people unemployed and broken. As a result, everyone turned on Big Daddy and thought that he was the reason the company lost their money and shut down. His family even left him.

After that, he lost his decency. He began building a new family by kidnapping homeless boys. His intentions were to help people survive, but his methods were against the law.

By the age of five, I knew how to read, write, and pickpocket. Before I was allowed to try that last skill in the streets, I had to practice taking something from each of my comrades without their knowledge. Took me a few months, but finally I took everyone's wallets in one day; even Big Daddy's.

"Well done," Big Daddy said as I returned the belongings. "I think you might be ready for your first run. You just have to go with one of the other boys and pretend he's taking you on a city trip, all right?" He poked me in the chest with his thick, dark finger. "You can go with Brand."

I nodded excitedly and ran to find the boy who was to take me. I wove through the tiny corridor of the underground bunker. Our concrete home was musty and disgusting but I loved it. The grimy, cold stone walls were covered in rusty signs and a few paintings one of the boys stole from a museum. The low ceiling dripped with slime and was covered in mold. It was fantastic. I jumped up and tried to high-five the dangling lightbulbs as I ran back to my room.

I was about to smack my fifth bulb when Big Daddy's right-hand man stepped out of the kitchen and blocked my way. Landing off balance, I fell to the cold ground and looked up. "Sorry, Mason," I apologized timidly.

Bending over, Mason stared me in the face. "Sorry won't cut it. Just what do you think you're doing?" he asked, his breath reeking with alcohol.

Frightened, I sat there staring. To be honest, Mason scared me more than Big Daddy. He was a skimpy, pasty fellow with a bad attitude. He had scars and tattoos going up and down his arms. He had three earrings on each ear and two on his right eyebrow… which I couldn't stop staring at.

Mustering courage, I sat up straight and said, "Big Daddy is sending me on a mission."

His glower softened and he chuckled. "Well in that case. What are you waiting for, kid? Go steal some stuff!" He pulled me to my feet and forcefully patted my back. "If you have any questions, you can always turn to the expert, Mason Couch." With a wink, he slid back into the kitchen.

"There you are, stupid," a boy with a thick urban accent called from behind me. Turning around, I found Brand—who was twelve at the time—standing in the hallway with his tattered sneakers on and a backpack flung over his shoulder. "I don't have all day," he complained.

"Sorry, I'm ready," little me replied. Excited, I ran up to him and was ready for my first mission.

Rolling his eyes, Brand jerked his head towards the door and reluctantly led me on. He led me up slippery stairs to a closed hatch.

Entering a code on the wall to his right, I heard a click and the metal above us slid aside. Shielding my eyes from the light that poured through, I followed Brand up and out to the surface.

I hadn't been out since I was brought to Fallout as a baby so you can imagine the excitement in five-year-old me. However, reaching the top step, I was slightly disappointed. We were in a disgusting alleyway.

"Is this what it all looks like?" I asked, confused as I kicked a beer can across the ground.

Brand reentered the code and a large metal garbage dumpster slid over the entrance. With a scoff, he replied, "No, the rest is out there." Once he was sure the door was hidden, he said, "Let's go, loser," and together we ventured into the city streets.

I was amazed at what I saw…and what I was looking at wasn't impressive. We were walking down the streets of Brooklyn. All the while I was enthralled by the massive brick buildings. Going into the middle of the street, you could see Manhattan Bridge over the water. I stood and gawked while all the people swarmed around us. Wanting to move on, Brand forcefully grabbed my arm and commanded me to follow him. We had some walking to do.

I clutched onto Brand's backpack as we navigated through the crowded streets. Everyone brushed past us and ignored our presence entirely.

"Do they see us?" I asked innocently as another lady bumped into me and said nothing.

Without looking at me, Brand replied, "Usually not; that's why pickpocketing is the easiest task. Let me show you." I let go of him and watched him do his thing. It was rush hour and we walked with the flow of the crowd. Brand closely followed one woman who was talking on the phone. She had a large purse flung over her shoulder and, conveniently, part of it was open.

Unnoticed, Brand slipped his hand inside and pulled out the woman's wallet. No one saw. No one said anything.

Amazed, I almost complimented him, but he quickly put his hand over my mouth. "They can't know we are doing this."

"Why not?" I asked, pushing his filthy hand away. I had no idea stealing was wrong.

It took him a moment to think of an excuse. "Man, you should know better! Because if they knew that they were helping us, they'd become prideful and too much pride can be bad. We don't want to hurt anyone." Looking around, he leaned over and whispered, "Listen, you must never ask questions. It shows people that you're stupid. So just do what they say, okay?"

Not being able to see through his lie, I smiled and nodded. "Should I try now?"

"Yeah, go crazy," he said unenthusiastically as he fixed the snapback cap on top of his curly brown hair. "Remember your assignment: ten items from different people. It doesn't have to be anything big like a wallet. Even jewelry will do."

I was determined to do better than that, and I succeeded. Along with sneaking behind people and taking things from their back pockets, I also put on acts. I tend to have incredible acting skills... as you may be able to tell from my time with you on the Isles. My main performance was the little lost boy looking for his brother. When the ladies brought me back to Brand, I hugged them goodbye and stole whatever I could.

By the end of the day I had a lot more than ten items in my little backpack. I ecstatically brought them back to Fallout to show Big Daddy. His brown eyes widened as I emptied my bag onto the table. Everyone else gasped.

Big Daddy rubbed his brown hair and simply shook his head. "You did this?" he said finally. Looking up at him, I nodded. The tall black man stooped over and stared me in the face. His angular features made him intimidating, but I was unafraid. After a few moments, he began laughing and gave me a bear hug. "Well done."

Impressed, a lot of the other boys clapped. I made some closer friends that day, but, unfortunately, I made a few rivals too; especially Brand.

After that, my training continued rapidly. Big Daddy thought I mastered pickpocketing and went right into hacking. He taught me everything he knew from working for the computer company.

That was a bit of a challenge and took me about two years. By the age of seven I was hacking into the police station and deleting any evidence of Fallout. They were getting close, but now they had to start over.

That was huge.

After accomplishing that, I earned my first ear piercing, which was a big deal for me. The other boys were ten years old at least.

Every time a boy passed a test or reached a certain age, he would receive an earring. By the time you were twenty one you should have six earrings, three on the top of each ear.

"My boy, you have really made me proud," Big Daddy said after piercing my right ear. "To be honest, I was unsure whether or not I could raise an infant, but I believe you're all right."

Smiling, I gave him a fist bump.

"Not bad, kiddo," Brand said flicking my silver earring. "Next time it won't be so easy; especially because I'm teachin' you."

I wasn't too thrilled at the sound of that. I was afraid he would teach me the wrong thing so I would take a step backwards.

"He will teach you how to pick locks," Big Daddy explained. "I would teach you, but I have to help Couch with the new recruits. Oh, and we're going to need your help. How is your rhythm?" Unsure, I shrugged. "Well, we will find out. You two have to play the part of street musicians and keep the public distracted long enough for the older boys to complete their *very* important assignment. I want you both to be the most impressive and entertaining musicians within three months. Understand?"

Accepting the challenge, we nodded.

The next day, Brand taught me the beginnings of lock picking. "Yo, little man, this is for you," he said handing me a small black case. Opening it, I found about a dozen metal picks and a few other tools. "Always keep these with you and don't lose them or let anyone see you with them," he instructed.

Picking a traditional lock was easy. After a few weeks of nonstop training, I was able to open doors, lockers, chains, and almost anything with a key hole. I was disappointed I couldn't get out of police handcuffs at that point. One day, I fell asleep chained to the wall because I couldn't escape. Brand had to unlock it for me with the key.

"You can't give up, man," he said putting the handcuffs on the scratched kitchen table. "These are an older model so they shouldn't be that hard to escape from. Keep trying."

I didn't want to try again just yet. My pride was crushed. Quickly, I changed the topic. "Should we practice that music junk?"

He totally forgot about that part of the assignment. "Oh, yeah…. Sure, I guess so. Do you remember what we have to do?"

"Big Daddy told us that we had to have a distracting killer drum act to play in front of that big weird science building a few blocks away. We have to keep them distracted for ten minutes. They have something we need inside."

Recalling that conversation, Brand nodded. "That's right. We have a buyer for *Couch's Concoction,* but he needs one more ingredient. Well, I guess we better get started."

I followed him as we walked to a room in the back of the shelter. Inside were two tattered couches, a small box television, and a few instruments in the back corner.

"I didn't know we had all these," I said gasping.

"Yeah, Big Daddy doesn't talk about them much," Brand told me, "He says it brings back sad memories."

Picking up a saxophone, Brand continued. "Along with his work in the computer company, he was also a part time sax player in a jazz band. Couch says his playing was awesome, but now he never comes back here." He rubbed the brass instrument. "This was his original sax. The rest of this stuff we stole from some visiting musicians." Looking at me, he said with a jealous tone, "Since you seem to be his favorite, maybe you can ask him to play for you."

I hated being called the favorite. It wasn't my fault he raised me like a son.

"Anyway, I call the bongos," Brand added, snatching the small wooden drums. "They are the easiest for me. Why don't you try the big set? When the day comes we will just use trash cans, but you might as well get familiar."

I grabbed the wooden sticks and plopped into the creaky torn seat. I had no idea what I was doing. I was just banging them like crazy until Brand ripped the sticks from my hand.

"I think we are supposed to make music," he said annoyed.

"Well, can you teach me how? I don't get it!" I cried.

Then, Big Daddy came in. Taking cotton out of his ears, he offered to help. "You really think I expected you to get it right away? I just wanted to see how you would do with no direction. To be honest it wasn't horrible…it was terrible, but not horrible."

He pulled up a chair in front of the set and grabbed an extra pair of sticks. "Now, just do what I do."  He pretended to play a simple rock beat.

Watching closely, I tried to copy his every move. After a half hour, I was able to keep the beat.

"Good!" he complimented. "Now practice that every day and you should be fine."

So I did. Every day I would practice and every day he would come in and teach me something new. He didn't play for us yet, only pretended. I made a bet with Brand that after the important assignment was a success Big Daddy would play his saxophone for us.

Finally, the day came for us to put our musician "skills" to good use. We were to perform while our buddies did their thieving. I was so excited.

Stop staring at me, guys, it's making me uncomfortable. Remember, I am still the same Mark you met on the Isles; Always was, always will be.

# CHAPTER 6
## Mark: II

Despite my excitement, I was still nervous the day we were to "perform". I never was part of a distraction team before. My small assignments were always taking people's things and hacking into security systems. Now they actually had to pay attention to me. I was so used to working in the shadows that the light scared me.

"Ready, dork?" Brand asked as he buttoned up his collared shirt.

Big Daddy said we had to dress "proper" to be taken seriously. By that he meant our clothes shouldn't be torn, and we needed to look clean. Brand wore nice blue jeans and a white button up that complimented his light brown skin tone. His blue snapback hat covered half of his short dark curly hair.

"I guess so," I said putting on my new sneakers. I wore black pants and a green t-shirt. I was jealous I didn't get a hat, but I didn't say anything. Besides, it looked better on Brand.

Grabbing his bongos, he said, "All right, let's head out." I snatched my sticks off the tattered couch and followed Brand up to the surface. We made our way down the streets of Brooklyn until we came across the massive crystal building. I looked up in awe, trying to find the top. Across the glass read "Powell Enterprises". Next to it, a golden lightbulb logo glistened in the sun.

Brand elbowed me to stop staring. I came back to my senses and did my best to get ready. However, setting up was trying enough. I wasn't allowed to bring the drum kit. I had plastic garbage cans from the alley and made a fake set. The different tones sounded cool, but it was still unfamiliar. I didn't want to mess up in front of so many strangers. The streets were crowded with people and individuals ventured in and out of the science building frequently.

I was so intimidated by the watching eyes that I almost forgot what we were going to do. I began shaking as my clammy hands clutched my sticks.

Calmly, Brand took out his bongos and laid out a money jar. "Relax, man," he said, noticing my anxiety, "We are only supposed to distract. If they like it that's great; if not, it doesn't matter as long as they aren't paying attention to anything else."

"But, I wanna play good!" I protested, swinging my arms down.

Annoyed, Brand stared at me with his brown eyes. "Seriously?"

"Yes! If we play good, we get more money."

"I guess you're right," he decided. "It's almost time. Ready?"

Without receiving a response, Brand began to play. First he tapped softly on the rims of his wooden instrument. He swung his head to the rhythm as he began to get louder. His hands jumped from drum to drum as he performed a complicated beat. He got faster and faster until his hands were a blur.

Impressed, a few people stopped and began to watch.

We were getting somewhere.

After a few minutes of freestyle, Brand slammed his hands on the bongos to end his rhythm. People clapped and my partner shot me a look as if to say, *"Can you do better?"*

That was my signal. All I was to do was copy him as best as I could and add my own flare at the end. I gripped my sticks and hit the cans on the count of four. I started with a quiet rhythm and slowly made a crescendo. I stuck with my simple beat and ignored the faces around me. Closing my eyes, I let myself get lost in the drumming.

Once I was finished, the people around us applauded and some began to throw money. Getting cocky, Brand and I continued playing, matching our rhythmic patterns to create percussive harmony. At times we would try and outdo each other, showing a glimpse of our fatal rivalry.

Our act went on for about fifteen minutes before we reached our finale. In unison we ended with a loud, dramatic solo and struck our drums in sync with a forceful head bang. The crowd cheered and applauded.

Out of breath and sweating through my green shirt, I raised my hand and waved my sticks in the air. The feel of drumming and being praised was invigorating… I wanted to do it always.

Wiping the sweat from beneath his curly hair, Brand said, "We did it, loser." He held up his damp hand.

High fiving him, I replied, "I think we did!"

A few people almost asked for an encore, but their lunch hour was almost over. Once the crowd dispersed, I put the garbage cans away and Brand cleaned up our spot. With his bongos under his arm, he grabbed the money jar and led us back to the shelter.

During our walk back, Brand counted the money. "We made thirty two dollars and ten cents," he said, flipping through the flimsy green paper with his thumb.

I was ecstatic. "Do we get to split it?" I asked with a grin.

Brand made a face like he didn't want to share. However, he sighed and gave in. "Yeah, I guess so." He reluctantly shoved my half of the money towards my chest.

Taking it from him, I exclaimed, "Yes! This is sick." I carelessly shoved the torn dollars in my pocket and added, "That was fun. Can we do it again even if we don't have to do it for a distraction?"

Brand smiled. "I think so. I had a good time, kiddo." He rubbed my head of thick brown hair. "Let's hurry back and see if Theo and Jordan got what Couch needed."

As we rushed back, I kept asking Brand about all the times we could play together just for fun. He was open to my suggestions and in the future he actually upheld his promises… in that regard. Thanks to him, drumming became one of my favorite *legal* hobbies.

Reaching the shelter, Brand entered the code and the door opened. We dashed down the stairs to see what the results were. Entering the kitchen, we found the two boys—Theo and Jordan—back from their assignment. The counters were covered in full clear bags and small boxes.

"I thought you only needed one ingredient?" Brand questioned as we came in.

"We did," Theo explained, slipping a suit jacket off his pale arms, "but you both gave us so much extra time we figured Couch could use this stuff."

"And I can indeed," Mason Couch replied looking at the contents of a plastic bag. He pulled out a vile and twirled it in his lanky fingers. "Our buyers are impressed with my newest concoction."

"What exactly are your concoctions?" I asked, standing on my tiptoes to see our spoils.

The pasty man just smiled. "You'll understand one day. It's a bit hard to explain."

"I could find a few ways to explain it," Jordan mumbled.

Couch hushed him. "No need for that. Now if you will excuse me boys, I need to take this to my lab." Scooping up all of his goodies, he placed them into an old shopping cart he had in the kitchen and wheeled it to his room.

"One day he is going to make something that will kill us all," Theo said as he left.

"He already has," said a low voice from behind me.

I almost jumped out of my skin. It was Big Daddy. For a large guy he sure was light on his feet. I guess all thieves had to be.

"Sorry, didn't mean to scare you, Mark," he apologized. "It's just…Mason is getting in over his head with this whole 'concoction' business. This soon will blow up in our faces."

"Probably literally," Brand interjected.

Big Daddy nodded and quickly changed the subject. "Brand, I heard you and Mark were a big hit up top. Nice job."

Pretending not to care for his compliments, Brand began to fiddle with the lightbulb dangling over the table. "Yeah, I knew everything would be fine. I was worried about Mark, but he turned out to be all right.”

“Hey!” I protested.

Big Daddy laughed. “I knew you both would be fine! Hey, maybe sometime the three of us can play together.” He winked and then walked out.

I looked at Brand and smiled. “See? I didn’t even have to ask.”

After our day of hard work, we were ready for some dinner. Brand cooked up some unhealthy snacks we stole from a local department store for Theo, Jordan, and I. Together, we ate and relaxed on the stained sofas in our living quarters. A few hours later, Couch came back.

“Oh perfect, just the boys I wanted to see,” he said coming in. He was carrying a large silver briefcase. “I want you four to join and me on my trip. We are going to bring our buyers my Concoction.”

Brand sighed as he threw his paper plate across the room. “Why? What’s in it for us?”

Couch smirked. “I like your thinking,” he said, pointing a tattooed finger at him. “Always looking out for yourself. Well, if you help me and my buyers like you, I can maybe put in a good word for you and Mark to get your next piercing. And maybe you can finally earn your brand, Brand.”

“Brand Brand? What?” I asked confused.

Brand knew and his face lit up. “I would be the youngest Fallout member to earn it,” he mumbled to himself. “Okay, I’ll do whatever I have to.”

Couch smiled sinisterly. “Deal.”

“Can someone explain what a brand Brand is?” I said impatiently.

Leaning forward on the couch, Theo unbuttoned his shirt. Over his heart was a large burn marking. It was three triangles with their points touching a small circle in the center. Almost exactly like the symbol on the signs we had hanging around the shelter.

“He meant that Brand will get a brand,” he explained, rubbing his marking. “Once you show true dedication to Fallout, then you get branded. You prove that you were always a part of us and always will be. The only way to get it is to show great excellence and undying effort."

A flame of rivalry sparked within me. I wanted to get my brand before Brand. I didn't care if I got my next piercing before him; I wanted the brand first.

Pulling some clothes out of a trunk behind the green chair Jordan was sitting in, Couch threw on a nice white dress coat and black glasses. "All right, you boys ready to go?"

Brand and I jumped up right away while Theo and Jordan sighed, agitated that they had to join us. Reluctantly, they rose from their comfy spots and followed us up to the surface.

Reaching the streets above, we walked for a while until we reached the subway. Couch hadn't explained that we were going to Manhattan.

Frustrated, Theo and Jordan tried to hold in their complaints as we entered the subway car. To keep us busy for the forty minutes, Couch instructed us all to pickpocket at least three things from different passengers… just for fun.

It was evening rush hour and the subway was crowded; my favorite scenario. I stole quite a few things. Being seven years old, no one would suspect it was me. I always was afraid my earring would make me suspicious so I made sure my hair was long enough to cover it until I was a little older.

I had stolen about two large wallets and three smart phones by the end of the trip. However, I wanted to score once more before getting off. I sat next to a young woman who had her purse at her side.

She was scribbling something onto a small card and then tucked it into her wallet. As she was putting the wallet back in her purse, she looked up at me and winked. I don't remember what she looked like, but I could never forget she did that.

When the subway came to an abrupt stop, I pretended to fall on the woman. While I was leaning on her, I snatched her wallet. She made it so obvious where it was in her purse… it felt too easy. Quickly, I apologized. She told me not to worry, rubbed my head, and then exited the train.

Discreetly, I opened her wallet and took a look inside. I hit the jack pot. There were about two hundred dollars inside. I almost felt sorry, but then I found a business card. It was what she was writing on: "*Don't spend it all in one place. Oh and keep this card, just to remember me by.*" She drew a smiley face underneath.

I was absolutely stunned. *How did she know I would take it?* She didn't have a name on the card; it only said "*Secretary*" in the center. If you tilted it a bit, you could see the shiny letters W-H-Y-P in the light.

I sat there in bewilderment until Brand interrupted my thoughts. "C'mon loser, time to go," he said from across the subway.

Placing my spoils in my bag, I jumped up and raced after him. They had a head start and were on the surface when I found them. The sky was dark but the bright neon lights of New York City lit the way for us down the dangerous streets.

Finally, we reached our destination: the basement of an old apartment in a rundown part of the city.

Before going down the rickety metal stairs, Couch looked down at his attire and fixed himself. "Everyone, make yourselves presentable. Tonight is a big night."

I did my best, trying to rub out the stains I received at dinner. I never really cared about my appearance or liked the way I looked at all for that matter. I was never sure if it was insecurity or I just didn't like myself.

"*Psst*, dork," Brand whispered to me, "your dog tag is hanging out. I could snatch that from you right now if I wanted to."

If he stole anything from me that would be the last thing I wanted taken. Big Daddy gave it to me when he told me the story of how I became a part of Fallout. I could never lose it. It had my full name, birthdate, and one sick letter H on the other side. Quickly, I grabbed the silver chain and put it inside my shirt.

"No talking!" Couch scolded. "Children should be seen and not heard. Be on your best behavior."

He led us down the stairs. Opening a rusted door, he brought us through a dark hallway. It was cold, eerie, and smelled like urine and a familiar drug.  I held a deep breath and pinched my nose with my thumb and forefinger to keep from smelling the unpleasant aroma.

Couch brought us to a room at the end of the hall. Entering, I found it was bigger and brighter than I expected. The floor was covered in blinding white tiles. Writing covered every inch of the light walls; there were scientific formulas, doodles, and many black Xs. Towards the back separating shelves of equipment and books was a bolted door leading who-knows-where. Five men stood by the three tables in the center of the room.

"Ah, welcome back Mr. Mason Couch!" the first man greeted us. He was a scholarly looking man with a black tie. "I see you have brought some helpers like you promised."

Couch shook his hand. "Of course, Mr. Devin Page, I could never let my best buyer down! Allow me to introduce you to my boys." He had us all line up. "Here with me is Jordan, Theo, Brand, and little Mark."

"How do you do?" Mr. Page said, bowing slightly. He was a proper man with tan skin and dark hair. He had soft kind eyes and a handsome face one could never forget. "Allow me to introduce you to my partners."

His friends weren't dressed as nice and didn't seem to be men of business. The two closest to Mr. Page were wearing leather jackets; the guy examining the notes on the wall, a flannel. The one standing furthest back wore a tie-dye shirt under his lab coat and had long shaggy blond hair. I think he was the one that made the place smell awful.

"These are our scientists," Mr. Page continued, "whom you have met, Mr. Couch, but this fellow in the back is a newcomer. His name is Mr. Carl Mallory."

Yeah, yeah I know; it is crazy and it only gets crazier. Didn't you notice that Mr. Mallory was always indifferent towards me while I was in custody on the Isles? He never really had an opinion.

Anyway, that is enough storytelling for one day. We have to set up camp and get some rest. Shane can start with his story again once we get on our way. I know our stories might be confusing for a bit, but try to keep up. They will all coincide soon.

# THE MAINLAND

# Chapter 7

## Shane: III

Okay, my turn again! So, picking up after my first day with the circus:

The following week had the same thing in store each day. All I did is what the other performers asked.

The last day, we had a lighter crowd so Daniel Jenkins—Shocky the Clown—took me around the fair on the lunch break. I felt a little awkward walking around in my sparkly blue suit with a clown, but I ignored that feeling and had fun. We took a few dollars and tried some games. We never won. I didn't care until I found the prize I really *really* wanted. Behind a booth counter hung a beautiful spruce wood acoustic guitar with a black pick guard. It looked almost exactly like my Uncle Chuck's. I stood there and stared.

Almost tripping over me, Daniel said, "Whoa! Watch where you're stopping buddy!"

I pointed to the prize and said, "I *need* that."

The clown scoffed and fixed his red nose. "You expect to win that? Don't you see the title? It's called 'The Impossible Game'. I am sure that means something."

I didn't care. I didn't even know what I had to do, but I wanted to win.

"Hello, boys, ready to try the impossible?" the booth man asked.

"Please, please, Daniel?" I begged. "It looks just like my uncle's."

Under the makeup, you could see my friend got red in the face. He was listening when I told Duke and Edwin about my backstory when I joined them a few days earlier. He probably felt bad, because he finally gave in. "All right, I only have enough money left for three tries." Looking at the vendor, he asked, "What do we have to do?"

"It's easy," the man said, "You just have to solve this puzzle within sixty seconds. Once you solve it, you get a prize! Be warned, if you want a larger prize you need to beat the lowest time." The time to beat was fifteen seconds.

*Easy, I'm fast*, I thought to myself. I gave the man the money, he gave me the puzzle, and the timer started.

I had no idea what I was looking at. Was it a house? Or was it a person? It was just a bunch of geometric shapes and I had to match one of the examples hanging in front of me. So I had to figure out which one matched mine and then solve it as quickly as possible.

I didn't get it within the time limit. So I tried again, and failed again. I tried once more, and failed once more. "C'mon!" I shouted in frustration, slamming my little fists on the table. "I was so close that time! Can I try again?"

Daniel put his clown nose back on. "Sorry, sport, I'm out of money."

"I can run back and get some," I told him, desperate to win this prize.

"That's across the fairground," he replied pointing. "A long ways for an old clown like me to walk back and forth."

"I can be there and back in less than three minutes," I informed him with a smirk. "Time me."

Sighing, the clown agreed. Although, he felt timing me was pointless because it would be much longer. He didn't want me to have any more disappointments. Still, he decided to humor me and counted down from three.

As soon as he said one, I was off in a flash. I pumped my legs as hard as I could as I wove through a crowd of carnival attendees. Despite my obstacles, I made it back to our booth sooner than I expected. I impress myself sometimes.

I skidded to a halt in front of Edwin. He stopped right in the middle of practicing a magic trick to stare at me in awe.

"Can I have a few more dollars?" I said panting.

Edwin looked at me as if to say, "*Where did you come from?*"

Duke was oblivious to what was going on. With his back to me, he said, "Sure, there's a five in the bucket."

Thanking him, I snatched it and raced off. Behind me I heard Edwin asking Duke if he saw how fast I ran. That really built up my pride. I made it back in two minutes and thirty seconds. I was proud of myself…until I saw the guitar was gone.

"What?!" I shouted in exasperation. My heart pounded in my chest as I tried to catch my breath to complain. "Are you serious? I ran as fast as I could!"

"Not fast enough," the man behind the booth said. "The guy who was waiting for his turn behind you just beat the high score."

I was so annoyed I hadn't noticed Daniel staring at me. "How did you get back so fast?" he asked, amazed.

I ignored him. "How could someone beat the high score? It's not fair," I complained.

"This guy was a genius," the man at the booth said shocked. Left on his wall were only the small prizes. That guitar was his attention grabber and he never expected it to be won.

Disappointed, I shoved my hands in my sparkly pockets and walked back to our booth with Daniel close behind.

When we returned, the clown put his hand on my shoulder. "It's okay, there will be other fairs! Maybe if we get enough money, I can buy you a new guitar."

I managed a smile. "Thanks, Daniel, but I wouldn't want you to do that. I should earn it myself."

"I actually think you could," he said as he fixed his obnoxiously large tie. "You've got talent, kid and I am going to make sure it's known to the world." With a wink, he walked over and began speaking with Duke.

Sighing, I slumped over and stomped away to wallow in self-pity. While I was going for a walk, I heard a little voice crying: "Help, help!" My head shot up and I looked all around, but saw nothing. Then, I heard it again: "Help me, help me!"

Without hesitating, I ran towards the source. After a few more cries, I finally found it. It was a little boy sitting outside the perimeter gates. He somehow got himself locked out of the fairground. "Please," he begged.

"Hey, there, are you okay?" I asked, approaching him.

The boy, who had to be about one-year-old, said, "Lost. Stuck."

"Don't move, I will get you back in," I told him. Taking a few steps back, I ran hard and leapt. I didn't clear the fence, but I was able to grab the top of it and hoist myself over. On the other side, I met the child face to face. He was a cute little blond boy with bright blue eyes and fair skin. His knuckles were turning white as he clenched the fence.

"Relax, I will help you," I told him with a smile. Picking him up, I said, "Let's go find your family."

He rubbed his face and sniffled. "Thanks," he whispered, hugging my neck.

When he pulled away, I walked along the outside of the fence until I found the way in where we searched for his parents. As we walked, he told me all sorts of stories which surprised me. I thought kids that young couldn't talk or walk, but he seemed to be lecturing me in all sorts of things… in his own childish words. He spoke mostly about science and machines.

Looking at my outfit, the boy patted my shoulders and asked, "Circus guy?"

"Yeah, I guess so," I replied. "The Regal Circus; entertainment fit for a king.' I'm new, though, so I don't do too much yet."

He just smiled. Then, out of the corner of his eye he saw his parents. "Mommy! Daddy!" he shouted and pointed, trying to reach for them.

His parents came running. His mother scooped him up and his father kissed his head.

I was about to introduce myself when I noticed what the father had. Even though I did a good deed, I was disappointed when I saw that the father gripped the guitar I wanted so badly

"Thank you so much for finding our son," the mother said to me, tears in her eyes. Before I could say anything, the boy explained the entire story in his broken baby words.

"Wow, not only did you find him, but you saved him," the father said appreciatively, understanding his son's gibberish. "I don't know how we can thank you."

"Give toy?" the little one asked his dad. He pointed to me and smiled. "Best friend."

"Of course, son," he answered, "whichever one you don't want."

His mother was carrying large bags full of stuffed toys and trinkets that they had won from the games, but the child had already chosen the one to give away. He pointed to the guitar in his father's hand. "That," he said.

My face lit up.

The father wanted to protest, but the mother interrupted. "Myles, you told Junior whichever one he didn't want. No going back on your word. Besides, don't you have two of those at home?"

The father—Myles—sighed and reluctantly held out the instrument. Then he noticed my outfit. "Weren't you that boy who was before me in line?" I nodded excitedly. "I watched how fast you ran. That was pretty impressive," he complimented. With a smile on his face, he gave me the guitar. "I think you can learn *faster* than I can." He chuckled to himself. "No pun intended."

Laughing, I said, "Thank you. You don't know how much this means to me."

"You don't know how much it means for us to have our son back," the father replied. Reaching in his pocket, he pulled out a bumper sticker. "Here, something to remember us by."

Without reading it, I peeled it off and slapped it underneath the bridge of my new guitar. "Now I can never forget," I said with a grin.

"That's very kind of you," the mother said. "Now, I'm afraid we must go; it's time for Junior's nap. Say goodbye!"

Junior waved. "Bye-bye!"

I thanked them again, bid them farewell, and ran back to my comrades. "Daniel!" I called as I came to a short stop. "Look, look! I earned it, I earned it!"

Shocky stared with his jaw open. "Did you solve the puzzle?"

"No, the son of the owner was lost and I returned him. Look, here is his sticker." I pointed proudly to the label on my guitar.

"Did you steal the kid and then return him or was that just mere luck?" James Green—Boggles—said.

I was offended that I would be accused of something so ridiculous. "No, I swear."

Daniel took my instrument and looked it over. "It really is a nice one. Very generous of them to just give it to you."

His clown partner came over and read the sticker. He tapped it and said, "Now I really know you stole the kid. Do you know what the father's first name was?"

"Myles."

"Did you read this bumper sticker?" he asked. I shook my head. "Well, you just ran into Myles Powell Senior;" he explained, crossing his arms, "the billionaire owner of 'Powell Enterprises'."

I had no idea who he was talking about.

"He is just an owner of a big company," Daniel said handing me back my prize.

I took a closer look at the bumper sticker. It said "Powell Enterprises" and to the left of that was a detailed lightbulb logo with a letter *P* inside it.

[Yup, that's how Myles and I became best friends. If you call him Junior, Aaron, he will probably kill you. I am surprised he hasn't zapped me yet with some sort of death ray gun. I call him Junior all the time.]

Okay, continuing:

"Shane," Edwin called, "Duke and I would like to speak to you." I flung the strap over my head and carried it over to them. It was too big for me, but I didn't care. "I think we already found an act for you to do," the magician said.

"Really?" I asked, stunned.

"Yes," Duke confirmed. "Right now it will only work at fairs, but I think we can integrate it into our show. Also, we have decided that each member is going to teach you a few tricks they do in their acts."

I was ecstatic. It had only been a few days and I was already on my way to being a star. I grabbed the ringleaders hand and shook it. "Thank you, thank you, thank you," I repeated.

"Of course, my boy," he replied as I vigorously shook his hand. "Now you will need some practice so we will add your act to the next season of fairs. But tomorrow, we will start training you for our next show. Do you think you will be able to handle that?" I nodded. "All right, then it is official," Duke said standing up. "Let's finish here, pack, and get on the road again." We closed up, said goodbye to the fairgrounds, and were on our way.

When we were on the road, Edwin started counting up our money. "We made $2,453.12."

I stood on my tip toes and peered at the dirty coins and crinkled bills scattered across the counter top. "Is that good?" I asked.

"Not exactly," Daniel said, disappointed. "The other booths probably make twice that."

James sat back in his seat and crossed his arms. "It's because we don't offer any prizes or activities they can participate in."

"He is right," one of the sword swallowers called from the back. "It is difficult though, because I can't just give a kid a sword and say, 'Hey, swallow this and I'll give you a prize'."

"That's true and that's why Shane is going to fix that problem," Edwin said with a smile.

"Seriously?" James said. He looked at the magician, then me, then back at him. "What can he do?"

"He can run fast," Daniel told his clown partner. "He made it across the fairgrounds in less than three minutes."

"And we can use that for an act that the spectators can participate in," Edwin chimed in. "They pay three dollars to race the little fellow.

If they win, they get a prize, if not then try again."

"How will that work?" Robert Ferguson—the young trapeze artist who hated my guts—said. "He is just a kid. I am sure the adults could beat him easy."

"He is not too much younger than you, Robert," his mother reminded. "Have faith in the boy."

"I can do it," I affirmed. "I outran the cop cars all day before I came here."

"I don't think you—" Robert was interrupted by a glare from his mother.

"With some more training, he'll be fine," Edwin reassured. "Our acts will help him build up his stamina and reflexes, especially doing trapeze with the Ferguson's."

"What?" Robert began to protest. "No way I'm teaching some loser kid things that took me forever to master."

"Robert, enough," his father scolded. The boy silenced, crossed his arms, and stormed off.

"He's almost as bad as a teenage girl," James muttered under his breath.

"Anyway," Edwin protested, trying to get everyone back on track, "we will start your training once we find an open spot to practice. We are ahead of schedule so a few stops won't hurt. For now, you get to sleep. You need your energy."

"I am always energetic," I said with a smile.

That's where my cockiness started. Sometimes it gets out of hand, but I'm working on it.

# CHAPTER 8
## Shane: IV

"Everybody up!" Duke banged cymbals together. "We have a big day of practice ahead of us. Up and at 'em."

I sat upright and stretched. "What time is it?" I muttered. Looking out the window, I couldn't see anything. "It's still night time."

"Performers begin practice before the break of dawn," the ringleader said chipper.

James—Boggles—just moaned and rolled out of his bed which wasn't smart. He had a top bunk. *Thud.* "Bad idea," he said with his face smashed into the ground.

"How many times do we have to remind you that your bed is in the air?" his partner said standing up.

"Enough chat," Duke said, combing his curly mustache. "Time to get dressed."

After everyone was ready, we brought out the equipment and set up as if we were performing. They had a lot of stuff for their big shows. The tent, wire nets, platforms, knives, swords, Edwin's magic kits, and the two show dogs.

It was a little after dawn when we finished. We ate a quick breakfast and then they began my training.

I am not going to go through all of what happened during those few months. You'll be bored to death. They just showed me stuff and I did it…over and over and over again. Basically by the end of it all I could do flips on the trapeze and on the ground, sword fight, ride a unicycle, and clean up show dog droppings. Yeah, that last one wasn't much fun.

Then, the time finally came. My first season in the circus.

To be completely honest, every show was a blur. I was in every act, even with the clowns, and it was exhausting. I remember I did my very best and everyone was impressed. I guess a seven year old boy doing flips and sword fighting was enough to leave people in awe.

The other thing I also remember was Robert constantly yelling at me. He was a pain to work with, because he hated me. That was something I could never forget. Every day he would remind me that I was an annoying pest.

At the end of it all, despite those troubles, I always enjoyed it and the audience loved me. I lived for the attention. I would do whatever I could to get it.

The season came and went and we were successful. Edwin believed I brought them all good luck. "Once again, you were the star of the show," he told me as we drove from another venue. "I guarantee they'll be talking about you for a while."

I liked the sound of that. "Thanks, but I just did what you all told me to do," I reminded. I reminisced about the event as I sat and stared out the window as the city lights raced by.

"And you pulled it off as usual," Daniel said, rubbing my head as he walked past. "To be honest, I thought we were overworking you, but you sure proved me wrong."

"Next I want to teach you how to swallow a dagger," one of the marksmen told me excitedly.

Duke laughed. "I think we should hold off on that for a bit. I want him to train for his own performance."

"I have to train for that?"

"Of course; you need to stay in shape and make sure you really are the fastest," Edwin reminded, playing on my ego.

After that final show, I continued to train every day: for their acts and my own. I would practice running for hours nonstop. I had to run carrying objects, people, with weights on my legs, and I had to try not to lose my breath or even break a sweat… that was almost impossible.

I prepared for six months straight before our next fair gig. I felt I was finally ready. I was so excited I couldn't sleep the night before. Imaginative scenarios just played in my mind all night, keeping me awake.

The next morning I had everything set up in a flash. I had a station with its own sign, big electronic timer, prize rack, everything.

To complete it all, Duke gave me my own costume: new running shoes, tight slick black pants and a shiny blue track jacket with my stage name bedazzled on the back: Zippy Presto.

[Shannon, stop laughing. Guys, not you too…cut it out. That was my circus name, okay? Everything there is ridiculous. I was about eight when I picked that. They helped me come up with it! Zippy because I am fast and Presto because I was mostly seen with the magician.

[Are you done laughing, Shannon? Can you breathe now? Good, I shall continue.]

Finally, people began to arrive. I was expecting them to line up by the hundreds as soon as the fair opened, but I was disappointed.

After about the first two hours, I began timing myself. I ran back and forth for about twenty minutes before some kids stopped by and watched. The little ones were amazed. "He is super-duper fast!" a boy exclaimed to his older brother.

The teen scoffed. "It just looks fast from here. It isn't that impressive."

Overhearing them, I taunted the older boy. "That's just an excuse because you aren't as good as me."

He got red in the face. "No, it is not! I am way older and bigger than you, kid. I will leave you in the dust."

"Then give three dollars and find out," Duke chimed in. "If you beat him, you get a prize. We have nice big ones here."

Grumbling, the teenager gave Duke the fee. "You're just going to lose money on those toys you have here."

I smirked. "Ready to be proven wrong?"

Duke counted down and rang the bell. I totally left that guy in the dust. I made it there and back before he reached his bell.

"I demand a rematch," he said, trying to catch his breath. "I went easy on you." He gave Duke three more dollars. He tried and failed again. We got fifteen bucks out of him before he gave up.

He sank to the ground and stared. His face was red and dripping with sweat. "You aren't even a little tired?" he asked.

"Nope," I said. I held out my hand and helped him to his feet. "Never get tired."

His little brother and some other onlookers were quite impressed and many were in disbelief. Some so much that they needed to race me just to see, making that first day a huge success for us.

After that, I was the talk of every fairground we had a booth at. All the attendees needed to come and check me out. At one fair, a local newspaper hungry for any story came to interview me. All of that really fed my ego.

I raced so many people I couldn't keep track. My act was an impressive accomplishment. We earned back the money for the timers and prizes plus a profit.

After months of fairs and other gigs, we finally went to a fancy restaurant for a well-earned meal.

"I am just in awe how much money we made these past few months," Duke said, fixing his nice jacket. "Between doing fairs and now school events and fundraisers, we have made more than we usually do in a year."

With a mouth full of chicken, Edwin said, "I'm telling you, this kid is our good luck charm."

Standing, Daniel held up his wine glass. "Well, then I propose a toast. To Shane, the answer to our prayers. May you always be happy and safe with us." Everyone cheered.

I felt so at home there. They accepted me as their own and were always there for me…except for Robert.

That night after dinner, I was about to get back on the bus

when I was cornered. Robert grabbed me and pinned me up against the side. "Listen kid," he sneered. "You think you are some hot shot just because you can run back and forth all day? Well, you better listen closely and not forget." He leaned closer. I saw the anger and bitterness in his eyes. "If you don't get out of here soon, I promise you that you will regret ever coming to us that night when you were hunted down." He gritted his teeth and breathed in my face, "I will make you wish that you were dead."

Cocky and not impressed, I grabbed his arms and threw him to the ground, causing him to land on his face. "The Bailey brothers taught me a bit of fighting, too, along with using a sword. So to put it into words," I bent over and stated, "you don't scare me." Hopping over him, I went inside and went to bed.

After that night, I remained with the circus until I was about thirteen years old. We became quite famous and even performed in Europe. Every new place we went to, I bought a souvenir sticker and slapped it on my lovely guitar. It's so banged up and covered; you can barely see the wood now.

With all that going on, I was finally enjoying myself. I owed a lot to my circus family; they gave me a home when no one else would.

Unfortunately, I am never meant to be happy. Robert kept his promise.

It was a dark night and we were packing up from a week at the fair. "Another successful adventure," Edwin said as we packed his magic chest. "I wonder what next week holds."

"One thing at a time, Edwin," I reminded as I picked up my guitar. "That's what you always tell me."

The magician chuckled. "That's because you are barely able to sit still. This incredible talent has affected your brain as well as your feet."

Smiling, I said, "Can't argue there."

He locked his chest tight and added, "Well, that's why Duke and I signed you up for the junior Olympics."

I almost dropped my guitar. I had been talking about it for over a year and didn't think it would actually happen. "Shut. Up."

Edwin stood upright and grinned. "It's not for another year or so, but that doesn't mean you stop training and practicing." He wagged his pointer finger at me. "You are a teenager now, I expect you to be even more responsible."

A grin spread across my face. Clutching the neck of my guitar and swinging the blue strap over my head, I replied, "I don't need the practice, but I won't let you down."

He winked and turned to pack the rest of his things. While he worked, I played my guitar. Several songs in, Robert came out to meet me. He was older and more mature. I thought maybe things were over between us, but sometimes I could still see the hatred in his eyes.

"Hey, squirt, need help?" he asked quietly.

"You know I am almost as tall as you," I told him as I finger-picked a quiet melody on my stringed instrument.

"To me you're still a squirt," he teased… but the tone of his voice sounded sinister. He had his hands in his pockets and kept looking off into the distance. He tapped his foot repeatedly, destroying the green grass beneath him. He was twitchy and anxious. The way he was acting gave me an uneasy feeling… the same feeling I had the day my foster parents were murdered.

I abruptly stopped playing. "What's going on?" I whispered.

Surprised, Robert stared at me, unsure of what to say.

"What did you do?" I said louder.

"Boys, what's wrong?" Edwin called from behind me.

That's when the first shot was fired and I heard a body fall. Turning around, I found Edwin on the ground in a puddle of blood.

"What did you do?!" I shouted at Robert.

"They promised," he whispered as he staggered backwards.

Crashes and bangs were heard from inside.

"They're in the bus!" I exclaimed.

Fear fell upon Robert's face. "They said this wouldn't happen… I told them to take you and only you."

"What?" I screamed.

Duke came stumbling out of the bus and motioned us to get away. "Run, save yourselves," he warned as he clutched his wounded side.

Robert bolted, but I protested. "I can't leave you all."

"It's too late," Duke said softly. "Please, run."

I looked into his eyes. It was too late. "I'm sorry," I said crying as the ringleader fell flat on his face.

His murderer then revealed himself. He stared at me with such hatred. I couldn't believe it. It was happening again. It was one of the two men who killed my family. I'd recognize the demonic eyes of the man with the dark hair anywhere.

Frightened, I flung my guitar over my back and ran. I raced long and far; never looking back. Finally, I caught up to Robert at the edge of a hill. He was slumped over with his hands on his knees, panting to catch his breath. He looked horrible. His clothes were tattered from running through thickets and his eyes were red and damp from tears.

I threw my guitar down. Anger and sorrow boiled up inside of me. I screamed and tackled him with all my might. Together we went tumbling down the steep hill and got all battered and bruised. I landed on top of him at the bottom.

"What is your problem?!" I bellowed as I pressed my hands up against his throat.

Gasping for air, he tried pushing me off. With a quick shove, he managed to get my hands off and gasped, "They promised… that this wouldn't happen."

I was outraged. "You think murderers would listen to a puny teenage boy? How did you even find them anyway?"

"I didn't; they found me," he cried. He attempted to push me off but repeatedly failed. "I put on the internet that you were with us and I figured someone would find it eventually. It took them years to find it so I thought that no one read the message… until this morning at least."

I loosened my grip and stared. "You...what?"

Robert rubbed his throat. "I told you to leave, but you didn't listen," he explained. "Now, we both face the consequences."

"I didn't do anything wrong!" I shouted.

"Well, you obviously did. Otherwise those men wouldn't be after you," he said. He shoved me off of him.

I couldn't believe what I was hearing. Before Robert got to his feet, I punched him in the face as hard as I could. Full of rage, I ran back to grab my instrument and raced off. I left him there. I didn't care for his safety. I didn't care if he died. So, once again, I ran for my life.

And that concludes my life with the circus. Ta-da.

# CHAPTER 9
## Aymie: III

Thank you, Mr. Depressing. I'm grateful the rest of my young life isn't *as* tragic.

I had just gotten off the plane and found the two women who were to take me to the orphanage. They led me out of the airport and signaled a taxi. The entire ride, I was silent and watched the state of Tennessee rush by until we arrived.

The beautiful large house was old and had a colonial style. A brick pathway parted the freshly cut lawn, leading to the front door. The area had a tall black fence surrounding it; reminding me of my old home.

When the taxi came to a stop, the young woman in the brown skirt opened the door for me and led me to the house. Approaching the front porch, I stopped before going up the steps. I looked up at the white door and was terrified. I wanted to run away and find Blake.

With a deep breath, I remembered Abigail's words again: "*A true princess is obedient.*" I mustered up enough courage and followed the two ladies inside.

I walked at a quick pace across marble floors to keep up. As we went, I quickly glanced at the images on the crème walls until a large portrait caught my eye. I stopped mid step to stare at a painting of a girl holding white lilies. *She's beautiful,* little me thought.

The lady in the brown skirt looked over and noticed my utter admiration. Coming back to me, she explained, "That is our patron, Maria Goretti. She's known for being an image of purity and is a great model for all girls."

"She is very lovely," I said. "Was she a princess?"

Chuckling, the woman in black said, "She is now. Before she died she was just a simple farm girl."

"How did she die?" I asked innocently.

The two women just looked at each other. "You will learn in class when you are a bit older, my dear," the one in black said. "Mia, can ya show Miss Aymie to her room?"

"Of course, Sister Maria Stella," Mia said, slightly bowing. "Come with me, Aymie."

That was the first I learned of their names. They had forgotten to introduce themselves.

As we walked through the dim corridors, we met other women in long dresses like Sister Maria Stella. Mia called all of them "sister" when she said hello or introduced me. I was confused as to why she had so many sisters. I also didn't see any young girls. "Am I the only kid here?" I asked.

Mia smiled. "No, of course not. The other girls are in class. School is almost out so you will meet everyone, but first to your room."

She brought me to a small square room with wood floors, beige walls, and two beds. *Hope she's nice*, I thought, looking at the occupied side.

"Make yourself at home," Mia said, gesturing to the room with one arm and holding the doorknob with the other. "I will be right back." She gently shut the door behind her and I heard her feet shuffling away.

I plopped myself on the bed and looked around. There was one small window in the middle of the back wall. Above the head of each bed was a wooden *T* with a Man on it. I looked carefully at the Man and became upset. *Who would do such a thing? Why were people so cruel?*

As I gazed upon the Man's broken body, I began to think about the family that was taken from me: Mr. and Mrs. Quartermane, Abigail, Mr. and Mrs. Bain, and especially Blake. I wondered if that Man's family felt what I was feeling as they watched Him be hurt like that.

Clutching my dog tag and Blake's ring, I began to cry. I curled up onto the bed and sobbed. I pulled my knees to my chest and shut my wet eyes. I missed them. I wished I could go back in time and tell them how I felt; how much I loved them.

A few minutes later, Sister Maria Stella walked in on me crying. "Oh, no dear," she exclaimed, her chocolate eyes filled with concern, "please, don't cry!" She sat next to me and pulled me close to her bosom. I wasn't going to fight her. I needed the affection. "Sweetheart, I know it's hard, but I promise we can help ya make it better," she said as she rubbed my shoulders.

"How?" I said mid sob. "Everyone I love is dead, Blake left me, I look disgusting, and—" I couldn't finish; I was crying so hard.

Sister Maria Stella rocked me back and forth. "I know. I know. Listen, hon, I don't know exactly what you are going through, but I know someone who does."

Looking up at her, I became hopeful. "Who? Can they help me?"

She chuckled. "Of course He can. Look right there." She pointed to the Man on the *T*. I was confused. "He was abandoned. He was betrayed. He was attacked. He looked disgusting. He died. Do you wanna know why?" I nodded. She wiped the tears from my eyes. "Because He loves you, Aymie. He did it for you."

Without explaining anything else, the Sister kissed my forehead and stood up. "Now, no more crying. He doesn't like it when ya cry. Put on a smile and let's meet your new friends."

I took three deep breaths and stood to my feet. I was a little lightheaded from sobbing, but I didn't want to tell her that. So, I obediently followed her out.

With a skip in her step, Sister Maria Stella joyfully led me to the backyard which was just as beautiful as the front. There were lovely gardens full of vegetables and flowers to my left; to my right was a small pond perfect for skipping stones. Straight ahead was a brick path leading to a large white gazeebo where they did class on nice days. Behind was a mysterious forest where the Sisters would take the students on hikes and have scavenger hunts.

Sister Maria Stella concluded her brief tour just in time for me to watch about a hundred girls flood out of the gazeebo. They were on their way to greet me. They were all wearing long black skirts, gray collared shirts, and black flats. Their ages ranged from five to seventeen.

"Ladies, I would like to introduce our newest student," Sister Maria Stella announced once the girls stopped before us. "This is Aymie Quartermane."

The girls smiled and waved, but I was so frightened I couldn't move.

"She is just a little shy, but I am sure y'all will get along very well," she said, patting my back. "Aymie is just in time for lunch, isn't she girls? Let's eat."

I've never seen so many people excited over lunch, especially what they had. They had homemade grilled cheese sandwiches with soup and water to drink. I wasn't familiar with eating like everyone else, so I did my best to enjoy it. I was accustomed to ordering whatever I wanted for lunch and having an abundance of it. I had to learn to be careful and eat only what I was given. *"A princess is obedient"*, I thought, recalling Abigail's advice.

I sat down with a group of girls at my left. They ignored me and whispered when I approached the table.

"Why does she wear that?" I heard one girl say to another about my head wrap.

"I don't know, but it looks ridiculous," the other chuckled.

"Her outfit looks like she just came out of a dumpster," someone joked.

I slumped down into my chair, trying not to be seen. I felt so small and wanted to cry again. Before I could, I was startled by the sound of a tray slamming on the table. "Enough, girls. Don't be rude," a voice said.

Looking up, I saw a beautiful girl about two years older than me with smooth black skin. She plopped herself in the seat across from mine. She flung her thick long braided hair behind her and wagged her finger in the air. "They are gonna get it one day, but for now just ignore them. I think you are wonderful." She looked at me kindly with her dark brown eyes and held out her hand. "Janelle Arends. It is a pleasure to meet you."

I shook her hand. "Thank you. My name is Aymie."

"*Love* the name," she said chuckling. "You know it means 'love', right? Ya see what I did there?" She clapped and laughed at her own joke. Her laugh was hilarious. It was loud, hearty, and genuine. I couldn't help but join in.  I barely knew her, but I knew I wanted to hang out with her every day.

Wiping the tear from her eye, she said, "Sorry 'bout that. I find myself funny sometimes. Anyhoo, so you're the newbie. I'm sure you will be just fine. No one here is that horrible I don't think. We all have good respect and the Sisters here are awesome."

"Is everyone related to these 'sisters'?" I asked confused.

Her laugh started up again. "No, silly! That's their title. They're a group of Sisters; a religious order." We didn't really talk a lot about religion in the Quartermane mansion. I knew I had a lot to learn. "Don't worry if ya don't understand," she explained, noticing my confusion. "That's why we take classes. We actually gotta pretty sweet getup here. We learn, we get fed, and every so often some of us get adopted." I wasn't sure how I felt about that last part.

We chatted all throughout lunch…well, she talked I listened. She sure was a talkative one, but I didn't care. She helped me take my mind off of everything.

Then another sister came in ringing a bell. "Time to clean up, girls," she announced. "Next class starts in five minutes."

Janelle stood up. "Well, I guess I will see you around, love." She chuckled and headed off.

Mia—the lady in the brown skirt—came back to get me. "You

are going to take a few tests to see what grade we need to place you in," she explained. "Our curriculum is a little different, so we want to make sure you aren't lost in any of the classes."

With a nod, I rose, returned my plate, and followed her to a vacant classroom. I sat down in a beige desk and immediately began an assessment. I think the only thing I understood was the math. The rest of the subjects they had were completely different than what I knew; Latin was one of them. I was so confused.

"Don't worry dear, you just have had a modern education," Sister Maria Stella said after grading the lengthy test. "We do things more traditionally here. I hope you don't mind. To be honest, we wish the world would go back to this education. The kids in the schools seem to be learnin' all the same things; like they are becoming those robot thingamabobs from the alien movies."

I shook my head. "I don't want to be a robot, but I won't be too lost, will I?"

She smiled. "Of course not, from what I see here you are a bright student and a hard worker," she complimented. "You will catch up in no time." Glancing at the clock, the sister gasped. "Oh, I am sorry! We missed dinner. I wanted you to socialize with the girls a little more." With a frown, she added, "I think you will have to eat in your bedroom while we are saying *Compline*. I hope you don't mind. You will be on schedule with the rest of us tomorrow, I promise."

Nodding, I went to my room and quietly ate the dinner that was left for me on my nightstand. The entire time I stared at the other bed, wondering who it belonged to.

I was just about finished when my roommate burst through the door. "Hey, love," a familiar voice shouted. It was Janelle. You have no idea how excited I was when she came in. I couldn't have asked for a better roommate. "I had no idea you were my roomie! This is gonna be crazy awesome." She jumped onto the bed next to me. "My other roommate was adopted and I've been kinda lonely. But now I have you. This is gonna be amazing."

She showed me where everything was and explained what the days were like. The way she spoke stirred excitement within me. She made life sound like it wasn't as bad as I thought. I just hoped she was right.

# THE MAINLAND

# CHAPTER 10
## Aymie: IV

I awoke the next morning to the sound of melodic church bells. Their angelic singing filled my room, gently awaking me from my tired sleep. I rubbed my eyes and yawned.

"Mornin', love," my roommate greeted. She was already up and dressed in her uniform; ready to start the day.

"Good morning," I mumbled. I slipped out of bed and fumbled around for my new clothes. As I was pulling on my shirt, my head wrap fell off. I had slept with it because I was ashamed. Embarrassed, I held back my tears and quickly slipped it back on my bald head.

Janelle noticed I was upset. "Aymie, don't worry," she said seriously. "I ain't never gonna judge you or think less of you 'cause of whatcha look like. Don't worry about what the other girls say, they don't understand."

I swallowed the lump in my throat. "Thank you. It means a lot."

She smiled. "That ain't no big deal, love! I have been dealing with them ever since I arrived. Those city girls used to make fun of me all the time until I showed 'em I could not be torn down so easily." She winked and motioned me to follow her to the restrooms.

After freshening up, we walked down the long hall until we

reached the back door. Exiting, we followed a rubble path to a small wooden house. It had a tall steeple where the bells continued to play their joyous tune. Inside were wooden benches facing the front and colored windows with pictures on them to either side. In the center was a marble table with the poor Man on the *T* above it. Behind the table was a golden box holding the Greatest Mystery within.

"Hope ya don't mind bein' here a little early," Janelle whispered as she put a white laced cloth over her head. "I have a little trouble focusing so I need more time."

Unsure of what was going on, I just nodded. "Do I need one of those things too?" I asked, pointing to her veil.

Smiling, she looked at my head and said, "Your head wrap makes up for it, don't worry."

After fifteen minutes of sitting in silence, more girls came in. They were very reverent and knelt down quietly. I was still confused so I just did what they did.

Then the "Mass" (as they called it) began. To be honest, I didn't understand anything. Mostly because the man leading us spoke in Latin. When he gave his sermon in English that helped, but I got lost so many times.

Halfway through, Janelle gave me a red booklet. "This is the explanation of what is going on," she whispered. "It's really helpful and makes you think more.

I thanked her and opened the book and followed along. It was actually very interesting even though I was unsure of what to make of it. After all I was only about nine. So, I sat through it patiently, mimicking Janelle's movements as closely as possible. However, when she went up to eat the Bread that the man had, she told me to stay put. I was a little upset, but as they were going up I repeated to myself, "*A princess is obedient.*"

After the man dismissed us, we walked out and to the cafeteria for breakfast. Receiving food, I followed Janelle again and sat down with her at a small table in the corner.

While we were eating, I asked, "Why couldn't I go up with you guys?"

"Because you aren't ready yet," she said with a mouth full of oatmeal. "They'll teach you in class."

I wanted to demand that I be taught at that moment, but it was not my place. "*A princess is virtuous*," I remembered.

After breakfast that day, things went downhill. I was separated from Janelle until dinner and had six nasty girls in my class. They didn't even know my name yet and they already made my life miserable.

The day dragged on and I diligently attended my classes. Some I needed to catch up on, others I excelled at. Whenever I did well, the six mean girls glared and talked about me. If I made a mistake, they laughed and made a bigger deal out of it. What really made them angry was when we reached the final class of the day: Music.

The teacher asked if I could read music or play any instruments. After I told her I knew piano, she invited me to come up and play a piece for everyone.

I think you can tell what was going on in the minds of the girls as they watched me perform a complicated classical piece at age nine. They *hated* me. I also regretted telling the teacher about my photographic memory and how that helped me remember sheet music. That made my situation even worse.

Exiting the hall after music, the leader of the mean girls, Sophia, ran up behind me and tore the head wrap off, leaving me exposed. Embarrassed, I threw my hands over my head and cried, "Please give it back!"

Sophia wagged the black fabric above my head. "Oh, Cinderella, Cinderella," she taunted. "Just ask your fairy godmother to bring your hair back." Sophia tossed it to the girl behind me who caught it with one hand. With a menacing glare, she stared at me as she tore the head wrap in half. Without another word, the six of them disappeared as I sunk to the floor in hysterics.

Hearing my cries, Mia came running. She almost tripped on her long brown skirt. "What's wrong, darlin'?"

Unable to speak, I weakly gestured to the torn fabric on my lap.

Horrified, she asked, "Who did this to you?" I shook my head.

She helped me up and gently took the wrap from my trembling hands. "Let's go fix this." With care, she led me down the white hall.

She brought me into a new room where I found folding tables covered in fabric, sewing supplies and machines, and more.

Sniffling, I walked inside and looked around. It amazed me. "This is how clothes are made?" I asked softly.

Mia chuckled. "Well, it's how ours are anyway." Sweetly, she smiled and pointed to an empty table to her right. "We could always use some extra help. I heard you've got a knack for memorization. Want to try and learn a few things?"

I nodded and followed her over. After setting up my table with supplies from behind her, she immediately got to teaching. I won't tell you all of it; it would be a lot for you to remember. For me, it was a piece of cake. I memorized the cutting patterns, the way she stitched, the parts of the machine, basically everything she showed me within that hour. In no time, I had completely restored my head wrap and even made a new pink polka-dotted one.

Unfortunately, our time together was short and the bell rang for dinner. Taking my new garments, I turned to the postulate and asked, "Can you teach me more tomorrow?"

With a kind smile, she replied, "Of course. I will teach you every day if you'd like." I leapt for joy and wrapped my arms around her. I thanked her a million times then finally ran off to find Janelle.

Entering the cafeteria, I spotted her at the same table we ate at during breakfast. "How was your first day of school?" she asked

"The end was good, but it would have been better if people didn't hate me," I confessed.

She looked around at the girls. "I'm sure not all of them hate you."

"No, they all do," I cried. The happy moments of the day flew from my memory, replaced only with the glares and torments of the other girls.

Janelle exhaled heavily. "Ya'know, love? These girls all have problems. You'd think since we have it good here they'd appreciate things and be kinder to others, but that ain't how it works. No matter what you do to help somebody, if their hearts are hard, they ain't gonna change. Our Sisters here do everything they can and more to help these girls and many of them don't care." She sighed and added, "Despite that, we gotta remember though we all have had hard lives and no one knows the whole story." Pointing, she sincerely said, "Just be yourself and when they grow outta their insecurity, they'll come around. I promise ya. Just stay strong."

I let that soak in. At nine years old, I was shocked to hear those words come from a peer. "That was a very grownup thing to say," was my only response.

She chuckled. "Don't worry; I didn't make all that up myself. I experienced the same problem you're havin' and that's what the Sisters told me. So now I tell you!"

With that in mind, I tried to be a little more tolerant from then on. It was very hard.

From that day, time passed like rushing sand in an hourglass. Two years went by and is now only a memory. During that time, my education was easier and I grew as an individual in my talents, especially with music and sewing.

However, my life was tough too. The six girls continued to torment me. It wasn't like they didn't let me sit with them or slightly offended me; that was normal and I am stronger than that. No, they embarrassed and physically abused me. For example, they would put tacks on my seat or hide my clothes when I took a shower or hit me, knowing I wouldn't fight back because I wanted to be better than them. I was always afraid to tell the Sisters, so I kept it all in. I would rarely even tell Janelle; I didn't want her to see that I wasn't strong enough.

Every day, something would rob my peace. Whenever I was calm either the girls would stir me up or my mind would wander back and remind me of what I had lost.

When I was eleven years old, I had a nervous breakdown. First, I was stressed about completing the religious part of my education. Second, I was very depressed thinking about my dead family and how they really weren't my family (again). It would hit me every now and then. I wondered if they *truly* loved me. Third, I couldn't stop thinking about Blake. I wondered if he was going through the same abuse where he was.

On top of all that, it was adoption day so the girls were brutal. They overheard one of the Sisters complimenting me saying how every parent would want to adopt me. That really boiled their blood.

They devised a plan to keep me hidden from the couples coming in. They found me finishing up a sewing project and caught me by surprise. They grabbed me and pulled me away from my work. That time, I tried to fight back but six against one isn't exactly fair. They dragged me down the hall with their hands over my mouth. My legs were flailing and I tried to bite. It was no use. They were too strong. They roughly brought me to the end of the foyer where a girl held the door open to a broom closet, bowing as the others threw me in. My body knocked over the buckets and brooms. They slammed the door shut and locked me in the dark.

I banged and screamed for an hour until my throat and fists bled. No one heard me. I fell to the ground, put my head in my knees, and sobbed. I wept until there were no more tears and then I passed out.

Hours later, I woke up in my bed. Janelle hovered over me with a worried expression on her face. "My goodness, Aymie! I am so happy you are awake," she exclaimed, giving me a tight hug. "I was lookin' for you all day. I was sure there was somethin' wrong."

Mia came in with a large glass of water and some food. Placing it on the table beside me, she bent over and looked at my face. "You poor thing, your eyes are all puffy," she noticed, gently stroking my face with her delicate hand. "Who did this to you? Was it Sophia and her friends?"

Looking down, I nodded.

Mia sighed and fixed her white veil. It was less than a week since she became a novice. I felt awful that she had to deal with this. Usually we would have several days of lovely celebration and her last day seemed ruined. "Have they treated you like this ever since you came here?" she asked.

"Yes," I whispered.

"I knew it," Janelle said. "Why haven't you told any of us the truth? We could have done something about this!"

I started sobbing whatever tears I could muster. "I wanted to stay strong, like you said," I cried, letting it all out. "A princess should always stay strong and help others." They tried to comfort me, but it didn't work.

Finally, Sister Maria Stella came in. "Oh, honey, you are awake! What happened?"

I couldn't get it out, so Janelle told her for me: "Those nasty brats locked her in the closet. They have been bullyin' her for years and she never said anything. I always knew somethin' was up."

"I knew that they were," the sister said quietly, "but I never knew how harsh. I have spoken to them before about this matter, but I believe I only made it worse. Now I think I know what to do."

"No, don't punish them!" I cried. "That will make things worse. I am tired of being hurt. I try to be a princess like Saint Maria but I can't. It's too hard."

Sitting on Janelle's bed, Sister Maria Stella said, "My child, becoming a princess is not easy, but that doesn't mean you aren't. Saint Maria Goretti was bullied too... in a way."

I looked at her. "Did mean girls lock her in closets or embarrass her in front of people?"

"Not exactly," she explained. "I think you are old enough to learn how she left this world."

I became nervous. I had asked how she died the first day I got there. I was afraid that the way she died could happen to me.

"She wasn't 'bullied' by her peers," she began, "she was 'bullied' by an older teenage boy. He was unchaste whereas Maria was a beautiful, pure twelve-year-old girl. However, he didn't see the beauty inside her; he only cared about the beauty outside. He wanted to take something from Maria and tried many times, but she always refused.

"One day, the older boy cornered her into the kitchen. He wanted to take away her purity, but she still refused telling him it was wrong."

Before finishing, she took a deep breath. "So... he hurt her... very badly. He wasn't even sorry but feared the cops so he took off and left her dying. It took them hours to find her and even longer for the ambulance to come. When she was at the hospital, they operated on her with no pain killer. The last thing she said before she died was 'Momma, I forgive Alessandro' and then she went to heaven."

I sat there in silence. *No wonder they didn't want to tell me before.* I was older, but still shocked. I didn't know what to say.

Sister Maria Stella's eyes met mine. "She forgave her murderer before she died. That's what being strong is about: fortitude and forgiveness. Being strong is not about letting them succeed in their wrongdoing. It is about standing up for what is right and forgiving those who knocked you down."

Standing up, the sister came over and kissed my forehead. "We are always here to help you through all of this and don't forget the One who is always with you." She pointed to the man on the $T$ and stood up to take her leave.

The sisters shut the door behind them and I sat thinking for a while. Janelle finally told me to eat, so I finished my dinner on my bed while we both sat in silence.

Okay maybe my story was a little depressing. At least it wasn't as bad as Shane's. I had some awesome times there too and eventually found peace.

# Chapter 11
## Mark: III

My turn again. Yes, Yared, finally. Well, we have to take turns otherwise we wouldn't get anywhere.

After our introductions to his buyer, Couch put his briefcase onto the table. "Here it is. Like you ordered," he said, gesturing to the chrome case.

Mr. Devin Page came over and examined the contents. He nodded approvingly, tugging on his black tie. "So it seems. You haven't let me down," he replied with a smile. "These were some difficult ingredients. How did you manage it?"

"It was actually easier than I thought," Couch confessed. "We had the people at the front desk quite distracted by these young men here." He gestured to Brand and me. "They've proved themselves to be quite capable of whatever plans you have in mind."

The man wearing the leather jacket who had been nervously glancing at us the whole time walked over to Mr. Page. "Are you sure you can trust these kids here with this task?" he whispered.

"Relax," the boss replied out loud, causing the man in the jacket to jump. "They are part of Couch's gang. They can handle it." Unconvinced, the other man crossed his arms and kept an eye on us.

"So, how can my boys be of service?" Couch asked finally.

"I think our newcomer will explain that to you," Mr. Page replied with a smile.

The smelly guy came forward, holding a wooden clip board in hand. "Okay, so here is how it's gonna work," Carl Mallory began, pushing the long dirty blond hair out of his eyes. "I take two of your boys back into my little operating room there and we see if this 'concoction' of yours works with a little something I've been working on." The four of us became a tense.

Couch thought it over for a moment, flicking an earring on his eyebrow. "All right, but what are you going to do exactly?" he asked, finally. "Where is your whole explanation speech?"

"I didn't write one," Mr. Mallory confessed, "but have you ever read any comics or stories on how people obtain super human powers?"

Couch nodded. "Yeah, but I don't see how that is relevant."

"Let's just say, I can give your boys these powers. Well, sort of."

Couch's eyes widened. "I'm listening."

"Awesome. Okay," he took a deep breath before continuing. "So what I have been working on is a way to give humans animal traits."

He was interrupted by the man in the flannel. "Are you serious? You hired this guy so we can act like *animals*?"

"Enough," Mr. Page scolded. "Mallory is onto something, just hear him out." Throwing his hands in the air, the man in the flannel stepped back and kept quiet.

"Thanks, man. Okay where was I?" Mr. Mallory recollected his thoughts and began again: "Oh right, so animal traits. Listen, there is an old theory. After the fall of Adam, humans lost part of their divine nature. However, the animals did not. So, I believe," he tucked his clipboard under his arm and interlocked his fingers, "that if we combine humans with animals, we can evolve into the most perfect being." Couch looked at him like he had ten heads. Sighing, Mr. Mallory added, "And it would give the kids rad abilities that animals have. Such as super speed, night vision, excellent hearing, etcetera. Any trait an animal has, they can have."

"Now we're talking," Couch said excitedly. "My boys are up for it. What do you need? Who do you need?" Theo stepped forward to protest but stopped immediately after Couch shot him a menacing, intimidating look.

"Right on," Mr. Mallory exclaimed. "Now, I've never done this before on a human so I don't know how it should go." Pointing to Theo and Jordan with a lanky finger, he said, "I would like your two oldest as test subjects if that is all right."

Theo and Jordan looked at each other, then at Couch. With no hesitation, Couch jerked his head towards Mr. Mallory. Reluctantly, the boys followed the smelly, crazy, scientist.

"Wait, I want to do it!" Brand called before they got very far. The other men were surprised by his eagerness. Mr. Mallory looked back, smiled, and kept walking. "No, please," Brand begged. "Let me prove my dedication to you and my brothers."

"Sorry, kiddo, I need to see how it works with the most developed brains first. You're still growing so you might turn into mush," Mr. Mallory said not looking back.

Then, they disappeared into the next room with the three men following behind; leaving Mr. Page, Couch, Brand, and me alone.

"How long will it take?" Couch asked.

Mr. Page shrugged his shoulders. "Not sure. This is his first time doing it."

"So in other words we have no idea what to expect," Couch said with a sigh.

"Unfortunately not," Mr. Page responded. "He told me his serum should only inject the subject's DNA with only one ability from the animal of his choice. He said he is starting with mammals. So you won't have to worry about having to keep one of your boys in a fish tank."

Couch laughed. "That's a good thing."

Mr. Page wrapped up the meeting. He went to the back and grabbed a large black leather bag. Inside was money; a *ton* of money. "Here you are," he said, "thirty-five-thousand cash just like we agreed. Keep this up and there will be more. I will double it if Carl's experiment works with your boys, and we get more like them. That, however, is on Mr. Mallory. Let's hope for both of our sakes he pulls this off."

Shaking Mr. Page's hand, Couch replied, "I hope so too. We will be back in a week to check on the boys. Is that reasonable?"

"Very," the man with the tie said. "Until then, farewell."

The journey home was quiet. Brand and I didn't speak at all even after we were back at Fallout. I changed and lay in my cot, staring at the ceiling. I could *not* sleep. I kept thinking about what that scientist was doing to my brothers, how that man had so much cash, the woman on the train, and a billion other questions. I lay on my back and held the business card the woman gave me high above my face. I read *WHYP* over and over, trying to figure out what it meant.

After dropping it on myself a few times, I decided to get some rest. I put it on the ledge next to my cot and forced myself to sleep.

I just went through the motions for the next few days and anticipated seeing Theo and Jordan again. Finally, weeks passed and the day arrived for us to check up on them. Thankfully, Couch agreed to let Brand and me accompany him.

Arriving in the same basement, we were greeted by Mr. Mallory bursting through the door towards the back and skidding to a stop before us. "You're here already?" he asked frantically. He was sweating and his lab coat was torn. "Look, they're fine, but I need more time and more ingredients. The rest of your concoction is shipped to its actual destination; I only received a bit of it. However, I don't just need *Couch's Concoction*, but the ingredients it contained."

Unsure of how to react to Mr. Mallory's episode, Couch agreed, hoping it would bring more money. After that meeting, the days continued and a few other boys, Brand, and I were given Mallory's list and went on a shoplifting spree. We stole things from pharmacies, science labs, all that jazz.

We got the final ingredients just in time for the next meeting with Mallory. Couch brought the items alone and told us to stay put. After he returned, I waited another week in agony, wondering what was happening. Theo and Jordan were with the scientist for three weeks and we were clueless as to what was going on.

Finally, it was time to see them. We returned to Mr. Page and Mallory at the end of the third week and found the scientist happy as a clam. "I think they are ready, Mr. Couch," Mr. Mallory said excitedly. Despite his good attitude, he looked horrible. His tie-dye shirt was stained and ripped. His once long white lab coat was covered in grime and half its size. His dirty blond hair was untamed and seemed to not have been washed since we first met him.

"All right Carl," Mr. Page said, "bring them out." You could tell by his stance and behavior that he was just as anxious as we were.

With a skip in his step, Mallory ran into the back. He came out of the hidden room with the two boys close behind. As they approached, I didn't know what I was looking at.

*Is that...really...them?* I wondered. Theo's white skin became tanner and his arms and head were *covered* in blond hair. His locks were long and matted. His blue eyes turned a dark brown and seemed very nervous. He was munching on a turkey sandwich with his new sharp pointy teeth. I also saw something dangling from behind him... he grew a *tail*.

Jordan's dark skin stayed the same but his body was covered in more hair and his fuzzy head had golden highlights. His arms were wrapped in medical gauze at the elbow. His eyes were a lighter brown and they became three-times bigger. Seeing our horrified and confused reactions, he smiled, revealing his sharp teeth.

"Meet, your new and improved friends!" Mr. Mallory exclaimed, gesturing to his new creations. "Theo here has been experimented on with *Soricidae* and Jordan, *Nycticebus*."

"Which means?" Couch asked impatiently.

"Shrew and Slow loris," Mr. Mallory replied, annoyed.

"Seriously? So no super speed? No flight ability?" Couch grumbled, walking around the boys and examining them.

"I wanted to start small," Mr. Mallory explained, trying to be patient. "Both of these animals have deadly bites. They both can inject venom, but in different ways." Mr. Mallory gestured to the boys' mouths and added, "The Shrew has venomous saliva while the Slow loris has to actually suck the poison from the glands located on the inner elbows." He pointed to the gauze wraps on Jordan's arms. We all stared at him.

"It's nasty, right?" Jordan added, subconsciously rubbing his inner elbows. "It works though."

"You've tried it?" Couch said surprised.

"Of course," Mr. Page explained. "We needed to make sure it's effective and if they can handle their new abilities."

Confused, Couch asked, "How did you conduct these tests, if I may ask?"

"Let's just say there are less people here tonight, if you hadn't noticed," Jordan replied smugly.

"Uh huh," Couch said, staring at him. Shaking off the thought, he addressed Theo. "How about you? You test out your venomous bite?"

"You don't want to know," he said with a mouth full of sandwich.

"Yeah, there is something you should know about Theo over here," Mr. Mallory said slowly. "A shrew needs to eat three times its weight every day."

Couch paused for a moment. He laughed. "You're not serious," he said, chuckling nervously.

"Don't worry, don't worry, man," Mr. Mallory responded with his hands out. "I reduced it to half. Just keep him fed or he will go berserk."

Flabbergasted, Couch didn't know what to make of it. "He weighs 180 pounds," he told him. "That would be—"

"Two-seventy, I know, I know." Mr. Mallory took a deep breath and continued, "Look, I know there are side effects, but we talked about this. Thanks to these boys, I now know how to give the new test subjects less physical characteristics. I will soon be able to have a 'pick-and-choose' ability serum."

"Mr. Couch," Mr. Page interrupted, before anyone would argue, "this worked. I got results. That's what I care about. Now, will we keep our deal and double your pay for more subjects or leave it where it is?"

Couch took a deep breath. "We can keep our deal," he decided.

"Besides, I will need the money for Theo's grocery bills." After shaking Page's and Mallory's hands, it was finally time to take Theo and Jordan home. Mallory gave them oversized sweatshirts to hide themselves. They pulled the hoods over their heads and we made our way back to Brooklyn. It was difficult but we managed to walk them down the city, onto the subway, and back to Fallout without being spotted.

Big Daddy greeted us when we came in and was happy to see Theo and Jordan home…until they removed their jackets. The moment he saw their eyes he was terrified. Instead of his warm welcome, his mouth gaped open and he stared at the two.

"Nice to see you too," Jordan said, rubbing the side of his fuzzy temple.

Immediately, Theo brush past Big Daddy and headed straight for the fridge. "Food, food, food," he mumbled as he rummaged.

"How much more does he need to eat?" Brand asked Jordan as Theo consumed an entire jar of pickles.

"Not too much more," he replied. "He ate almost all he needed back with Mr. Mallory."

After a few minutes of just gawking, Big Daddy finally spoke. "What did he do to you boys?" he asked softly.

"Lots of things," Theo said before chugging a carton of milk.

"I'll give it to you in brief while the shrew finishes its drink," Jordan said crossing his arms. He took care not to touch his bandages. "When we went in, we had no idea what to expect. We thought he would inject us with some serum or zap us with gamma rays like in the comics. We were dead wrong. He actually needed to operate on us."

"So these new teeth and glands," Couch said, pointing to his arms, "were implants? Not side effects from the serum?"

"Not exactly," he replied. "To be honest, we aren't sure what he really did. We were knocked out and he refused to tell us. Frankly, I don't wanna know." He rubbed the sides of his face. "But, when we woke up we were freaking out. Our bodies… didn't really feel like our bodies. I don't feel like myself anymore. I was in so much pain..." his mind was lost in thought for a moment. Bringing himself back, he added, "I can't even describe it. We were strapped to operating tables and just screaming our lungs out.

"We did have more side effects than he'd like to admit," Jordan continued. "Theo actually went nuts. When we were released, Theo jumped up and ran around the room; scratching at the walls and chewing on stuff. He actually attacked one of Mr. Mallory's workers and bit him…" Jordan almost didn't finish his sentence. Taking a deep breath, he stared Big Daddy dead in the face and stated, "and then Theo ate him."

I stood there in awe as he finished his story. Hearing that last part, I wasn't sure if he was telling the truth, but the expression on his face told me he wasn't joking. Looking at Theo, I had horrible scenarios running through my head. My little brain imagined him going crazy and violently tearing the flesh off of a human…

Unfortunately, my imagination was too graphic and it made me sick to my stomach. So ill in fact that I had to rush to our bathroom and throw up. I didn't get to hear the rest of the story; they were done when I came back. Frankly, I'm glad I missed it.

One thing is for sure, I could never look at them the same again. To think that they actually killed and *ate* human beings was insane. I'm not going to lie…I was afraid of them and wanted to ask Mr. Mallory why he did it. But, I always kept quiet and listened to Brand's advice about *never* asking questions.

Yeah, Lucas, I am happy you Mutants didn't go crazy like that too. I feel so bad for you guys, you have no idea.

# CHAPTER 12
## Mark: IV

Getting used to our new friends was tough. The next couple days were especially difficult. Everyone woke up that morning to Theo rummaging through the fridge and eating everything. He was sitting on the floor in the kitchen, shoving whatever we had into his mouth.

Big Daddy was not too thrilled about his new behavior, but he tried not to show it. "What are you doing?" he asked firmly, his thick arms crossed.

"Um, eating?" Theo replied sarcastically with a mouth full of bread.

Looking around at his mess, Big Daddy was too upset for words. He tried to keep it in but finally, he spat, "You ate everything! We just went shopping two days ago."

Belching, Theo said, "Sorry, Big Daddy. I just need to eat. If I don't I'll go nuts."

Big Daddy sighed and rubbed his head of dark hair. "I understand. I guess this is our price to pay." He thought for a moment and looked at Jordan, "Next week, once you two are more relaxed, I have a big assignment for you and two other boys. For now, just keep covered and do your normal routine."

Brand's face lit up. "I can go with them, Big Daddy. Whatever the task I can handle it. I am sure Couch told you how I offered to take one of their places for the experiment."

"Yes, yes he told me," he replied, waving the boy's comment away. "I will think about it, Brand."

I became jealous. I didn't want Brand to do more assignments than me. I kept forgetting that I was seven and he was fourteen. But before I could say anything, Big Daddy ordered Theo to get up and for us to get started on the day's "work".

Brand's and my usual job was pick-pocketing people on the surface. We had quotas and everything. On top of that, we put card scanners on all of the ATM's on our streets. We were able to bring in thousands of dollars from those scanners without anyone knowing and we were never caught.

That day we worked in Manhattan. Everything was normal until Jordan met us on the streets a little after lunch time. He was running faster than I'd ever seen. He was wearing a blue jacket with the hood hiding his face. His sunglasses almost flew off as he skidded to a stop before Brand and me. "Guys, I need your help," he said panting.

"What's your problem, man?" Brand said annoyed as he shoved a woman's necklace into his old backpack.

"It's Theo," Jordan replied seriously, taking off his sunglasses. His giant light brown eyes filled with desperation. "We were just doing our stuff when he smelled some food and ran off. I need help finding him and dragging him back."

Brand thought over it for a moment. When he realized what he could get out of the situation, his face lit up. He decided to use this as an opportunity to get his brand. "Okay, we will help you catch him. And *I* will personally pay for his lunch."

"Are you serious?" Jordan said confused. "You are one of the cheapest guys I know."

Brand shrugged. "I've done some good business today," he said smugly. He looked at me and pointed his thumb over his shoulder. "Mark, grab the scanners and let's get him."

Nodding, I casually walked around to each ATM, slyly removed the scanners, and met them back on the last block where Theo was. "What if he gets caught?" I worried as I placed the machines in Jordan's empty pack. "We'll be in danger looking for him."

"No matter what, we look out for our own," Jordan reminded, throwing the bag over his shoulder.

Thankfully, it didn't take us long to find him. We only needed to follow the sound of screaming people. Running down the city streets, we located him in a bakery. Theo was behind the counter, eating all of the food like an animal. His hoodie was torn in half and lay covered in jelly at his feet. His sunglasses had been trampled; their pieces scattered across the tile floor.

Theo was exposed.

Everyone could see his hairy blond head and almost black eyes. My only consolation was his tail was still tucked in his pants…

In fear, the customers had fled and the owner was in the corner of the shop holding a kitchen knife.

"Theo!" Jordan called as we burst through the door.

"Almost done with this cheesecake," he yelled back, waving a sticky hand above his head. "Then onto the doughnuts." He licked his lips with his unnaturally long tongue. He ignored everything else and kept his focus on the food.

"Who is that?" the owner screamed, trembling in fear.

"We are so sorry, sir, we will get him out of here," Jordan apologized.

"No you will not, I am calling the police," he replied, shakily. "Where is my phone?"

Brand began to panic. "What will we do? They will arrest us all," he whispered.

I had an idea. I rushed up to the counter, leaned over, and gently grabbed the owners arm before he could find his telephone. "Sir, please our friend is ill. The police will make it worse," I explained as he watched me nervously. Letting go, I flipped my backpack around and pulled out the wallet with the most money.

Holding out a chunk of cash, I offered it to the frightened store owner. "Please, take this to pay for the food our friend is eating."

He hesitated, watching the money with scared eyes as if it were dangerous. The man finally snatched it and motioned for us to get out of there. While I was negotiating, Jordan and Brand had knocked Theo out and grabbed him. Once the man told us to leave, I thanked him and we bolted home, carefully trying not to be seen. We were forced to take the long way back. We had to dip through alleyways, climb over rooftops, and even go through the sewers. Carrying a 180 pound Mutant-shrew through New York City and back to Brooklyn is not fun.

Finally, we reached Fallout before we collapsed from exhaustion. Brand entered the code in the keypad behind a large dumpster. Like normal, the entrance on the ground slid open and we all descended, shutting the door tightly behind us.

"What happened?" one of the boys, Louis, asked as we carried Theo inside and plopped on the kitchen island.

"He's fine, just knocked out," Jordan explained, rubbing the sweat off his furry head. "We need more food though. He is going to wake up and go into another feeding frenzy."

"What time do Couch and Big Daddy get back?" I asked, fanning my sweaty body with my green t-shirt.

"Big Daddy gets back at six; Couch at eight," Louis responded.

"That gives us three hours to get Theo more food," I concluded. With determination, I added, "We can do it."

"Are you a moron?" Brand yelled. "Wait, let me rephrase that. You are a moron," he forcefully poked me in the chest. "How are we supposed to get enough food? We can't buy enough and we certainly have no place to hide it if we stole it."

Rubbing the new bruise on my chest, I smirked and replied, "I have an idea for that." Quickly, I explained my plan. My colleagues had mixed feelings about it but we were out of options and time because Theo woke up. Quickly, the five of us returned to the surface and carried out my clever plan…well, I thought it was clever.

"Bad idea, bad idea," Brand was telling me as he drove through the busy streets with his newly stolen food delivery truck. While we were rushing to bring Theo home, I noticed our favorite grocery store in Brooklyn was having a delivery today. They always came in threes to that store. So, we knocked out the drivers and took the trucks. Easy as pie…but Brand didn't think so.  He was not as cool under pressure as he makes out to be. His brown face dripped with sweat and his eyes were filled with anxiety as he keenly watched the road.

"Dude, seriously, we are so gonna get caught," he worried, "I don't have my license."

He amazed me sometimes. Cocking my head to the side, I stared at him. "Really? We just stole—*stole*—three trucks and you are worrying about not having a license?"

He ignored me and followed closely behind Jordan and Theo, who were following Louis, the only member of Fallout who knew how to drive. He also was the only one who had access to our abandoned warehouse that we usually stashed bigger goods.

We got there without any complications just like I had said. They drove fine, no one stopped us. We did almost hit a few old ladies, but they're okay… I think. Regardless, no one was after us; no one stopped us. You'd be surprise how little the police cared during my time.

When we arrived, we pulled the trucks right into the old, brick warehouse and began unloading. We separated the food into two piles: Theo and everyone else.

"We have locks and cameras all over this place," Louis told us as we finished unloading. "Anyone tries to come in here, we'll get 'em."

"Thanks, man," Jordan said, shaking his hand. "This means a lot."

"Yes, yes, yes," Theo began chanting. He danced around his pile of food and sang, "Time for dinner, time for dinner!"

"Relax, man, we gotchu," Jordan said picking up a loaf of bread.

Sitting on a crate of watermelons, Brand wiped the sweat from his forehead and watched Theo scarf down the loaf in one bite.

Shaking his head, Brand looked at Jordan and said, "It's sweet that you didn't turn psycho."

"Yeah, me too," Jordan replied, subconsciously rubbing the glands on his inner elbows. "Don't get on my bad side, though; just in case."

Brand smiled. "Never wanted to."

After taking a breather, we separated Theo's food into how much he needed per day. Thankfully, we had enough for two weeks. We gave Theo more to eat and he sat down in the middle of the warehouse and munched away.

It was the middle of the night when he finished; time to dump the trucks. Carefully, we drove them to the other side of town and left them in an old lot. When we finally returned to Fallout it was three in the morning.

"Where have you boys been?" Big Daddy yelled when we came back. He was in his ratty pajamas and looked exhausted.

"Grocery shopping," Theo told him with a sharp smile.

We were each carrying about five bags of food to restock our own shelves. The look on Big Daddy's face was priceless. It was a mix of shock, horror, joy, and disgust. "How did you do this? And why isn't Theo eating it all?"

"I ate my fill before," the shrew explained, patting his stomach.

Jordan placed his bags on the kitchen island. "We stole some delivery trucks and stored the food in our warehouse."

"Just the five of you?" he asked confused, pointing to each of us.

"Yeah, but it was all this little man's idea," Louis said, referring to me. Everyone except for Brand gave me the credit.

"We also rationed Theo's food so he will have enough for two weeks," I told him. "Now he won't have to jump over bakery counters and eat all their food."

Ashamed, Theo had to explain what happened and how Jordan, Brand, and I saved him despite the risk. He even told him how it was me who stood up to the owner and persuaded him not to call the cops on us.

Impressed, Big Daddy smiled and clapped for us. With a smirk, he went to wake up Couch. We heard some grumbling and moaning before Couch lethargically made his way into the kitchen wearing only boxers and bunny slippers…as per usual. In his pale hands was a kit of needles. Behind him, Big Daddy came in carrying three silver earrings. Looking at Brand and I, Big Daddy said proudly, "You boys deserve these."

Saying nothing else, Couch pierced Brand's and my ears as a sign of our accomplishment. However, I didn't get just one. I got *two* piercings. That was unheard of!

Once Couch finished cleaning my ear, Brand looked at me with such distaste and hatred. Now, we both had three earrings on the same ear. Looking at Brand, I knew that our relationship would never be the same.

After that day, things began to change. Every day was a new adventure and new risks were taken. Theo and Jordan finally tried their abilities. We broke into high security facilities, in New York City and out. We made ourselves *millions* and gave Mr. Mallory and his partners all they needed for their business. I never found out what they used it for while with Fallout, but I discovered it later.

As our numbers grew, we offered more boys for test subjects to Mr. Mallory's super serum, but they never came back. Mr. Mallory took them and kept them for further study. They would come around occasionally if we needed extra help with an assignment, but that was it. Theo and Jordan were the lucky ones who stayed back with Fallout.

I am not going to tell you everything that happened. I don't want you to get bored…or horrified at all the crimes I committed... uhm, let's go with the first thing. Before I stop, I want to quickly tell you about how I got the Fallout brand on my chest that Alison likes to stare at.

[Yes, I did see you that time you guys saved me from Wally.]

I was thirteen years old and Brand and I were on an assignment with Theo and Jordan. It was the usual ingredient smuggling. Brand and I were just the getaway drivers, but we took our job seriously.

This time, something went wrong. There was gunfire and shouting. "What should we do?" I asked, slightly panicked, looking outside the window of the passenger side.

"Wait," Brand said impatiently, gripping the wheel. "We aren't supposed to interfere with them. We could get hurt."

Then the alarms went off in the building.

"We should grab them and get away now!" I yelled.

"No!" he bellowed, forcefully grabbing me by the arm. "We wait two minutes or leave without them. That is final."

I tore myself from him, threw on my ski mask, grabbed my gun, and ran into the building.

I found them surrounded. Security guards circled my friends and aimed their weapons, ready to fire. Theo was down on the ground and Jordan seemed exhausted. As fast as he could, Jordan sucked the poison from his inner elbows and covered himself and Theo in it for defense.

I hated when he did that. It made everything a mess and it was nasty.

I hid in a doorway and randomly fired at the ceiling. The lights shattered and littered the chrome floors below. Those surrounding my friends panicked and dropped to the ground; they didn't know what to do. This never happened.

Amidst the confusion, Jordan grabbed Theo and ran past them.

In the blinking light, I saw the guards get to their feet and prepare to fire, but I wouldn't give them that chance. I shot them down with no remorse and followed my friends out.

Quickly, we made our escape and leapt into the car. The moment we were in, Brand drove us back to the shelter. I panted in the front seat as I listened to the alarms and shouts of angry guards fade away.

Finally, we were at Fallout. We were safe. The moment we stepped foot into the kitchen, Jordan and Theo told everyone in Fallout the story of how I saved them. For my bravery, Couch took out a metal branding iron with Fallout's symbol; three triangles pointing to a circle in the center.

I had proven myself in excellence and undying effort.

Without saying anything, I removed my shirt and stood up straight. With a smile, Couch pressed the burning metal over my heart. I clenched my fists and grit my teeth as my chest burned. I didn't cry and tried not to show that it hurt… but it did. Finally, Couch slowly pulled the iron away and pressed a cool cloth over my chest. I was now branded and a true, high member of Fallout.

Everyone was thrilled for me…except for Brand, naturally. He was twenty-years-old and still never got his. He was furious. He did not speak to me for months and abandoned me on our daily duties. I never got a chance to confront him and try to talk things over because he had left Fallout before I could do anything. He went and volunteered himself to be a subject for Mr. Mallory and *never* came back.

I was devastated. He was my closest friend and I felt like it was my fault that he left. Unfortunately, a lot of the other kids began to treat me as if it was. I don't know why. Brand had taught all the new boys and they looked up to him. He was their role model. They were hurting and they took it out on me. Everyone had forgotten about my heroics and used me as a scapegoat.

Because of their constant cruelty and Brand's abandonment, I slipped into depression and even went through an "emo phase". I shaved half of my head and barely spoke to anyone. I felt like a nuisance and the only reason I helped out was because Big Daddy favored me the most. Without him, I wouldn't be doing anything important. I coped in my thievery, hacking, and drumming. I sincerely thought that *that* is how I would feel the rest of my life.

Little did I know that soon the day would come that would change my life forever.

# THE MAINLAND

# Chapter 13

## Shane: V

My turn again. This is Shane; the one whose circus family was killed and the two bad people were after me again. Please don't be confused with emo Mark. I hope you guys don't get too lost with us jumping between stories. I promise you they will connect eventually

Another attempt had been made on my life and I was running. First my aunt and uncle, now the circus I called home. I was never safe. I thought things were finally turning out okay and everything fell again.

I had no idea where I was going and I barely rested. A few miles from where we parked the circus were woods and only woods. Having no choice, I went straight through them. I had been going for days with no provisions and no direction, but that didn't stop me. There had to be another side…and I was right. After a week, I found the edge of the forest. Beyond it was a house on a hill.

Seeing it in the distance, I ran through the backyard and up to this dark brown log home. I dropped my guitar and put all my strength into my feet, but it was no use. Exhaustion took over and I passed out before I could reach it.

What happened next was something I can never forget.

The first thing I remember was hearing classical music. My eyes slowly fluttered open and I began to come to my senses. Looking around, I found I was in someone's family room. To my right was a small television hanging on a beige wall with a sofa and sitting chairs facing it. To my left were pictures of girls all across the wall; girls everywhere. I looked at every single one and only found one boy… who was an older man, presumably the head of the household.

Shaking my head, I decided to try and stand up, but I couldn't. I was tied to a chair. I tried to loosen my bonds but it was no use. The rope was tight and coarse. Not to mention I was exhausted and practically *dying*.

I struggled for a moment but to no avail. My head dropped and I began panting. My throat was dry, my arms weak, and I couldn't keep my eyes open. I was about to try one last time when a little girl in a pink dress poked her head around the doorway in front of me. Her soft dark hair was pulled into pig tails and her skin was pale and smooth. She stared with her big brown eyes.

I froze and watched her carefully. Trying to be nice, I smiled, but I think that made it worse.

She gasped. "It's awake!" she yelled.

I heard two other shrieks from the back and watched her and two other girls run down the hall. "It's awake! It's awake!" I heard the three of them chanting. Their screaming ceased, and they ran back into the room and hid behind me. I tried to turn around and see them, but I could barely move my head.

Then, two more girls came in carrying bowls of food and water. They looked a few years older than the others; both had brown eyes and brown hair. They were wearing long black skirts and t-shirts: one orange the other yellow. The one in orange held the large bowl of water to my lips. I was so parched that my brain forgot about my Aquaphobia and I gulped it down messily. The girl in yellow took the pretzels out of her bowl and shoved them forcefully into my mouth. It hurt but I didn't care. I was starving.

As I gobbled the whole bowl, the girl in the yellow whispered to the other, "How much does it need to eat?" The one in orange just shrugged her shoulders.

Finally, the oldest came in to meet me. She was a short, solid girl with long brown curly hair and gorgeous blue eyes. She had beautiful pale skin and nine freckles on her cheeks. She wore white shorts and a lavender short sleeve shirt. Around her neck was a leather cord with seven silver rings and a key with an intricate Celtic knot design. The key split the rings into groups of three and four. I thought it was really cool.

She crossed her arms and asked, "Who are you and what do you want?"

Unsure of what to say, I stared at the pretty girl. Getting impatient, she asked her questions a second time. "Who are you and what do you want? Are you alone?" Slowly, I nodded. "Okay, so you are alone," she said as she paced back and forth. "Are you hiding from something? Running from something maybe?"

Confused, I asked, my voice cracking, "Why would you think that?"

One of the girls behind me yelled, "It can speak! It can speak!"

The eldest hushed them. "Why don't you go put on your playlist? It's your turn."

I heard the pitter-patter of little feet running back and forth. When she came back, I heard a very familiar classic rock song playing throughout the house.

"My favowite song," she explained, still hiding behind me. "'Thunder-duck' by *ABCD*."

"Close enough," I said, trying not to laugh… even though I was so weak I couldn't anyway.

"Anyways, I think that," the oldest continued again, referring back to my question, "because you passed out in our backyard. People who are willing to come up this way need something desperately. Also you had no bags, just a guitar." As she mentioned it, I heard the sound of my instrument being strummed.

"Hey! Leave my guitar alone," I cried, my voice cracking.

"They're fine; they know how to take care of instruments. They will just try to play 'Thunder-Duck'," she reassured. "Also, judging by your guitar, you have been around a lot. On the run or whoever you were with liked to travel?"

"Both, I guess you could say," I replied hesitantly.

"All right, we are making progress," she said with a smile, clapping her hands together. "Now, either I can give you my guess of who you are or you can just tell me?"

I was afraid of what she was going to say, but I told her my story anyway… well, a story. I twisted some of the facts a bit. I basically told her I got separated from the circus; nothing more.

"Dang, my story was close, but not exact," she said disappointed, showing no concern that I was lost. "Well, that doesn't matter. Practice makes perfect. Anyways, I guess we can trust you enough to tell you our names. My name is Shannon. Shannon Hollinger."

[Yes, yes, that's how we met. I am not answering that, Aaron. Shannon is sitting right next to you.]

Anyway so the rest of the girls began their introductions. They gave me their names and ages. I didn't really care how old they were I just wanted to be set loose.

The one after Shannon was seven year old Peggy in the orange shirt. The one in yellow was Lucy who was a year younger. The two girls who screamed when they heard I was awake came out from behind me; carrying my guitar. They were wearing similar blue dresses and both had reddish-blonde hair, freckles, and blue eyes. The taller one in the lighter blue dress was Carol-Ann who was three. The shorter—who was one—was Agnes.

Last but not least was the two year old girl who let her sisters know I was awake: Rebecca. "What's your name?" Rebecca asked, looking up at me with her big eyes.

"My name is—" I started to say.

"Maybe it doesn't have a name," Carol-Ann said, interrupting me.

"No name?!" Agnes shrieked.

"Can we name it?" Rebecca shouted. They kept bickering back and forth about what to name "it" while I sat there awkwardly…still tied to the chair.

They stopped when they heard a knock at the door. Shouting in delight, the three younger ones ran to it, completely forgetting about the argument they just had. I heard the voice of another girl greeting them in the hall.

*More girls*, I thought. I was surrounded by girls. I wouldn't have minded so much if I wasn't tied to a chair, being called "it", and eating food out of dog bowls.

"Shannon! Where are you?" the new girl called.

"In here Johanna," she replied.

"I want to see this 'new pet' the girls are talking about," she said before entering.

"Hey!" I croaked in protest.

She stopped mid step when she saw me. She covered her mouth and began giggling. "Where did he come from?"

"Its name is *Clarius*," Carol-Ann told her, with a smug look on her face. The other girls protested and so did I. I was not a fan of being called *Clarius* whatever that meant. Despite our pleas, it was official. Carol-Ann had dubbed me "Clarius" and that was forever my pet name. She had been reading too many stories about the Romans when we first met. She wanted a Roman knight in shining armor but got me instead.

"Girls stop!" Shannon yelled. "So what is your name, really?" she asked when we stopped our fighting.

"Shane. Shane Hodgins," I said, peering at Carol-Ann who blew a raspberry at me.

"Nice to meet you. Welcome to our home," she said, untying me effortlessly.

"Hi, I'm Shannon's best friend, Johanna," the new girl introduced. She was a few inches taller than her friend, but they were both eleven. She had long dirty blond hair and green eyes that matched her shirt.

They seemed like nice girls; all very pretty too. Standing up, I stretched and rubbed my rope burnt arms as I tried to follow them into the kitchen. It was hard. Not only because I was dead tired but also because Agnes was latching onto my leg. With whatever strength I had left, I dragged myself and the little girl into the kitchen. Don't ask me how I managed it.

The moment I walked in, they gave me a sandwich. I scarfed it down in seconds. When I was finished, Shannon pointed out how tired I must've been and led me back to the room I was first held hostage. It was right by the back door in case I needed a quick escape if their parents' didn't approve of me upon their return. Agnes let go of my leg and ran to get me a blanket.

She came back dragging a big pink quilt with her sister, Carol-Ann. "You can use this," Carol-Ann said, handing it to me. "You'll sleep on the couch for now, but when Mommy and Daddy get back, you can sleep in a box by my bed."

Too tired to argue, I accepted it graciously and thanked all the girls. Once they left, I lay down on the couch by the TV and fell fast asleep.

When I woke, I could hear adult voices conversing in the kitchen. The parents were home. Sitting up, I looked at the clock underneath the TV and gasped. *Three* days had passed. I couldn't believe it. Slowly, I rose from the sofa and walked down the hall. Entering the large kitchen, I found the parents standing around the round stone island counter.

"Our guest is awake," the father said with an Irish brogue. He was a skinny fellow with short reddish blond hair and blue eyes. His skin was frail and covered in freckles. He was wearing black pants, a white collared shirt, and blue tie.

His wife walked over to me with a bowl full of pasta. She was a beautiful woman with long dark hair and brown eyes. She was the same height as her husband and had a solid appearance. "Are you hungry, *bambino*?" she said with an Italian accent.

I was so confused. One was from Ireland, the other Italy, and they have American children. I tried not to dwell on it and slowly accepted the bowl of spaghetti. I sat down at the table to my left and politely ate in quiet as the two continued to talk as if everything was normal.

After I finished, I glanced over at the clock. It was past ten. "I am so sorry, I hope I didn't disturb you," I apologized.

The wife smiled. "Mr. Hollinger just came home from work and I was just doing dishes." Clearing my plate, she said, "Shannon told me everything, but I think there is more to the story, no?"

I looked down at my lap. There was, but I was afraid to admit it. I didn't want people to know. I wasn't sure if I could trust them. *Still*, I thought as I looked at the couple.

I let out a deep breath and told them everything. The whole truth. They were so shocked by my story that they didn't know what to say.

"*Mio Dio*," the wife said finally with her hand on her chest. "Well, that settles it then. You are staying here until we find you something else."

"Veronica—," the husband began to object.

She glared at him before he could finish. Knowing the fury of his wife, he remained quiet. "The world is a dangerous place, Quinn," she reminded him. "You of all people know that. Not only are those people after him, he could catch a cold or starve." She began mumbling to herself in Italian as she cleaned the dishes.

Not going to argue any more, Mr. Hollinger stood and beckoned me to follow him. He brought me to the bathroom and gave me more comfortable clothes. At thirteen, I was practically the height of Mr. Hollinger so he gave me his pajamas to wear. After freshening up, I was led back to the family room.

"I hope you don't mind the couch," he said fluffing up the pillows. "If you stay for a while, maybe I can arrange to get you a bed."

"Don't worry," I assured him. "This is enough. Thank you for doing this for me."

Smiling, the man ruffled my full, brown hair and said, "Ah, go way outta that. Besides, I always wondered what it would be like to have a son." He thought about that for a moment and looked at me caringly. As if remembering a horrible memory, he quickly shook his head and tried to put a smile back on his face. Before I could say anything, he quickly added, "You will be put to work around here though, understand?"

I nodded. "I will do whatever I have to."
He bid me goodnight and I passed out immediately.

# CHAPTER 14
## Shane: VI

I woke the next morning to three pairs of eyes staring at me closely. They scared me so I screamed, and then they screamed. It was chaotic. Mrs. Hollinger came charging in to see what the matter was. When she saw it was just the girls, she cursed a few times in Italian and told them to get into the kitchen for breakfast.

"Sorry about that, Shane," she apologized, rubbing her hands on her apron. "The little ones love to hang out with strangers. Then they frighten them so they never return." The woman shook her head. "You'll get used to them."

After she left me, I got dressed and headed to the kitchen for breakfast. The four youngest were sitting around the long table waiting for the older ones and their mother to bring them food.

"Morning, *Clarius*," Peggy teased. Trying not to get annoyed, I faked a smile.

"He doesn't like it when you call him that," Shannon told her.

"Yeah, how would you know?" Lucy challenged, flipping her long braids behind her.

"He pretended to smile to not hurt our feelings," she replied, carrying a tall plate of pancakes to the table.

Lucy tried to pick a fight but her mother stopped her. I settled in the seat next to Agnes. She was sitting on top of a stack of books so she could reach.

I learned so many knew things just at breakfast that day. First, Italian mothers will *never* let you leave the table until you have eaten over twice the serving size. Also, they said something called "grace" before eating. I had never done that before so it was nice. The kids were very quiet and respectful at the table; I did my best not to give a bad impression.

As we were cleaning up, there was a knock at the door. It was Johanna. "Ready for school, *bambina*?" Mrs. Hollinger asked as she came in.

"Happier we are almost done with this year's work," she replied, dropping her heavy blue backpack to the floor.

"Wait, you don't go to school?" I asked confused.

"No, mom homeschools us and Johanna," Shannon explained. "The things they teach us in school nowadays are a little 'weird' let's just say." She made a face that showed she didn't want to talk about it. Brushing it off, she added, "Our mom is a part-time school music teacher though. She teaches us our stuff in the morning and goes in for the afternoons."

I guess I could have been considered homeschooled in the circus, but I didn't really learn anything among the normal school subjects... unless sword swallowing was a thing.

Once breakfast was all cleaned up, the little girls grabbed their books from the next room and brought them to the table. I sat next to Mrs. Hollinger across from Shannon and Johanna. For the next several hours, we all did homework together. To my surprise, Mrs. Hollinger had extra books for me to use. Kindly, the woman began to teach me. Turns out I didn't know much, but she didn't mind. Her brown eyes looked at me with such kindness and her voice was sweet.

In those several hours, I realized how serious this family was about taking care of me.

Two o'clock rolled around when we finally finished our day's work. Mrs. Hollinger had instructed the girls to put their books away.

"I'll be back late tonight. There are leftovers in the fridge," she said as she put on her jacket. Kissing each one of us goodbye (even me), Mrs. Hollinger hurried out the door and left us alone for the day. I was so shocked… I never received that kind of affection before. The last time was from my Aunt Monika…

Not wanting to remember the pain, I closed my math book and asked, "What now?"

"Time for chores," Shannon said handing me a mop with a smug look on her freckled face.

Rolling my eyes, I took the mop from her frail hands. "Make sure you do a good job," she reminded, playing her favorite classical tunes over the speakers. I wanted to talk back, but I remembered I should try to be decent. They were letting me live in their house after all…

Reluctantly, I began to mop the sections of the house I was assigned while the girls went about their own work. I hadn't done chores since I was six years old…with Uncle Chuck and Aunt Monika. Looking into the mop bucket, I saw my reflection in the sudsy water. Immediately it was replaced with the horrified faces of my foster family before their heads were plunged into the cold, deadly stream.

I panicked. I let out a silent scream and knocked over the bucket. Trying to back away, I slipped on my mess and fell on my back with a *thud*. I lay there and wait for my anxiety attack to pass. I closed my eyes and tried to wish the Aquaphobia away…

As I steadied my breathing, I heard the stomping of little feet. Someone was ignoring sections of the floor I had just finished and proceeded to paint the white tiles with her footprints. The footsteps stopped and I felt someone's breath touch my face.

Cracking open an eyelid, I saw two dark brown eyes looking intently at me. Her long brown braids tickled my chin as she leaned closer to my face. Out of the corner of my eye I could make out bright yellow fabric. It was Lucy.

With a mocking tone, she said, "You scream like a girl. What's your problem?"

Embarrassed, my face turned bright red. I wasn't going to tell her I was afraid of water… "There's no problem," I told her firmly. "Get on with whatever you're doing."

Standing straight, she threw her hands up. "Whatever, you big baby," she replied. "Just hurry up. You're probably the slowest person I've ever met."

As a kid who made a living off of being the fastest runner ever, I took high offense to that. "I'll show you!" I called as she walked away. Frustrated, I snatched the mop off the slippery floor and hastily went back to work, ignoring the cold memories that flooded my mind. "I'll show them all," I muttered, thinking about the men who murdered my loved ones.

Two hours flew by before I was finally finished with my chores. I wiped the sweat from my forehead and went to the kitchen to put the supplies away. Inside, I found the girls sitting around the table, finishing a snack. "When did you guys get done?" I asked.

"Almost an hour ago," Johanna told me, tossing a grape into her mouth. "You'll get used to it."

My competitive side was rather upset the girls were much faster at cleaning than me…but I refrained from bringing it up. I took a paper plate and sat down to eat with them. After grabbing a handful of chips, I changed the subject. "So, do you guys ever leave the house to see, um, people? Are you guys trapped here like princesses?" I asked, trying not to sound rude. I was curious.

"Me princess!" Agnes shouted.

"No, me," Rebecca argued.

"I wanna be the dragon," Carol-Ann roared, jumping on top of her chair. She wielded her fork in the air, ready to slay herself. They almost started fighting again.

"No, no, no," Shannon repeated, swiping the fork from Carol-Ann's hand. "You can play dragons and princesses, but no pointy things. Promise?"

The three girls whined, but finally agreed. Clearing their plates, the youngest ones went off to play. "I don't know why you won't let them play with pointy objects," Lucy asked, poking Peggy with her spoon. Irritated, Peggy swatted the utensil away. The two were about to bicker until Shannon shot them a look. They stopped and jumped up to go on to another activity.

"We do more than most kids," Shannon finally explained once they left. "Most go to school and come home just to do hours of homework before rushing to sports or something. We get out and see friends, do volunteer and community work, and stuff like that."

"I guess that makes sense," I said, crushing some potato chips on my plate. "So what do you two girls do for fun?"

"Shannon spends most of her time with her books and case files," Johanna told me as she tied her dirty blond hair into a bun. "I like to read too, but also sleep and eat and other things. Really we are good with doing anything."

"Case files?" I asked confused.

"My dad is a detective," Shannon replied, standing up to clear her dish. "I like to go through his old files and try to solve them from the evidence given in the reports. When I think I got it, I check their results with mine." Bending over, she whispered, "Not to brag, but most of the time I am right."

"She is quickly following in her father's footsteps," Johanna said smiling as she handed her friend our plates.

As we finished tidying up the kitchen, we continued to chat about random stuff. However, one conversation led to another and the subject of siblings came up. I mean how could it not? It turns out Johanna is an only child and you already know Shannon is the oldest of many. For some reason, I was comfortable enough to tell them about my missing siblings…

"Wow, I am so sorry that happened to you," Johanna said sympathetically after I told them my story. Wiping the granite counter, she thought for a moment and added, "You know, no matter how far away you are or what your influences are, siblings always tend to like and do the same things."

Amazed, I replied, "Really? Is that a thing?"

"So the studies say," Shannon said. "You play guitar right? It is possible both of your siblings play an instrument or are interested in music as well." Shannon's face lit up, "Maybe we can help you find them."

"Shannon," Johanna said, "Don't you have—,"

"No, we can do it," she interrupted. "Shane, let's go write down all the facts and see what we can determine."

"Um, okay?" I replied unsure as she grabbed my hand and dragged me through the hall and into their tiny library. Being pushed inside, I stumbled over a pile of books on the floor. Steadying myself, I looked around. The left wall was lined with shelves and the right with metal filing cabinets. The back had a large map covered in sticky notes, push pins, and strings. My curious mind wanted me to wander over and see what it was for, but I held back.

"I am so happy you cleaned this room," Johanna said as she admired the cleaned floor. She ignored the books I almost killed myself on. "It was getting messy."

"Mom doesn't understand my thinking methods," she replied as she opened a hefty, dusty filing cabinet drawer. Flipping through files, she pulled out some yellowed, musty paper and brought it to the desk.

"'Methods'?" Johanna said, quizzical. With a laugh, she continued, "I think you are reading too many detective novels."

Shannon pulled out some paper and a pen from the mahogany drawer. There was a glint in her eyes as she hastily scribbled down all she knew. The way she wrote and proudly taped her notes on the wall proved her love for a good mystery and her desire to solve it.

I admired her determination. I walked over and wanted to watch her work, but my eyes caught something on the map behind her. I noticed many newspaper clippings, reports, and pixelated images of a young boy with curly brown hair. Taking a closer look, I realized that he was also missing.

Noticing my curiosity, Shannon explained, "My dad and I are working on that one together." She looked at the pixelated image longingly for a moment but shook it off. Quickly, she covered the notes on the missing boy with the information about my siblings. "This one," she said, tapping the first note, "I'm hoping we can do on our own."

"We?" I asked.

"Yeah, I need to know all you know," she replied, pointing to my chest. "So you said people are always out to get you, right? Well, then it is possible people are out to get your siblings too, especially if they chased your mom."

A puzzled look crossed my face. I only told that to her parents the night before. I didn't think she realized that important detail. Either she was eavesdropping or her mother couldn't stop talking about it. I decided to ignore that fact. She was trying to help, but I wasn't sure how much faith I could put in a young stranger…

"So," Shannon continued, rubbing her pale hands together, "We can research all the abductions, abduction attempts, accidents, attempted murders, all of that on children ages zero to thirteen in the USA."

"Sounds like a lot," I said, scratching my head.

"It is, but it will be worth it," she replied with a smile. In a flash she ran out of the room and returned with three laptops. Handing me a little pink one covered in flowers, she said, "Let's get through what we can today."

I looked down at the girly laptop and sighed. *This might just be a waste of time*, I thought as I sat down and opened it. Immediately, the three of us got to work on our research. Throughout it all, my feelings varied. I was excited that there was a possibility of finding my family, but I didn't want to get my hopes up. *How much can an eleven year old girl do?* I wondered, watching her work intently. Her pretty blue eyes were glued on the screen of her chrome laptop. She didn't let anything distract her…not even Johanna's snoring after she fell asleep.

We sat on the floor searching for hours before the clock chimed. Next on their schedule was music practice: my favorite. We put our investigation on pause and the girls led me to their beautiful music room that was home to many different instruments. Each girl could play. Shannon preferred Viola; Johanna, the piano. They performed together like a little orchestra. They even taught me to play with them on my guitar. Our practice ended abruptly when Rebecca and Agnes started whining because they were hungry. Dinner time.

After we ate was the hour of silence; I *hated* that part of the schedule. We sat in the sitting room either reading, thinking, whatever.

The girls usually caught up on their homework or took their time reading enlightening books. I am a very impatient person and have no need for sitting around doing nothing.

Despite my attitude, I decided to try that first night. I was struggling for the first five minutes and apparently was complaining to myself. Hearing my murmurs, Shannon got up from her chair and sat next to me on the wooden floor by the fire place. I will never forget what she told me:

"In this hyper, distracting world, true happiness and peace are rare," she began. "As people jump from one thing to the next, they wonder if it all means something. They wonder if they actually found their place in the world or if they're lying to themselves." She looked into my eyes. "They continue to wonder and be miserable because they never sat down to listen." Leaning closer, she whispered, "It's only in the silence that we can truly hear. Only in the silence will we find the truth. Once you realize that, peace and happiness will follow." Ending with that, she stood up and went back to reading her book.

Soaking that in, I stared at the flames flickering in the fireplace. First of all, that was intense for a tween girl to say. *Happiness?* I wondered. I was never sure if I truly felt happy. *Was I tricking myself? I didn't know the answer.* Then I understood what she said. I took a deep breath and sat in the silence.

I'm not going to lie; I wasn't able to sit in quiet for an entire hour. That first night I did it for less than three minutes and then had to get a book which was fine. I didn't mind starting off slow. I also didn't get the answer to my question either, but that was all right. Over time, I knew I would hear it.

Finally, the hour was up and it was time to get rowdy. To be honest, the girls surprised me. I had no idea how fun they could be. We played games all night. It wasn't like old people board games or shuffleboard or something, we played some intense games.

That particular night was clean and cool so we went outside and played capture the flag. I showed off the entire time. They could *not* catch me. Shannon did trip me a few times. She was pretty good… not that I was super impressed or anything.

We played about five games before the younger ones had to go to bed. We brought them inside, tucked them in, and then went back downstairs. It was only Shannon, Johanna, and I that were still awake. So, Johanna decided that we should all play video games. I would never have guessed a family like that to even know what video games are.

Well, I shouldn't be talking; I never actually played video games unless it was an arcade that we stopped at while on tour.

"You are really fast at running," Johanna complimented as we played some character fighting game. "How do you do that? You also don't pant or lose your breath after. It isn't really humanly possible."

"I'm just that awesome," I responded as she knocked my character off a cliff. "I trained every day in the circus. In fact, my ringleader got me into next year's national Junior Olympics." Recalling that, my mind flashed back to that night Edwin told me…the night he was murdered. The sights and sound of his body collapsing to the ground relayed in my mind. I got so distracted that I stopped playing the game for a few moments. I didn't snap back into reality until Johanna threw my avatar off the screen again and won the game. Shaking my head, I added, "Well, I guess I'll never get to put my speed to the test."

"Sure you will," Shannon told me as she played with her Celtic knot key necklace. "I don't think my dad will mind training you and making sure everything is okay."

My eyes widened and I stared at her. I just met this girl three days ago. "Are you serious?"

Her blue eyes looked back at me. "Why not?" she replied, shrugging her shoulders. "You have talent, Shane. You should show it off."

I didn't know what to say; so I stared awkwardly. She smiled, and my heart began to race. At the time, I wasn't sure why.

Trying to ignore my beating heart, I grinned and said, "You know you girls aren't so bad yourselves. To be honest, I wasn't sure what to expect, but I have to say. This is pretty sweet."

Shannon laughed. "Well, I guess we can take that as a

compliment."

Before I could answer, Mrs. Hollinger came back with her husband and Johanna's parents. It was time for Johanna to go home and for us to go to bed. Shannon bid me goodnight and they all went up to sleep.

That night, I lay on the couch, staring at the ceiling. In one day, so many things happened. I found a home, friends, and people who wanted to help me. I thought about the horrors of my past but what joy the future might bring. My imagination drifted to the idea of being reunited with my siblings. *We will find them. I know it*, I thought as my eyelids got heavy and I fell into a deep sleep.

# CHAPTER 15
## Shane: VII

Aymie said she wanted me to go again because she doesn't have much to say until our stories connect. Hope I don't confuse you all! To be honest, I could talk about my life with the Hollingers for weeks and never tell you all the stories. I will narrow it down to the most important events... especially when we visited New York City.

It had been a year since the Hollingers opened their home to me and a lot had happened. I pretty much became a part of their lives. I even adopted their beliefs. That will forever be one of my favorite experiences. At first I was scared because I had to have water poured on my forehead, but it was still amazing. The feeling I had after participating in their Celebration and receiving the Greatest Mystery for the first time was incredible and beautiful. On that day, I felt a peace like never before. I wanted to experience it every day, but it was harder than I thought. I understand I still have a lot to learn, but I am happy to have my foot in the right direction.

Even before I adopted their beliefs, I was still treated as a brother. They gave me my own room which the little ones were jealous of. The girls also enjoyed beating me up. It's hard to avoid it since their dad is a cop and teaches them many different self-defense arts especially boxing. Shannon and I became sparring partners and, I have to say, we are almost evenly matched.

[No, Yared, I'm better. Don't listen to her.]

Speaking of, Mr. Hollinger's work began to get busier. Good for them because they needed the money. Bad because that meant the crime rate increased *five times* in one year. It was awful and only getting worse.

Good news though, Mrs. Hollinger had another baby. Of course it was another beautiful girl. They named her Rachel. She had light curly hair and brown eyes. I felt like I lived in the middle of the fairy tale, twelve dancing princesses… except there were only seven of them.

Even with taking care of the baby, we still were able to make progress with Shannon's case of finding my siblings. We narrowed down about one hundred events that could possibly be connected to mine, but we were still looking.

After that year passed, we took a trip to New York City to visit the Hollinger and Capello family (Mrs. Hollinger's side). Apparently, both families immigrated there when they were very young and that is where they met. Business would have been better for Mr. Hollinger in NYC, but they moved away so they could raise a family in a more comfortable location.

"Ever been here before?" Mrs. Hollinger asked as we walked down the city streets.

"Once when I was with the circus," I replied, looking around at the tall buildings and crowded sidewalks. "Didn't get to do much sightseeing though."

Carol-Ann—who was four—held my hand and said, "I forgot Clarius was in the circus. Can you do any tricks?" She looked up at me curiously with her cute blue eyes.

Smiling, I rubbed her golden hair and said, "I told you I can do many tricks. I can do flips, hand stands, swallow swords—,"

"Swords?!" Agnes shrieked, trying to run away from Mr. Hollinger. "Where?! I want a sword!" Tearing her hand from her dad, she began to run down the street. The short cop yelled as he chased after her, snatching her before she ran right into traffic.

When Detective Hollinger returned with Agnes, she began bickering with Carol-Ann and Rebecca about who got what sword and what kind.

"You've gotta stop setting them off," Shannon complained.

Fortunately, they only argued and didn't try to attack each other in public like usual. We couldn't have been more appreciative when we reached their grandparents' house before there was too much screaming.

Going in, I was greeted by their friendly, welcoming family. Immediately, I felt at home. Sitting around the table, we sat and talked with them for over an hour. I was surprised I stayed still for so long. I guess it was because I enjoyed the way the grandmother and Mrs. Hollinger talked. Mostly with their hands, but their accents made it just as entertaining.

After eating enough pasta to solve world hunger, Shannon asked if she and I could take a walk a little further into the city to look around before her other grandparents' came over for dessert. Her father agreed as long as she kept a phone close by. Heading out, we ventured down the streets of New York City.

As we walked, we noticed that there were many homeless people. I knew there were usually poor folks, but it seemed like more than ever. The scariest part was most of them were children about Carol-Ann's and Lucy's age. Moved with pity, we gave them whatever pocket change we had. They were highly grateful. Sadly, we couldn't help them all.

"Why isn't the city doing anything about this?" I asked.

"I think they are, but there are too many," Shannon replied. "They just can't do enough. I have been doing some research and it seems like the parents are just disappearing."

"'Disappearing'?" I said as we walked. "I doubt that."

"So do I," she said sadly. "I think the same thing that happened to your family might be happening to others or something like it. Children separated and/or abandoned by their parents. This is happening all over the country; all over the world even."

"How is that possible?"

"I don't know, but I want to find out." Looking back over her shoulder, she said, "Care to ask around?"

I couldn't believe what she was saying. "Wait, you want to talk to the homeless children? I thought giving them money and walking away was enough. Doesn't your dad say never to talk to strangers?"

"I tied you to a chair and talked to you when we were strangers, right?" she replied smugly.

Grumbling, I agreed and we questioned some of the kids.

After speaking with a few, I couldn't believe the stories. It was odd. Most of their pasts revolved around three scenarios: First, broken homes and childcare fell apart. Second, given up for adoption or abandoned. Third, parents killed or taken and they were runaways.

"Your story sounds more like our last category," Shannon said quietly as we walked away from another child. She scribbled a few more things into her notebook and placed it back into her brown over the shoulder purse.

Suddenly, the two of us got knocked over by some kid who was coming the opposite way. Shannon fell over and her bag dumped.

"So sorry! So sorry," he apologized as he picked it up while I brought Shannon to her feet. His face was covered by his long hair and he quickly placed the contents back in her bag. When he finished, he handed Shannon her purse and took off.

"Shane, he just stole my wallet," Shannon said shocked, watching him run.

"Wait, what? You didn't even check your purse," I replied unsure.

"I observe things, you know that," she snapped. "And now he is getting away!" She pointed towards his direction.

Trusting her, I chased after him in a flash. I raced down the crowded city streets, trying my best not to knock into anything. In no time, I spotted him waiting at a busy crosswalk. I skidded to a stop and took a closer look. I noticed him reach around the woman standing next to him. I watched as he slid his hand into her purse and pulled out a crimson wallet.

Catching him in the middle of his crime, I shouted, "Stop, thief!" I darted towards him.

He ran across the street, not waiting for the walk light. Cars screeched to a halt as they tried to avoid hitting him. Still running, I wasn't going to let the vehicles block my way. I ran and leapt over the nose of each one with ease, leaving the bystanders in awe behind me.

We had an epic chase, I have to say. We ran between people, past street sellers, down alleyways, across streets, and back again. I had to jump over carts, kids, and even did a back flip off the wall when he changed direction. (That was pretty awesome.) He seemed cool under pressure, but whenever he looked back I could see a bit of fear in his eyes. I guess I am just *that* intimidating.

Finally, he went through an abandoned building and lost me.

Looking around frantically, I tried to see where he went. The dusty building wasn't very big, but it was dark and eerie. Thankfully he wasn't very good at closing doors. A faint light found its way in through a small opening in the back. I found the stairs to the roof. Without thinking, I went up.

I found him with his foot resting on the low wall at the edge of the roof and his arm resting on his knee. He was looking off into the distance at the cityscape and twirling Shannon's wallet on his finger by the strap. I took a few steps forward and was about to tackle him, but stopped when he opened his mouth. Someone who had kept me on the run for that long deserved my attention. Also, there was something about him, but I couldn't put my finger on it…

"Ah, New York City," he said with his back to me. Just by the sound of his voice, I knew he was from a borough outside of Manhattan. "The Big Apple. The place thousands flock to everyday. Many people pass by but aren't actually there." He grabbed Shannon's wallet mid twirl and pointed it to the citizens below. "I watch them every day as they go through the motions; never actually being in the moment. Sometimes I'm able to slip through crowds entirely unnoticed. It's as if I am a wolf in a sheep's pen. I'm the predator and they're the prey, but they don't know it until I attack." With a sigh, he shook his head and went on, "To be honest, sheep are more attentive and alive than these humans. That doesn't really bother me though. Makes my job easier. They don't know and don't care until I am gone."

He took his foot off the ledge and turned around, looking me in the face. He had bright blue eyes and long dark hair that was shaved on one side. The top of his ear on the shaved side had three silver hoop earrings. He wore a baggy green t-shirt with ripped jeans. He looked like a dirty street rat.

"You know," he continued, staring at me, "You and your friend are the only ones to notice something was wrong before it was too late. You're different than the other sheep. Why is that?"

I shrugged. "When you have the past that I've had, you learn to always be on your toes."  Becoming serious, I added, "Now, you're lucky I let you get away this long. Return my friend's wallet and we can pretend this never happened."

The thief laughed and gripped the wallet tighter. "I have a quota to make," he said as he jumped off the building.

Running to the edge, I threw my head over and expected to see his body free falling. To my surprise, he was running down the long fire escape. I chased after him. While I was descending the rickety, rusty, stairs, I heard some grunting from below. I slid down the last staircase to find Shannon with her forearm across the thief's throat, pinning him up against the building. It was amazing watching this short twelve year old girl threatening a fourteen year old guy who was so much taller and stronger than she was. *She really is something else*, I thought.

The crook tried to pull her arm off his neck, but had no luck. "Geez, what's your problem?" he spat, gasping for air.

"My problem?" she yelled in defense, pushing against him harder. "You stole my wallet and thought you could get away with it."

"I usually do!" he retorted, struggling.

She scanned him up and down until her eyes fell upon his neck. She let out a subtle gasp. She looked back up at him and smirked. Peering into his blue eyes, Shannon added, "But you are too ignorant to know my friend here stole something from you."

He scoffed, his hands still grabbing at Shannon's tiny arm. "Thieving from a thief? I don't think so, beautiful."

"Want to bet?" she wagered.

"Sure, sweetheart," he said with a smile. "Now, what did he take from me?"

I was about to protest, but she glowered at me. Within the past year I learned to trust her and not mess things up.

Raising her head, she said smugly, "He took your dog tag."

He stopped struggling and stared. "No, that isn't possible," he told her, "I am still wearing mine."

"Yours has your name, birthdate, and last initial on the back, doesn't it?" she asked.

Chuckling nervously, he held his hands up and replied, "Cutie, I don't know what game you are playing but I don't like it. I won't believe you until I see it. You probably just saw mine around my neck."

I couldn't believe what I was hearing. I had to be sure of it myself. "No, I really did take it. Look," I said taking off my dog tag. I held it in front of his face, careful to cover my first and middle name but leaving the rest revealed.

His eyes scanned it for a moment. "No, no, can't be," he muttered. I turned it around and showed him the *H* on the other side. That's when he began panicking. "That's mine! Give it back," he cried. Holding out Shannon's wallet, he said, "Here take it back. I'm sorry just give me back my dog tag, please."

Shannon had the biggest grin on her face. Laughing, she released him and threw her arms around him, hugging him tightly.

The thief got red in the face. "G-geez, sweetheart," he stammered, patting her back. "It's not like I offered it to you without anything in exchange."

Stepping back, she laughed and said, "Check around your neck."

He put his hand on his neck and he froze. He ran his fingers down the silver beaded chain that left a red imprint in his neck from Shannon's arm. "Wait," he said pulling off his own dog tag. "This one is mine. Then, whose do you have?"

"I have my own," I said showing him the side with my name on it.

"Shut. Up," he replied in shock as he looked at his own and to mine again. He snatched my dog tag and held them both side by side, searching for some possible flaw. Looking up at me, he asked, "Who are you?"

"I was just about to ask you the same thing," I told him.

Shannon was grinning from ear to ear. "Shane, I think I just found your brother," she whispered.

The thief and I stared at each other. We did look alike: same hair color, shaped eyes, height, build. "My name is Shane Hodgins," I introduced, holding out my hand.

Hesitantly, he shook it and replied, "I'm Mark Hodgins." He walked around and inspected me up and down. He tugged at my uncle's brown work jacket that I was wearing. He poked my high cheekbones and then at his own. "Are you really my brother?" he asked, fluffing my hair while he played with his own, comparing the textures. "How can we be so sure?"

Quickly, Shannon explained my story and how my mother left the note of the three babies she abandoned at different locations.

When she finished, Mark remained silent. He couldn't believe his ears. "That's so weird," he replied softly. "I mean, I was found. Your story sort of matches up with mine."

"Guys, you both have identical dog tags with the exact same illuminated letter *H*," Shannon said impatiently. "The way that it is designed is like none other. Trust me I have looked everywhere for it."

Looking at her, Mark said, "Who are you anyway?"

"Oh sorry," she said slapping her palm to her face. "My name is Shannon Hollinger, daughter of Detective Quinn Hollinger. I am a detective in training."

Mark became nervous. "I think I've heard of him," he said.

"I know you have, because you are part of Fallout," she retorted.

His eyes widened and he began to sweat. "Wh-what?" he stammered, taking a step back.

"A few years ago, my father almost exposed your group to the police, but one of your members deleted all of his research before he could prove it," she explained. "You guys don't leave too many physical traces." She pointed to his right ear. "But your earrings and the brand on your chest which I saw when you bent over gave you away. If you don't want people taking your dog tag or seeing your brand, I would suggest I tighter shirt."

"Oh yeah, I remember that with the police," he recollected, subconsciously pulling his t-shirt up. "My first hacking job."

"That was years ago. You had to be younger than ten then," Shannon said unbelieving.

Mark smirked. "I guess you can say I am gifted."

"Makes two of us," I said.

He looked at me, then back at Shannon. He held out her wallet. "Here take it," he said, "I didn't have time to empty it so everything should be in there."

"Thank you," she replied taking it from his coarse, dirty hands. She looked up at him and kindly added, "Come with us. There is always room for another Hodgins at our place."

Mark shook his head. "This is all too weird for me right now. I feel like you might turn me in or your dad will contact his police bros."

Shannon opened her wallet and pulled out an old receipt. Rummaging through her bag, she found a pen and scribbled down her information. "If you change your mind, please let us know. Maybe we can arrange a day for you guys to see each other." With more sincerity, she added, "You have to believe me; I know for a fact you two are brothers."

"Not sure if I believe that yet," he replied, "but I will keep it in mind." Taking the note, he shoved it into his pocket, looked at both of us, and ran off without saying another word.

"What do you think, Shane?" she asked. "Do you believe me?"

"I think I do," I replied unsure, looking towards the direction that he ran. "I did feel something: a weird connection between the two of us."

She smiled. "Well, we won't tell anyone just yet. Let's give him time to take it in." She shook her head and sighed. "I wonder what it must be like, living the way he is. I read my dad's notes on Fallout and it doesn't seem like the best thing to be part of."

"You mean there is something worse than thieving, hacking, and breaking the law?" I said chuckling.

"Yeah, actually," she said upset, pushing her curly hair out of her eyes. "If the members are unneeded, they are bumped off or sent away. I hope they find him useful enough to stay alive."

That made me nervous. "I sure hope so." After that, we went back to her grandparents' house.

We stayed with her family in NYC for about two weeks. Every time Shannon and I went out walking, she said she could see Mark occasionally spying on us or doing his every day thieving. I tried hard to find him, but never could. He was right. The world seemed to ignore people like him and didn't even care. The problem is, I did care and still seemed to "ignore" him. I hoped that one day, he would accept the fact that I was his brother and he never would have to feel unnoticed ever again.

# CHAPTER 16
## Aymie: V

Yay, stories are connecting! To be honest, the different perspectives are confusing me; and one of the perspectives is mine.

The day after I was locked in the closet went better than I expected. We walked into the chapel that morning to find the mean girls getting scolded by one of the Sisters for what they did to me. She wasn't yelling at them. She was speaking softly and pointed to the man on the *T* and then back to them. I wasn't sure what she was saying, but it seemed to be working.

That week was the best I've had. No torment, no teasing, and no one destroying my work or reputation. A few times I saw the girls scurrying about with the new jobs they received as punishment, but they never stopped or even looked at me.

"Are you feeling better, Aymie?" Sister Maria Stella asked.

"Much better, thank you," I replied. "I've barely seen the girls since it happened."

"They are busy reflecting and doin' their chores," the Sister explained. "Also, they are a bit besides themselves since Sophia got adopted."

My jaw dropped. "She was adopted?"

She chuckled. "Yeah, she was! You won't have to worry about her anymore," she said joyfully. "The family seemed nice, but strict; in a good way. They'll whip her into shape, I promise."

I was jealous yet happy. I wanted to be adopted, but she was gone so my life wouldn't be as miserable. Although, a part of me was glad for her too. I think a family is what she needed.

After that, things perked up. The years that passed after that were wonderful. I was becoming more well liked by my peers and people outside the orphanage. Word got out from some of the Sisters that I was an "excellent" seamstress, and I received many requests for clothes, linens, and the like. It was easy for me because I was able to recall all different patterns thanks to my photographic memory. I could do it in no time at all. This helped out the Sisters a lot with their finances. Also, the girls eventually apologized for what they had done to me and began to follow Janelle and me around like we were celebrities. I loved feeling like a princess again. During those short years, I learned so many things and found a small feeling of peace inside of me.

Unfortunately, when I was fourteen, my life seemed to change again.

I was finishing the seams on a wedding dress that I had made for one of the women in the Sisters' parish when Janelle burst through the door.

"Aymie, Aymie!" she cried, out of breath. Her thick black hair was unkempt and sweat dripped down her dark face. "There is a couple here that wants to see you."

Immediately, I dropped what I was doing, raced up the stairs, and to the office. I screeched to a halt before the door to make myself look presentable. When I was ready, I took a deep breath and walked in. I found the couple sitting in the chairs facing Sister Maria Stella's desk. They turned around and faced me.

The man had a light olive skin tone and his black hair was nicely cut. His eyes were dark and they... scared me. His cold stare made me shudder. He gave me a smile that was meant to be friendly, but it looked sinister. The "wife" looked distressed. She had bags under her blue eyes and her light hair was a mess. She didn't smile until her "husband" elbowed her.

Something about the two of them frightened me. I wanted nothing more than a family, but these people made me want to run.

"Aymie, these are the Petersons," Sister Maria Stella told me. By the tone of her voice, it sounded like she was unsure of this couple.

"H-how do you do?" I stammered, holding my hand out.

The man gripped it firmly and shook it. "The pleasure is ours, Aymie," he said looking at me up and down. It made me uncomfortable.

"Aymie, would you like to give them a tour of our home while I deal with another matter?" the sister asked.

Slowly, I nodded and showed them around. While we walked, they didn't seem the least bit interested. The man kept his eyes on me and the woman looked around as if planning an escape. She also appeared to be shakily taking notes on a pad in her hand. I wasn't sure what she needed to write down…it wasn't like I was going to quiz her afterwards.

I had finished the tour when I turned to them and asked if they had any questions. The man had one: "What's your necklace, there?" He was referring to my dog tag that was hanging out of my shirt.

I clutched it tightly. "An old souvenir," I lied.

"May I see?" He reached for it.

"No, you may not," I said sternly, backing away from him.

The man became angry. Before he could say anything, he was called back by one of the Sisters. With a glare, he grabbed the arm of the woman and they walked back to the office.

As they were returning, I noticed the wife dropped something onto the ground. It was a note she tore from her notepad. Picking it up, I uncrumpled the small paper and read the frightening message: "*Run.*"

Then, Janelle raced over to me again. "I don't trust these guys," she said out of breath. "They gotta big black car out back with some bald guy covered in tattoos waiting inside."

"How do you know?" I questioned, fiddling with the note in my fingers.

"Imma detective when it comes to my best friend," she confessed. "I am not lettin' ya leave unless I like the family and right now I don't." She noticed me playing with the little piece of paper. She snatched it out of my hand and read it. "Who wrote this?"

"The wife I think," I told her.

Distress fell upon her face. "Go. Listen to her," she commanded. Janelle had fear in her dark eyes; fear like I'd never seen before. "She seems scared; you have to go, now!" She shoved me hard down the hall.

Janelle had never yelled at me before so I decided to obey. I rushed to my room and packed a bag with the snacks we hid under our beds. I still wasn't sure why I was doing it…but it didn't feel wrong. I ran back to Janelle who was keeping watch.

"What are you waiting for?" she cried, pushing me away.

"I can't leave you!" I screamed, throwing her back.

"Go to the city and hide," she said. "In a week, give a call and ask for me. If everything is okay I will reply, 'The snakes have slithered'. Understand?"

With tears in my eyes, I nodded and ran out the back, not knowing what else to do.

I snuck through the gardens and around the side of the home. Peeking out, I saw Janelle was right. There was the van with the tattooed man inside. I studied his features closely, making sure to memorize every last detail. The tattoo that was the clearest to identify was a double edge sword that's hilt was behind his left ear and the blade crawled down his chest, disappearing behind his black leather jacket.

Terrified, I realized the only way I could get to the city was to sneak past him and follow the main road. With no way out, I took a deep breath and ran for it.

The man saw me in his side view mirror. Before doing anything, he looked at me, then at something he was holding, and back again.

I was almost at the end of the driveway when he jumped out of the car and chased me. I pumped my legs as hard as I could. My backpack continued to smack me as I ran. I felt my head wrap slipping off, but it didn't matter. I raced past the black fence and down the street.

I ran to the city. When I arrived, I looked back and saw I wasn't being followed anymore. I leaned against a store window to catch my breath. I was exhausted and wanting to go home. I was alone and afraid. I didn't know where to go so I hid in an alleyway for an entire week, careful to hide from strangers after dark. I ran out of food by day three and had to beg. People were generous in Tennessee; especially to an orphan girl with no hair… but no one wanted anything to do with me. No one took me to the police, offered to help me, or anything. It was as if they were afraid of me…

Finally, a week passed. Time for the call. With the few coins I took from the orphanage, I shoved them into the rusted slot of a nearby payphone. It rang and rang until finally a sister answered. I asked for Janelle, but the she told me that she was no longer with them.

She said that Janelle had been adopted.

I froze and the receiver almost slipped from my hand. Shaking, I hung up without saying another word.  I sank to the floor and sat on the sidewalk. *How is that possible?* I thought, distressed. *It was only a week.*

I sat there in shock as tears streaked down my dirty face. I was there for a while before someone forced me to my feet.

"Don't lie on the ground, it's dirty," a man said holding my arm. I looked up and saw a kind face smiling at me. He had salt and pepper hair topped with a black baseball cap with the word "Veteran" embroidered on it. He had brown eyes and slightly wrinkled pale skin. He wore a black track suit and had a tall posture even though he was a shorter man.

Pulling loose, I apologized, "I'm sorry sir. My friend was taken from me."

"Taken from you?" he asked, concerned. "How?"

Wiping the tears from my eyes, I replied, "They say she was adopted, but I don't think so. It happened too quickly. I wasn't gone that long."

The man scratched his temple. "Gone from where?"

I realized I said too much. "Sorry, sir, I can't tell you anymore."

"Please, my dear, I want to help you," he said kindly. "Are you alone?" I nodded. He thought for a moment and asked, "Your name doesn't happen to be Aymie Quartermane, does it?"

Taken aback, I stared at him. "How did you know that?"

"I know Sister Maria Stella," he replied smiling. With a sigh, he quickly added, "You are right, something is wrong. She called me to come take you to another home. You are old enough. Besides, I can't say no to a sister."

I was afraid it was a trick. "I don't trust you," I told him, taking a step back. "Let me speak to her."

"Not here," he replied quietly, looking around. Putting a strong hand on my shoulder, he bent over slightly and whispered in my ear, "I can let you speak to her in person one last time, but only if you agree to come with me as she asked. I can save you from those men who were chasing you."

I thought for a moment but refused him. My mind decided it was a lie. I gently removed his hand from my shoulder, thanked him for the offer, and began to walk away.

"Please, don't let those men burn down your home again," he called.

I stopped dead in my tracks. *That's impossible*, I thought in disbelief. *How does he know about that? Could it have been them?* I turned and stared at the man in the cap who looked at me sympathetically. Not sure what to think, I slowly walked back towards him and agreed to go only after I saw Sister Maria Stella. He promised and led me by the hand to the library. There I waited alone in agony until he returned and it was time for him to fulfill his word.

That night, we went to a small café a few miles out of town. Sitting in a red leather booth, I waited anxiously for the sister to arrive. I swung my feet back and forth and tapped my finger impatiently on the glossy table. The man with the cap was very tolerant of my behavior and didn't say a word to stop my irritating mannerisms.

Finally, Sister Maria Stella arrived. The moment she walked through the clear front doors I jumped up and ran to her. "Sister!" I cried, throwing my arms around her. At fourteen, I had surpassed her in height, but I didn't care. I still felt like a kid.

She held me tight. "Dear child, I am so happy you're safe," she whispered, her voice cracking.

Pulling away, I looked at her dark smooth face and desperately asked, "Who were those people? And what happened to Janelle?"

With tears in her eyes, she said, "They took her."

I couldn't believe what I was hearing. "Wh-what? Why?"

With a sigh, she explained: "While I was out looking for you, another sister helped signed the paperwork for Janelle's adoption. She didn't know; they told her that I was out. I spoke to her and she said Janelle *willingly* went with them."

Tears welled in my gray eyes. I staggered back and put my hands on my head. "No, no, no, Janelle," I repeated softly. "She probably did it for me…"

"I think so too," the sister replied, putting a soft hand on my arm. "But for her sake, get away from this place. If we are right and not just being paranoid, then you need to go with my friend here. He will protect you and take you to a new home."

"Okay," I whispered, sniffling. "I'll do it for you; for Janelle."

"Thank you." She kissed my forehead. I wanted to start bawling in the midst of the café but I contained myself. Inhaling sharply, I threw my hands around her and whispered, "Thank you, Sister Maria Stella, for everything."

"You're welcome, child," she replied, rubbing my bald head. "We will be praying for you." She let me go and wiped the tears from her beautiful face. The man shook sister's hand and then left to go get the car.

Peeking out the dirty glass doors, I saw he had the car at the base of the sidewalk. I grasped the handle and was about to exit when I had the urge to tell sister something. Looking back, I let her know who I really was in case I never saw her again. "Sister Maria Stella?" I called, subconsciously grabbing the beaded chain around my neck. "I just wanted to tell you that, my last name isn't really Quartermane."

She smiled. "I know. Now be good, Miss Hodgins."

Before I could say anything, the man came back and urged me to leave. "I'm sorry, Aymie, but we need to move."

I turned to Sister Maria Stella one last time. Her kind smile was enough to give me the courage to continue. Taking a deep breath, I stood up straight and went to the man's car, ready to start over once again.

The ride to the airport was quiet and depressing. We said nothing and I didn't even know this man's name. When we arrived, we didn't park. We drove around back.

"Aren't we supposed to go inside to catch the plane?" I asked, looking up at him.

The man smirked. "Not when you have your own jet."

Stepping out of the car, I gasped at the sight. I tilted my head back as I tried to see the entire plane that was before me. The outside was gray and seemed to go on for miles. On the side of it was a large lightbulb logo with a *P* inside it. I assumed it was a company jet.

Carefully, the man led me up the stairs to go inside. The vast interior was just as impressive. The floors were wooden and all the seats were leather. I felt like I was actually in someone's house. They had a television, kitchen and table, couches, bar, everything.

As I sat on the sofa, the pilot came out to greet us. "Ah, you are back my friend, and you have brought our guest." Looking at me, he smiled and asked, "What is your name my dear?"

"Aymie Quarter—" I stopped myself. "Hodgins. Aymie Hodgins," I corrected, holding out my hand.

He shook it. "What a lovely name," he complimented. "Sounds very familiar, too. If I can think of where I've heard it, I'll let you know." Straightening his yellow tie, he pointed to himself and added, "You can call me Mr. P and I will be your pilot for today."

"Don't worry, you are in good hands," the older man said. "Mr. P is an old friend of mine. We work together in fact."

Mr. P smiled. "That is true, old fellow. I would love to stay and chat but we have to get moving. My pal here will show you to your seats." He was about to walk away when he remembered something. "Oh, and please don't mind my son if you see him scurrying about. He is training with me today."

"Of course not," I told him. Now, I was expecting his son to be eighteen or so, but I was wrong. A little boy ran past us and followed his dad into the cockpit. He seemed only about eight years old.

"He isn't going to be flying, is he?" I asked as the two shut the door behind them.

"He might," the older man replied smiling. "Don't worry, he can handle it. We say Junior there is a child prodigy. He is one of the smartest kids in the *world* right now." He shook his head and chuckled. "He is estimated to graduate college by eleven years old. He won't be the first kid to do that, though. I guess you can't be best at everything."

I didn't exactly believe him, so I just nodded.

Walking towards the bar, he called back, "So are you ready to go to your new home?"

"Um, I don't know where we are going or who you are," I replied snootily.

He cocked his head to the side and twirled a small glass in his rough hands. "Really?"

"Yeah, that is kind of important." I said with an attitude.

"Sorry," he said, fixing his cap with his free hand. "Getting old is ruining my memory. I am taking you to a community home called 'Wyght's Home for Young People' or 'WHYP' for short."

"Who is Wyght?" I asked.

"I am, my dear," he replied with a bright smile. "My name is Stanley Wyght."

# THE MAINLAND

# Chapter 17
## Mark: V

Yeah, Aymie found out what "WHYP" stood for before me, and she didn't even get his business card.

Meeting my so called "brother" filled me with anger rather than joy. I wasn't ready to believe that I magically found my long lost sibling. He was just some kid who had the same skin and hair color as me. Other than that, there weren't many similarities… that I could see anyway. His eyes were green while mine were blue. Our styles were completely different. He wore an old brown work coat over a blue flannel, jeans, and running shoes. His hair was full and wispy…much different than my half shaved style.

While he was still in NYC, I followed him and the pretty—but intimidating—girl around. I thought I wouldn't get caught, but I am certain she noticed me. Several times she would look at me, smile, and keep moving. *What do I mean to her?* I wondered, passing by them one day.

It didn't matter, though. They left for home a few weeks later which didn't improve my mood. In fact, it made it worse. Don't ask me why but not being able to stalk them every day made me angry.

During one of my fits of throwing things around my room, Big

Daddy barged in and asked what the matter was.

"None of your business," I spat through gritted teeth.

"Yeah right," he said, making himself comfortable on the edge of my bed. "I know when something's wrong." He looked around at my trashed room. "Also looks like a bomb went off in here. So spill it."

I took a deep breath and pushed my hair out of my eye. "Do you remember anything when you saved me as a kid?"

Big Daddy gave me a confused look. "I've told you everything. Why ask?"

"I met some people a few weeks ago," I explained, picking up a pair of broken drumsticks. "They noticed I stole one of their wallets."

Surprised, Big Daddy replied, "They noticed *you*? My number one thief?"

"That's what I was thinking!" I exclaimed. "Not only that, but they caught me. The dude was ridiculously fast. I had to create obstacles just to have some distance." Rubbing my shaved head, I continued, more quietly, "The girl whose wallet I stole knew exactly where I was going to be and pinned me up against the wall."

Big Daddy snorted. "She must've been twice your size then." He held his arms out for measuring. He laughed and then asked, "Was it his mother?"

I kept my eyes on the ground and shook my head. "No," I started, "She was two years younger than me…and short."

My caregiver laughed heartily. "No wonder you're in a bad mood," he stated after calming down. "But that can't just be it. What did she say to you?"

Hesitantly, I explained, "She tricked me into thinking her friend stole my dog tag," I grabbed my chain subconsciously, "but he actually had the same one."

Big Daddy raised one eyebrow and leaned forward, placing his forearms on his knees. "What does that mean?" he asked curiously although he believed he knew the answer.

"She claimed that her friend, Shane Hodgins, was my brother," I whispered.

He took a moment to let that all sink in. "Your brother?" he whispered. "Wait, your brother?" he repeated, louder this time.

"Please don't tell anyone," I begged. "About Shane, the girl, any of it. If they knew who he was staying with who knows what Couch would do to them."

"Why would Couch care?" he asked. A joyous grin crept across his face. "This is incredible."

"Because the girl was Shannon Hollinger," I answered. "Daughter of Detective Quinn Hollinger."

Big Daddy's face fell and his smile disappeared. "No wonder she found you," he replied, quietly. "Do you think he is after us again?"

I shook my head. "No, they don't live here anymore. They were visiting family. She knew of us because she went through her father's files."

"How did she know you would be here?" he inquired, concerned. He was dreading the day the police came and separated him from his boys.

"I don't think she did," I told him. "I was watching them question all those homeless kids. She seemed to be doing some research of her own."

Letting out a deep breath, Big Daddy replied, "That's good news." He scoffed. "Your brother, huh? I think… I believe it. Although, I'm not ready for you to ditch us, okay? We gotta stick together."

Nodding, I replied, "Ain't planning on leaving."

He chuckled. "Good and I won't tell anyone," he promised with a wink. He stood up from my bed, patted the side of my pale face, and walked toward the door. Before leaving, he turned and added, "I almost forgot. You are going on another assignment this evening with Theo and Jordan. It's an overnighter, so pack your things."

As he mentioned my task, I got a weird feeling in my stomach. For a few months the boys were mentioning a big, dangerous job. *This must be it*, I thought, worried. Despite the feeling, I obeyed. I placed everything I would need into my backpack. I packed so much I felt like I was overdoing it, but the feeling I had made me think I wasn't coming back.

Picking up my bulging bag, I flung it over my shoulder; knocking over one of my many beer bottles onto the floor. I bent over to pick it up when I noticed a small piece of paper peeking out from beneath my metal bed. I pulled out the small card given to me on the subway years ago by that 'Secretary' woman. I rubbed my thumb over its silver title and tilted it into the light, revealing 'WHYP'. I stuck it into my wallet and went out to meet the others.

While we were in our black van and on our way, I asked Jordan to fill me in on the details.

"The first part of the assignment is the usual," he started, his hairy hands gripping the wheel tightly. "Couch and Mallory need more ingredients. However, this one is worse than last time. This guy is tight with the folks who owned the last building we broke into. If they listened, it will be guarded. Second, we gotta hand deliver half of the ingredients to Mallory himself. Third, we are the front men for some new buyers."

"Wait why are we talking to people?" I asked, frustrated. "We are supposed to be 'seen, not heard.' Remember?"

Theo laughed. "You forget Jordan and I are older than twenty five," he reminded me as he tore into a large sandwich with his pointy teeth. "If we want to stay around, we have to step it up."

I became worried. "What do you mean 'stay around'?" I asked my Shrew-friend.

Jordan smacked Theo on the arm. "Nothing, kid. The three of us are fine," he reassured. He fixed the dark glasses over his giant eyes. "We are the favorites. As long as we do our jobs, we'll be fine."

That wasn't very convincing. *What about the rest of the boys? I* wondered. *We have so many now. Will they 'stay around'?*

Quickly, my Mutant friends tried to take my mind off of it by singing obnoxiously loud along with the radio. After a few songs, I sang along to the heavy metal with them until we reached our destination.

Going in was a minefield. Security cameras, guards, sensors, they had everything…but nothing we couldn't handle.

It was the normal routine: I hacked into the systems, disrupted the security while Theo and Jordan did the rest.

This time, it didn't go as planned.

As I was sitting in the control room, a guard came in behind me with a gun to my head. "Back away slowly, please," he asked, polite yet stern.

Putting my hands in the air, I stood up and did as he asked. Once I felt the cold barrel against my head, I quickly made my move. Abruptly turning around, I grabbed his gun with my left hand and shoved his wrist downward with my right. As his arms went down, I knocked his legs out from underneath him, causing him to go crashing down and lose consciousness.

I sat back in my seat and continued my work. Typing as fast as lightning, I had disabled all security. I let out a victory cheer and jumped up to help my friends. As I searched down the dark, eerie building I heard the echo of a scream.

"Theo?!" I called, racing down a hall with its floor decorated in broken glass. At the end, I saw him come running.

His hood had flown off and his tail dragged behind him, leaving a trail of blood on the white floors. "MARK, MARK!" he screamed, terrified. "Jordan's hit!"

"Let's get him," I yelled back. The Shrew skidded to a stop and turned to lead the way. Jordan was lying on the ground behind a desk, bleeding profusely from a bullet wound in his side.

I tore off a part of my green shirt and pressed it into the hole, momentarily stopping the bleeding. "Keep the pressure," I ordered as I grabbed his legs. When Theo had a grip on his torso, the two of us carried Jordan out of the building and to the car.

As we placed Jordan across the back, we thought we were in the clear, but the cops were on us this time. I slammed the doors shut and Theo jumped in the front. He hit the gas and we started our escape. He drove as fast as possible on the bumpy dirt road while I tried to clean Jordan's wound in the back of the moving vehicle. Thankfully, he didn't cover himself in his toxin so I could work without getting killed.

"How is he doing?" Theo called with a worried tone of voice.

"Focus on driving!" I barked, applying more pressure to my

friend's wound. I was covered in blood and Jordan was fading. "I don't even know how to treat him. I don't know the makeup of Slow loris."

"Keep him alive until backup comes," Theo commanded. "I notified Mallory of our problem, and he is more than happy to help."

As he finished his sentence, three white vans came into sight and were headed in our direction. Cursing, Theo slammed on the brake and tried to prevent us from having a head on collision. Behind us, the officers also stopped and skidded across the road.

Thankfully, the vans ahead weren't interested on hitting us. They stopped as soon as we did. When all cars were at a halt, the headlights before us went dark and two dozen people emerged from the vehicles. They lined up in a neat row in front of the vans and stood perfectly still. I couldn't see them in the dark; the police car lights couldn't reach them. However, there was one figure I could identify: Mr. Mallory. He came out last and carried an electric lantern that illuminated his pale face.

The cops rushed out of their vehicles and formed their own line behind our van, their guns aimed and ready. They shouted and waited for orders. They were afraid to make the first move in fear that the individuals with Mallory were hostages. The lead officer yelled to Mallory over the loudspeaker asking for information, but all he got was silence.

After the cop repeated the questions with more threats, the scientist was finished playing games. Casually, Mallory held his hand in the air and his people shifted into fighting stances. His crazed green eyes glared at the cops. Sick satisfaction shone in them. Then, he quickly and dramatically dropped his arm and pointed all his fingers towards the direction of the cops. His people charged.

The cops screamed and fired, but Mallory's soldiers kept on coming. Some of them even scrambled over our vehicle. We were in the middle of a battlefield. When they reached the cops, hell broke loose. I heard shouting, crying, and inhumane sounds. I didn't know what was exactly happening, but it wasn't pretty. From what we could see out of the rearview mirror was gruesome.

Curious, I opened the back of the van a crack and tried to see what was going on. The ones attacking the cops were Mutants like Jordan and Theo... but lacked sanity and humanity. They were savage beasts tearing these poor policemen limb from limb. Tackling them, biting them, and beating them senseless. No matter what the cops did, their efforts were futile. They tried to retreat, but it was too late. The Mutants let *none* escape.

During this horrific display, Mallory came into our van and treated Jordan's wound. I was in too much of a shock to pay attention to him or dying Jordan.

"He lost a lot of blood," I finally heard Mallory say with no sense of worry in his voice. "He'll survive though." In no time at all, Mallory stitched up our friend. Jordan was screaming throughout it because he had no anesthesia. However, Mallory gave him a pill to help with the pain and blood loss afterwards. The man was so unperturbed it worried me.

Finally, the battle was over. Every cop was down and the monsters were still standing. The lights of the sirens illuminated the scene with an eerie purple glow. The Mutants stood amidst their destruction and threw their heads back, howling and screeching at the starry night sky. After their victory cry, they scurried back into the vans.

Mallory led me outside to look around at the carnage they had left. I was stricken with horror, disgust, and sorrow. Those poor police officers, who were just doing their job, were shown no mercy by a mad scientist's pets. Their families would not even be able to recognize who was who by whatever was left of them. Every drop of their blood was either spilled or consumed by the Mutants.

"Isn't it beautiful?" Carl Mallory observed, looking at the scene.

The man was truly psychotic. I looked at him with disgust. "'*Beautiful*'? That was messed up!" I bellowed. "Those things killed so many innocent people."

Glowering at me with his stern green eyes, he stated, "You are not innocent and yet I spared you and your friends. Your role in the divine plan was greater than theirs. Consider yourselves lucky." He watched as the last Mutant scurried back to the van like a frightened woodland creature. "We are imperfect," Mallory continued, "I am trying to make us perfect again. This lovely display is just a result of our progress."

He walked away and left me to gaze upon the destruction our wrongdoings had caused.

"Oh, one more thing," he called back, "if you change your mind about helping me that is fine. There are many other ambitious young people out there. Whether they are test subjects or item retrievers it doesn't matter. I'll work with what I get." Turning around, he looked at me and added, "Just remember, Mark Hodgins, no matter what you do or where you go, I will always welcome you. I have always been grateful for your services and will never forget you." With that, he took the ingredients we stole and drove off with his monsters.

Once he was gone, Theo jumped out of the van and walked over. "Man," he gasped as he gazed upon the disemboweled bodies. "I thought I was bad when I lost it. This is nuts."

"Let's go now," I growled, not wanting to continue the conversation. With clenched fists, I marched to the van and hopped in the back. I looked out at the mess we had made one last time before shutting the doors. My eyes welled up with tears and I thought to myself, *Do I really want to be responsible for things like this?*

# CHAPTER 18
## Mark: VI

We drove away from the horrific scene and parked for the night in an old lot. We were scheduled to meet our new buyers the next day and we needed to be well rested. However, that night was a sleepless one… for me at least. Theo and Jordan were out cold in the back of the van.

Trying to get my mind off of everything, I went outside, climbed up the hood of the van, and sat on the roof. The sky was beautiful that night. The stars danced around the moon as they lit the way for us down below. The wind blew gently against my skin, calming me down. We never had those kinds of nights in the city.

I sighed. "What am I supposed to do?" I whispered to myself. I didn't like Mallory's way of doing things. Not one bit. Yet, I didn't know what I could do. *I could leave*, I thought. *I could go find my brother.* Quickly, I shook off the feeling. Theo and Jordan needed me. So did Big Daddy. I pulled the weight of almost all of the boys at Fallout. Without me, they would crumble to the ground...even though most of them hated me and treated me like trash. Besides, I didn't know for sure if Shane was my brother. He could be related to that girl Shannon and the two of them were trying to capture Fallout.

With all these thoughts swarming through my mind, I lay down on the roof and clutched the dog tag that hung around my neck. *If we are brothers, I hope to see him soon.* Finally, my eyes shut and I went into a deep sleep.

The next morning, Theo beeped the horn to wake me up. Startled, I yelled and almost fell off the roof.

"Found him," Jordan exclaimed as he poked his head out of the front window to see me. His big, light brown eyes looked at me with concern. "You worried us, man."

I rubbed my head. "Sorry, Jordan. How you feeling, by the way?"

"Let's just say I'm kicking," he said, winking. "Now c'mon we're going to be late."

The ride to our meeting spot was long and rough. It was almost sunset when we reached our destination: an old fairground. Ancient, rusted rides were scattered on the property.

Walking across the trash ridden lawn, I saw two men in dark clothing at one of the picnic tables in the center of the park. The one on the left was reading an old brochure for a circus he found on the ground. He had light brown skin, a bald head, and had wicked tattoos on his chest that crawled up to his head. One that was clearly identifiable was a detailed sword starting from behind his left ear and pointing to his chest. He had a bigger stature than his skinny friend who watched us intently as we approached. The skinny weasel-looking man was lighter and he had clean cut hair.

"Evening, gentlemen," Theo greeted the way he was instructed to. "The night wind is crisp this time of year."

Smiling, the man with the hair replied, "Quite so, but it doesn't bother me. I always wear extra layers."

Theo chuckled and held out his hand to the man, who shook it firmly. "Good to see we found the right place," Theo said. "Kinda spooky joint you chose."

"We like spooky," the man replied. Putting his thin hand on his chest, he introduced himself. "I'm known as Masdit. This bigger fellow over here is called Gerrior." Gerrior looked up, raised his eyebrows, smiled, and then went back to his reading.

We sat down and talked business. Well, Jordan and Theo spoke business with Masdit while Gerrior and I remained silent. Gerrior occasionally would look up at me and glance at his "Regal Circus" brochure then back at me as if he was comparing something. Every time I noticed him, he would quickly look away.

*What's his deal?* I wondered.

After an hour, we all stood up and prepared to leave. "Thank you, Theo, Jordan," Masdit said, shaking their hands. "I believe that this is just what we are looking for." Turning to me, the man apologized. "I am so sorry. I have forgotten your name."

"Mark. Mark Hodgins," I reminded him.

His face lit up and he smiled creepily. "Ah, Hodgins. That's right. Well, I hope we see you all again soon." Masdit nodded politely and left. Gerrior shook our hands, shoved the brochure in his coat pocket, and went off with his partner. Once they were out of sight, we returned to the van and began our journey back.

"Is it just me or did those guys seem freaky?" I asked on our way home.

"Crooks weirder than us? I doubt that," Jordan joked as he drove. His bullet wound hadn't caused him any pain that day…whatever was in that pill from Mallory worked.

"Speaking of weird, this shrew needs to eat," Theo said as he pulled out his ninth sandwich of the day.

We got back to the shelter safely and relayed to Big Daddy all that had happened. He seemed satisfied with the deal. However, he and everyone else ignored my rant on how Mallory murdered those officers in cold blood. Frustrated that no one cared, I stomped back to my room, placed my bag in the corner, and stayed there until I was needed.

Several months went by before Masdit and Gerrior contacted us to meet again. They had ordered a large sum of *Couch's Concoction.* They also wanted the contact information of that psychotic hippie scientist, Carl Mallory.

I grabbed the bag I never unpacked from months before and prepared to leave. Big Daddy gave us what we needed to trade and a list of what we should come back with.

While I was on the stairs following the others up, I turned to Big Daddy who smiled kindly. He had a satisfied look on his smooth, black face. He was proud of us…especially me.

"Big Daddy, if things go south tonight," I started, slowly, "I just want you to know that I always thought of you as my dad and I couldn't be more grateful for all you've done."

Taken aback by this unexpected remark, my caregiver replied, "Of course, Mark. I'd do anything for you. But why bring it up now? This assignment's like all the rest."

I shrugged. "You never know when things could get screwy." With that, I left him and joined my companions.

In no time, we arrived at our destination. The sun had set and the street lights had flickered on, bathing the abandoned lot in a yellow hue.

"Wait in the car until we get the money," Theo told Jordan and me as he put the van in park. Leaving the keys in the ignition, he unbuckled and opened the door. "I don't trust these guys waiting to make a deal with us after so long." Then, he stepped down and went into the lonely building.

Jordan and I sat together and conversed about why we thought Masdit and Gerrior had failed to contact us before now. We tried to touch base with them several times, but it was as if they dropped off the face of the earth. Now they suddenly show up and pretend everything is okay?

Twenty minutes went by before we got the call from Theo. Jordan removed the vibrating flip phone from his navy jacket pocket and opened it with his thumb. Once it was on speaker, Theo gave us instructions:

"*It's okay guys,*" the shrew said, "*Jordan, send Mark in first with the goods and you be ready with the car. Apparently this place isn't as abandoned as we thought.*" Immediately, Theo hung up.

Jordan and I looked at each other. That wasn't the comforting message we had hoped for. He helped me unload and I made my way to the building, alone.

As I carried the heavy packages, I realized I was shaking. I felt the glass contents in the boxes clank together from my quaking body… *Why am I so scared?* I wondered, clutching them tighter. *I've done this a million times.* Something unnerved me that night, but I had no idea what.

I approached the rusted door of the warehouse and slammed my shoulder against it. Forcefully pushing it open, I entered the dusty building to find Theo standing beneath the only light in the center. "Hurry up, kid, we don't have much time," he said with a shaky tone of voice.

Walking up to him, I gently placed the boxes down at his feet. "What's wrong?" I asked.

His dark eyes darted back and forth. "Nothin's wrong," he reassured. Biting his lip, he winced and then reached behind him. Before I understood, he had pulled out his pistol and pointed it at my chest. "Make a sound and we both die," he whispered.

I couldn't believe what was happening. "Theo, what's going on?" I asked, trying to remain calm.

"They wanted something else with their bargain," he explained, looking me in the face. "Either they lemme go without food for days and then leave me in a room with Jordan until I was full or let you go with them quietly."

I shook my head and started to back away. "You don't have to do this."

Theo's eyes became watery. "It was either Jordan and I or only you," he explained, his voice cracking. "I had to make the smart choice."

"He is right, Mr. Hodgins," a familiar voice called from the shadows. "Listen to us, or experience the same suffering your brother had to."

I couldn't believe my ears. "What about my brother, Masdit?" I bellowed. I glanced behind the Mutant to see the crook.

Theo was amazed. "Wait, *brother*?"

"Shut up, Theo, or I take you too," Masdit yelled. "Hurry along now. I have my new daughter, Janelle, to go back to."

I thought it over for a moment. "Fine, I will go with you. Only if you promise to give them what you owe and not harm anyone."

Emerging from the shadows, Masdit looked me in the eyes. "Deal," he said smirking. "Gerrior, lead Mr. Hodgins to our truck while I finish business here."

Theo stuck his gun back in his pants and Gerrior came out, motioning for me to follow him. Glaring at Theo, I stood up straight and marched towards my kidnapper without fear. Unafraid, I followed the tattooed man out to the delivery truck.

"You have to ride in the back," he said. That was the first time I'd heard him speak. His voice was deep and hoarse, but it didn't sound threatening. "I hope I made it comfortable enough for you." He gripped the rusted handles and opened the back with a grunt. Inside were an old cot, boxes of food, and different crates of supplies they had gathered. I clutched onto the straps of my back pack and went inside.

"Oh, before I forget, I need to search your bag and take your cell phone," Gerrior told me kindly. I liked him better than his sinister friend. Reluctantly, I took off my backpack and handed it to him. I reached into my pocket and tossed him my disposable flip phone. He looked over it and smiled. "I like your style, kiddo." He then rummaged through my bag. He took out my knife and the lock pick set Brand had given me…I was not happy to lose that but I didn't protest. "I'll let you keep your laptop for entertainment purposes. You'll be bored out of your mind without it," Gerrior said, returning my bag. "Now if you do as we ask, we won't give you any trouble."

"Can you tell me what you know about my brother?" I asked sternly.

He reached into his coat pocket and pulled out that brochure he was reading the night we met. "This is what we currently know about him," he explained, tossing the paper at my feet, "but we've been following you, your brother, and your sister since you were born."

I gasped. "Wait, I have a sis—," I was interrupted when he slammed the doors shut.

I froze and stared at the metal exit. With a jerk, the truck started moving and I staggered to remain standing. Where we were going, I had no idea. It all happened so fast, I couldn't believe it. I slumped down to the ground. On the cold floor was the torn, colorful brochure. I picked it up and held it in my pale hands. I didn't dare open it. Instead I held it as I rested my head on my knees. For the first time in a while, I cried.

I dozed off and had no idea what time it was when I awoke. There was a small light, but no clock to tell whether I had slept through the night. I rose, went to the cot, and plopped myself on it. It creaked and shook beneath my light weight… I was afraid it would snap. Trying to ignore that thought, I slowly opened the "Regal Circus" brochure Gerrior gave me. I wanted to see if he was telling the truth.

To my surprise, I didn't have to look very hard; he was right there. A younger image of the boy I met several months ago. He was the star of the entire show:

*THINK YOU'RE QUICK? COME RACE*
*THE FASTEST BOY ALIVE.*
*YOU BEAT HIM, YOU WIN THE GRAND PRIZE*
*AND MORE. GOOD LUCK!*

"'Zippy Presto'? What a ridiculous stage name," I ridiculed. I ran my fingers over the bold, embossed title. I took a closer look at the pages and found his real name. "'Shane Hodgins'," I whispered to myself, "He wasn't lying."

Suddenly, I remembered I had their contact information. I grabbed my bag and rummaged through it. *Where is it, where is it?* I panicked. After dumping the contents onto my cot, I remembered where it was. Slapping my hand to my forehead, I pulled out my wallet. Next to the WHYP card was the little slip of paper with Shannon's number. *If I can get away from these men, I thought, I could call them for help.*

With that as my plan, I decided to try and make contact if we stopped at a gas station. Unfortunately, it was a few hours before then. I waited anxiously the entire time but played it cool when they came to get me.

"You try to run or scream we blow your head off. Understand?" Masdit threatened as he opened the doors.

"I am fond of my head," was my rejoinder. My plan wasn't to do either. Shoving my hands into my pockets, I casually made my way into the gas station and went into the bathroom. I locked myself in a stall and pulled the paper out of my wallet. Then, I remembered my next problem. I didn't have a phone.

*Idiot*, I called myself. Internally, I was panicking until I heard familiar clicks coming from the stall next to me. *He's on his phone*, I thought I looked at the two feet in the stall next to me. It was an awkward situation, but I had no choice. I took a deep breath and casually asked the man in the stall next to me if I could borrow his cell phone.

The clicking stopped for a moment. Then, the phone slid by my feet. "Sure man, it's distracting me anyway. Just don't drop it in the toilet or anything."

I stood there staring at the phone on the floor. *I didn't think he would actually lend it to me. People actually help and trust each other?* Thanking him, I picked it up and first looked at our location. Then I dialed the number as fast as I could. I got the answering machine. I left them a message quickly explaining who I was and telling them I needed help. I told them where I was and hung up the phone. I thanked the man again and slid the phone back under the stall.

"Anytime," he replied, picking it up. "Stay out of trouble, kid."

"I'll do my best," I replied, flushing the toilet. After washing my hands and trying to make myself smell better. I went back out to meet my kidnappers. Masdit did not look pleased that I took forever.

"Sorry, I was having some trouble," I told them.

Masdit looked disgusted and held his hand up. "Too much information, kid. Just get in the truck."

Reluctantly, I hopped in the back. As they slammed the doors, I prayed that the Hollingers and my brother would get the message. *They're my only hope right now,* I thought as I sat on my cot.

I was traveling with them for an entire week before anything happened… at the time I wasn't sure if it was good or bad. We were taking a backroad when we ran into an obstacle.

Cursing, Masdit opened the back where I was to grab some tools that could help them move a fallen tree. I mean, they did have a chainsaw. As he dragged the tool out of the back, I poked my head out to see what was happening.

"Try to run and I shoot you!" Masdit yelled as he walked towards the tree.

"Always with the violence," Gerrior sighed as he grabbed some rope and followed his partner.

Doing as I was told, I sat on the edge and let my feet dangle. I felt like a little kid as my legs swayed back and forth. To be honest, it just made me homesick. Not that I ever really acted like a kid at Fallout…but still.

"*Psst,*" a voice said, interrupting my nostalgia. Startled, I looked around trying to find the source. "Up here," it whispered. I saw a man wearing a dark ski mask leaning over on the roof. "Want help or not?" Slowly, I nodded but jerked my head back to where my "traveling companions" were.

"Don't worry about them," he reassured, "Head into the woods. I will meet you there." Then, he disappeared. I didn't care who he was or what his objectives were; I just wanted to get out of there. So, I grabbed my backpack and carefully went away from the truck.

I didn't go unnoticed. Masdit was just about to start the chainsaw when he saw me sneaking away. "Hey! Where are you going?" he bellowed. Before he could do anything, he was knocked to the ground by a black blur.

I don't know what happened after that. I ran away as fast as I could. I raced through the forest with no care where I was going and no intention of slowing down. I was put to a sudden stop when I looked over my shoulder and ended up slamming into a tree. Staggering back, I held my head and rubbed my new bruises.

"Hey are you okay?" the man who saved me called from behind. He was dressed in all black from his mask to his combat boots.

I rubbed my face. "Just peachy," I grumbled. "What'd you do to them?"

"Just knocked 'em out," he replied, taking off his mask. He was a taller young man with smooth black skin. He had a big friendly smile and kind eyes. "Not a fan of killing. Friends call me Thyme. Pleasure to meet you, Mark."

"Are you a friend of the Hollingers?" I asked, thinking that's how he knew my name.

He looked confused. "The whos?"

"The Hollingers," I repeated. "Detective Quinn Hollinger? I met his daughter and a friend a few months back and I called them for help. I left a message on their answering machine."

"Never heard of them, sorry," he apologized. "I came because we got a signal that you were leaving home."

I took a step back. "A signal? Who are you exactly? How did you know my name?"

He held his hands out in front of him. "Relax, I am a good guy. I know you have one of our business cards," he explained, pointing to my pocket. "Each one has a tracking chip."

Hastily, I fumbled in my pocket and pulled the card out of my wallet. "That's impossible," I marveled. I was amazed and horrified that I was being tracked by a thin piece of paper.

"Technology is advanced these days," he explained with a shrug. "Now hurry, I will take you somewhere safe."

With no other choice, I put the card away and followed Thyme.

# Chapter 19
## Shane: VIII

We kept that encounter with Mark to ourselves… and by "ourselves" I mean we only told Johanna. It was too risky with Shannon's dad wanting to bring down Fallout and all. So, we kept everything on a need to know basis. Shannon hid the information we had about this mysterious "Mark Hodgins" from her father.

We returned back to the countryside like nothing ever happened and went back to our normal routine…sort of. Shannon wasn't kidding when she mentioned her dad would help me train for the Junior Olympics. Mr. Hollinger was so impressed that I even was qualified for the events that he followed up and made sure I was still in the roster. He signed me up for the Junior Olympic track team to ensure I was prepared. He also got me a sponsorship and everything!

Even on top of my track team training, he personally worked with me nonstop for months. I went with him basically everywhere. The Irish detective and I became close friends over the course of that time. I felt like I had a father again. We worked so diligently that I barely had time to do things with the Hollinger girls.

"We had a big turnout tonight," Shannon told me the day before the games. They had just come back from performing at another venue. She, Johanna, Peggy, Lucy, and I occasionally played together for extra money at some local cafés and restaurants. She unclicked the torn case on her viola and gingerly took it out. With tired fingers, she decided to play a sad song as an attempt to make me feel guilty. "We wished you were there," she said, watching me as she sweetly moved the bow against the wire strings.

"I'm sorry," I told her, "but with the big day coming up tomorrow…I need to be ready."

"That's right, darling," Mr. Hollinger said, rubbing Shannon's curly brown hair as he walked by. "This could be his big chance to show the world what he can do."

I was still in awe that Mr. Hollinger was so persistent in training me. With his job, I had no idea how he made time. He would take me to work with him and have his police buddies help me train. They were amazed at what I could do. Some of them even called me a prodigy. I mean I knew I was awesome, but never considered myself quite like that.

With a smile, Shannon dramatically bowed the final note of the piece. "Well, this all better be worth it tomorrow, dad," she added, putting her instrument away.

Her father grinned, his blue eyes filled with excitement. "Tomorrow will be hatchet," he said.  Rubbing his hands through his reddish-blond hair, he added, "Well, you all must be knackered. You should go to bed or else I'll batter ya." Playfully, he threw a few faint punches at his daughter who deflected them as she was taught. After giving me a wink, he disappeared into the hallway.

Shannon chuckled. "I've never seen him so happy," she said. "He's taken a liking to you. You really are a part of the family now, aren't you?"

The way she looked at me made my heart race. The corners of her mouth reached her sparkling eyes as she smiled. Clearing my throat, I stood up and said, "I guess so…but it's probably only because I have such an Irish name."

She punched me in the arm, but I didn't block it. "I doubt it. You have an English last name, and my dad's family *hates* the British people. If names were taken into consideration, I think you'd be treated a lot worse."

I laughed. "Well, I truly am grateful then." I looked at her pretty freckled face and thought over how much her and her family took care of me. This twelve year old girl had done more for me in a year than I could repay her for.

Noticing my staring, she waved her hand in front of my face. "Shaaaaneee," she whispered. "You have to go to sleep."

I snapped back into reality. After bidding each other goodnight, we went to our rooms.

I had a hard time sleeping; I was too anxious. However, the fear of letting the Hollinger's down was the pill that put me to rest.

Finally, the morning came…frankly, I don't remember much of it. I recall the girls had everything ready when I woke up, so all I needed to do was get dressed and jump into the van.

After we arrived, Mr. Hollinger immediately checked me in. Once I was all set, he wished me luck and went to sit with his family in the crowd. I went over the rules and itinerary of the events with the track and field coach. The prep ended and all the contestants waited anxiously for the games to start.

I was about to go over for my race when someone behind me started causing ruckus. I saw two guys of bigger stature arguing and yelling about something. "I will show you up when it's time!" one guy shouted as he staggered backed into me.

"Hey, watch it!" I exclaimed as I was almost crushed.

"Oh, sorry buddy," he said backing away. He wasn't a brute like I initially thought. He was a few inches taller than me and muscular. He had sweet blue eyes and short blond hair. "Things can get kind of tense before the events."

"Tell me about it," I said with a smile, fixing the number on my shirt. "I'm Shane Hodgins. I'm doing the hundred meter. What about you?"

"The name's Nicolas Eerkens; Nic for short," he said, pointing his thumb to his chest. "I'm about to kick butt in the weight lifting event."

[Yes, Nic was originally blond with blue eyes. You think he was *born* with violet eyes and weird red hair? No! I am not saying red hair is weird! Just Nic's. Uh huh, sure, guys. I hate redheads. Think what you want.]

The two of us talked for a while before it was time for me to race. "Best of luck!" my new friend called out. "I'll be rooting for you."

I thanked him and went to the track. At the starting line, I did some final stretches before the countdown. I scanned the crowd and found the Hollingers and Wattersons. The little ones had a homemade banner that read "*Clarius*" across it.

I shook my head. *Oh, girls…what am I gonna do with you?* I thought, looking at all their smiling faces. Next to them, Johanna and Shannon were waving and shouting. Seeing all of them there for me touched my heart. I found a family who was proud of me. I wasn't a nuisance or a problem…I meant something to them. I was determined to win. For them.

Finally, it was time. "On your mark," the starter began, counting down. I got down in my stance and took a deep breath. After a moment of suspense, they fired the pistol and I pushed myself off.

I felt like I was going in slow motion. My entire life I was preparing for that moment and yet it would only last a few seconds. My heart beat hard in my chest and my nerves caused me to fall a little behind at the beginning. I couldn't lose. Not after everything I'd been through. I pumped my legs harder and gave it all I had. In no time, I dashed past every contestant.  I was the first one across the finish line.

The crowd went insane. The time was 10.08 seconds; the new junior record. I stood on the track looking around at all the screaming faces. The announcers were yelling over the speaker system and acclaims filled the stadium. Getting cocky, I waved to everyone and blew them kisses. All the attention…I loved it.

While I was soaking in the praise, I could hear my competitors whining behind me: "How is that possible?" one shouted.

"He was behind! How did he catch up *and* beat the record?" another baffled.

"This must be rigged," someone complained.

While they were throwing tantrums, my friends came down to the track to congratulate me. "You did it!" Shannon exclaimed as she tackled me.

"Thanks to you guys," I said as I caught her and spun her around.

After I put her down, her face turned red and she backed away.

Laughing, Mr. Hollinger gave me a big hug. I was taller than him at that point. He had a grin on his freckled face that I could not describe. When he let go, he put his hands on my shoulders. "Lad, I haven't seen a feat like this in donkey's years." He shook me gently and said with sincerity, "You've made us proud."

Before I could thank him, his wife pushed him out of the way. With tears of joy, Mrs. Hollinger embraced me. Kissing me on my sweaty cheeks, she kept praising me in Italian. She stepped back and pushed her long brown hair out of her eyes. "Quinn is right, you make us very proud."

I thanked them both repeatedly as the younger girls came to hug me one by one. I picked up little Rachel and held her and looked past the crowd to see Nic on the sidelines. He was jumping and waving. When I acknowledged him, he gave me a thumbs-up and then ran off to prepare for his event.

That was a long yet amazing day. The reward ceremony and celebration was like one I could never forget. I couldn't believe it was all real. I wished that Duke and my other pals in the circus were still alive. It was thanks to them that I was able to do all this in the first place…

*I owe this to all my past families, too*, I thought, standing on the first place podium as the medal was draped around my neck. Thanking everyone, I picked up the shiny gold medal and rubbed it between my fingers. I could hardly comprehend it all. Then again, I didn't have time to let any of it sink in. The moment I stepped down I was bombarded by individuals who wanted to sponsor me for the real Olympic Games in four years when I turned eighteen. Unsure of what to say, I told them I would keep it in mind.

Finally, it was time for the official celebration. It was meant for all the participants and their families. About halfway through the party, I decided to find my new friend, Nic.

"Who are you looking for?" Shannon asked after I walked around the hall aimlessly.

"I met someone today and I wanted to see how he did," I explained, looking through the sea of faces.

"Is he a strong fellow with blond hair and blue eyes?" She mimed his stature by flexing her muscles…which weren't half bad.

Scoffing, I said, "Did you 'observe' me talking to him before?"

"No, he asked me where you were," she replied. "He is over there." She pointed to the far corner of the hall.

I said thanks and ran to him. When he saw me, he smiled and waved, but his grin faded quickly and he looked down.

"Hey, Nic. How did you do?" I called as I approached.

"Fifth place," he said disappointed.

"That's not bad at all," I encouraged. "How many contestants were there? Over twenty?" I knew how much he wanted to win, but I guess things don't always go as planned.

"Yeah, but for me it's horrible," he replied, shaking the ice in his glass. "I have been training for years and I thought I finally had what it takes to at least get a bronze."

I put my hand on his shoulder. "There is always next time."

"Of course there is," an unfamiliar voice said behind us. I turned and saw a man in a suit with long shaggy blond hair holding a glass of champagne. "I'm sorry I couldn't help but overhear," he apologized, strolling towards us. "I know of some way I can assist you."

Nic perked up. "We're listening."

The man smiled. "I am a scientist and I am doing some experiments on human genetic enhancement. So if you need help with a particular skill just let me know and I can assist you."

Confused, I asked, "Are you offering us some sort of steroid?"

Insulted by my question, the scientist replied as nicely as he could: "I guess you could call it that."

"Aren't those illegal?" Nic inquired, still intrigued.

"I know all the loopholes," the man replied smugly. He twirled his champagne glass. "Besides, these are natural. It isn't illegal to take vitamins now is it?"

Nic ruffled his blond hair and thought about it. "Do you have a card?"

"I knew one of you would make the right choice," he replied. He pulled out a small crisp business card. Addressing me, he said, "You know, I could give you speed that no one will ever be able to top in human history."

"Thanks, but no thanks," I replied with my hand up. "I already intend to do that, but the right way."

"Always the good boy," he replied, pointing to me. "Well, it was pleasure speaking with you Mr. Eerkens, Mr. Hodgins, but I am afraid I must go." He tapped the card in Nic's hand. "If you need me, you know where to find me." With that, he spun around on his heel and went out of sight.

*Wait, how did he know our names?* I wondered. I immediately shook off the thought. *He's probably a sponsor who pays close attention to the contestants.* I turned to my new friend and asked, "Are you sure that's a good idea?"

Nic read over the card. "Not at all, but I have no other choice. I need the help. I can't go any further alone."

Perplexed, I looked at him and asked, "Why? Why push yourself and live in fear of getting caught?"

"You wouldn't understand," he said shaking his head. "I've been caught and done my time." He hesitated for a moment and then explained, "I was the biggest guy in juvie so no one picked a fight with me twice, but things are different now. The world is going south. Juvie is filling up and kids are being sent to *real* jail. I want to be ready to protect whoever I can and prevent that from happening."

I was shocked at his story. "How can you keep them safe though?"

He took a deep breath. "I wanted to do it like my father did, but my reputation destroyed that chance. Now I have to do it my own way." He held out his hand and bid me farewell. "I hope to see you again. Best of luck to you."

I shook it firmly. "Likewise," I said, smiling.

After he had departed, Shannon came up to see me. "What were you guys talking about? Who was that man?"

I scoffed. "Like you don't already know?"

She shrugged. "Tried to sell you stuff? Nic took the offer."

"Something like that," I replied. Saying nothing else, I put my hand on Shannon's back and led her back to her family where we enjoyed the rest of the evening.

That event passed by in an instant as did the months that followed. With that over, the weight of the world seemed to be lifted off my shoulders...

That is until I was arrested a few months later.

I was framed, I swear. I was just so petrified of being taken away from my family again. Normally, I wouldn't tell people this story, but the culprit of my crime is one we know too well (yet somehow not well enough).

That day I was arrested I sat in the cold interrogation room with my hands on my lap. My foot tapped incessantly as I sat in silence, waiting for the officer to go over what happened. The man was not happy to be there; he had a bad day and then to deal with me was not a good way to end it.

With his forefinger and thumb pinching the bridge of his nose, he explained, "So not only did you have a weapon on your person, but you assaulted an elderly woman *and* were smuggling drugs in your backpack." He sighed and flipped the pages in front of him. "We have one witness, the backpack with the drugs, and the unregistered gun in our possession." He looked up at me and casually added, "You also have no ID on you or anyway to prove who you really are. No birth certificate, no family. Can you tell me how we are supposed to *not* suspect you?"

"Because I didn't do it. I am not that kind of person," I replied.

"Sorry, kid," he said, "but I don't know you."

"Please, where is Mr. Hollinger. He can tell you," I begged.

"The detective is busy with another case," he reminded.

"Not too busy," Mr. Hollinger said entering the room. "Let me speak with the boy." More than happy to go, the officer motioned for the detective to come in and left, shutting the door behind him.

"So, how did you end up in this mess?" the detective asked as he sat down.

"I know it looks bad, sir," I began, the cuffs on my wrists clanking against the metal table, "but I can assure you that I am innocent. I heard the woman shouting from inside and ran in to see what was the matter. I bumped into some guy, apologized, and kept going. When I got there the woman was shouting at me saying *I* had knocked her down. The clerk called the police and didn't let me leave. When the cops arrived, they searched my backpack and found a gun and drugs." I shook my head. "I swear I have no idea how it happened, it's seriously the dumbest situation. I don't know what idiot comes up with something like that."

Sitting back in his chair, the detective began chuckling. "That's a fret. A boy like you smuggling drugs, weapons, and then harassing old ladies? My daughters beat you up and you never fight back."

"Thank you, sir," I said relieved. "How will I get out of here?"

Rubbing the reddish-blond scruff on his face, Mr. Hollinger replied, "Unfortunately, we have to catch the one who framed you. Do you know what he looked like?"

I shrugged. "I only caught a glimpse of him. I know he seemed to be wearing all black and he was pale."

The detective placed his elbows on the table and rested his chin on his fists. "Peculiar. Was anyone with you when this happened?"

I smacked my palm to my forehead. "In front of that store was where I was supposed to meet Shannon and Johanna. If they got there on time maybe they saw someone."

The detective grinned. "If my Shannon was there then she's got something. I'll go give her a call. Sit tight."

After an hour, they took me out of the interrogation room and left me in one of the cells. I stayed there until the detective came back the next evening.

Spending a night in jail was not fun. Thankfully, my cellmates were pretty chill. The weirdest part was they were kids younger than me…practically the same thing that happened to me happened to them. *Someone has to be framing all of us*, I thought, looking at the others.

"Sorry to leave you in here for a day," Detective Hollinger apologized. "You're off the hook, though. We caught him, and we think he framed the other boys."

I jumped up and the guys behind me gasped. "Seriously? Who is it?" I asked, ready to give the culprit a piece of my mind.

He clicked his tongue. "That's the thing. He doesn't have any identification either and he isn't talking. However, we found a few more samples of the same drug he planted in your bag." He chuckled and added, "Along with that, the old lady felt so ashamed she confessed that a pale boy with black hair *bribed* her into telling the police you assaulted her. For some reason, this boy wants to get kids in trouble. You are free to go." Solemnly, he looked back at the other boys and added, "Unfortunately, we need to confirm that you all were framed by the same individual. Hopefully, that won't take too long." Frustrated, the kids cursed and swore at the detective as we left.

After he returned my things, the two of us walked through the station to leave. While we were on our way, I saw the kid to blame. He was a pale, thin boy with long black hair and crisscrossed bangs. He wore a leather jacket and black jeans. He shot me a look of disapproval with his reddish eyes as I walked passed him.

"If we get any more information, I will let you know," Mr. Hollinger whispered to me.

Outside the station, Shannon and Johanna were waiting for us. "You get him to talk?" Shannon asked with her arms crossed.

Her father shook his head. "Nope. He is a stubborn fellow."

"Maybe this will help," Johanna added, handing him a small envelope.

Inside was a torn letter that had been taped back together. "'Erik Patya'," he read aloud. "This letter asks a certain 'Erik' to dispose of the contents he was carrying and escape as quickly as possible. Whoever this boy is working for, they must have known he might get caught."

"You need to protect this boy," Shannon warned. "If they find out that Erik's been arrested, they will come after him. He seems to be the tie back to them and they will possibly leave no loose ends."

"Very good, my dear," he complimented as he rubbed his daughter's head. "Now you three head on home. I'll be with you tonight."

Thanking him again, I walked back to the girls to find Johanna's aunt waiting for us by her car. Her parents were out again so she usually stayed with Johanna and kept her company.

Once we were settled and on our way to Johanna's house, I cleared my throat and said, "Thanks, girls. If it wasn't for you following him, I don't know where I would be."

"We're your friends. We'll do whatever it takes," Shannon said. "I hope they keep Erik safe. While we were following him, we knew something was wrong. He saw us, but didn't do anything about it. I think he *wants* our help, but can't ask for it directly." She thought for a moment. "He tore up the note and carelessly threw it behind him. If he was really in that sort of business, he would've destroyed it permanently."

"So you're saying he is in more trouble than we know?" I asked. The girls nodded.

"We don't know how long he has," Johanna said with a worried tone. "Hopefully, he will survive the week."

The remainder of the ride we sat in silence; pondering the fate of the helpless Erik Patya.

Okay, we thought you were helpless, all right? Geez, way to ruin an ending. Excuse us; we didn't know that wasn't your real name at the time.

# THE MAINLAND

# Chapter 20

## Shane: IX

It had been a month since Erik's arrest and, thankfully, he was still alive in juvie. Detective Hollinger checked on him every week and he reported no suspicious activity… at least that's what the guards said. The detective and his daughter thought otherwise.

"He hasn't gotten into any fights, he never speaks, he rarely eats; there is something wrong," Mr. Hollinger said one night after dinner. Mrs. Hollinger was out with Johanna's parents so he, Shannon, and I were up having coffee to wait for her while the other girls went to bed. "This kid was smuggling and dealing drugs for someone, and he hasn't made a peep. Not to fight back, not to throw us off, nothing no matter what we do. A drug dealer who doesn't put up a fight? Now that's hen's teeth."

I never understood some of his Irish sayings, but I got the gist. "So what should we do?" I asked, grabbing the handle of my mug. "There has to be something he isn't telling us."

"There is everything he isn't telling us," Shannon corrected. "Why is a fourteen year old boy in such deep trouble dealing drugs? I mean I know times are tough, but this is ridiculous."

"Actually, we aren't even sure they were drugs," Mr. Hollinger confessed. "We tested them over and over and the results came back the same. Maybe they were drugs at one point, but now they are something we don't even know."

Suddenly, there was a loud banging at the front door. As Mr. Hollinger got up to answer it, Shannon and I stayed behind and discussed a different matter.

"Have we heard anything from *him*?" I whispered, referring to my so-called brother.

She shook her head. "Not since the message," she told me. "I wish we could actually do something about it. I feel like we should tell my dad, but then again I fear we will only make matters worse."

I clenched my fists. "I can't believe this. Why did they want him? Have your cop friends found anything?"

"Nothing," she said disappointed. "They are doing all they can to keep this quiet. My dad's the head detective; it's really hard for them to hide things. No one has reported a kidnapping so they feel like they are chasing a rumor. After all, we are just a bunch of kids."

Before I could say anything, I overheard another man speaking to Mr. Hollinger in the hallway. At the sound of his sinister voice, my heart stopped. That uneasiness came back. "We have to go," I whispered. "We have to go now."

"What?" Shannon asked confused as I pulled her out of her chair and pushed her towards the back door. Grabbing my arms, she forcefully shoved me back. With her hands still clenching my biceps, she stared into my eyes. She knew why we had to escape. "Let's get my sisters," she said as calmly as she could.

I grabbed her hand and we snuck out of the kitchen, down the hall, and up the stairs to their rooms. We gently awoke all six of Shannon's siblings… well, we carried baby Rachel while she was still sleeping. Thankfully, the girls were better behaved than they seem. Shannon calmly explained that we had to leave. They were scared and confused, but cooperative. They kept quiet and followed us down the stairs.

While I was helping the girls shuffle outside, Shannon called Johanna and left a voicemail telling her what was going on. I went back in, grabbed the single flashlight on the counter, and dragged her out, leaving Mr. Hollinger alone with what was most likely one of my old pursuers. As we were leaving, we heard arguing and threats. I felt so guilty for abandoning him, but we had no choice.

We snuck our way across the backyard towards the forest. "We can go to Johanna's house were my mom is," Shannon whispered as she held Rachel close.

"But how will we get there?" I asked as I scooped up Agnes, Rebecca, and Carol-Ann. I gave Rebecca the lone flashlight to guide our way.

"We hide in the woods until—" she was interrupted by the sound of gunshots.

The girls began to scream, so we ran.

For the third time they had found me and I was running for my life, but I was not going to let anyone else die. As we approached the edge of the eerie forest, we heard an engine revving and men shouting. Their voices were all to familiar. I heard them when I was little and every night since.

I stopped dead in my tracks, almost dropping the girls. "It's them. It's them," I said, my voice shaking.

Peggy and Lucy were still headed towards the trees. Shannon skidded to a halt, careful not to drop the baby. "The ones who are after you?" she asked, panting.

"It must be," I replied with tears in my eyes. "I am sorry, I did this to you. I am sorry."

"This isn't your fault, now keep going!" she ordered, urging me forward.

I told the three girls to hold on tight and we raced to catch up to Lucy and Peggy. We ran through the dark woods until we were unable to go on. Lucy and Peggy could barely keep up, I couldn't carry the three girls anymore, and Rachel was getting restless in Shannon's arms.

Not able to run with the struggling baby, Shannon stopped and plopped herself on a boulder. "I don't think they're following us," she said out of breath, trying to rock screaming Rachel.

I put the three girls down. "Maybe… not…" I tried to say as I caught my breath, "but do you think... Johanna got... your message?"

Uncertainty fell across Shannon's face. It was a look I had never seen. She always knew the answers, she was always positive. Now, she wasn't the brave one she sought to be. "I…I don't know," she stammered, choking back tears. "What if something happened to them? What about my father? I…I," her voice faltered. Her blue eyes became watery as she looked to me for help, but I couldn't give it to her.

Her sorrow was my fault.

In an attempt to comfort her, I sat beside her and wrapped my arms around her trembling body. "I won't let anything happen to you or your sisters," I whispered into her ear. "I promise."

She took a shaky breath. Saying nothing, she rested her head on my chest and held Rachel close. Wanting comfort, the other five girls sat around me. In no time, the seven girls were sleeping, and I was left awake, reflecting in the silence. The only time I could truly hear. In my head I heard the screams and cries of the loved ones I lost…

With wet eyes raised to the starry heavens, I whispered, "Please, spare them."

I stayed awake to keep watch for another two hours until I heard a whisper through the trees. The voice was soft and kind, giving me a sense of comfort rather than uneasiness.

Then, the whisper gradually rose into a cry and I saw a glimmer of light. "Hello? Shannon? Shane? Girls?"

Realizing who it was, I screamed, "Here Johanna!" I flicked the flashlight on and off, hoping she would see. Gently, I shook Shannon and the other girls awake. The girls opened their eyes and looked up to see Johanna running towards us.

"Johanna!" Peggy cried, jumping to her feet and running to her with the others following. Johanna dropped her flashlight, opened her arms and let the five girls crash into her. She sobbed and kissed each one of their heads.

I helped Shannon stand up and we walked over to them. Johanna rose to her feet and hugged Shannon and me. "I thought you were dead," she whispered.

"Did you see if my father made it?" Shannon asked desperately.

She shook her head. "I didn't see much. I overheard that there was blood, but no bodies. Maybe that's a good thing."

"That means one of many things," Shannon said, crossly, "not sure if any of them could be categorized as 'good'. Either my dad escaped, he was abducted, or killed and they took his body."

I elbowed Shannon and gestured towards the girls. Their big eyes stared at their eldest sister with fear and sadness. Not wanting to scare them anymore, Shannon shut up.

Johanna sniffled and wiped the tears from her eyes. "My aunt is here to drive us back to my house. Your mom and my parents are talking with the police."

Mustering up our energy, we made our way back. When we finally got out of the woods, we climbed up the hill to see a line of cars in the driveway. We found police vehicles with their sirens still flashing in the dark, but no police. We went around to the front where Johanna said their parents were waiting, but they weren't there. The place was deserted.

Looking in the cars and around the house, I began to panic. "What happened? Where did they go?" I cried, coming back to the girls.

Shannon thought for a moment. Then, her face fell. "Shane, what if it's happening to us?" she asked, solemnly. "The same thing that happened to those kids on the streets of New York City?"

I didn't want to believe it… Unfortunately, I couldn't come up with a better explanation. There is no way they would have abandoned us at a time like this. *But how can someone abduct so many adults without anyone noticing?* I wondered, glancing back at the red and blue lights.

"Could the people after you have taken them too?" Johanna asked.

"It couldn't be." I thought for a moment then shook my head. "No, they only wanted me, no one else. They killed the other adults that got in the way."

"Not helping," Shannon said through gritted teeth as she tried to calm her sisters. Taking a deep breath, she reminded us we weren't safe in the house. "We need to get means of survival and then hit the road."

The fear in her voice made me angry. Not at her, but at the men that did this. I led Johanna, Peggy, and Lucy inside to pack some things.

The house was in shambles. Furniture was knocked down, photographs shattered, and there were bullet holes in the walls. I couldn't even imagine what happened.

After gathering food, clothing, money, weapons, my guitar, random things that Shannon wanted, toys for the girls, and anything we may need, we headed out to meet the other girls.

Before exiting the house, I remembered something I wanted to bring. I told the girls to go on ahead. I ran back into the library where all of Shannon and Detective Hollinger's research was. I wanted to take anything we had on my siblings. *Maybe we can find them. Make something good out of us leaving*, I thought, hopeful.

As I was taking the notes off of the corkboard, I noticed Shannon's old case that was hiding behind some newspapers. She briefly mentioned it when we first met, but brushed it aside. I tried to find clues as to what they were looking for. It took a few minutes, but I pieced the information together.

There was a crime of child abduction fifteen years ago. Four children were taken off of a playground during their recess time. No one had seen or heard anything since. In one newspaper clipping, it said Detective Hollinger had been assigned to the case when it first started but made no progress and admitted defeat.

*Shannon is trying to finish his case*, I thought. *But why?*

Searching a little more, I found the names of the children, but only one caught my attention. I knew it too well.

Pietro Hollinger.

Seeing that familiar last name made my heart stop. I stumbled back and leaned against the desk. *She had lost her older brother and she didn't tell me?* I thought, staring at the wall of notes. She had dropped her case to find *my* siblings. I felt so guilty.

My wallowing was interrupted by the van beeping. Snapping out of it, I grabbed all the information on both cases, put them into a bag, and dashed back outside.

Shannon sat at the wheel and said, "Thankfully we have a full tank. Are you ready?"

"Hold up, *you're* driving?" I scoffed, leaning in the window. I pushed the thought of her dropping an important case for me out of my mind. "I am two years older than you, I should drive."

"You may be older, but I am more mature," she stated. "Besides, I know how to drive this thing *safely*. You are a reckless thrill seeker who could put us all in danger."

"Ouch," I retorted. "That was a very complex insult."

"Well, I am a complex person," she said as she started the van.

Before driving out, I showed her what I packed for her to make sure I didn't forget anything. "This stuff good? I even grabbed your little box." It was a small wooden chest with a silver lock. I always saw it on the shelf but never realized it had such value.

She panicked for a second and put her hand on her throat. Feeling that her key necklace was still there, she let out a sigh of relief. "Yes, that's perfect."

"What's in this box?" I questioned shaking it.

She tore it out of my hand and put it back in the bag. "Secret. Now don't touch."

"Yeah, hands off, boy," Johanna scolded, flashing her own key necklace that Shannon had gotten her for her previous birthday. It was on a leather string, lined with silver rings and a key; same as her friend's. What was different was her key was  heart shaped and she only had two silver rings on each side.

"Are the rings and key supposed to mean something?" I asked, flicking the key around Johanna's neck.

"Yeah, the key represents me and the rings, my family," Shannon explained. She rubbed the key between her fingers. "It's an old Hollinger tradition."

Without explaining it further, Shannon instructed us to get the girls settled. When they were strapped in, Shannon backed down the driveway and onto the main road. Shifting gears, she hit the gas and we were off. Where to, we weren't sure yet.

We drove throughout the night and didn't stop. The entire time, we sat in silence. I didn't want to bring up anything yet; it was too early. Thankfully, Johanna and Shannon's sisters all fell asleep. It was a lot to handle and we didn't know what would come next.

I sat in the passenger seat with my guitar beside Shannon. To my surprise, she was a smooth and responsible driver. She kept her eyes locked on the road and didn't say a word.

At three o'clock in the morning, I finally offered to drive. "Do you want to pull over and take a rest? You haven't stopped."

She shook her head and gripped the wheel tighter. "I won't be able to relax. I have too much on my mind." With a sigh, she added, "I can think of reasons for abducting adults with power or intelligence, but I don't understand why they would take 'unimportant' people so to speak."

"Maybe they're aliens," I said joking. "That British alien said he never met someone who wasn't special. He also abducts random people."

Shannon smiled. "I don't think my parents are flying away with an alien-in-the-box."

After that, the two of us sat in quiet. Eventually, I fell asleep, only to be haunted by nightmares. Practically every time I closed my eyes to sleep I was tormented by my dreams. This time, they were about the girls' lost brother and whatever those monsters had done to him. I woke up with a start and nearly caused Shannon to crash.

With a scream, she swerved back into her lane. None of the girls in the back woke up, thankfully. "Warn somebody when you're going to do that!" she yelled.

"Sorry." I put my hands on my face. "I just can't seem to have pleasant dreams."

"I noticed," Shannon said. "I wish we could do something to help."

I thanked her and we sat in silence again. The sun was just

coming up…and Shannon was still driving.

"Wait, did you stop at all?" I said after realizing.

"I took a quick nap, don't worry. I also stopped  to get gas and use the bathroom," she replied. "I can't believe how much gas and food prices have gone up! It's like we aren't drained of our income enough. Anyway, we just had to keep going. We have to get there."

Johanna poked her head between our two seats. "Wait, you actually know where we are going?"

"Good morning to you too, Johanna," Shannon replied sarcastically. "And yes I do know. We are going to the place where Mark sent us his S.O.S."

# CHAPTER 21
## Aymie: VI

The plane ride to WHYP was more enjoyable than I expected, so you can imagine how disappointed I felt when it was over. I was afraid that this "community home" was going to be a dumpy nursing home for teenagers.

The plane landed on a private runway, I guess you could call it. "Why didn't we land at the airport?" I asked, peeking out the window.

Smiling, Mr. Wyght replied, "Wouldn't you rather land in your own backyard?" He grabbed my things, opened the door, and led me down the stairs.

I looked around at the property and couldn't believe my eyes. His backyard was huge. The mansion in the distance looked nothing more than a small farm house. There was also a barn, animal pen, and fields of crops. To the far left was an enormous training ground covered in equipment, wooden towers, sandbags, tents, and different obstacles.

I stared with my jaw dropped until Mr. Wyght commented, "It's nice, isn't it?"

I nodded. "It seems like a far walk though," I added, pointing to the mansion in the distance.

He chuckled. "It is, but that's why we don't have to walk." He pointed in the direction of the mansion where a vehicle that was just a blur came into view.

Two teenage boys rolled up in a mini, army truck. The boy who was driving looked about sixteen and had straight black hair that went below his ears. He had friendly brown eyes and light brown skin. He was fit and wore a white t-shirt and gray cargo pants.

The other in the passenger seat looked older and stronger, but seemed less confident than his friend. His blue eyes were timid and he had a nervous smile. He wore a dirty gray jumpsuit and welding goggles on top of his full blond hair.

"Evening, Grath. Flicks," Mr. Wyght greeted.

"Evening, sir," they said simultaneously. The driver hopped over the side and approached me. "Hello, Miss. I'm Zander Grath," he introduced, holding out his hand.

I shook it gingerly. "Nice to meet you. I'm Aymie."

"The pleasure is all mine," he replied. Taking my bags from Mr. Wyght, he went back to the truck. "Gregory Flicks, let the lady sit there!" he scolded his friend as he threw my belongings into the back. Grumbling, Flicks got up and went to sit in the bed of the truck.

Zander shook his head and sat back in his spot. With a smile, the teen looked at me and patted the seat next to him.

Before I went over to sit down, Mr. Wyght said, "I will have to catch up with you in a bit. The boys are very nice and will explain how things work around here." He began to walk away, but then remembered something. He whispered, "Just a warning: Zander has a soft spot for pretty ladies."

My face turned bright red. *Me pretty?* I thought, baffled. The thought of a cute boy finding a pale, bald orphan attractive was beyond me. Still, I smiled and went to sit down.

He started the engine. "All right here we go," Zander exclaimed, gripping the wheel. "Hold tight back there, Flicks." With that, he hit the gas and off we went.

Zander wasn't the best driver, but I tried not to say anything. I was in a strange place surrounded by cute boys and I had no idea what to expect.

Thankfully, Zander was talkative so there was never a lull in the conversation. He glanced over at me and said with a smile, "Well, I guess I could start the tour." Clearing his throat, he began: "Welcome to 'Wyght's Home for Young People' where 'the youth of today transform the future of tomorrow'. At least I think that's the slogan." He acted as a safari tour guide that really didn't know what he was doing. "As you saw behind you, there were mountains. We climb those sometimes. Straight ahead you will see a barn and a pen with animals in it. We have a farm and grow food and stuff. Behind you've got the mansion where you live and the warehouse where some of us work. To your left you will see our training field. We do random drills every other day."

"Wait," I interrupted, holding my door handle tighter as he roughly jerked the truck, "training? Drills? We have to *do* that?"

"He didn't tell you, did he." He chuckled. "In order to live here, you have to learn quite a few things. Think of 'WHYP' as a cross between a military academy and an awesome foster home."

I was astounded. "Please tell me you are joking."

"I asked Mr. Wyght the same thing when I came here," Flicks yelled from the back.

"Yeah, sorry," Zander apologized. "You are going to become some sort of soldier. Think of it as a way to pay your rent." I slumped back in my seat. I wasn't cut out for that nor did I want to be.

We reached the first stop: the warehouse. Driving through the open garage, Zander turned to the right where we parked next to several other vehicles. The vast building was filled with a variety of things; I couldn't comprehend them all. There were work tables, high shelves covered in supplies, cars, tools, guns, and more. Teenage workers scrambled about their business. They were so engrossed in what they were doing, they didn't notice us come in.

Hopping out of the vehicle, Zander ran around and offered to help me down. I took his hand and stepped out. Flicks jumped off the back with my bags. He led the way in silence.

"Don't mind Flicks," Zander explained, "he has been here ever since he was nine and tends to do his thing. None of us newbies mess with the Veterans."

"When did you get here?" I asked.

"About three months ago," he said. "The two of us will be in a few of the same classes." That was a relief that I would know somebody. It all seemed very intimidating.

Flicks led us to the back of the warehouse. I was so in awe with everything around me, I almost bumped into one of the kids working. She quickly sidestepped before our shoulders collided. "Hey watch it!" she shouted as she cradled the objects she was carrying. "These are fragile explosives!"

Quickly, I backed away, "Oh my gosh, I am so sorry!"

She laughed and harshly patted me on the shoulder. "I'm messing with ya. They're only spark plugs." With a grin, she said, "The name is Alexandrea McCracken." Alexandrea was about my age and height, but had a stronger build. Her blue eyes had a mischievous look and her hair was pulled back into a blonde ponytail. She had the same outfit as Flicks only no goggles. She wore heavy fire proof gloves instead as her added accessory.

"I'm Aymie," I replied timidly. "I'm new here."

"Yeah, I can tell," she replied. "Don't worry. I am still kind of new too. Zander and I got here around the same time."

"Let's keep moving," Flicks urged. "Introductions later."

Alexandrea rolled her eyes. "Well, then. I will see you later, Aymie." With that, she went off with her spark plugs.

Irritated, Flicks gripped my bags tighter and kept moving. We stopped at the back of the warehouse where boxes of extra supplies were kept. "I'm sorry, but what are we doing here?" I asked.

"We need to get you uniforms," Zander explained as he lifted a box off the shelf. He plopped it down. He was about to lift the lid when he paused and looked at his friend with a puzzled expression. "Wait, did Mr. Wyght say what Branch she would be working in?"

Flicks shrugged. "What are you good at?" he asked me.

My face got red. I didn't really know. "Um, I know how to sew and make things. I can also play piano if that counts for anything."

"You have good hand eye coordination and you're creative,"

Flicks said. "How fast can you sew things? Are you personable?"

I was so overwhelmed. "Yes to all I suppose? I also have a photographic memory if that helps."

Flicks looked impressed and turned towards his friend. "What do you think?"

Zander smiled. "Definitely a Polymath," he concluded. Holding his hands up, he exclaimed, "Congrats, girl!"

"Polymath? What is that?" I asked, perplexed.

"Polymath is an old term used for someone who can do many things," Zander told me. "Since you do not quite fit in any of the other Branches, and you are definitely not an Umbrella, you are going to be with the other Polymaths and help out in a little bit in each branch."

Noticing my utter confusion, Flicks explained with further detail: "There are six Branches that you can be in: the Combatants, the Drones, the Nerds, the Polymaths, the Agricolae, or the Umbrellas. Remember, everyone here learns the same exact things, but each Branch works harder in different subjects."

Pointing to his friend, Flicks continued, "Zander here is a Combatant. That means his main focus is fighting, survival, defense, and other things military like. Alexandrea and I are Drones. We focus mainly on creating and fixing tech, weapons, automobiles, and machines. The Nerds work on the computers doing whatever it is they do; hacking and junk." With a bag still in his hand, he pointed to me. "The Polymaths don't have a main area of focus, but assist the other Branches and usually do their own thing. The Agricolae are the smallest group, because no one really grew up learning that stuff; finding an Agricola is rare. They are the main caretakers of the farm and its animals. However, everyone has to learn how to farm to help out. There are just a few who do it all day, every day. Finally, the Umbrellas. They are a more generic category for kids who haven't found their talents yet. They help with the house chores, make the food, and mainly do schoolwork."

Chuckling, Zander said, "Let's not let the poor girl's head explode. All you have to know is you are a Polymath. Now, let's get your uniforms."

I hoped I had a large closet, because Zander handed me one of each. As a Polymath, apparently I needed the attire of all the Branches, because they didn't have their own outfit. They all kept slipping from my grasp. Thankfully, I was given some of Mr. P's official company merch to carry it all. I carelessly shoved my new clothes into the black bag with the lightbulb logo and followed my guides to the house.

We had to walk farther than I thought; my legs were killing me…as was the suspense. I looked around at all the kids going about their work. We passed through the giant barn where the Agricolae rendezvous to get their tasks and check in. It smelled disgusting and they all looked filthy.

"Evening, Marian!" Zander called to a girl in the center of the crowd.

With a smile, she waved back. Her pale face was covered in dirt and her blue overalls looked almost black. "Got a new recruit for me?" she asked.

"Not exactly, she's a polymath though," he called back.

She clapped. "Congratulations! So excited to have you."

Unsure of what to say, I smiled and waved. Many of the kids turned to return the gesture. No one shot me a judgmental look because of my head wrap or anything. The sweaty, stinky teens all seemed welcoming. *Why are they so nice?* I wondered, suspicious.

After another long walk, we were out of Agricolae territory and to the front of the manor. Tilting my head back, I couldn't even see the top of it. "Oh my goodness," I baffled. The gorgeous white building glimmered in the sunlight like ice. "This is bigger than my mansion was."

"You lived in a mansion before this?" Zander asked surprised as we went up the front steps.

"Yes, the Quartermane Mansion," I said quietly. "It's just ashes now along with my family."

Zander's smile faded. "I am sorry; I didn't mean to bring it up."

"No, it is okay," I replied. "It's nobody's fault." I took a deep breath. "So, may I see the inside?"

Pulling the door open, Zander motioned for me to go in before him.

I stepped foot into an enchanting hallway. The floors were polished mahogany and everything was clean and beautiful. Young teens strode along about their business. Straight ahead was a staircase with walnut railings. It curved from the left side of the hall up to the hidden second floor. Beneath the center of the stairs was another hallway leading to more small rooms. To my left was the entrance to the kitchen and dining area. To my right were more enclosed rooms and a staircase leading to a lower level.

"Breathtaking isn't it," a familiar voice said. It was Mr. Wyght. He came out of the dining hall and was holding a plastic clipboard. "So what do you think so far?"

"Incredible yet confusing," I confessed, looking around in awe.

The older man chuckled. "I would hope so. This is a one of a kind program that not many outsiders know exist. However, I think you will find some things similar to your time with the Sisters."

"Which Sisters did she stay with?" someone said behind me. Turning around, I found a shorter man wearing a dress-looking outfit of all gray. It was similar to the Sisters' but without a head covering. He had rough light brown skin and a long dark beard. His eyes were small but full of life.

"Father Edgar, meet Aymie," Mr. Wyght introduced. "She was at Saint Maria Goretti's."

The man thought for a moment. "Unfortunately, I don't know the Sisters down there," he confessed. "Perhaps one day I'll get the pleasure." He turned to me and held out his hand. "Pleased to meet you. The students here call me Papa E."

Shaking it, I replied, "Thank you. Do you live here?"

"I do," he told me. "I maintain the chapel and am here whenever someone needs help or just a listening ear which reminds me," he turned to Mr. Wyght, "I am putting in a request for an assistant counselor. With Father J gone, I am a little shorthanded. Even a mature student whom I can train will be fine."

The older man nodded. "Of course, I'll see what I can do. I wouldn't want to put too much on your plate."

The priest held his hand up. "Please, it's no trouble. I just would like to offer help as soon as a child needs it." He looked at me. "It was great to meet you and I will hopefully see you Sunday."

Telling him he would, he took his leave. Once Papa E was gone, Zander spoke up. "Permission to speak, Mr. Wyght?"

"Granted, Grath," he replied.

"We placed Aymie in the Polymath Branch. Was that all right?"

"Sounds fine to me," he stated. "To be honest, I wasn't quite sure about that myself."

Zander let out a deep breath. "Okay good. We were worried it wasn't what you wanted."

"We were?" Flicks asked before he was elbowed by his companion.

"It's fine boys," Mr. Wyght said. "Now, take Miss Hodgins to her new bedroom." He handed him a slip with the room number on it.

Zander thanked the founder and led me up the staircase and to my room. Approaching it, I suddenly became very nervous. *What if they don't like me? What if they are just as mean as the girls from the orphanage?* The thought of having no kind friends made me miss Janelle. I feared that those people were hurting her…

My mind snapped back into reality when we reached the last door in the center of the back wall. Zander knocked. "Any ladies in there?" he called. No one responded, so we went in.

I was once again blown away. The floor was layered in a blush pink carpet and the wall ahead of me had glass display cases showing off elegant handmade outfits. In the center was a doorway leading to a walk in closet, master bathroom, and a supply room. To the left and right of the cases were white stairs with wooden railings leading up to eight beds. It was a bedroom for a princess fashion castle (if that is even a thing).

Zander seemed just as surprised as I was. "Wow. This is so big and pink. Why do the girls get bigger rooms than we do?"

"Their rooms are almost exactly the same. Only this one is different," Flicks told his jealous friend. "Since we can't really order our clothing without arousing suspicion, there is a special team of female Polymaths who make it for us as well as whatever else we need. This is their workshop and bedroom." He gestured to all the supplies on the tables around. "I guess Mr. Wyght thinks your sewing talent is top notch because only a select eight girls get in here."

"Or is she one of the only ones who actually *knows* how to sew?" Zander thought aloud.

Flicks smacked him in the back of the head. "Anyway, make yourself at home. I think the first bed on the left is for you."

Suddenly, a female voice made an announcement over the P.A. system that was connected throughout the house: "*All Royals to the meeting room. All Royals to the meeting room, thank you.*"

"Well that's my cue," Flicks said, dropping the bags at his feet. "I'll catch you all later." With that, he left Zander and I alone in my new room.

"Who are the Royals? You never mentioned them," I asked as I put my new duffle bag down.

"The Royals are a select few who excel in their duties as well as other things," my friend explained. "Flicks isn't just a Royal, though. He is a Royal *Veteran* or RV for short. As an RV, he leads all the Drones, has other duties, and better privileges. He earned the Royal title a few years ago when he heroically ran into a misfire in the warehouse to save a few newbies. Also, he is the greatest welder that anyone has ever seen." He leaned closer and whispered dramatically, "Legend has it he welded over one hundred machines in a twenty four hour period for a customer who paid for a lot of our equipment. Those are the reasons why he became the RV." Zander glanced over his shoulder to made sure no one was listening before he went on. "I mean welding is a rare talent, but I think they are over exaggerating."

That was pretty cool, but I still couldn't understand his character. "Why is he so grumpy?"

Zander sighed. "The reason why people come here is because bad things have happened to them. Flicks is having a harder time than most to put it behind him. The main focus of this school is to help us cope with what has happened. We are taught to use that experience to move forward and help others."

"I'm sorry, I didn't know," I apologized.

"It's all right, you don't have to keep apologizing," he replied, smiling. "We all have been through a lot, right?" Bending over, he picked up my bags. "Now, let's get you settled in."

# CHAPTER 22
## Aymie: VII

After putting my things away, Zander left me to go get ready for dinner. While he was gone, I changed into my casual uniform: a flowy white long sleeve blouse tucked into black dress pants and shiny flats. My pink head wrap didn't exactly match, but I didn't have any other and I was not going to take it off. I tucked my silver chain that held my dog tag and Blake's ring into my shirt. The cold metal pressed against my warm chest and I could only think of Blake and my family...and the fact that I was alive and living in a place as WHYP.

Thankfully, Zander came back before I could get too depressed. His casual uniform was similar to mine. Instead of a blouse, he wore a white button up dress shirt with a badge that had his last name on it. "You almost ready?" he asked, doing the last button on his top.

"As ready as I'll ever be," I replied.

"It's okay to be nervous," he said. "This is all big and new, but I am sure you will fit right in." Reaching into his pocket, he pulled out a small black badge with my name on it. "I almost forgot to give you this. Make sure you have it pinned to that uniform at all times. You are going to have to monogram the others."

I took it from him and rubbed my finger over the letters.

"*Hodgins*" it read. This was the first time people would know who I really was… even though *I* didn't even know who I really was. Nevertheless, I pinned it over my heart and followed Zander back downstairs to the dining hall.

The long room was filled with many rows of wooden tables and chairs. People scurried from the buffet in the back of the room to their seats, but no one sat down. Zander and I got plates of food and went to a table. Rather than sitting, we put our trays down and stood behind the chairs.

"What are we waiting for?" I whispered.

"The Royals, the older staff, and Mr. Wyght," he replied. "We don't sit down until they are all here and they give a toast."

After standing for about five minutes, Mr. Wyght made his way to his seat at the center table with Flicks and a few older members. Lifting up his glass of soda he began the toast. "Friends, we thank Heaven for another day on this earth. We are grateful for everything we have, our new members, and those to come. Thank God for life, friends, and the will to fight on for the future of tomorrow!"

We raised our glasses, let out a short cheer, and took a sip of our drink. Finally, we sat down to eat.

"Is that your version of grace?" I asked, curious.

"Uh, I think so," Zander replied unsure as he shoved his face with steak. With his fork, he then gestured to Alexandrea and two others who were sitting across from us. "Anyway, meet some of your new classmates."

"You already know me," Alexandrea said, licking her lips. "So what Branch did they put you in?"

"Please tell me you're an Umbrella," the boy next to her said. He looked at me desperately with his big brown eyes. His dark hair was shaved on his round head. He must have been twelve at the most because his skin was smooth and he still had a lot of baby fat.

"No, I'm a Polymath," I replied.

"If you weren't so scared, Dylan, you would actually go make friends with the other existing Umbrellas," the other girl next to him said. Turning to me, she introduced herself. "My name is Roxanne

Pontiff—Combatant." Roxanne had dark hair shorter than Zander's that was shaved behind her ears and curly on the top. Her skin was tan and smooth. Her eyes were hard and the color of night. She didn't really have table manners and gave the impression that she was the toughest one in the hall.

"Oh yeah, I am Dylan Cheatle—Umbrella," Dylan said glumly. "It's not my fault I can't make friends."

Roxanne belched under her breath. "Kinda is."

"Anyway," Alexandrea interrupted, growing impatient, "what room are you in?"

"The big pink one at the end of the hall," I replied.

Roxanne's jaw dropped. "What? Girl, I am jealous. Although, I don't like the pink part."

"What's so great about the pink room?" Dylan asked.

"It is the biggest one, has the most closet space, they have their own bathroom," Alexandrea explained. "Only the girls who are the best at sewing sleep there. It's their workshop. The stuff they make is incredible, so you must be one of the best."

I blushed. I hadn't even shown Mr. Wyght anything I could do. I wasn't sure if I could match those girls.

"Wait, why do only girls get that?" Dylan complained. "Guys can sew too."

"Of course they can, moron," Roxanne insulted. "The guys who sew work with the Drones. They handle heavy duty materials like leather and whatever. They are really good at what they do. Their time is better spent than making linens and wedding dresses."

For the rest of dinner we talked about our pasts and how we came to be with WHYP. They were all newbies like me. Each one told me about how they became orphans. Well, almost all of them told me voluntarily. Roxanne had to smack it out of Zander for some reason. I said it was okay and he didn't have to share, but they insisted. He basically said that his family didn't get along. So, he decided to go live with his uncle. He never told us what exactly happened after. He said he would rather listen to my story than go through his.

After they shared, I felt inclined to share my past. I told them about my old life in the Quartermane mansion. I also spoke a lot about my best friend, Blake. As I talked about him, Zander's expression changed. I wasn't sure if it was out of curiosity, jealousy, or what but he asked a lot of questions. Then, I told them about my life with the Sisters and how I met Mr. Wyght.

Before we knew it, dinner time was almost over and Zander had forgotten that he was supposed to brief me on what was to come. I won't even begin to explain to you what he told me. However, as you can already tell, what we experienced isn't that different than the Isles you grew up on.

[I figured you were wondering about that, Alison. Trust me, there is an explanation. Also our system was safer, more trustworthy, and all around better. No offense.]

After dinner was free time. We could go wherever we want and do almost whatever we wanted. If something was illegal or immoral we had to scratch it off our to-do list. That didn't stop some kids though, let me tell you. However, they were quickly disciplined.

"That's why we gotta listen to the rules," Roxanne said. She pointed to a few kids whom Mr. Wyght was leading into his office. "No one wants to get on Mr. Wyght's bad side."

"I thought it was because we are growing as human beings and have to be the better example?" Dylan questioned.

Roxanne sighed. "Yeah, sure there is that too."

After watching the boys being led to their punishment, they showed me around. I never had an official tour so they took me through a few rooms in the far wing. It was absolutely incredible.

The first room on the right was a ballroom large enough to fit all of a king's subjects. It had wooden floors and pictures covering the walls. They were framed photos of the events they had held. There were wedding photos, homecomings, parties, and old fashioned ballroom dances. I could not wait to participate in one of those events.

Next, we entered their music hall.  Music was part of their curriculum, so that room was a big deal. The walls were white and had a large music staff painted across the perimeter. The floor was pearl tile, making all the instruments stand out. They had an entire orchestra in one room. I stood there gawking.

"I heard you play," Zander said, motioning to the grand piano in the center of the room. Before I could go over to it, he remembered something. "Wait! You said you had a photographic memory?" I nodded. Going over to white bookshelves, he pulled a random music book off. "Look at this, memorize it, and play it."

"I don't think it works like that," Alexandrea doubted.

Smirking, I studied the page and went down to the piano. I closed my eyes and rested my fingers against the keys. I took a deep breath and began the piece I had never heard before.

I felt myself get lost in the music; completely ignoring the people around me. My fingers danced across the ivory keys and childhood memories flooded my mind. The piece reminded me of my Quartermane family, making me homesick. I wanted to stop and cry…but I wasn't going to. They asked me to play, so I would play. Hearing Abigail's voice in my head, I recalled, "*A true princess puts others before herself.*" I set my sorrows aside and played for their entertainment.

Striking the final chord with finesse, I ended the piece. Everyone clapped. I stood up, took a bow and went back to my new friends.

"Aymie, that was incredible!" Zander exclaimed, grinning from ear to ear. He wanted to say something more but saw someone behind me and became quiet.

"So you are the new girl?" an unfamiliar voice said.

I was startled. "Uh, yes?" I replied, turning around.

It was an older girl with sandy curls. Her eyes were sky blue and her skin as soft as cotton. Everything from her build to her face made me think of a princess. Laughing sweetly, she said, "Relax, we were all tense our first couple days. You'll get used to it."

Looking at her made me upset and insecure. I once was a princess and now I felt like the bald frog. "Thank you," I said softly.

"I heard you're our new seamstress," she continued. "I thought I'd introduce myself. I am Adeline Zarra; the Royal Veteran Polymath. I've been around for what seems like an eternity."

"How long is an eternity?" I asked.

"Let's see," she replied, thinking. "I am almost twenty three and I came here when I was twelve. So eleven years I believe?"

I was shocked. I thought foster homes could only care for kids until they were eighteen. "And you are still here? Isn't there an age limit?"

She giggled. "Not for Mr. Wyght. Once he thinks you are ready, he sets you up with a place to live and a job to start your own life. That is what is so great about WHYP. There is no limit. I think it's rude that once kids reach a certain age they are abandoned. Here, we can take all the time we need." She wagged a finger. "But that doesn't mean we can take advantage of the free life here. Once we turn eighteen we work triple time in case anyone gets any ideas."

We talked for a little bit about the work load. It was a lot, but I knew I could take it. Adeline seemed ecstatic that I had previous experience.

"We are so understaffed," she confessed. "There are quotas we can barely fill even if our deadlines were pushed back by months. So, we will be expecting big things from you." She shook my hand and exited the room.

"She seems nice," Dylan slurred as if under a spell.

Roxanne smacked him. "Keep dreaming kid."

An hour or so later, we had our final "class" of the day: meditation. This was the time where everyone found their own little corner of quiet, sat down, and thought about the day. We were supposed to go over what we had done, who we had met, and what impacted us. If we thought it necessary, we would write it down or talk to Papa E. This was supposed to help us settle down and learn more about what makes us tick. It was also part of Psychology class. I was used to it because of my life with the Sisters who had special times of the day dedicated to just thinking.

[Oh my goodness, it *is* kind of like you guys having to keep record logs each night. Maybe that is why Mr. Nik made you do it… sorry, I'll explain what I mean later. Yes, yes I will explain! Ethan, you're making me get out of order.]

Finally, it was time to go to bed. I barely spoke with any of the other girls while we were getting ready. I made sure I didn't take off my head wrap while I was around them. Adeline noticed my caution and almost said something, but held back. I was embarrassed so I slept with it on. It was so uncomfortable. I lay in my new bed and stared at the ceiling. Despite my efforts, I could not sleep that night.

*This new life…what will it hold for me? What do You have in store?* With that question swirling in my mind, I finally closed my eyes and fell asleep, not sure what the future to hold.

The next couple of weeks were an interesting experience. Before I was assigned jobs with the seamstresses, I had to make sure I was caught up in the normal schoolwork. I was used to some of the curriculum. Unfortunately, there was much I had to learn. I think I had the hardest time when we had class learning about technology. In the Quartermane mansion, I never had to fix anything. The servants did it for me. Living with the Sisters, we didn't really have too much of that. I was also terrified something would catch on fire. I did not want to go through that again.

After the first month, I really enjoyed my time there. Zander, Alexandrea, Dylan, Roxanne, and I became really close. I even got to know Flicks a little better too.

[Don't worry, Axel, if you don't remember all their names. There are a lot of people you are getting introduced to; I'm sorry if you get lost. Yeah, I know it's tough. Maybe I'll make a list for you or something.]

The day came when my life changed once more. Only this time, I didn't even know it.

I was assigned to hospitality with Alexandrea to meet this new kid one of the Royals saved from abduction. It was a bright, sunny day and the two of us waited on the front porch for them to drive up to the door.

They approached in a banged up pickup truck. Hopping out of the driver side was a handsome, young man with black skin and a built figure. His clothing was shredded. *More stuff for us to sew,* I thought, annoyed.

His passenger was about my age and had pale skin like mine. His hair was brown and cut weird. Half of his head was shaved while the other half went far below his ears. The ear on the shaved side had three silver earrings. His clothes were in just as bad of a condition as his friend, but he was covered in dirt and smelled worse.

"Alexandrea," the older one greeted when they were at the bottom of the steps.

"Welcome back, Thyme," she replied. "This is Aymie; another new recruit."

"Nice to meet you," he said walking up the stairs, the other close behind. That climb took its toll. They were both already out of breath. "Can you help us? We haven't stopped for days."

Alexandrea took Thyme's bags and I grabbed the other boy's.

"Thank you," he said. He kept his pretty blue eyes on the ground.

"You're welcome," I replied hesitantly. I tried not to breathe in his foul body odor. "I'm Aymie."

Glancing up, he looked at my face, then my badge, then back at me. "Mark," he said, almost uncertain.

Yes, that is how we first met! To be honest, I didn't really like you at first, Mark. What? It isn't my fault! You smelled terrible. Yeah, you better give them a good explanation for that.

# Chapter 23

## Mark: VII

Let me provide you with the explanation for why I stink. Well, it all starts when a little boy's body begins to blossom into manhood.

Totally joking, guys. Relax. I'll give you another explanation.

I was running away from my abductees with a guy who was named after an herb. Nevertheless, wherever he was taking me had to be better than the back of a truck. We ran through the woods for miles with Masdit and Gerrior close behind.

"This way," Thyme instructed as he made a hard left through some sharp shrubbery. We didn't care about faces getting cut by the thorns or the rips in our clothes. We kept going. As we ran, my rescuer pulled out a gun that was in his pants. "Stop here," he said finally. Ducking behind some trees, we waited to see if they were still following.

My heart was racing. This wasn't my first chase, but this time I wasn't sure of the outcome. I tried to steady my breathing to keep quiet, but I couldn't stop.

Finally, we heard them.

"Mark Hodgins!" Masdit screeched. "Come out now, or they die. We will kill them *both*. We will say it's an accident. They will both die the same way their foster families did. Shane will die alone in the woods and his body will drift down the river; never to be seen again. Your sister?" He cackled. "Well, first I will have some fun with her. Then, I will burn her slowly and painfully."

I covered my mouth and tried not to curse him aloud.

He came a few steps closer. "You've never experienced a loved one die, have you? You've never watched your family drown or be slaughtered in front of your eyes. You never saw your entire house burn down with hundreds of people inside. I guess you were always the different one; the odd one out. We have watched the three of you grow and—I have to say—I can't tell which one I like the best."

I was about to run out and tackle him until Thyme shot me a look.

"Come out, come out wherever you are," Masdit continued to taunt.

"The kid's gone," Gerrior said finally. "Let's just go."

"No!" Masdit bellowed. "The boss wanted them now. He said it was time."

Without warning, Thyme seized the opportunity and jumped out of hiding and shot Masdit.

Masdit howled, grabbed his shoulder, and stumbled towards Gerrior. "Kill him!" He commanded his partner.

Pressing his hand on the wound, Gerrior made sure Masdit couldn't escape his grip. "Run," he mouthed to us without his comrade noticing.

We listened and got out of there as fast as we could. We reached Thyme's beat up truck and hopped in. Revving the engine, Thyme slammed on the gas and we were on our way. Neither of us spoke until we were about an hour away from my pursuers.

"Why did you help me?" I asked finally.

"You needed it," he replied, gripping the steering wheel. "That's what we do."

"Who's we?"

"You'll see in a day or so. It takes some time to get there."

I was impatient and ungrateful. "Well, if it takes time, Thyme, then you can tell me now. Save the rest of 'we' the trouble of explaining it."

He chuckled. "I like you kid. You're edgy. All right, I will explain a little bit of it.

"We are a special foster care system for all kinds of kids: criminals, addicts, suicidals, homeless, and so forth. We provide them with a home, education, and hope. The destruction of the family these days is disgusting. Kids are abused, thrown on the streets, and even killed when they are just born if not before." He sighed. "Lately, most cases have *not* been the parents' fault like the past. Adults are disappearing like crazy, getting killed, and are losing their minds due to God knows what.

"That's not even all of it. The children are being taken away from their parents because of the government. They are apparently getting 'information'," he made air quotes with one hand, "that their parents are doing 'illegal' things and must be stopped. So somehow they have manipulated the children to give testimonies against their parents, separate the families, and throw the kids on the streets."

I thought for a moment. *Is he lying?* I saw adults and children in the city every day. It didn't seem like they were disappearing.

"I know this is a lot to take in," he said after a while, "and you are probably confused. Just know that this is happening. We are doing our best to fix it, but we haven't saved as many children and families as we had hoped. We only have one spot for our organization, and we have to keep it secret. If the wrong people found out, many could be in jeopardy."

After that depressing conversation, we sat in silence for a little while. It didn't help, so Thyme did his best to break the ice. We conversed but tried to keep the topics light. We learned a bit more about each other during our forty-eight hour car ride.

Thyme apparently was one of the original kids in WHYP (the place we were going). There were several Branches that you could be placed in plus one special one for those who proved themselves. Thyme told me I would most likely be a Nerd. I didn't really like the name but what they did was pretty much up my alley. Although, I would have considered myself a Polymath. However, pickpocketing and thievery was not a categorized skill. Thyme told me he was the Royal Veteran Combatant; a hard-core fighter.

When their founder was in the military, he took Thyme overseas with him to an army base after it had been attacked from an unknown group. Thyme assisted in the rebuilding and was assigned to aiding another soldier with his tasks.

"I'll never forget what that soldier told me," he recalled. "He was a pale Russian guy with a dark mustache and thick accent. He said, 'The world needs more people like you. If I can't find any, I'll make some.' I was kind of inspired by it at the time, but now that I think about it, it was super creepy. "

After that last story, we were reaching the end of our journey. The final road to the house was a dirt path stretching up the side of a mountain.

"Isn't this a little dangerous?" I asked, holding on to the handle above me for dear life.

"Dangerous? I thought you told me you liked thrills," Thyme teased. He violently jerked the wheel to compensate a sharp turn.

"I said I *lived* for thrills," I corrected. I caught the papers that fell off his dusty dashboard. "I don't die for them."

When the road levelled out, we drove underneath the umbrage of colorful trees. The leaves flew gently down and were swept away as we zipped past. Coming out of the tunnel of foliage, we went up the driveway towards the mansion.

"Whoa," I said, gawking at the sight. "Is this what normal people live in?"

"'Normal people'?" Thyme questioned. "If you are referring to the middle class and lower than no. This is what a rich person's house looks like."

"This is *not* a house," I told him. "There are, like, five extensions the size of schools on each side." Looking over to the right, I gasped. "They have a jet? Is that a *freaking* jet?"

Thyme laughed. "You are going to have fun. Wait 'til you see what we've got on the inside."

We parked right in front of the main doors where two girls waited for us. They were around my age and neatly dressed in white blouses and black pants. One was blonde and the other wore a black head wrap. Not hard to distinguish the two, but they also wore nametags to make it easier.

However, I wasn't in the mood to try and make a good impression, so I decided not to make eye contact at all. Getting out of the car, I let Thyme do all the talking while I followed behind.

I almost made it through the door without speaking to them, but the girl with the head thing took my backpack from me and introduced herself.

Not wanting to be rude, I looked up. Something seemed so familiar about her… then I glanced down at her name badge. "*Hodgins,*" it read. My heart skipped a beat. *Could it be?* We shared the same name. *Masdit swears I have a sister…*

Not knowing what to say, I replied, "Mark," then quickly went inside.

The girls gave their spiel about who they were and what I was to expect and blah, blah, blah. It was boring, I was tired, and I was hungry. I didn't even have the energy to admire the beautiful place I was staying in. To be honest, I was just happy to not be abducted anymore.

After giving me a quick tour, they brought me down to the lowest level where the boys' dorms were. Inside my room were two beds side by side and nightstands next to each. On the navy wall to the bed on the right was a small mirror above a dresser. Next to it was a small empty closet. On the left wall was another closet and dresser but overstuffed with clothing and random junk. That mirror had been shattered and the pieces were still around.

"Can't wait to meet my roommate," I grumbled. Going over to the cleaner side of the room, I picked up the uniforms that were folded neatly on the bed. Since I was in the Nerd Branch, I only received two, but they were similar. The Nerd uniform was a short sleeve white button up with a blue tie and black dress pants. The casual uniform was pretty much the same; just long sleeves and no tie.

Holding the up a shirt, I turned to the girls and asked, "So, do we ever get normal clothes or do we always dress like Shakespeare?"

The blonde girl—Alexandrea—chuckled. "Good one. You can wear regular clothes during free time and on weekends, but if you don't have any you have to put in a request to the Polymaths." She motioned towards Aymie who had an agitated expression.

Looking at the Polymath, I nodded and said, "I might need a new green t-shirt." I looked down at my torn and tattered attire. "Probably some new jeans, too."

"I'll see what I can do," she said, crossly.

Not wanting me to get upset, Alexandrea quickly added, "Will you need anything else?"

"Yeah, when do we eat?" I inquired, rudely.

Impatient and irritated, Aymie hastily replied, "In two hours. That's just enough time for you to make yourself decent and get some rest."

"All right, chill," I responded with my hands up. "I hope you have okay pizza here. I have no idea where *here* is, but I'm from New York so I am only used to the best of the best. I don't want any of that frozen garbage."

"From the city?" Alexandrea asked, her eyes filled with curiosity.

"Yeah," I replied smirking. "To be honest, I have no idea where I was or where I was going when Thyme picked me up, but I know it was *not* New York." Not knowing what else to say, the girls told me where to meet them and then left to finish their duties.

Once they were upstairs, I looked around and took a deep breath. *I can't believe this is happening,* I thought. Then, it hit me. I had just been abducted, threatened, and stolen away from everything I've ever known.

Remembering everything that I went through, I collapsed onto the edge of the bed, put my head in my hands, and cried. I sobbed so much I couldn't anymore. I was in a place that could save kids from the life I had and yet there were more than ever leading miserable ones. I saw them firsthand on the streets. *Could they have a chance at this better life?* I was even lucky to have Fallout even though I had to be a criminal to live there.

*Do they understand what I've done?* I thought to myself, reflecting on my lifestyle at Fallout. I know Thyme said they accepted people like me but would my peers accept what I've done? Would my *sister* if that's who she was?

Wiping the tears from my eyes, I took a deep breath and got up to shower. Thankfully, everyone was in class so I had the ginormous bathroom to myself. To be honest, I don't think I ever took a shower that actually got me clean. The water we used at Fallout and the homeless shelters was never exactly the clearest.

I stood in the shower and tilted my head back, letting the water run down my chest and drip to the floor below. The black water swirled down the drain beneath my feet like a whirl pool. I stared at the chrome showerhead and became lost in thought. As I continued to think about my past, I subconsciously rubbed the Fallout brand over my heart. *They'll never accept me,* I thought, bitterly. *No one here will understand.*

When I was finished, I dried off and changed into my casual uniform. As I combed the long part of my hair, I stared at myself in the mirror. I never did that before. I mean sure I would see my reflection in store windows and stuff, but I never *really* looked at myself. In the mirror I saw an ugly, scared, teenage boy. I didn't know who it was.

Not wanting to look any more, I lay down onto the bed, folding my arms behind my head. I was exhausted before, but now I couldn't sleep.

I lay there staring until the bell rang for dinner. I began to walk towards the door when I remembered my backpack. It had my laptop on it with files from Fallout. Not wanting anyone to find it, I shoved it under my bed and went up to the dining hall.

Inside, hundreds of kids flocked to the counter and went back to the tables with plates of food. Being a city boy, I never minded crowds. I went in line and got my fill. Seeing all the choices they had amazed me. *So many people are starving...how do they have so much?* I wondered. Before I could dwell on it, Thyme found me.

"Hey, Mark. There you are," he greeted. "How is everything?

The girls treat you well?"

"It's good. Nice to take a shower with hot water and have a real bed," I told him. "The girls were fine."

"Are you happy with all of it?"

"Yeah, for the most part," I replied honestly.

"You can give me your complaints later, I promise," he said sincerely. "But I wanted to introduce you to some people you will be working with." He brought me over to a group of guys who were standing behind their seats, waiting to eat. "This here is Mark," Thyme began my introduction. "He is one badass computer guy, so you better watch out."

They laughed which made me feel good. I hoped we were off to an okay start.

"We will see about that, newbie," one of them replied, smiling. He meant well, but it looked intimidating. His teeth were straight and sharp and the edges of his mouth went higher than they should. Other than that, this red head seemed like a decent guy. "I'm Clive Foxwood," he continued. "Here is Derek Rocks."

"Sup," Derek said. Derek was a shorter, rounder teen with black hair and dark almond eyes. His skin was soft and his round face had a relaxed expression. "Welcome to the coolest Nerd table around."

"It would be even cooler if Vandewater could sit with us," Clive replied.

"Who is that?" I asked.

"Oh, that's the Royal Veteran Nerd," Thyme explained. "Man, that sounds really weird. Anyway, he is the best of the best."

"And if you are as good as you say you are, you will definitely get noticed by him which is hard to do," Clive informed, raising his eyebrows.

"Good luck with that," a little voice said behind us. Turning around, I saw a young boy no older than ten carrying a tray of mac and cheese. "Can I sit with you guys?" he asked.

"Anything for mini Mr. P," Derek said, gesturing to the seat next to him.

Putting his food down, he held his arm out across the table. "I am

Myles Powell Junior. Who are you?"

I shook his small hand. "Mark Hodgins. Nice to meet you, Myles."

His eyes got wide. "Wait, your name is—,"

Before he could respond, Thyme exclaimed, "That's what I forgot!" He rummaged through his pockets and pulled out a small plastic rectangle. "Your very own name badge." After I put it on, Mr. Wyght said the toast, and we sat down to eat.

"Now, wait, are you sure that is your last name?" Myles asked before touching his food.

"There are many people with the same last name," Derek explained while he ate his soup. "There is another girl here with Hodgins."

"Wait, there is?" Clive asked.

"Yeah, I met her on the way in," I said, shaking my cup that only had ice left.

"But, but, there is still a possibility," Myles ranted. "You have to! I can't find him. I think something terrible happened to him."

"Relax, man," I said. "You will find this person one day. What's his name?"

"Um, I don't remember exactly," he confessed. "I am pretty sure that his last name was Hodgins and he was in the circus. It was a few years ago, but he is my best friend."

My heart raced. *No...that's impossible. It's just a coincidence*, I told myself. *But still...*Shane was technically a celebrity. Just to make sure, I said, "The circus? I think I met him once when I stole his friend's wallet when I was in New York. Does he look like me, but with green eyes and thicker hair that kinda stands up?" I mimed combing my fingers through thick hair.

Myles was ecstatic and hopped up and down in his seat. "Yes! Yes! That's him! You look *just* like him! Do you know him?"

"Is he like your cousin or something?" Clive asked. He and Derek were interested in our conversation.

Looking at him and then back at Myles, I replied softly, "No. I think he is my brother."

"Shut up," Clive said. "Myles has been talking about this guy for years; it's not possible."

"His name is Shane Hodgins and he has this exact same dogtag," I told him. I pulled the metal necklace out of my shirt. "He was an act in the Regal Circus."

Myles' eyes got wide and continued to bounce. "Yes! Yes! That's the circus. That's it! My dad will tell you, it's him! It's him!"

Derek closed his fists and then opened them while mimicking the sound of an exploding bomb. "Mind blown. The possibility of meeting a long lost sibling is one in a million."

"It was destiny," Myles exclaimed, slamming his tiny hands on the table. "Do you have his information? I have been looking for him everywhere. I thought after what happened to his circus friends he would be in trouble."

I shook my head. "I don't think he is in trouble. I have no clue what happened to the circus he was with, but I do know that he is staying with this cute chick and her family. She was the first one to know we were related. As for contact, I actually gave them the address to a gas station I stopped at about a few weeks back." I thought about that. "Wow, I was stuck with those dudes for a month at least. I wonder if they got my message."

"We can send an Umbrella to look for them," Myles said confidently. "Zander already sent someone to find a friend of his friend." He looked over my shoulder to the table he was sitting at. "I think he is just trying to impress her, to be honest," the little boy whispered.

As dinner went on, I told them more details about Shane and Shannon. They were interested in helping me, and I was never more grateful. I didn't tell them about Aymie possibly being my sister, however, but I asked them to keep everything else quiet.

That night I slept better than ever before; even though my roommate was a self-righteous Combatant who thought he owned everything (and he only arrived two months before me). The people I met were incredible and were willing to help. For the first time, my life was looking up.

# Chapter 24
## Mark: VIII

"Wake up, Nerd," my roommate said throwing his dirty uniform on my bed.

Groaning, I sluggishly sat up. I looked at the clothes and back at him. "Seriously?"

"What?" he asked. "I did this for two months; don't change my routine, city boy."

"My name is Mark," I told him as I threw his XL outfit off my bed.

He walked towards me until we were less than six inches away from each other. He was only two years older, but looked more mature. He was brawny and way taller than me (and I'm over six foot). His skin was light, but his arm hair was unnaturally dark. His bangs had deep red highlights and were styled into a Mohawk. Kind of strange, but who am I to judge hairstyles?

He looked at me with bright violet eyes and replied, "I am Nic, and I call you what I want." He noticed me staring at his appearance. "All of this is natural. Well, natural after the experiments of course." Pointing a large finger at me, he looked closer at my face and added, "You actually look familiar. Ever been to jail?"

"No, because I am too good to get caught," I replied with a smirk.

Nic smiled. "Ooh, nice. I think I am actually going to like you." He bent down to grab his giant backpack. "But I have met you somewhere. I will let you know when I remember!" With a wink, he left for breakfast.

[Yes, Nic and I were roommates. I had no idea he knew my brother. No, Ethan, It wasn't terrible; we had similar habits when it came to room cleanliness. Johanna, we are guys; it's what happens.]

It was my first day with the Nerds and it was not that exciting. After my normal boring classes were done I sat in front of a computer screen at my new desk waiting for something to happen. No hacking, no coding, just staring.

I do have to give them credit; they had a pretty sweet tech lab. The silver computer monitors and white glass tables gave it a futuristic feel. Covering a third of the back wall were one large monitor and many tiny ones beside it. That was the RV Nerd's station. It made a lot of noise and would talk in a weird beeping fashion to whoever was sitting at it.

I went to my new computer station in the middle of the room. I could barely see the items on my desk because the room was dim. There were blue LED bulbs scattered around the room. I am pretty sure they didn't mean anything. They were just for show and to make us feel cool, but not practical at all.

Despite the new setting, my mood didn't improve. "This is pointless," I sighed as I twirled a pen between my fingers like a drumstick.

"Nothing is ever pointless," Derek whispered a desk down from me.

"What are we waiting for then?" I grumbled back.

"If you don't have another assignment, you wait for signals. Signs. Anything to let us know that someone is in danger or needs our help," Clive explained from the row behind me. "How do you think we found you?"

"You found me because that lady on the train gave me your

business card along with some Benjamins," I retorted.

"You met the Secretary? No way," Clive gawked. "No one has ever seen her or even knows her real name. What we do know is she is the one who keeps track of us all and makes sure we are all in place."

"That's nice, but seriously, is anything supposed to happen?" I snapped.

"Quiet back there!" someone up front shouted.

"Sorry," Derek apologized. He turned to me and whispered, "You are going to get us in trouble."

Grumbling, I almost stabbed my desk with the pen until I thought of something to do. *Duh,* I thought to myself. *Find my brother.*

I started my search from the beginning: my family. I never had a reason to look them up before. Now, I had one and the resources.

I didn't have to dig far to find something. Was it entirely helpful? No, but it was something. It was an old article referring to a missing family of five. That was it. Could've been my family, could've been someone else. Never said. The police who tried to investigate also went missing, so they dropped the case.

Next, I tried searching my brother's name. The first thing that came up was a website for a Junior Olympics Association. "What?" I said aloud. "He is a record breaking athlete?"

"What is going on back there?" the man shouted again.

"Nothing, Vandewater," Derek covered up again. "Dude," he mouthed to me.

Ignoring him, I continued to scroll down the site. There he was. I saw a picture of my brother with a golden medal around his neck and I found his astonishing record time. Articles relating to it said that the time was almost as fast as the actual world record. Not bad for a six-foot white boy. I found another photo of him at the rewards ceremony. A picture of him, Shannon, and her family I guessed.

*Man, he is living the life,* I thought jealously. He was standing with pretty girls and I was sitting in the dark surrounded by computer loving nerds. No offense to them or myself.

Looking closely, I saw another familiar face in one of the pictures. *Is that my roommate?* I questioned as I did further research in the weight lifting section. It definitely was. "*Nicolas Eerkens*," it read beneath his fifth place picture. His appearance was just a little different.

*No wonder I looked familiar. I will bring this up to him.* I printed out what I found and shoved it in my backpack.

My final searching was looking up where the Hollinger's lived. I was distraught with my findings. Their home had been broken into and the family was attacked. The children ran out the back and were never seen afterwards. Police and friends came to the Hollinger's aid, but all were reported missing.

Frustrated, I abruptly stood up. I could not believe that WHYP wasn't doing anything about it. I began heading toward the front of the room where Vandewater sat.

"Mark, what are you doing?" Clive called.

"Hey, Vandewater!" I shouted. "Aren't we supposed to be finding people? Well then what are we doing staring at a bunch of screens?"

Without turning around in his chair, the Royal Nerd held up his pudgy left hand and hushed me. He typed a few things and then finally spun around to face me. He was a larger guy in his early twenties. His brown hair was slicked back and neatly trimmed. He wore very dark round glasses.

He was blind.

"Um, are you Vandewater?" I questioned awkwardly.

The Nerd chuckled. "The one and only, kid. Yes, I am blind. Yes, I work with computers and I am good at them. Any other questions about myself before we begin?"

Slowly, I shook my head no. "Oh wait, I mean no," I said out loud.

"I actually knew you were shaking your head," he replied smiling. "My guess is you have long hair going down one side of your face. I heard it rubbing against your shirt. But from now on, just speak okay?"

"Okay," I replied.

"Good. So are you looking for someone?" he asked. "I hear you and Junior are looking for the same guy, yes?"

"That's right, Guy!" a little voice said from behind me. Myles came in carrying a box of papers. "This is his brother. We need to find all of the Hodgins family before it is too late."

"Too late?" Vandewater questioned. "Too late for what?"

"For them," he said quietly. "As Mark just found out, Shane and his friends' house was ransacked and no one has seen them since."

"How did you—," I started.

"You left it up on your screen," the boy said smiling. "Now, I already have someone on the case, but we need to make sure we give him the right clues."

"Allow me to help any way I can," Vandewater offered. "However, for now we must continue our assignments. Can we begin at free time?"

"Of course," Myles agreed. "Meet me in my workshop."

"You have a workshop?" I asked.

"Yes," he replied. "I have and know many things. However, kids tend to make fun of me so I try to act my age. In the end I just end up in my workshop with my inventions and blue prints."

Without explaining anymore, Myles gave Vandewater the box and walked out of the room.

Vandewater rubbed his hands over the papers. "These are for you, Mark; your first official assignment," he said. "You better prove that you are as good as you say."

Cocky, I replied, "I'll prove I am even better."

I took the box to my desk and began going through it. The instructions at the top read, "*Delete, destroy, and decode all information and/or promotion regarding this group.*" There were old newspapers, articles, and websites about something called the "Order of Xenophon". Apparently, they are an extremist cult filled with people of different races, religions, cultures, etc. that wanted to "cleanse the world of impurities".

I searched the normal internet for them and could find barely anything. So, I decided to dig deeper. The internet goes further down than people realize, and that's where all the bad stuff hides.

Finally, I found it. There were millions upon millions of videos, articles, and pages referring to this group. They were all promotional and offering people benefits if they joined. Their recurring motto was "*We are Organized Chaos. We will fix humanity.*" The content I found never mentioned anything that I received in my instructions. I read some articles and two words kept reappearing, "strange voices". *So an 'organized chaos of strange voices'*, I thought to myself, not impressed. I wasn't sure what they were getting at until I watched the videos:

Overlapping *O* and *X* symbols were painted on the sides of buildings in blood. Men, women, and children lay dying in the street. These people didn't care what happened to them or who saw their faces. They were shot at by the police, but they continued to walk towards the barricades like some sort of zombie apocalypse.

Watching a tenth video, I noticed a recurring theme in the background. There was always a group of people who seemed to be leading these mindless robots from the sidelines. You could only catch a glimpse of them, but it was a good theory.

I must have gone through an hour's worth of information before I decided I had enough. I began to erase their work from the internet. *No wonder he gave this to me*, I thought to myself. *This is almost impossible.* I had to go through firewalls, security programs, and crazy stuff before I could even delete one full video. Thankfully, Fallout had prepared me to do exactly that.

I got more done than I expected. *There's got to be a better way to do this*, I thought as I finished up, but that could wait. Free time was next. I packed my things and ran off to meet Myles and Vandewater.

"Hodgins, wait up!" Derek panted as he and Clive chased after me.

"You know where I am going!" I yelled back.

Vandewater and Myles were already there when I arrived… after a few wrong turns. Myles' workshop was a large hidden room in the back of the warehouse. It had all sorts of gadgets, plans, and tools cluttering it. In the center of the room was a complex prosthetic looking machine.

Derek and Clive finally caught up. They put their hands on

their knees and started panting. "I really need to do more Combatant exercises," Derek wheezed.

"I second the motion," Clive said as he stretched.

"Good luck with that," I mumbled.

Clive was about to give a snarky remark when he saw Vandewater was already there. Noticing their superior, the two quickly made themselves look presentable. They admired their RV and now they were getting a chance to work with him. It was a big moment for them.

Rolling my eyes, I went over to Myles' work bench in the middle of the room. I began examining the complicated robotic body part that lay on top of it. "Are you building that?"

"Not by myself," he replied, putting some of the extra wires away. "My friend from Scotland and another from the states are helping me. We are working together." He sighed. "They had to go back home for a bit, so I haven't gotten to work on it. I made everything else though."

"What do you have for us to work with, Myles?" our blind friend asked as he approached the table.

"Lots of things," he laughed. "We have the articles Mark found, Shane's last known locations, and the coordinates Mark sent to them when he was kidnapped."

"All right," Vandewater said. He put his white foldable cane down and clapped his hands together. "Let's get to it."

# THE MAINLAND

# CHAPTER 25
## Shane: X

Okay, so continuing my side of the story. For the fastest human here, I am sure taking the longest to catch up.

Speaking of getting places, we should be reaching our destination in a week or so. I know you are probably all cramped up on this train, but it is almost over. However, what is going to be waiting for us is something you might not expect.

Anyway, so the Hollinger girls, Johanna, and I were on our way to the location Mark sent us a month back. We knew he most likely wouldn't be there, but Shannon hoped to get some clues as to where he was headed.

The ride took longer than anticipated, but we made the most of it. I played my guitar and sang songs, we played those silly road games, and saw incredible sights.

The most frustrating part was Shannon's stubbornness in not letting me drive.

"Please just let me take over for you," I whined. We just left a gas stop on our final day of driving. "I look older and we reduce the risk of getting caught. Not to mention that you are probably still exhausted. You've barely gotten any sleep since we've been on the road." I could see the deep bags under her blue eyes. She was drained and it was going to get the better of her.

I was denied…again. Her stubborn Irish side was not going to give in. "No way," she said, gripping the wheel tighter. She was about to yawn but stopped herself. "There are almost no cops on these roads anyway," she added, changing the subject. "Something must have happened to them too. Because of it, people around us have really taken advantage." Warily, she looked in her rearview. "Also there has been some guy on a motorcycle following us for who knows how long."

I looked in the mirrors to see if she was just being paranoid. She wasn't. In the distance I saw a character in all black cruising behind us. "I've seen plenty of motorcycles during our ride this way," I told her, resting my forearm on the car door. "It's a nice day, I'm sure he's just out for a joyride. This is no excuse for not letting me drive."

She rolled her eyes. "Fine, here's a better point: if someone tries to get us to drag race at a stop light again, you will be the person dumb enough to do it."

She did have a point, but I wasn't going to let her know that. I was just as stubborn as she was if not more. "C'mon, Shannon. Let me driiiive," I whined.

This bickering went back and forth for that entire rest of the day. Johanna was ready to jump in the front seat and shove our faces through the dash board.

Thankfully, we ended that conversation by reaching our destination: a dumpy old gas station in the middle of nowhere.

"I thought our tank was full?" I joked as we pulled into a parking spot.

"It is you idiot," Johanna insulted. "We're here."

If there is one lesson to be learned from this story it's this: make sure Johanna gets enough sleep before you try to be funny.

We instructed Peggy to hold down the fort while the three of us went to the shop. Courteously, I opened the filthy glass doors for the girls and followed them inside. We walked through your typical, run down gas station shop and made our way to the main counter where we found a young cashier. He was anxiously tapping his finger against the cash register. He didn't notice we were standing there until Shannon cleared her throat, snapping him back into consciousness.

He looked at us speculatively. "Sorry, may I help you?

"Yes, I'd like to ask you a few questions," Shannon replied. She looked closely at him as she spoke as if trying to figure out who he was.

It didn't take me long to come up with my own conclusion. This guy was nervous. Sweat dripped from his forehead down into his brown eyes. He quickly took off his glasses and began cleaning them frantically. He looked like a mess in general. His shirt was half tucked in and his dark hair disheveled.

"I guess that all depends on what you want to ask, young lady," he said.

"Are you okay?" she first asked.

Taken aback by her question, he stopped in the middle of cleaning his glasses. Resuming his mindless task, he replied, "I'm not having the best day. "

"I could tell," she said eyeballing him up and down. "I apologize for taking your time, but we were wondering if anyone reported any suspicious activity about a month ago? There was a boy here whom we think may be in trouble."

"He looks a lot like me," I chimed in. "Except half of his head is shaved and his eyes are blue."

The cashier's eyes widened. "Follow me," he instructed.

That was not the answer we were expecting. As he was out of earshot, Johanna whispered to Shannon, "This is creepy. Can we trust him?"

"No, but we can give him a chance," she replied.

Cautiously, we followed him to the back and into the musty storage room. The young man began rummaging through some boxes. Without looking back at us, he asked, "How did you first meet this boy?"

"He stole my wallet," Shannon replied, hesitantly.

He let out a deep breath and relaxed his tense shoulders. "See,

Joshua? Not so hard; although you should've stuck with acting. At least *that's* not real," he rambled to himself. Turning to us, he held out a small box wrapped in newspaper. "Don't open it here. Get in your van and open it while you are driving. It will take you to him." I snatched it without thinking.

Johanna put her hand on my shoulder. "Come on, we can't just take gifts from strangers. What if it is a bomb or a tracking device?"

"It's a tracking device," the cashier—Joshua—said. "Not for you though. Trust me, your brother is safe."

"What choice do we have?" I snapped, pulling away from her.

"Thank you," Shannon said graciously. "My name is Shannon and this is Johanna and Shane."

"Nice to meet you. I am Joshua Wolfrum," he replied smiling. He carelessly threw his glasses into the garbage. "Now, hurry along. I will see you again soon." Without saying anything else, he ducked into another room and didn't come out.

Thinking we received the answer to our questions, we left the store and went back in the van. I opened up the box to find a small black GPS. Not having any other options, I plugged it in. The machine made an ascending tone and came to life. Directions and the ETA appeared on the screen. Unfortunately, it was another long car ride. With no other choice, Shannon put the van in drive and we were off to find my brother.

"Is it just me or is this all *really* weird?" Johanna asked once we were back on the road.

"Lots of things are weird," the third oldest Hollinger girl— Lucy—pointed out. "Like everybody leaving, no one pulling shorty Shannon over for driving, and stuff like that."

"Don't forget sporks," Peggy—the second oldest—added. "Sporks are downright weird."

"Sporks scare me," Rebecca shouted.

"Sporks?!" Agnes cried on the verge of tears.

"I am going to devour all of the sporks!" Carol Ann interjected.

For the rest of that day the younger girls were freaking out and discussing the topic of sporks. I think the only well behaved one was the baby, Rachel. She just giggled and slept the whole time.

At one point, the girls were getting so restless Shannon unleashed her "secret weapon": their father's Gaelic lullaby. In the midst of their bickering, Shannon took a deep breath and began her soothing, enchanting song:

*Codladh mo ghrá*      *Sleep, my love*
*Tá Lá ag deireadh*      *Day is at an end*
*Heaven thuas*      *The Heavens above*
*Ag breathná thar tú arís*      *Watch over you again*
*Codladh mo daor*      *Sleep my dear*
*An chuid eile I mo glacadh*      *Rest in my embrace*
*Nuair Tarrain maidin in aice le*      *When morn draws ever near*
*Céimnithe me le bánú an lae*      *I fade with break of day*
*Codladh mo ghrá*      *Sleep my love*
*Fiú nuair a théann i*      *Know even when I go*
*Tá mé fos an ceann*      *I'm still the one*
*Chun grá agat mar sin*      *That always loves you so*

[Yeah, it is pretty, Donnie. Thanks for the compliments. I hope me singing it did the song justice. Sorry I don't have the translation for you all… I never really knew what it meant so I hope the Gaelic was enough. What do you mean Aaron? The recording thing translated it for me? That's incredible! Now I will finally know what it means. Yeah, you're right, Shannon, I could've just asked…]

After she ended her tune, the girls fell asleep. I loved listening to her sing, especially that song. Her voice was so calming and melodic.

It was evening when the girls woke from their nap and I noticed Shannon started nodding off. She slapped herself a few times to keep herself awake, but it was no use. We were still far away. Finally, Shannon gave up.

"Okay, Shane, you win," she said, pulling over. "I hate admitting defeat, but I can't go on. I need to sleep." She sluggishly opened her door and hopped out.

I did a victory dance as I jumped into the driver's side. After I fixed the seat's settings from gnome to normal person, I gave the girls in the back an announcement. "All right, ladies, this is your favorite boy ever speaking. We have now swapped drivers so things are going to run a little smoother from here on out."

"Just drive!" Johanna shouted.

Obeying, I started us on our journey. I will admit it was rougher than I anticipated, but I quickly got the hang of it. Thankfully, no one threw up.

"We switched so I could sleep," Shannon complained as she clutched onto the handle above her.

Night had finally fallen and all the girls were asleep except Shannon. Of course. The one time she gets to sleep and she doesn't.

"Just shut your eyes," I whispered.

"I can't," she replied. "Too much on my mind."

"You can always confide in Johanna or me if you need to," I reassured her.

Sighing, she rested her head against the seat. "I'm actually worried about you," she said. I felt her eyes locked on me. "Are you okay"

My face got red. "I actually don't think so," I whispered. "I've been feeling so guilty lately."

"About what?"

Taking a deep breath, I confessed, "I know about your brother, Pietro. I feel so guilty that all this time you are missing your sibling and you have been doing everything to help mine."

She began chuckling. "I seriously thought it was something else. However, my deductions aren't always accurate; well, *yet*. But don't worry about it. I can't get far without my dad on that anyway. He seems to have lost hope, but I haven't." She took a shaky breath and tried not to dwell on the fact that her parents could be dead. "Besides, finding your brother makes me think I am making up for it."

Not knowing what to say, I rubbed the side of the steering wheel and asked, "So you knew I knew?"

"Of course I did," she replied confidently. "You had to have seen my notes especially since you grabbed all of them that night. Besides, you were acting funny when you came back."

"Am I that easy to read?" I asked, looking over at her.

Her smile was adorable. "You still have your mysteries, Shane." Her bright blue eyes shined in the moon light and her freckles danced on her cheeks in its glow. Finally, she drifted off into a sleep.

"'Wake up, Shannon. I love you'," a voice from behind me mocked after she fell asleep.

My face got beet red and I became uncomfortable. I brought my attention back to the road. "What're you talking about, Johanna?"

She didn't speak again.

I drove through the night, only stopping twice. As the sun rose, we were approaching our destination. I accidentally hit a bump in the road that caused all the girls to stir.  "Good morning, lovely ladies," I said as they woke up.

"I'm not lovely," Rebecca corrected, rubbing her brown eyes. "I'm magnificent."

"Well, I'm a majestic unicorn," Carol-Ann said putting her hands on her hips.

"Me princess!" Agnes shouted.

"Please tell me we are almost there," Johanna complained as she banged her head against my seat. "I can't take another freak out session."

"Yes, we are," I confirmed as we drove up a winding mountain. It was terrifying but looked beautiful in the sunrise. Reaching the top, we traveled on a long road underneath the shadows of dead trees.

"This looks like something out of a horror movie," I pointed out, looking around at the spooky environment.

"Horror?!" Agnes screamed. Once again, they all started freaking out.

"Thank you so very much, Shane," Johanna said sarcastically. "You are the most incredible human being on the planet. You make children cry. You will be a wonderful father."

I ignored her and drove out of the "creepy-forest-of-monsters". We all stared in amazement as we drove up to a mansion.

"That's like five times the size of museums I've seen," Johanna observed.

"This is a castle," Lucy pointed out.

"Castles have food, right?" Rebecca asked.

"Food! Food!" Agnes yelled, jumping up and down in her car seat.

We parked at the base of the steps leading up to the beautiful front doors. Once the van was off, I immediately jumped out to help Johanna and Shannon with her sisters. One by one we let the girls down which was a terrible mistake.

Shannon took baby Rachel out of her seat and handed her to Johanna. Looking around and then at me, she slowly asked, "Where are they?"

I spun in circles looking for them. They were gone. "Oh no."

Without hesitating, we all ran separate ways looking for the five other girls.

I barged through the front doors and into the hall. The place was huge, but I didn't have time to sight see. Thankfully, I caught a glimpse of a small girl with reddish-blonde hair wearing a light blue dress. I found Carol-Ann.

I followed her, but she thought I was playing tag. She turned to me, laughed, and ducked through the nearest door. I chased her through rooms, down corridors, until finally she decided to talk to one of the kids.

"What's your name?" the boy asked her.

"Carol-Ann," she said with confidence, looking up at him with her blue eyes.

"Aw, do the TV people need your help?" he mocked. "Are they going to suck you into the walls and ask you to lead them to the light?"

She shook her head and replied sadly, "No, the TV people haven't talked in a while."

Weirded out, the boy just walked away.

She looked at me and shrugged her shoulders. "You told me to say that when people mentioned the TV people. Why do they walk away?"

I felt like a proud parent. "You did it perfect," I said as I snatched her and ran back to the hallway.

Shannon and Johanna had found Peggy and Lucy. Lucy had gotten into the trophy room, knocking down and breaking a few while Peggy watched for amusement. Even though they were older, they were just as immature.

Three down, two to go.

"I'll stay here and make sure they don't go anywhere," Johanna offered, trying not to let Rachel crawl out of her arms. "Go find them."

We felt like we were searching for eternity. What was odd was not many people were seen around the house… a good thing and a bad thing.

"For a place like this, you think there would be more eyes watching," I pointed out.

"The kids are all in class," Shannon quickly explained. "But that doesn't matter. Did the girls say anything to you before they disappeared?"

"They said they were hungry," I recalled.

We looked at each other. "The kitchen!" we shouted simultaneously. We ran back towards the hallway then into the dining area until we finally found the chrome kitchen.

"Okay, now we must be careful. These are hot," we heard a boy say.

"Cookies! Cookies! Cookies!" two small voices chanted.

Making our way through the maze of counters, we found the girls with one of the students. They were sitting by the boy's feet; their faces covered in cookie crumbs.

"Do these girls belong to you two?" the boy asked as he placed his tray on the counter.

"Yes, thank you, thank you," Shannon repeated, shaking her folded hands.

"You are welcome," he said smiling. "These kids are hysterical. Hey, if you ever need something to eat, just ask for Dylan Cheatle of the Umbrella branch. I can hook you guys up with something good." He gave the little girls a wink. They looked up at him and giggled.

Thanking him again, we snatched the two and went back into the hallway. When we returned, we were in an odd situation.

# THE MAINLAND

We reunited with the others and found hundreds staring at us. The kids must have gotten out of their classes and came rushing to see the cause of the commotion. Also, it didn't help that Lucy and Peggy started fighting and Rachel began crying.

"There are those eyes you were talking about," Shannon whispered. Taking a deep breath, she addressed all of the students. "We were sent here by Joshua Wolfrum in search of Mark Hodgins."

We all stood there in an awkward silence until five boys came running towards us.

One of them was Mark.

# CHAPTER 26
## Shane: XI

When Mark reached us, he stopped and stared. I couldn't believe it. I looked him up and down. The expression on his face and the look in his blue eyes told me he knew I was his brother and he was mine. A few moments of silence passed as we stared at each other in the midst of hundreds of students. Then, we laughed and gave each other a manly hug.

"It's so good to see you again," I confessed as I patted his back.

"Yeah," he replied, not knowing what to say. Pulling away, he put his hand on my shoulder. "Man, you look terrible."

"And you look different," I said pulling his tie. "Why so formal? What happened to the ratty t-shirt?" I flicked the long bang out of his face. "You even brushed your hair."

He smirked and looked over my shoulder to see Shannon, Johanna, and the little Hollingers. His jaw dropped. "Did you live in the same house as all of these girls?"

"Clarius is our pet," Carol-Ann explained.

"No, he's not," Shannon told him, shaking her head. "Anyway, I'm happy we found you, Mark."

"Happy you found me too, beautiful," he greeted. "I'm sorry

about your folks."

After she thanked him, a boy ran up to me and buried his face in my stomach. "I found you! I found my best friend!" he exclaimed.

Confused, I patted the blond boy's head and said, "Um, yes you found me."

"It's me, Myles," he explained. "You saved me at the fair a few years back."

Once he looked up at me, I recognized his blue eyes. I couldn't believe it. "Myles? What are you doing here?"

Stepping back, he held out his arms and said, "Welcome to Wyght's Home for Young People! My dad and Mr. Wyght own it."

"We sure do," a familiar voice said. It was the boy's father, the one who gave me the guitar. Seeing my familiar face, he grinned and said, "Nice to see you again." He looked down at his child and rubbed the boy's blond hair. "Incredible work, son. You, Vandewater, and Hodgins make a wonderful team."

"Thank you sir," a round young man with black glasses and a white cane said. He was not facing the right direction.

Coming over, Mr. Powell offered to take us to Mr. Wyght. Before doing so, he addressed the crowd of people still staring: "Attention everyone. You have just witnessed something people deemed impossible. The reunion of blood brothers separated at birth. Please welcome the newest members of our family." The room was filled with acclaims as we followed Mr. Powell to see Mr. Wyght.

We found him downstairs in the indoor dojo training a group of girls. The floor was covered in a red and black mat and there was training equipment everywhere: punching bags, monkey bars, boards, nunchakus, you name it.

The class was ending and the girls were packing up. As they passed us, one of them caught my gaze. I couldn't keep my eyes off of her. She had light skin like mine, but her gray eyes seemed so familiar. She wore a black head wrap that matched her dark fighting uniform. She stared back but said nothing and continued to walk. I placed whatever that was in the back of my mind and followed the others inside.

"Mr. Powell," the man greeted, wiping the sweat from his slightly wrinkled forehead. "So, they found their way here, did they?"

"Yes, they sure did," Mr. Powell responded, smiling. "Joshua Wolfrum handled his mission just fine. He will handle his second one just as well."

"Good." Turning around, the other man looked at us and said, "I am sure you were welcomed upstairs, so there is no need to be redundant. My name is Mr. Wyght, and I hear that one of you is related to our newer student, Mark."

"I am," I said. I stood upright and fixed my brown jacket. "How did you know we were looking for him?"

"He told us, so we helped him," he replied, smiling. Then, he began explaining everything we needed to know about WHYP.

To be honest, I didn't pay any attention. I was always so bad like that. I *was* listening in the beginning, but I got distracted by the younger Hollinger girls playing with the equipment behind him. Carol-Ann thought it was a wonderful idea to give Rebecca and Agnes weapons so they could fight. Peggy and Lucy were too busy poking the abs on the punching dummy to pay attention to the three girls attacking each other. Carol-Ann was instructing her younger sisters how to hit each other "properly". Thankfully, they were tough; the few clonks on their heads didn't make them cry.

Eventually, Shannon interrupted me not listening when Mr. Wyght's explanation was finished. "Shane, didn't you hear what he said?" she asked sharply.

"Huh?" I shook my head and snapped back into the conversation. "Of course I did," I lied. "I think that's incredible. Thank you for helping him."

Johanna slapped her palm to her face. "He literally just explained everything we were to expect here and what Branch you are going to be in."

"Yes, I did," Mr. Wyght said kindly. "You are going to be an Agricola. You will take care of the farm."

"Wait, what? Why?" I questioned.

"Because you have had experience with the subject," he

explained. "You should be honored. Not many people become Agricolae."

"Where are the girls going, though?" I asked, looking at my friends.

The man chuckled. "You will still see them at your other classes as well as meals and free time. The younger girls are going to stick with the Umbrellas who do mostly housework and caregiving."

"That's my Branch," Johanna said. She turned to the man, put her hands together and shook them. "And thank you again for giving me such a high position, Mr. Wyght. I will do my best as caregiver and counselor."

"Don't thank me yet," he informed. "Not only can you go even higher, but I hope you won't get too overwhelmed. Papa E needs help and I think you are a perfect fit."

"She will do awesome," Shannon confirmed. "She is a great leader, and I think Papa E will agree."

Looking at her I asked, "Are you an Umbrella, too, Shannon?"

She shook her head. "No, I am a Combatant. Not only will I focus on fighting and defending, but I can continue to pursue the same career as my father. There are no detectives in that group so I will be the first."

Jealous, I replied, "Wait, there is a fighting group? Why am I a stupid farmer? I am probably faster than everyone in that Combatant Branch." I was being insensitive and ungrateful, but my pride was hurt. I could *not* have that. I looked at Mr. Wyght and went over more reasons why I should be with Shannon: "Also, I have had experience fighting from the Hollinger's. Not only that but I have incredible balance, reflexes, and know stuff from the circus. I would be better as a Combatant."

"Fast or no, you couldn't keep track of five little girls," Mr. Wyght said as nicely as possible. "How will you be able to protect yourself and others in the heat of a fight? Especially if all you care about is yourself. From what I know, you have run from fights all your life. How will you stand your ground?"

That cut me through the heart. *How could he say that? Like he knows what I have been through*, I thought bitterly.

Ending the conversation, Mr. Wyght sent us upstairs to unpack our van. Insulted, I followed the girls quietly and said nothing as we brought our things inside. Myles met us in the hallway with a box of uniforms.

"These are for the girls," my self-proclaimed best friend explained, pointing to the large box. "Shane, your Agricola and casual uniforms are waiting in your bedroom downstairs in the men's dormitory."

Peggy and Lucy immediately ripped the box open and went through it. "Why are there only four cool black uniforms?" Peggy asked, holding one up. "One of them better be mine."

Myles giggled. "Yup! Lucy gets one too, but she'll be in my division." He pointed to himself with his thumb. "I'll try and go easy on you two."

"You better watch I don't break you in half, skinny," Lucy challenged, punching her palm.

Nervous, Myles gulped. "I'll be careful." Inching away from her, he went to Johanna. "Here is your room number," he said handing her a laminated card. "So, you won't forget."

Johanna took it and looked it over. "We all get the same room?" she asked.

The boy confirmed. "Yes. That's not a bad thing, right?"

"Not at all," she replied. She turned to her best friend and admitted, "I was afraid we would be separated from your sisters, Shannon."

She nodded. "I am very grateful you made that arrangement for us; especially because of baby Rachel." At the sound of her name, she cooed in her big sister's arms. She awoke from a long nap and began slapping Shannon in the face. Everyone around me was smiling, but I was still angry. I kept my arms crossed tightly and had a dissatisfied expression.

"Of course," Myles told Shannon. "We want to build families here; not break them." As he said that, his chrome, touch screen watch made a beeping noise. "Speaking of family, my dad wants me to finish preparing Shane's room." He tapped the screen and the noise stopped. "Will you be able to settle in by yourselves?"

"We can do it just fine, blondie," Lucy retorted. Her hard-headed nature would be something Myles needed to get used to.

Trying not to be offended, Myles replied, "Okay, I'll see you later then." With that, he ran off.

Peggy slapped Lucy on the back. "Why would you do that?"

She returned the slap. "Why not? We will be fine without his help!"

"We will be fine, but you don't need to be rude," Shannon chimed in, holding Rachel back from imitating their violence. "Although, we all know being rude is your way of showing affection, Lucy."

The eight year old's face got red. Peggy laughed at her, only to be slapped again. I rolled my eyes and put down my guitar that I was carrying. I picked up the girls' box of uniforms. "Let's get you settled in now."

While they followed me up the beautiful curved stairs, I could hear Carol-Ann whispering behind me: "Why is Clarius so cranky?"

Finally, we reached their room at the end of the hall on the right. Going in, we found a large space with wooden flooring and a long window on the light wall in front of us. On each side of the room were two sets of bunk beds and a baby crib. Each bed was covered with handmade light blue bedding.

"I call top bunk!" Peggy yelled as she raced towards the bed on the left closest to the window.

"Me too!" Carol-Ann called.

Leaning over to Shannon, Johanna whispered, "You don't think she will fall off, will she?"

"Fall off?!" Agnes shrieked.

I threw my head back and groaned, expecting another fiasco. A part of me was happy to be on a floor separate from the girls. Thankfully, Agnes was distracted before she could start whining. Rebecca brought her over to her bed and helped her unpack.

"I'll get the bunk above you, Shannon, next to the baby crib,"

Johanna told her best friend. "You need to be close to Rachel."

"Besides, Shannon can't reach the top bunk," Peggy teased as she dangled her legs off her new bed.

As much as I tried not to, I couldn't help but smile. They always teased Shannon about her height. She wasn't super short but short enough to be picked on. I always thought her height was adorable. Unfortunately, my smile faded when I remembered I wouldn't be in her "Branch" or whatever during the day. I had to do stupid farming.

I plopped the box down and went back to the doorway. "I'll see you girls later," I told them without looking back.

Shannon ran over and grabbed my arm. "You haven't walked in his shoes either, Shane." Without saying anything else, she brought the baby to her new crib.

*I hate it when she does that*, I thought as I left. I grumbled and complained as I walked down the stairs, across the long front hall, and down another flight to reach the guys' floor.

The hallway lined with closed doors was long and empty. The walls and flooring were dark blue and it wasn't well lit. *You would think the lighting would be better in a place like this*, I complained. My mood dampened further when I found my bedroom was the last one against the back wall.

My attitude changed once I went in.

Opening the door, I was almost blinded by the bright lighting. The room was massive and had a futuristic feel. The walls were white and the floor had silver carpeting. In the center was a glass dining table with two egg chairs on each side. On the left and right walls were king sized beds with electronic canopies. On the walls different things flashed on and off. To the back of the room were a flat screen television and a long white couch.

"I see you found it," Myles said coming up to me. "I arranged for us to be roommates, if that was okay."

"Totally," I said still gawking at the sight. "This is your room?"

He smiled. "Our room now, but, yes. My father said I could have anything I wanted in here as long as I designed and built it myself."

"Wait, you *made* all this stuff?" I asked, amazed.

"Sure did." He pointed to all his creations. "I designed and created the bed frames, the gadgets in the walls, the floating chairs, but not the television. That was a gift."

Taken aback, I asked, "How old are you again?"

"Six years younger than you. Do the math."

"You are *nine*?" I exclaimed. "You are an amazing kid."

"Aren't we all?" he humbly replied. "Anyway, you should get changed and head outside. The Royal Agricola is waiting for you in the barn. She is very passionate about her work, so try not to be a wise guy."

I went over to my bed and found my new uniforms folded neatly on top. I became upset again. Abruptly, I grabbed the overalls and went into the even brighter bathroom to change. Dressed, I pulled on my new work boots and threw my clothes carelessly on my bed. Well, except for my uncle's work jacket. I hung that up neatly on a wall hook. Once I was set, I headed outside.

I dashed across the lawn and to the high red barn. I found a girl sitting on the hay covered floor surrounded by chickens.

"C'mon, you have to be good for me this week," I heard her saying to them. "We are still short staffed, but I hope it will look up." Noticing me come in, she jumped up, came over, and held out her hand. She had light brown hair and kind blue eyes. "Marian Best, Royal Agricola. You must be Shane?"

I shook her rough hand. "That's me. So when do we start?"

She went in one of the stables and grabbed some things. Without warning, she threw me farming supplies. "Right now."

The entire rest of the day I followed her around and worked on the farm. It was typical stuff I was used to: cleaning up after animals, taking care of the crops, and stuff like that. After a few hours, I felt like I was going to pass out. I was so exhausted from being on the road for days that I couldn't handle anymore.

Marian noticed my fatigue as I almost fainted. "Man, did you get any sleep last night?" she asked after digging another hole.

I shook my head and rested on my arms on my shovel. "My friends and I have been driving for almost a week when our house was attacked."

"Boy, that is awful," she said as she fixed her light brown hair that fell out of its ponytail. "Usually Mr. Wyght lets the newcomers rest a day. He didn't tell me you had *just* come here." She reached into the pocket on her chest and pulled out a beautiful, silver pocket watch.

I peeked over her shoulder to try and see the time but instead I caught a glimpse of a photograph: a couple standing behind a girl who was holding a cute baby.

Checking the time, she shook her head and interrupted my staring. "You've been out here too long. Why don't you go and get some rest before dinner."

Overly grateful, I thanked her repeatedly, tossed my shovel aside carelessly, and dashed back to the mansion. Tracking mud into the building, I made my way back down the hall and to my room. I took a speed shower, like I normally do, and lay down on my bed. Within minutes I was fast asleep.

I awoke hours later to Mark and Myles hovering over me. "Good morning, Snow White," Mark teased.

Moaning, I sat up and rubbed my head. "How long was I out?"

"You slept through dinner," he explained, leaning on my bed post. "By the way, those girls are hysterical. The little ones had the entire dining hall in stitches."

"Yup, they do that," I replied, yawning. "Wait, I missed dinner?"

"Yeah, but Myles has stuff for you," he said, motioning to the glass table behind him. It was covered in delicious food. "But seriously, how does it feel to be Snow White?"

"What?" I asked confused.

"Dude, you lived in a house with seven chicks," he said chuckling. "That's, like, a parallel universe version of that fairy tale."

I thought about it. "To be honest, I always thought of the girls as the twelve dancing princesses."

My brother shot me a confused look. "But there are only seven," Mark corrected. "Snow White works better."

"To be honest, your whole situation is a fairy tale," Myles said bringing me over food, which I scarfed down, "separated at birth, living tragic lives, and finally reunited hopefully living happily ever after."

"We aren't reunited yet," I said with my mouthful. Swallowing my food, I looked at my brother and added with a serious tone, "Mark, we have a sister."

"I know," he started. Plopping himself in an egg chair, he explained. He told me his whole situation with Masdit and Gerrior and how he told them about me and our sister. As he described the men to me, my glass almost slipped from my hand. I knew immediately that it was the men who killed my aunt and uncle.

"It has to be them," I told him, putting the cup on my nightstand. "But why are they after us? What do they want with our family?"

"I don't know," Mark confessed. "But if they are the same people, I guarantee you that they were after our sister."

"How can we tell if Aymie actually is our sister?" I asked.

Myles, who was quietly listening, stood up from his bed and chimed in, "You said that this Masdit guy burned your sister's house down?"

Mark nodded. "Yeah, and he said some other nasty things…but I'm not going to mention those."

A thought crossed Myles' mind and a disgusted expression appeared on his little face. "Don't want nasty, nope, no thank you," he repeated, shaking the thought from his head. "Dylan and I were talking and he told me that Aymie said her mansion was burned to the ground with her family inside. That's why she is an orphan."

Mark stared at the blond boy. "For real?"

With a smile, he nodded. "I promise. I can even show you the newspaper articles." He strode across the room to the monitors in the back wall. With tiny fingers, he tapped their screens and began typing away. In no time, he pulled up several articles about the Quartermane Family. Getting to his feet, Mark went over to take a closer look. I copied.

Myles scrolled through a few articles until he found the one he was looking for. "See?" he announced, pointing to an image of a little girl. She had gray eyes and long, brown hair. She was standing next to a little boy with…gray hair.

"Who's the old kid?" Mark asked.

"Her best friend, Blake," Myles told him. "The Aymie here talks about him all the time. She says he has old hair because he's sick."

"Gotcha," Mark replied.

Glancing at another monitor, I saw what Myles was talking about. An image of ash and rubble was slapped on the front page of a popular newspaper. "Hey, Junior is right. Aymie's mansion was burned down."

Mark took a closer look. "And look who the suspects are." He pointed to a sentence several paragraphs below. "Two men were spotted fleeing from the scene but have no identification for them."

*I can't believe this*, I thought to myself. "This has to be our sister," I decided.

"Man, I think you are right," Mark replied. He rubbed the shaved side of his head. "This is so weird…not sure if I believe all this is happening."

"Well, you better believe it," Myles demanded. "Aymie Hodgins is your sister. I bet my brain on it."

"Well, we'll find out for sure soon," I told him, rubbing his blond hair. "I appreciate you helping us out, Myles."

The boy smiled. "Anything for my best friend and his brother."

After that, Mark and I decided to catch up. We had missed 15 years of each other's lives. So, we sat down on my bed and exchanged stories and experiences. Mark didn't talk too much about what he did with Fallout. He was probably ashamed.

I on the other hand tried to lighten the mood by telling them happy experiences of my life before and with the Hollingers. I didn't want to tell him the terrible parts about what Masdit and Gerrior did to the circus I was staying with. He knew about my aunt and uncle, he didn't need to know about them too. After hearing the life he lived, I felt bad "competing" with him…on this at least. We became competitive at almost everything else; music especially. Once I heard he was a drummer, I immediately needed to hear him play something.

"They have one rad kit here," he said after keeping a beat on the side of my bed while I played along with my guitar. He was pretty good. "When I first started, I used garbage cans and whatever was lying in the street."

"You're not bad," I told him. I didn't want him to think I was impressed. I rested my forearms on my instrument. "We should jam like this often."

Myles couldn't help but interrupt when he saw I still had the guitar his dad gave me. "Look at all the stickers you put around it!" the boy marveled as he ran his fingers over its base. "You've been to all of these places?"

"Yup," I said proudly. "It's thanks to the circus that I've been everywhere." I thought back to those days and smiled. "I owe a lot to them. My life for one; this guitar another. Not to mention it's thanks to them that they helped train me to be a runner. I wouldn't be the record holder of the hundred meter dash without them. It may be for Junior Olympics, but it was pretty close to the real Olympians," I said, smugly.

After we talked about my Junior Olympic experience for a bit, Mark remembered something he wanted to tell me. "Oh, by the way I think you already know my roommate." Mark flexed his slender arms to describe him. "Big, brawny, super hairy, has violet eyes, and brown and red hair styled in a tiny Mohawk?"

I shook my head. "I think I would remember someone like that."

Mark scratched the shaved part of his head. "Oh, what's his last name." He snapped his fingers. He pulled out a piece of paper he had in the backpack at his feet. Reading over it, he stood up and sat next to me on my bed. He handed it to me, pointed to a picture of a boy, and asked, "Does the fifth place weightlifter Nicolas Eerkens sound familiar?"

I couldn't believe my ears. "Nic is here? How?" I asked, baffled. "Why does he look like that?" Remembering our first meeting and pointing to the picture, I said, "He was blond with blue eyes when we first met."

Mark shrugged his shoulders. "That's weird. He told me it was all natural...although he mentioned something happened to him first, but I don't remember." I handed him back the paper so he could put it away. "Anyway, you should ask him tomorrow. I'll let you surprise him, though. I'm not one to start a conversation." He thought for a minute and remembered, "Although, I think Shannon and Johanna were talking to him at dinner. He took a liking to Johanna right away so I hope you don't got a thing for her."

When the warning bell for curfew rang, Mark stood up from my bed. "Well, it was good catching up, bro, but I have to go." He gave me a fist bump. "See you tomorrow. Sleep well, Snow White." With that, he left.

"I like him," Myles said as he was pulling on his dinosaur pajama pants. "I'm happy we found him; he helped us find you."

Looking at the young boy, I remembered his face from when I found him at the fair ground. His cute blue eyes were still full of life and wonder. The fact that I was reunited with him and my long lost brother was a miracle in itself. Too lost for words, I smiled and whispered, "I'm happy too."

Finally ready, the two of us crawled into our beds and Myles clapped twice to turn off the lights, but he had his canopy LEDs on above him. They bathed the room with their gleaming colors, but I was so tired it didn't matter. Rolling over, I stared at the wall. It was a weird feeling; finally being safe from harm. I liked it. However, I did miss Shannon, Johanna, and the girls. Even though we were in the same house, I knew things would be different. *This will take some getting used to,* I thought as I drifted off to sleep.

Of course with my luck, I didn't get to sleep. At three in the morning an alarm blared throughout the entire mansion.

Someone had broken in.

# Chapter 27
## Aymie: VIII

I woke in the early morning to a blaring siren and announcement: *"Intruder alert. Intruder alert. All members prepare for situation eight."*

Jumping up, I immediately put on my black combat uniform and prepared for dispatch. *First those two brothers find each other here. Now this?* I thought as I pulled my shirt on backwards. Too exhausted to care, I threw my jacket over it and waited for orders. *I wonder how things can get crazier.* Looking around at my roommates, I was kind of disappointed. The other girls weren't as diligent as I was.

"I'm sure this is another drill," one girl mumbled as she rolled in bed.

*"This is not a drill. Repeat: this is not a drill,"* the announcement said.

Adeline Zarra, the Royal Veteran Polymath, went over to the other girls to hastily wake them up. Smacking one on the head, she shouted, "Girls, this is serious! We have to get up."

Once everyone was ready, we headed to our sections' meeting point. Since I was newer, I met with Alexandrea, Zander, and about thirteen other newcomers.

"Over here," Alexandrea called as I shuffled into the music room.

Seeing where they were, I tip toed my way toward them. They were huddled by one of the tall white bookshelves behind some other kids. The lights were off and the stars glistened through the back windows.

"You ready for a fight?" Alexandrea asked out loud.

Zander elbowed her. "Quiet. We are on stealth, remember?"

Alexandrea rolled her eyes and put her blonde hair into a low ponytail. "Well, that new kid didn't get the memo." She jerked her chin to a boy who was standing in the open, making a fuss.

Peering through the dark, I saw gorgeous green eyes glowing in the starlight. It was the boy that I bumped into the day before. He was freaking out that we had to engage in actual combat. He was ranting to Flicks and another kid. Frustrated, the RV grabbed him and the other boy and dragged them to duck with my friends and me. Throwing them behind us, Flicks told him to keep quiet and went back to his monitoring.

"Are they seriously handing us weapons?" he said to his friend, too loudly as he loaded his pistol. "I mean it's awesome, but I thought this was foster care, not the military."

I grew impatient. I whipped around and yelled at him to shut up.

As soon as he saw my face, he smiled and elbowed his friend who was that kid I helped a couple weeks back. Mark was his name. I remembered they were the long lost brothers. With the two boys next to each other I realized how eerily similar they were.

I didn't notice how long I was staring until Zander poked me. "If you are going to look at boys it better be me," he whispered jokingly. Embarrassed, I turned back around and kept my head down.

We waited there in silence until the alarms stopped blaring.

"Was it a dud?" Alexandrea asked.

Suddenly, we heard gunshots and screaming in the hallway. Flicks yelled to stay put, ran out, and shut the large doors behind him.

"Should we go check?" I exclaimed, jumping to my feet.

"No, we have to wait for instructions from our RVs," Zander told me, grabbing my hand. I listened and squat back down next to him.

The firing continued and it sounded like a campus wide fiasco. Internally, I was terrified. *What is happening out there?* I thought, nervously glancing at the exit.

Just then, that new girl, Shannon, came barging through the door, startling me. I held my breath and hid behind Zander. Frantically her eyes darted back and forth until they fell upon the boys behind us. She ran to them and grabbed the guy with the normal hair. "Shane, Carol-Ann is missing," she panicked. Her blue eyes watered as she shook her friend's shoulders. "No one has seen her all night."

Fear fell over Shane's face. He turned to his brother—Mark— who stared right back, looking just as nervous. Not saying a word, the three of them jumped to their feet and decided to ignore their orders. Together, they ran out of the room and into the gunfire.

"Should we go after them?" I asked.

"No," Zander stated immediately. He squeezed my hand a little tighter. "It's too dangerous, Aymie." His dark eyes were filled with concern. He was genuinely afraid.

And then there's Alexandrea. She cocked her pistol, jumped to her feet, and motioned for us to follow her. Without hesitation, Roxanne went right behind.

I shook Zander's arm. "Please, we can't let them go alone."

Sighing, he finally gave in. He gently pulled me to my feet and together we ran to catch up to our friends.

In the foyer, we found many male students on the ground screaming and trying to stop their bleeding wounds. None of them looked fatal, but they were hurt pretty badly. A few girls were panicking and went to get help. Roxanne scoffed. "Boys. Can't even get shot right." Zander shot her a look, but she shrugged. Not wanting to linger around the graphic scene, we continued our search.

"Now if I were a new kid with a missing sibling, where would I be?" Alexandrea thought aloud as we walked.

We were about to go down the hall to the classrooms when we heard rapid gunshots behind us. They were in the dining hall. Rushing in, we dove behind a table that had been knocked over. I peeked out and couldn't believe what I saw.

It was just *one* man. Not even a man, he was about fifteen—my age at the time. His hair was long and black as night. A scarf was pulled over his pale face, revealing only his eyes that glowed red in the dark. He stood to the far left of the dining hall and fired his machine gun at a few teens hiding behind fallen over tables. Three were who we were chasing. They wanted to fire at the intruder but couldn't. Behind their attacker was a crying little girl.

"They need help," Zander observed, pushing his long slick hair behind his ears. Cautiously, he waited for an opening. When the intruder needed to reload his gun, Zander motioned for us to go. Alexandrea and I swiftly ran to where the other students were sitting. I slid behind a table next to Shane who was unpleasantly surprised to see me.

"What are you doing here?" Shane whispered. "It's not safe."

"Yeah, like you know what you're doing," I ridiculed as I loaded my hand gun.

"I have a good guess," he said. He carefully peered around the table. "Look, he is holding my friend's sister as a hostage. I need to get her back. Can't let him get you too."

"You hardly know me," I replied as I gripped my weapon.

Before an argument could ensue, the girl Shannon called to her friends: "Shane, Mark, Nic, can you distract him while I grab Carol-Ann?"

"I can do it by myself," Nic boasted, flexing his beefy muscles.

Rolling his eyes, Mark cocked his gun and said, "Let's just go."

Nic chuckled. "Watch and learn, Nerd." He crawled over to a long upright table. Getting to his feet, he bent over and gripped it. He effortlessly raised it and used it as a shield.

Everyone paused; intruder included. Those tables were hefty and it normally takes four people to move one across the floor. This guy raised it over his head like he was preparing for a pillow fight.

Returning to her senses, Shannon tried to sneak around and grab the girl. Unfortunately, the intruder noticed her out of the corner of his eye. He aimed his gun at her. Terrified, she stopped dead in her tracks and stared at him. Maintaining eye contact, he turned his gun away from her and she kept running.

While he was distracted, Nic threw the table at him.

The trespasser saw it coming. He threw his machine gun, grabbed the girl, and dove to the side. He landed on his feet and decided that that was enough. Pulling out a pistol, he aimed it at Nic and put his finger on the trigger, ready to fire at any moment.

Without hesitation, Shane dashed over and tackled him to the ground. He did it so fast I didn't even realize what was going on. Mark and Nic ran to his aid and tied the villain up with curtain tiebacks they stole. Meanwhile, Shannon snatched the little girl and backed away. The boys secured the intruder so he couldn't move.

Seeing this, the little girl in Shannon's arms yelled at the boys. "No! Let him go. He saved me!"

Shannon rubbed the girl's head to calm her down. "Relax, it's okay. We just need to make sure he doesn't run away."

She wriggled out of Shannon's arms and went to untie the prisoner

"What are you doing?" Nic said. He picked up the little girl with one hand by the back of her shirt as if she were a rag doll. He held her up so they were eye-level, her feet dangling in the air. "He's crazy," Nic argued with her.

"You're crazy!" she shouted, poking his large nose.

"No, you are!" he yelled back, determined to win the childish arguement.

They two of them went back and forth until Zander turned on the lights. When he rejoined us, we went over to the four teens around the gift wrapped intruder. Shannon's sister jumped out of Nic's grasp and stood behind me. Peeking out, she blew a raspberry at the big guy who returned the gesture.

Shannon squatted down and examined the teen's face. Gasping, she tore his scarf off. "It was *you* who were following us this whole time?"

"No way," Shane marveled. "You put me in jail."

"Whoa, you went to jail too?" Nic asked, too happily.

"No," Shane denied, ignoring the excited expression on his

friend's face. "Well, not exactly. This kid framed me." He pointed to the intruder. "Tell them what you did to me." The boy said nothing and glared at Shane.

"I don't think he speaks English," Shannon said. She turned back to him and tried communicating with him in Italian. Not getting a response, she tried again in French.

"I didn't know you could speak French too," Shane marveled.

She smiled. "There are many things you don't know, Shane Hodgins."

My heart stopped. *Wait, that's...* I subconsciously looked at my nametag. *These boys have my last name?* I thought, trying to figure it out.

Before I could ask him or his brother, our prisoner spoke up. Not in English though. He responded to Shannon's French.

"Language!" Shannon scolded, smacking the boy's knee.

"They couldn't understand me," the boy replied, smirking. His voice was deep and raspy as if his throat were bleeding. "Sorry *you* had to hear it though."

"Wait, hold up," Nic said, holding his massive, hairy hands in the air. "You can speak English?"

"Whatever language you can think of, I can speak," he replied rudely.

"Where are you originally from then?" Mark asked.

Mr. Wyght interrupted before the prisoner could reply. He stormed through the dining hall doors with the Royal Veterans and Papa E behind him. Adeline did *not* look happy to see me with the trouble makers. Her blue eyes looked at me with such disappointment. I dared not look at her or Flicks...I felt so ashamed.

"You've been here one day and you cause a ruckus!" Mr. Wyght roared to Shane and Shannon as he approached.

Shane began to protest but Shannon put her arm on him. He held his tongue and remained silent. The culprit of this whole situation just sat there with a smirk.

Sighing, Mr. Wyght said, "I will deal with all of you tomorrow. Right now you are going to tell me what is going on."

"This kid followed us here," Shannon explained. "He was sent to juvenile detention for drug dealing as well as framing Shane for it. My guess is when my dad was taken," she paused for a moment. The pain of losing her family finally starting to show in her eyes. Carol-Ann also started sniffling and latched tighter around my leg.

Shane finished her deduction: "I believe Shannon thinks that when that happened, people came after him knowing he was vulnerable. He must've escaped prison somehow."

The older man looked at the boy on the floor. "Is that true?"

Expressionless, he replied, "She'll be as good of a detective as her dad someday."

"I'm guessing yes," Nic clarified aloud.

"So can you tell me your name then, son?" Wyght asked.

"Yes," he replied, but didn't say anything afterwards.

Shane groaned. "His name is Erik Patya. That's what we saw on the letter, right?"

"'Patya'?" Mr. Wyght repeated. "Are you sure?"

"No, he is not sure!" the so-called Erik barked. "That is *not* my real name."

Shane began arguing with the boy about his real name until Carol-Ann left my side and went between the two teens. "Mr. Wyght was right," she said pointing. "His name is Sun."

"Sonny," the boy corrected. "Sonny Wilcox. Erik Patya is an alias I guess you could say."

Still confused, Mr. Wyght paused and thought for a moment. "Patya, Patya, I know a Patya. What was his first name again?" The older man pressed a finger to his lips and tried to remember. "Nikita!" he exclaimed when it clicked. "Do you know a Nikita Patya? Dark hair and eyes, thick accent, has a little mustache growing in? Always hangs out with a German soldier?"

For some reason, you could see anger burning in Sonny's eyes, but he remained mellow. "Can't say that I have," he said in a low voice.

"Eh, I haven't seen him since I was overseas," the man said chuckling. "He probably went back to Russia. Anyway back to seriousness." He paused for a moment and cleared his throat. "What in the world are you doing shooting my students?!" he bellowed.

"He was protecting me!" Carol-Ann shouted with tears in her eyes. "I got up for a snack a-and then I heard a cat outside so I wanted to get it. So I opened the doors and the lights starting blinking and a loud voice was yelling at me. Sun was inside looking around and he found me crying. Th-then all these people in black came out and held their guns at me." She began crying again and ran to Shannon.

"We weren't going to hurt her," one of the RVs shouted from behind Mr. Wyght.

"Look," Sonny said pulling off the restraints Carol-Ann untied earlier. "I would never hurt any woman or child. I am not a monster. I only shot the guys who came after me and it's not like I killed them." He carelessly threw the cords off his lap. "Besides, by the looks of the world out there you're going to need me."

"Whatever for?" Mr. Wyght asked, curious. Taking a deep breath, Sonny stood to his feet, and we aimed our guns just in case. Unafraid, he stared right at the man and replied, "I was raised as a member of the Order of Xenophon."

Mr. Wyght's eyes widened. He took a step back and motioned for us to get behind him. "Why are you here?" he asked sharply. He held his arms out to shield the students he stood in front of.

"I've been trying to escape them ever since I was born," the boy said defensively. "There is no need to explain it. I was raised as a spy and a murderer, and now I betrayed them. I was doing a mission for them when I tried to escape. Plan *A* was to make it look like I was arrested. Plan *B* was to get help from an outsider. Plan *B* worked better."

"So you did want us to find that letter," Shannon said.

"Why couldn't *that* have been plan *A*?" Shane replied, crossing his arms. "Not very well thought out if you ask me," he grumbled.

Mr. Wyght thought about the intruder's words while Shane and Sonny bickered. He turned to Papa E and whispered, "What do you think?"

Stroking his gray beard, the priest replied, "I am not totally sure.

If I was able to speak with him in private, maybe he'll open up." He sighed and scanned the boy in all black who was arguing with Shane. "We can't turn him away especially if he is telling the truth, but that doesn't mean we don't have to take precautions."

Mr. Wyght went over to the teen. "Turn around and show me."

Knowing what he was talking about, Sonny turned and lifted up his long slick hair. He showed the man a brand. The Order of Xenophon symbol and the number 0 was burned into the boy's neck. Inside the *O* was a small incision. "It's gone," Sonny told Mr. Wyght. He tapped the back of his neck. "No tracker. They don't know I'm here."

Mr. Wyght stepped back and sighed. "Fine. You can stay here. However, you will be watched around the clock until I find a reason to trust you, understand?" He wagged a finger at the dark haired teen. "We will have Mr. Powell take a look at your brand to double check for the tracker." Motioning to the robed man beside him, he added, "Also, I would like you to get acquainted with Papa E, here. Deal?"

Sonny nodded. "If I were you, I would do nothing less."

"Good," he replied. "You will receive your uniforms in the morning. You will room with Zander Grath and stick with him and the other Combatants."

"Yeah, welcome to the Combatant Club," Zander exclaimed holding up his hand for a high five.

Ignoring it, Sonny asked, "How advanced are your fighters? I don't think there is much they could teach me."

Mr. Wyght scoffed. "You'll be surprised." Turning to the rest of us he said, "You all go to bed. You will not be punished for this night, but I expect better behavior in the future."

After we agreed, he, Papa E, and a few Royal Combatants left to announce to the other students everything was all right.

"A third new combatant in two months," Zander said excitedly. "And you guys already know how to fight, so this will make my job much easier."

"I know more than all of you combined," Sonny mocked.

"Don't be so sure about that," Nic replied, crossing his

brawny arms that I couldn't stop staring at. "I'll be the judge of that tomorrow."

With that, we headed out the door. Alexandrea and Zander went ahead of me while I walked alongside Adeline and Flicks.

"You shouldn't have run in with them," Adeline rebuked. "You are a Polymath, not a Combatant. Besides, you disobeyed orders."

"I'm sorry, but I was just following Alexandrea," I replied.

Flicks chuckled and fixed the goggles sitting atop his blond hair. "Alexandrea is the *last* person to follow. I watch her as she helps the other Drones and, trust me, she gets everyone into trouble."

I promised I wouldn't do it again, and I was off the hook. Adeline and I said goodnight to Flicks and headed upstairs. As I was undressing, Adeline came over. "Hey, I just wanted to let you know that you are going to be on hospitality again with a new Umbrella. Wolfrum recruited someone else."

"Okay," I replied. "He was the one who brought in all those newbies today, right?"

"Yes, he did. He is really giving the Umbrella branch a good name. He was always insecure and shy so it was a surprise to everyone that he was assigned these tasks. He is going to be a Royal in no time."

"It's always the shy ones that accomplish the greatest things," I told her. Removing my head wrap, I put it on my nightstand and crawled into bed. Adeline took a look at the cloth and smiled. She wanted to say something but held her tongue. Telling me goodnight, she turned and went to her bed.

I was exhausted but my mind couldn't sleep. My thoughts drifted back to the two brothers and this new member of ours... *Why do they have the same last name as me?* I wondered. *Also, can we really trust that OX kid? He shot at our friends...Why does nothing make sense anymore?*

Finally, my brain gave up on my questions and I went to sleep.

This is all super crazy, right? Yes, Sonny was raised by the Invaders. No, he doesn't like to talk about it. Does that look like the kind of face that would open up about his life story?

# CHAPTER 28

## Aymie: IX

I woke up the next morning with bags under my eyes. I tried shocking myself with a cold shower, but that made me cranky. I sluggishly walked out of the bathroom, having only a fluffy white towel wrapped tightly around my torso. I was so exhausted that I didn't cover my bald head like I usually did. I let the water drip off my body and onto the pink carpet as I went to my drawers beneath the glass cases that displayed our most recent sewing projects.

As I was pulling out my uniform, I couldn't help but feel eyes staring at my head. Normally, the girls didn't say anything, but I felt like that day they wanted to.

And I was right.

I turned around to find Adeline standing right behind me. "Morning, Aymie," she greeted with her perfect smile. Her makeup was at its best and her hair was beautifully curled…I envied it so much.

"Morning," I mumbled as I rudely brushed past her to get dressed. I didn't mean to be impolite, but I didn't want to get upset for no reason. I slipped into the bathroom and closed the door. Once I locked it, I placed my clothes on the wooden shelf next to the sink and began to change.

I had buttoned the last button on my white blouse when Adeline knocked on the door. "Aymie, when you're done I want to give you something," she called from outside.

"Uh, okay," I replied, grabbing my makeup brushes. I was perplexed yet curious. *What does she have for me?* I wondered as I covered my blemished face in a powdery mask.

Once I had a pound of makeup on, I grabbed my things and walked back out into the room. I nonchalantly put my belongings away. I didn't want to seem so eager to find out what Adeline had. Out of the corner of my eye, I saw her coming from the supply room that was to the left of the bathrooms. She had her hands behind her back.

"There you are!" she called. A grin spread across her face. "You ready?"

Standing up straight, I replied, "Not so sure…"

She giggled. "I think you'll like it." Carefully, she brought her arms around. In her hands was a mannequin head wearing a beautiful brown wig.

I stared at it as if it were a foreign object. Slowly, I reached out and touched it. The soft hair was long and wavy with bangs cut straight across. *It looks exactly like what mine used to…* I thought, amazed. "What's this for?" I asked, playing dumb.

Adeline smiled. "Now, I don't want you to think that you need this to be beautiful. I just noticed that you always seem so embarrassed by your alopecia, but I don't want you to be. I want to make sure you are happy."

I was too stunned for words. I wasn't sure to be grateful or insulted because I was different. *Her intentions seem sincere,* I thought positively. Part of me wanted to wear it desperately, but the other half of me told me that it wouldn't make a difference. I took a deep breath. *"A princess is obedient,"* I reminded myself as I kindly took the wig from my Royal Veteran. "Thank you, Adeline," I told her.

"You're very welcome," she replied with a wink. "Put it on! I want to see."

I went back into the bathroom and shut the door. I didn't want the girls to watch. I carefully took the wig off the mannequin's head. Closing my eyes, I put it on my own. Once I made sure it was straight and secure, I opened them. I looked in the mirror and saw the nine year old girl that lived with the Quartermanes. I had flashbacks of Abigail, her parents, and Blake.

*Oh Blake...* I thought as I stared at my reflection. I wanted to cry, but I couldn't. My emotions felt...dead.

My mind returned to the present and I saw fifteen-year-old me again. Shaking off the past memories, I began to admire the wig itself. It felt so real and it matched my skin tone perfectly. I twisted a lock and let it fall in front of my shoulders. I smiled through tears and decided I would like it.

When I came out of the bathroom, Adeline took one look at me and gasped. She nodded approvingly. "It suits you. What do you think?"

"It's perfect, thank you," I told her honestly as I played with the curls.

"You're welcome," she replied. "Remember, we are always here for you."

I was happy to hear that. It was nice to be cared for after everything I'd been through. I thanked her again and went to get ready to greet our newcomer.

Going down the curved staircase, I spotted the Umbrella that I'd be working with. In the hallway below was a girl with golden hair pulled back into a bun. She was tall, like me, with leafy green eyes. *She was part of the group that came yesterday,* I thought to myself, going over to her. When she saw me, she smiled. I returned the gesture and asked, "Are you on hospitality with me?"

She nodded. "Yeah. I'm Johanna Watterson. You must be Aymie, right? Aymie Hodgins?"

"Yeah," I replied hesitantly. "How did you know that?"

"Shannon and the others told me you were there last night when the new kid broke in," she explained. "That was crazy you ran in with them like that."

"I couldn't stand by and do nothing," I replied. "Besides, I didn't think those annoying kids Shane and Mark could do anything to help."

Chuckling, she replied, "Hopefully they're not too annoying 'cause you might be hanging out with them more often." She looked around and leaned in as if she were telling me a dangerous secret. "Word got around to them that you are one nice pianist. The boys need another player for this band they wanna start."

Unsure of what to think, I nodded and replied, "I'll keep it in mind."

We talked a bit about music and this potential band while we were waiting. Turns out Johanna and I had more in common than I first thought.

Finally, we heard a car pull up to the front. That was our cue. I quickly made sure I was presentable and headed towards the front door with Johanna close behind. Going outside, I greeted an older boy who I presumed was Joshua. "Welcome home, Wolfrum," I said, adjusting my new wig.

He looked at me with his brown eyes and smiled. "Thanks. You Aymie?" he asked.

I was slightly confused as to how he knew my name but I didn't get a chance to ask. Behind him, the newcomer stepped out of the car and made his way towards the stairs. The moment I laid eyes on him, my heart stopped.

He was a cute fourteen year old guy with pale skin. He wore a gray sweater and a beanie on top of his head of white hair. His bangs stuck out of his hat and reached his bright blue eyes. Over his shoulder was a knapsack and around his neck was an expensive camera with a butterfly pin attached to the strap.

When he looked up, he froze. We stared at each other for a moment. "Blake?" I asked, slowly walking towards him. I couldn't believe it.

Subconsciously, he put his hand on the butterfly pin and smiled. "Hey, Princess," he whispered.

I put my hands over my mouth. *I can't believe this.* My prayers had finally been answered. Bawling, I ran up and flung my arms around his neck. He was finally taller than me—only by an inch, though. I buried my face into his shoulder and sobbed. "I've missed you so much," I cried through tears. "I thought I'd never see you again."

He held me close to him. "I knew we would. I prayed for it every day since we've been apart," he confessed. "A few weeks ago I dreamt of this moment and here we are." We stood there for a few minutes until he gently pushed me away. He looked at me caringly and then realized that I had hair. Confused, he was about to point to my wig but pulled his hand back. He decided to say nothing.

I laughed. "Yes, I have hair again," I said, answering his question. Wiping the tears from my face, I fanned myself and said, "I hope this mascara doesn't run."

"I'm happy I don't wear makeup," Johanna said, sniffling. She slapped the sides of her face and began to gently tug on her frail skin. "Gah! Man, I am so emotional!

Blake chuckled. "All you ladies are. I didn't realize how weepy teenage girls were until I left Saint John Bosco's."

"I knew nothing about guys until I left Saint Maria Goretti's," I said, giggling. Pulling myself together, I took a deep breath and added, "I still can't believe you are here."

Blake smiled, fixed his soft gray beanie, and replied, "Well, here I am. Let's enjoy it." He winked. "Anyway, will you ladies show a guy around?"

Eagerly, Johanna and I led him through the mansion with Joshua Wolfrum quietly shadowing us. Johanna did most of the explaining because Blake was going to be an Umbrella with her. Every so often Joshua would chime in or answer any questions about their Branch that Johanna couldn't answer. I wished Blake could've been a Polymath like me, but since his family was in the servant business I guess it made sense. He was going to spend time in the kitchen with Dylan and do housework.

Johanna and I had finished showing him the gallery of the Royal Veterans when he asked, "Will I be able to keep up my photography?" He peered through his camera's viewfinder and snapped his fiftieth picture; the sound of the shutter bounced off the walls. "I could manage a website or take photos for parties or something," he explained. He took a look at his image and nodding approvingly. "That's what I did to help out at the orphanage."

"How did you get into photography?" I asked, peeking over his shoulder to see the photo. He had snapped a picture of the RV Agricola's—Marian's—oil painting. It was so tasteful and aesthetic, I was surprised. "I never would've thought someone like you would be interested in something like that," I confessed.

To save battery, he switched his black camera off and smiled. "It makes sure I am not *in* the pictures," he explained slightly joking, but I watched as he subconsciously pushed his white bangs out of his face. In a more serious tone, he continued, "Also my dreams and the last time with our parents made me realize that time stops for no one. Pictures help me keep those memories forever. I never want a moment to pass by unappreciated."

"That's deep, man," Johanna said. "I am sure we could use a photographer. I'll ask Mr. Wyght personally." She winked.

For the first time in a while, Wolfrum spoke up. "You can do that?" he asked, stepping forward. "Mr. Wyght has special rules about who can contact him unless it is absolutely necessary. Only the Royals—no scratch that—the Royal *Veterans* have that privilege."

Johanna paused and thought. "He never mentioned that to us," she replied. "Maybe we are a special case. I mean, c'mon, Shannon and I were promoted pretty high in no time." Realizing that might have been a little rude, she quickly added, "But maybe it's because we have the youngest students to personally take care of. He said he doesn't want us to raise them on our own."

"How old is the youngest?" Blake asked.

"One," she replied, smiling. "To be honest I don't even know where she is. Everyone just wants to snatch her up which is fine by me. It's nice for Shannon, Shane, and me to get the break. We aren't ready to be responsible adults just yet."

"Yeah, but you are a caregiver *and* counselor now," I reminded. "That is a big job for starting only yesterday."

Wolfrum's jaw dropped. "You're taking those positions?" he

said, shocked. "How long was I gone? Last I checked it was the Royals who were given those responsibilities."

Johanna shrugged. "Apparently they're shorthanded because a few of the Royals left to start their own lives. I just told Mr. Wyght that my parents were in the medical field and I was going to be a Psychologist."

Wolfrum threw his hands up in disbelief. "There are special positions for psychologists, seamstresses, and possibly photographers but what about actors?" He began to rant. "I am five years older than you all and only have recruiting jobs. I want a cushy position with high esteem."

"You know you are the youngest Recruiter and the only non-Royal, right?" I reminded, remembering Adeline mention that the other day. "That has to mean something."

He held his finger up, paused, and then put it down. "Never thought of it that way," he said. He pinched his shirt beneath its collar and gave it a quick tug downward. "I am glad he noticed talent." With that he said goodbye and went to put his and Blake's things away.

Once he was out the gallery door, Johanna said, "So… he is an interesting character."

Blake shrugged. "He's nice and all. I guess he just feels underappreciated sometimes."

Quickly ending that conversation, we decided to wrap up the tour. We brought Blake into the kitchen to meet his partner and roommate, Dylan Cheatle. The moment we walked in, Dylan saw us and immediately started staring at my head. "Hey, Aymie! You look different today," he said pointing to my wig. "Looks, nice; I mean you looked nice before, but you know."

"Thanks. Don't worry I get it," I replied, dismissing his remark with my hand.

Then, I felt a tugging on my leg. A three year old girl with reddish-blonde hair and freckles was staring up at me with a cookie in her mouth. With her big blue eyes she looked at me, then at Johanna, then back at me. "Lady Clarius!" she said with her mouth full.

*"Lady Clarius?"* I thought, confused. I heard her call that boy,

Shane, Clarius. *What does he have to do with me?*

Johanna smiled. "We think so, Agnes. We're going to find out in a little while," she said without explaining. Now, I was utterly confused.

Before I could ask any questions, Blake complimented the little girl. "How cute!" he said, looking down at her. "Is she with you?"

"Sure is," Johanna replied. "She is one of seven Hollinger girls." Agnes waddled over to Blake and hugged his shins.

Picking her up, he held her in his arms. She chewed her cookie and proceeded to rub Blake's beanie. "Are the rest of them this cute?" he asked.

"Well, Shannon is almost your age so I won't answer that for you," Johanna said, chuckling. "As for the rest, I guess so. I practically live with them so it's tough for me when I know how they behave."

As she was speaking there was a loud crash behind Dylan. "Speaking of behavior," Dylan said marching over to the sound. "What have I told you?" he said firmly, looking down at the ground. The counter was blocking our view so we couldn't see who was behind it.

We heard giggling. Then, a girl with big brown eyes and dark hair ran out and revealed herself.

"Of course it's Lucy," Johanna said throwing her right arm in the air and back down again. "She is such a bad influence on the others. First she broke stuff in the trophy room, then she messed with the training equipment, now she is—," before she could finish she gasped and ran over to snatch a knife that Lucy had hiding behind her back. "Playing with knives," she finished. "You are eight years old; you should know better," Johanna scolded. "For crying out loud if you can play in a band at coffee shops; you should know how to handle kitchen utensils."

The girl shrugged. "I'm a rebel."

Blake laughed. "I think I am going to enjoy working in the kitchen," he said as Agnes tugged on his white bangs.

We stood around chatting until we were interrupted by Mr. Wyght over the P.A. system, and he did *not* sound happy. "HODGINS!" he bellowed. "Report to me immediately."

# CHAPTER 29

## Aymie: X

Okay, I think I'm going to go again because I feel like I might leave you all in too much suspense if I don't.

The tone of his voice made me nervous. *What did I do?!* I thought, panicked as I ran out to find him. I heard Johanna calling after me, but I was too worried. I didn't do anything wrong, but Mr. Wyght sounded terribly upset.

I ran all over like a maniac. I went to the barn then the warehouse, bumping into people here and there. Finally, someone told me he would be in the gallery. With no options left, I headed there as fast as I could.

Rushing in, I skidded to a stop in the center of the room. I was knocked down unexpectedly from behind by that kid Shane. To make it worse, Mark came too and tripped, falling on top of us. I was being crushed by two six-foot tall teenagers. I shoved them off me with all my might. My shirt was undone, my dog tag was hanging out, and my wig was crooked.

After fixing my new hair, I yelled at them. "What is your guys' problem?! What are you doing here anyway?" In the moment, I totally forgot Shane and I shared the same name.

Offended, Shane barked back, "My problem? Maybe you shouldn't stop without warning."

"Oh what, should I wear tail lights?!"

"Maybe you should've just slowed down, Shane," Mark told him.

"You keep quiet!" Shane yelled back.

While we were bickering, we didn't notice the five others that followed us in; Blake and Johanna among them. In the midst of me yelling at the boys, Mr. Wyght entered. We didn't notice until he cleared his throat behind us, making us jump.

My face reddened and we all became quiet. He raised his eyebrows and stared at us. Even though Shane and Mark were taller than him, he intimidated them, too.

Fixing his veterans cap, he said, "What is going on here?"

"You called for me, didn't you sir?" I nervously asked, trying to clear everything up.

"No, I called for Shane," he replied, looking at him. The man opened his mouth to yell at us, but he held back when he noticed something. He studied Shane, then me, and then turned to Mark. His eyes widened and looked back and forth at our faces. Pointing to us, he whispered, "What do you know. Hollinger is right."

"Right about what, sir?" I asked, confused. "So, you didn't call for me?"

Clearing his throat, he said, "I don't think this was supposed to happen until later." He looked over his shoulder and called to Shannon, "Weren't we supposed to do this calmly?"

The short Combatant ran over and stood next to him. She stared at the three of us and smiled. "Yeah, but Shane likes to screw things up," Shannon teased.

Shane didn't protest. Instead, he and Mark looked at me with wide eyes. Everyone watched us…me in particular. My heart began to race and an uneasiness washed over me. I felt their gazes piercing through me. All the portraits of the Royal Veterans that lined the walls didn't help; especially Adeline's.

"Wh-What are you all staring at?" I stammered, slowly backing away.

Shane looked at me up and down and then his eyes fell upon the dog tag that was hanging out of my shirt. Gasping quietly, he grabbed the necklace he was wearing. "I can't believe it," he said softly.

"What?" I yelled impatiently. "I don't have all day."

Mark laughed. "Yup, definitely our sister," he said. "Can't wait for anything."

It was my turn to stare. Shocked and confused, I looked at him like he had twelve heads. "*Sister*?" I repeated. "Who are you both?"

"Hodgins," they replied simultaneously.

"People can share the same name and not be related," I reminded sharply. "This is ridiculous." Turning to Mr. Wyght, I said, "Did you really call Shane here? If so, I would like to return to my duties."

Before the man could respond, I felt a hand on my shoulder. Shannon looked up at me with sweet blue eyes and said, "Please hear us out. This wasn't supposed to be told to you so soon, but now there's no way out." She turned to her friend. "Shane, tell her when she was born."

His green eyes looked at me kindly. "The twenty-third of June, but your foster family found you a little while after that day on the front porch of their mansion," he explained.

Taken aback, I just stood there. "No, no this isn't true," I whispered even though he was right. The letter I received from Mrs. Quartermane when the mansion burned down said that they had found me…but I never wanted to believe it. "They weren't my foster family, they were my real family and they're dead along with Blake's." I shook my head, not believing them. "You're not my family. You're lying."

Then, the two boys grabbed the chains around their necks and pulled out dog tags that were identical to mine. I grabbed theirs and yanked it closer, the boys jerked forward with the sudden motion. Taking out my own, I tried to find a flaw between the three. The same metal, *H* emblem, font, birthdate, chain, everything. They were identical.

*No…this isn't possible.* I looked up at them.  Everything from the shape of their faces to the creases of their smiles was familiar. *My hair was the same color as theirs, too*, I thought but quickly shook it off. This was all just a dream that I was going to wake up from.

"This is not possible," I doubted, throwing their tags back at their chests. "I can't believe it. I won't believe it." I pushed past them and headed to the exit.

Before I could storm out, the big guy, Nic, stood in front of the door.

"Don't do that in case I want to leave too," the intruder from last night, Sonny, said. "I only came because I thought Hodgins was going to get in trouble for something."

"Which one?" Myles—Mr. Powell's son—said laughing.

"This one," Mr. Wyght called, pointing to Shane. "You didn't come in vain."

"What did I do this time?" Shane whined.

I stared at the one who was blocking my way; desperation in my eyes, but he wouldn't budge. Slowly, I turned around and stared at each one of them. I can't describe what I felt, but all I know is that I was shaking. My palms were clammy and a lump was caught in my throat. "What is this? Is this a trick?" I asked, my voice cracking. I looked at the two boys. "I am finally happy and now you are going to make me a fool? What is your problem?"

"This is no trick, my dear," Mr. Wyght kindly said, taking a few steps closer. "You weren't supposed to find out this way, but we can't hide this from you now." He took a deep breath. "Shannon told me all about Shane's story and how she knew that you were—are—their sister. This may seem far-fetched, but you should believe in miracles more than anyone else."

I shook my head and tears began to roll down my soft cheeks. This wasn't a dream anymore. It felt like a nightmare. I whipped myself around and begged Nic: "Please, just let me go."

Pity fell over his face and he moved. The moment I could, I ran out and headed down the hall, up the stairs, and back to my pink bedroom. I slammed the wooden doors behind me and pressed my back against them. Sinking to the ground, I wrapped my arms around my legs and rested my forehead to my knees. My mind flashed back to my life with the Quartermane's and all the happy memories I had with them.

*Were they not my family? Were those great times a lie? Did they only love me because they had to?* All these questions swirled in my head as tears dripped down my face and dampened the plush carpet beneath me.

I sat there completely still for an hour before there was a knock at the door. "Aymie? Are you in here?" someone called from outside, jiggling the handle.

I wiped my tears with my forearm, stood up and opened it, revealing Shannon and Johanna on the other side.

Peeking in the room, Johanna complimented, "This place is pretty sweet. I think it's so cool that you guys sew the clothes for all the kids here."

"What do you want?" I interrupted sharply.

"I wanted to apologize," Shannon said letting out a deep breath.

"*We* wanted to apologize," Johanna corrected. "That was a lot to take in and we feel terrible for doing it so suddenly. That wasn't supposed to happen. We were going to tell you a little at a time, but that was a huge accident." She shook her fists in the air. "Curse Shane and his incapability to keep out of trouble for five seconds."

"You couldn't even have waited more than a *day* since you got here to play your stupid trick?" I replied coldly. "How did you even get Mr. Wyght to play along?"

"It's not a trick and we have data to support the theory," Shannon explained.

Johanna chimed in, "Yeah. Mr. Wyght believes it all, as do we."

"Fine. Tell me your 'theory' and whatever 'evidence' you think you have," I demanded rudely. "I just want to know the truth."

Shannon then explained the story to me; the whole story. She told me everything that was in the letter Shane's first foster family had. I learned how Shane watched people he loved die in the most traumatic ways. He was now diagnosed with Aquaphobia and suffers from it. He had perks of living with the Hollinger's and his new Junior Olympic record but even that had a sad ending. Mark on the other hand was a liar and a thief. I couldn't believe what they told me he *did*. I knew they weren't saying the worst of his crimes and that made me nervous.

Finally, she told me about the men who kidnapped Mark. They swore to Mark that he had a sister and that they burned her house down and were after her. They described the men and I immediately knew who they were. I had a photographic memory; I never forget a face. Their sinister glares and grins were engrained into my mind. They were the ones who were after me at the orphanage.

*No, it can't be them,* I thought, quickly pushing it aside. Then, Shannon mentioned one of the men had a "new" daughter… named Janelle.

My heart dropped to my shoes when I heard her name. That was the turning point for me. *That* made me believe. My photographic memory I could've brushed aside but my best friend? *Never*. There was no possible way that they could've known about Janelle and the exact features of the men…

When Shannon stopped explaining, I leaned against the doorway and reflected on the whole thing. "Why is this happening to us," I whispered, believing their far-fetched fairy tale.

Johanna shook her head. "No one knows for sure." A moment of silence passed before she spoke again. "Well, we should let you take all this in. Sorry this happened so suddenly," she apologized.

Shannon nodded. "We want you to know that we are all here for you and want to help you as much as we can." With a smile, she asked, "Will we see you at dinner later?"

Slowly, I nodded and they left me standing in the doorway. I was still trying to process it all. I *have a brother who is a runaway and another who is a thief,* I thought to myself. *What happened to our family?*

I sluggishly walked up the steps of the loft and plopped myself on the edge of my bed. With my arms folded across my lap, I looked down at the floor and stared. I replayed their whole story in my head, trying to find a different explanation for it all. I couldn't find one, so I accepted it.

My family was alive and we were being hunted.

I sat there for two hours when my thinking was interrupted by the dinner bell. Forcing my weak legs to stand up, I mentally prepared myself to go downstairs and face my new brothers. I took a shaky breath and headed to the dining hall.

I had missed the toast and everyone was seated and eating. After I got my food, I went to go find my brothers. They were at the longest table with my friends. Alexandrea and Roxanne were enthralled by Shane and the story of his record-breaking experience.

I found a seat saved for me between Blake and Zander, facing Shane and Mark. I took a deep breath, walked over, and sat down, not saying anything.

"What a crazy day, huh?" Zander greeted as I settled in. His dark eyes danced when he looked at me. "First I find your best friend then this detective finds your long lost brothers. What a happy ending!"

My sadness dissipated for a brief moment. Looking at him, I asked, shocked, "Wait, you found Blake?"

"Surprise," he said, smiling.

My face lit up and I couldn't believe it. "How did you do it?"

He winked. "Trade secret I'm afraid. Think of him as a present from me to you."

"I can't thank you enough," I said ecstatic. I gave him a tight hug and a kiss on the cheek. His face turned bright red, and he went back to drinking his soda.

"Wasn't that what you wanted?" Roxanne teased as she ruffled her curly hair.

After some banter, Mark spoke to me for the first time since I sat down. He cleared his throat and sincerely asked, "How are you feeling, Aymie? I mean about all this."

It was so weird hearing him say my name. I thought for a moment and replied, "I'm okay; seriously having trouble understanding it."

"So are we," he replied. He played with the three earrings on his right ear. "It took me forever to wrap my head around it. Frankly, I still can't."

"Well, we're together again and that's what matters," Shane said. Holding up his dark water bottle, he proposed a toast: "To taking on the future, together."

Everyone lifted their cups. "Together," we all replied clinking glasses. Sonny was the only one to spoil it by refusing to lift his glass; he left Nic hanging. To be honest, the only reason why he was sitting with us was because Shannon's sister Carol-Ann forced him to. She wanted to sit with the "big kids" and begged him to accompany her. He really had a soft spot for the little girl.

Standing up, Blake said, "This moment is worth remembering." He pulled out the camera that was sitting with him and was about to take the picture.

"No, let me," Zander offered, taking the camera. "You need to be in them for once."

Before he could protest, I grabbed Blake's arm and pulled him down, forcing him to sit next to me. Zander counted to three and snapped the photo. Checking it, Blake said, "That's a good one."

"Sonny, you aren't smiling," Zander complained, pressing his finger against the tiny screen. "Way to ruin it."

Sonny ignored him and continued to eat and listen to the nonsense Carol-Ann was rambling on about.

"That was a pretty profound toast, Shane," Shannon complimented after we all saw the image. "Never would have expected it."

"Aw, Shane is growing up to be a big boy," Johanna mocked as she rubbed the boy's thick brown hair. "Soon we will get him to drink from a normal person's glass."

"Hey, at least I am staying hydrated without hyperventilating," he replied, pushing her hand away. "Besides, it isn't my fault I am like this."

Remembering the horrible story Shannon told me about his foster family and circus being murdered, I offered my condolences: "I'm really sorry that happened to you, Shane."

He nodded. He then looked at me and said, "I'm sorry about the Quartermanes. They seemed like awesome folks."

I thanked him. After a moment of thought, I said, "I can't believe this is happening to us…why do they want us so badly?"

My brothers shrugged. "That's the mystery," Mark said, taking a bite of his pizza crust.

"I am going to get to the bottom of this, I promise you," Shannon said determined.

"Shannon, it's okay," Shane reassured. "You have helped us enough and we are safe now. Now you can focus on finding your own brother."

"You don't understand; those men are still out there. They won't stop," Shannon told him. "If Pietro is even still alive I am sure he can wait a little while longer. We have resources now, let's use them."

Mark nodded. "I'm game. These guys could come back and get us any time. Let's figure out what they want and stop it now."

We all agreed and promised to put an end to Masdit and Gerrior's chase once and for all.

Yes, that is how we all met. We all kind of stuck together after that. Sonny was always on and off, though. But that was to be expected.

# THE MAINLAND

# CHAPTER 30
## Mark: IX

So, the three of us finally met and we made friendships to last a lifetime even though we didn't know it. After that dinner we all had together, things began to change.

A month after that day, I woke up in the morning to the sound of Nic humming. Ever since he found out Shane was my brother, he backed off a little bit. The two of them immediately bonded the night Sonny broke in. Thanks to that, Nic began to open up to me a little more.

*He isn't so bad*, I decided. I sat up and brushed my long hair out of my eyes.

The moment that thought crossed my mind, he hurled my dark pants at my head. "Get dressed, city boy. We have another long week ahead of us."

"Mornin' to you, too," I said, my voice muffled by my clothes. Taking them off my head, I stood up and stretched.

"What was that?" he asked as he changed all his clothes right in front of me.

I quickly turned away. "Dude, I don't care if you change, but keep some underpants on that hairy body of yours."

"Sorry," he apologized, chuckling. "The animal inside of me forgets about the importance of being clothed sometimes."

I rolled my eyes and changed into my Nerd uniform. I was careful to make sure he never saw the brand on my chest.

I thought about how many times before he would talk of this "animal" as if it was a part of him like a second nature. As I was fixing my tie, I looked at my earrings in the mirror when my mind flashed back to when I saw Theo and Jordan as those creatures for the first time. They were so different in appearance and attitude.

My wandering mind was interrupted when Nic latched onto my arm and harshly threw me out of the way. I landed on my bed. "Stop hogging!" he bellowed. He stood in front of the mirror and combed his red Mohawk.

"Quit shoving, jerk," I retorted as I jumped up. "Bro, what's your beef anyway? One sec you're joking, the next you're trying to kill me."

Ignoring me, he growled while looking at the small comb in his massive fist. In a fit of fury, he chucked his comb against the wall, picked up his backpack, and stormed out of our room.

I rolled my eyes. *What is his problem?* I thought as I fixed myself. *He really is an animal.*

Then, a thought crossed my mind.

"He mentioned experiments when we first met…" I pondered aloud. Quickly, I shook off the feeling. *Not possible. There is no way he would know Mr. Mallory.* I thought about everything that had happened. Me meeting Shane and Aymie, them knowing others that were here, and it goes on. *It could be…*

Not wanting to dwell on it anymore, I packed my things, used the bathroom, and went up to breakfast. I saw the Nerds saved a seat for me at our usual table. The only time I got to sit with my siblings and their friends was when we met that month before. Mr. Wyght wanted them to get acquainted with people in their Branch before they started to break off. We hung out at free time occasionally. Recently, we talked about starting a mini band for fun. Shane and I were for it, but Aymie still needed some convincing.

As I walked to my table, I glanced around the room to see where everyone was. Shane was sitting with the Agricolae. He was the most popular guy and everyone was listening to him talk. It was only a month and he made himself more known than any newcomer. Despite his popularity, I knew he *never* wanted to be with them. He'd glance over his shoulder at Shannon who was sitting with Sonny, Nic, and the other tough combatants.

She was the smallest one at the table, and probably the whole group, but she was not intimidated. Shannon was confident spending time with the soldiers even while holding a baby on her lap. These ruthless, muscular guys laughed whenever the little girl—Rachel—did something cute.

*Man, they're wussies*, I thought as I watched them talk with Shannon and play with the baby. The only one unamused was Sonny. Then again, he always looked emotionless.

Aymie on the other hand was enjoying herself. She always sat with her usual crew: Alexandrea, Zander, Dylan, and Roxanne. Now, Blake, Johanna, and the other Hollinger girls joined them. They seemed to be having a good time, too.

Looking around at them, I sighed and brought my tray over to the Nerd table. We never really talked about anything too exciting. They mostly spoke about typical nerd stuff while I pretended to care. To be honest, the only reason why I was in that Branch was because I knew my way around computers. I wasn't smart, never had an education. So, if it wasn't hacking or thieving related, I usually didn't know what they were talking about.

The only plus was getting to know Myles, the billionaire's kid. (Although, he liked my brother more than me.) One thing is for sure, that kid could talk for *hours*. Thankfully, Clive and Derek could keep up. I daydreamed while he rambled. My mind kept drifting back to Nic and him possibly being an experiment of my old employer.

My thoughts were interrupted towards the end of breakfast when Clive shook me to wake up, abruptly snapping my back into reality. "Myles has been calling your name for almost two minutes," he said, taking his hands off my shoulders.

I blinked a few times. "Uh, what?" I looked at the little blond boy. "Sorry, what were you saying?"

He laughed. "It's okay. I was just asking how 'Operation OX Removal' was going?" I cocked my head to the side. I had no idea what he was talking about. "Getting rid of the Order of Xenophon stuff?" he clarified.

"Oh, duh," I replied. "It's okay. I've been working on it for over a month and haven't made too much progress."

"I guess you're not as good as you say," Clive muttered as he finished his coffee.

Taking offense, I retorted, "I am too. Hacking like this without getting caught is tough." I sat up straight in my chair. "It's tough but not impossible. After all, I did hack into a police station and erase all electronic evidence of my gang when I was kid."

Derek almost choked on his biscuit. "You did what? *Gang*?"

I regretted bringing it up. They didn't know much about my past, and I wanted to keep it that way. Thankfully, I was saved by the bell. "We'll talk later," I lied. I grabbed my tray and shot up from my seat. I wanted to get to my next class as quickly as possible in case they tried to follow me. I crossed the room to put my tray on the conveyer belt for the kitchen staff.

As I put it down, Shannon walked over to say hello. She was carrying garbage in one hand and little baby Rachel in the other "Hey, Mark," she greeted as she threw out a can of baby food.

I didn't want to talk, but I couldn't be rude. "Hey, sweetheart. How you doin'? How're things?"

"Interesting," she replied, honestly. Together, we started walking towards the door. "Good, but interesting. Life as a Combatant is odd in itself. Not to mention I have to take Rachel with me sometimes."

At the sound of her name, the baby cooed and reached for me. Her pudgy fingers wrapped around my brown bangs and she started tugging as if a bell would ring. It didn't hurt, and I loved to see her smile. Her little light eyes danced and she looked at me with love. That was a nice feeling…

"Play all you want, baby," I told the little girl. She giggled.

Looking at her big sister, I asked, "So, do you like being a Combatant?"

Shannon pulled the little girl away from me. Rachel immediately latched onto her sister's curly brown hair. Trying to get free of her grasp, Shannon replied, "I guess I mostly do. I always enjoyed fighting, but I never used my feet." She shook her right leg. "The training is brutal. I wanted to stick to my boxing."

"Well, you're pretty good, babes," I told her, rubbing my neck. I remembered our first meeting the year before. "I know from experience."

She smiled and her gorgeous blue eyes lit up. "Thank you, even though I didn't really get to fight you. I caught you by surprise."

Before I could respond, Nic came over and interrupted, "Hollinger! There you are. We're headin' out."

She nodded. "It was good talking, Mark. I'll see you soon." With that, she turned and left.

I wanted to follow but Nic put his hand on my chest and pushed me backwards. "Combatants first, Nerd," he told me as he and his friends followed him out. I glared at each one as they passed. I wanted to show them who was boss, but wasn't sure how well I'd fare against professional fighters.

Sonny was the last Combatant to exit. Before doing so, he grabbed me and yanked me through the doorway, my body almost crashing to the ground. "If you aren't assertive, you won't go anywhere," he stated without looking at me. Not saying anything else, he left.

Grumbling, I rubbed the arm he latched onto. "At least he had a better reason for hurting me," I mumbled. *But why give me advice? He doesn't talk to anyone...* I wondered.

Throughout the day, I paid no attention during my studies, did the minimum of what I was required, and ignored everyone. My siblings and friends were never in my classes so I didn't see a need for unnecessary human interaction. So... another typical day at WHYP. The only time I really focused was when I got to my actual Nerd duties after lunch.

Thankfully, Clive's and Derek's classes went over so I ate by myself. I didn't want to talk about my Fallout days just yet. I hoped to push it off as much as possible. The moment lunch was over I jumped up and got out of the dining area. I raced down the hall and into the dark Nerd headquarters.

I cursed under my breath when I saw Vandewater already sitting at his desk, listening and typing away. *Maybe he didn't hear me,* I thought as I tiptoed to my spot. I tried to sit down as quietly as possible, but my swivel chair made a creak.

"Good afternoon, Mark," Vandewater greeted without turning around.

*I still will never understand how he does that,* I thought before responding. He always was able to tell who was in the room with him before even hearing their voices. "Sup," I replied.

"Normal RV stuff," he said. The computer beeped and spoke to him in a code only he could understand. "How is Operation OX Removal going?"

"Is that what we're calling it, now?" I asked as I powered up my programs.

"What Myles is calling it anyway," he responded. "I don't mean to rush you, but you need to hurry."

"What for?" I asked. I hopped down the aisle stairs to stand behind him.

Sighing, my superior typed things on his keyboard. The noises ceased and bright white boxes appeared on the screen. Hundreds of windows displayed news articles, videos, and complaints from the outside world. One news anchor spoke about a horrific bombing that had taken place at a marathon. Another about shootings in movie theaters, schools, and marketplaces. Articles covered things from public attacks to kidnappings. They dated from the present back to almost fifty years.

One article that caught my eye recalled a vicious manslaughter that left dozens of police offers dead. It was a gruesome event and apparently they don't know how it happened, so they called it an accident.

Looking closer, I realized why I recognized it. I quietly gasped. *That was…* I thought, remembering the last day I saw Mr. Mallory and his army of demons. *That's my fault.*

I didn't want to feel guilty, so I moved on to the different atrocious articles. The most terrifying thing was seeing government officials and popular individuals *defend* the culprits of these attacks. Most of them denied that they were acts of terror. Many of them said that they were accidents from people with mental disabilities. Some tried to justify their unlawful actions. Rather than reprimanding the source of the situation, they blamed it on inanimate objects or ignored it all together.

"Do you see?" the blind man said. "The world is being thrown into chaos and people aren't accepting the truth. These 'accidents' have been going on for years and no one has publicly done anything." He pressed a button and everything was replaced by a large black and red flag that I recognized all too well.

Its crimson background bathed the computer room in blood. I recalled the screams and cries of the OX victims that I had seen in the thousands of videos I watched the past month. It was a symbol of destruction and chaos. My heart raced, my fists clenched, and hatred mustered inside of me.

"We need to stop them, Mark," Vandewater continued softly. "This group is a virus. They will stop at nothing until everything is corrupted or destroyed." He wagged his finger at their giant logo. "I believe with every inch of my soul that *they* are the people behind these accidents. *They* are the reasons why parents and children are being torn from each other. *They* are the reason the world is thrown into confusion and no one knows what's right anymore."

He grabbed and gently squeezed my arm with his soft, pudgy hands. "I entrusted this task to you because you know how to get on the inside. You know how to break the rules. Now, I am telling you." He lifted his head and faced me. His milky eyes shone through his dark glasses. Even though they couldn't see, they were filled with sincerity and hope. "Do whatever it takes to destroy their virtual presence. This is one step. Help us take it."

I was amazed at his passion and serious tone. I nodded and said, "Of course. Won't let you down."

He took his hand away. "I know you won't. Now, get to work." With that, he closed out of all the visible windows and went back to his normal duties.

I trekked over to my desk. The other kids filed in after I was seated. *I hope none of them saw those articles and videos*, I thought. I looked around at their faces. I didn't know who they really were or what they went through. But one thing was for sure, they didn't need to be burdened with things like that. *That's probably why I was given this job,* I thought as I went to one of the OX's sites. *I've been a part of stuff like this. Some of it's probably my fault.*

I shook off the thought and went to work. The most miserable part was whenever I deleted one site, two more would pop up. It was the Hydra monster of the internet. It was frustrating and it infuriated me. I had to take deep breaths and hold myself back before punching a hole in my computer screen. I spent another hour slowly deleting one site. After that, I became impatient. I couldn't wait anymore. *I need to try something else,* I thought.

I played Vandewater's words over and over in my head: "*This group is a virus. They will stop at nothing until everything is corrupted or destroyed.*"

Then, it hit me.

*How stupid am I?* I thought putting my hands on my face. *He called them a virus. Well, I'll give them a taste of their own medicine.* Immediately, I began jotting down ideas and ways to go about coding the most complex, dangerous, and illegal virus that has ever been comprehended. *I did it to the NYC police, why not the world?*

Engrossed in my new plan, I didn't realize how fast the time flew. I was at my computer for five hours straight just taking notes and researching. I went through meditation, first free period, and almost all of dinner. The only reason I noticed the time was because Clive and Derek came to find me.

"You're still here?" Derek asked, rushing over to my desk. His round face was covered in sweat as if he'd been running a marathon.

"Dinner is halfway over. What have you been doing?"

I looked at him and Clive, then at the clock on my computer, and back again. "Sorry. I've been working hard," I told them.

"That's a first," Clive said, crossing his arms and smiling his creepy grin.

I wanted to punch his straight, sharp teeth in but held back. "Let's just eat," I growled. I turned off my computer, abruptly stood from my desk, and stomped towards the dining hall.

Behind me, my two friends whispered to each other, not addressing me until we all sat down. I looked around again and saw everyone else at their usual tables like this morning. Only this time, Shane had Rachel. He was using her to get more attention from the girls. I was jealous. I know I shouldn't have been, but I was.

*Why can't girls look at me like that?* I thought bitterly. I felt like my anger for OX was being directed towards my brother only because it had nowhere to go at the moment.

"Mark!" Derek shouted for the third time.

I was startled and jumped a little in my seat. "What?!"

"Quit your daydreaming and pay attention for once," Clive scolded.

Derek repeated the question he asked when I wasn't listening. "This morning you mentioned you were in a gang and hacked the government when you were a kid. Can you explain yourself?"

He and Clive stared; it made me uncomfortable. "It's not something I like talking about," I mumbled.

"Too bad," Clive said coldly. "We're your friends; we deserve to know."

Taking a deep breath, I gave in. I told them a watered down version of my story. I never mentioned I smuggled drugs and supplies or was the best pickpocket. I only told them that I was an orphan with a man who lost his way. He raised us to keep people off our trail so that's what I did.

After I finished, they both stared at me. "I thought my life was bad," Derek mumbled. He looked at me with his dark almond eyes and apologized, "Sorry for pushing you. Sometimes we feel like we don't know you at all."

"That's because we don't," Clive muttered, but quickly added, "but that doesn't change the fact that we are friends."

"I'm sorry, I'm not used to knowing people who aren't out to kill me," I confessed. "Takes time to open up, ya'know?"

Derek nodded. "I get you. Besides, we've all had hard lives. You would think we would be more understanding." He glared at Clive who just shrugged his shoulders.

Clive was about to make a remark when a familiar deep voice spoke behind me. "Hey, Hodgins, can we speak with you?"

Turning around, I found Thyme and Vandewater standing side by side. "Hey, Thyme," I greeted, looking at the tall, dark Combatant. "Long time no talk."

He managed a smile. "I wish this was a friendly chat, but we have something else to discuss."

Nervous, I stood up and followed them out of the dining hall, leaving my confused friends behind. As we exited, I felt the eyes of hundreds of students upon us. Once we were out of the room and walking down the hallway, I asked, "Am I in trouble?"

Thyme chuckled. "Of course not." He and Vandewater led me to the gallery where we first told Aymie we were her family. I never had a chance to enjoy the large paintings of the Royal Veterans: present and past. I admired how well they were done. Each member was dressed in their casual uniform and sitting straight before a gray backdrop. They were painted with oil and protected by a glossy coating. One thing I never noticed before was there was no RV Umbrella presently.

"Hey, Thyme. Where is the Umbrella?" I asked.

Turning to the empty spot where the portrait should be, Thyme replied, "We haven't chosen one yet. We have to pick unanimously with Mr. Wyght and Mr. Powell. The last girl—Virginia Michaelson— was sent by Mr. Wyght on a special mission. After she completed it, she stayed in the real world to start a life for herself."

"I wonder how she's doing," Vandewater asked from behind me.

Thyme shrugged his shoulders. "Anyway, we should focus on why we are here." He turned back to me. "We need your help with an important task."

"Shoot," I replied. "I can handle it."

He smirked. "I thought so. We need some help keeping an eye on two people: your roommate, Nicolas Eerkens, and the so-called Sonny Wilcox."

Not wondering why they chose me, I immediately asked, "Okay, what do I need to keep an eye out for?"

"Anything you find suspicious," Vandewater chimed in. "We didn't entirely trust Sonny and his story of being an OX escapee to begin with. Nic on the other hand," he clicked his tongue, "he is worrying us. We diagnosed him with bipolar disorder when he arrived, but it seems to be getting worse and out of control."

I confirmed it. "Yeah, he literally threw me out of the way this morning and then chucked his comb across the room like a psycho."

Thyme's brown eyes widened. "Tell us immediately the next time this happens. Hopefully, we can figure out what's really wrong with him."

*I might have an idea,* I thought. Rather than telling them my suspicion, I nodded and asked if there was anything else.

"Not at the moment," Vandewater answered, gripping his white cane with his pudgy fingers, "but we will let you know if there is. Thank you, we are counting on you." With that, Thyme and Vandewater led me out of the room and went to enjoy the rest of their evenings.

That night, I didn't go find my siblings or Nic and Sonny at free time. Instead I went straight to my room and continued working on the virus on my personal laptop. *Coding tonight, stalking tomorrow,* I told myself while I worked.

Finally, Nic came in and, without saying a word, plopped himself on his bed and began snoring obnoxiously loud.

*I'll learn the truth about you sooner or later,* I thought looking at the monstrous teen sleep. Being tired too, I decided I should rest. I had made a little progress with my program but knew I had ways to go. I put my laptop under my bed, lay down, and drifted to sleep.

# Chapter 31
## Mark: X

The next morning, I woke before Nic and quietly got dressed, careful not to stir him. He was a heavy sleeper so it wasn't difficult. To be honest, I didn't really know where to start. Thyme and Vandewater only told me to keep an eye on him, but I was determined to figure out if he was an experiment of Mr. Mallory's. *I'll think of something*, I repeatedly told myself as I snuck out of the room and headed upstairs.

To my surprise, there were already people waiting for breakfast to start. They lined up neatly by the food counter. Nic and I were always right on time. The thought never crossed my mind about actually being *early*. They didn't serve the food until Mr. Wyght was in the room anyway, so why bother losing sleep?

As I reached the back of the line, Mr. Wyght entered. Everyone stood up straight and became quiet. He went to the front, received his food, and went to wait at his center table. After he put his tray down, the Umbrella's manning the counter began distributing food to the kids.

I took my tray, went to my usual table, and stood behind my chair, waiting for the toast.

"Well, look who is up," I heard Clive say behind me. He put his food down. "Couldn't sleep?"

I shook my head. "Nah, something just woke me up early."

"Well, I hate getting up early," a little girl's voice said to the left of me. I looked down and saw one of the Hollinger girls resting her forearms on the chair. "I wish we could just sleep all day."

I laughed. "Tell me about it."

She looked up at me with her big brown eyes and smiled. It was amazing how the Hollinger girls had similar appearances but completely different personalities. This one—Lucy—was always getting into trouble. Cute kid, though. Her long brown hair was in perfect braids and her Umbrella uniform was clean but wrinkled. Not that she cared. "So, you're Clarius II?" she asked, smirking.

"That would be me," I replied. I recalled the story my brother told me about how he got his pet name.

"You two look alike yet so different," she told me. "Is it okay if I sit with you guys? I'm mad at Peggy and Carol-Ann right now."

"You're always welcome to sit with us," Myles chimed in with a big grin. One thing I had noticed was if a Hollinger ever came up in a conversation, Myles would *always* mention Lucy, whether it was to complain that she beat him up in combat practice or to compliment her.

Instead of insulting him right away she thanked him… then insulted him: "Thanks. I'll go easy on your skinny butt in fighting later."

Finally, Mr. Wyght said the toast and we sat down. One thing that will forever surprise me is how much and how fast that little girl could eat. None of us said anything, but it was pretty funny. "So, what did Vandewater want to talk to you about?" Derek asked after watching Lucy inhale a third helping of pancakes.

"Just stuff about my project," I lied.

Trying not to be jealous, Clive asked, "Did he compliment you or tell you anything else?" His face was green with envy.

"Nah, nothing worthy of repeating," I told him. Clive's jealousy receded and he went back to his coffee.

Breakfast ended and we went our separate ways. The day passed as usual. This time, however, I had training with the Combatants mixed into my schedule. Being a Nerd, we only had it once a week. I never really cared for it. I already could handle myself and always had a weak partner.

After I changed into my fighting uniform, I went outside and was blinded by the sun. The day was bright and crisp. The cold wind blew against my face as I walked across the frosted fields. I passed the Agricolae working on the farm, preparing for a cold winter. *I am so happy I don't have that job*, I thought as I watched them work.

I reached the fighting area of the field where the others were. I was grouped with a few Nerds, Umbrellas, and Polymaths my age. Pulling my combatant jacket closed, I waited for instructions.

Thyme came out of the large warehouse carrying a large box of fake weapons in his strong black arms. "Defensive practice," he said. He dropped the box on the floor.

I grabbed a rubber knife returned to my place in line, waiting to be assigned a partner. When Thyme gave the word, we paired up and began practicing.

It wasn't really exciting. I already knew everything Thyme was showing us. My partner, on the other hand, had a harder time. He was a scrawny, timid kid with white hair that he covered with a gray beanie. I recognized him as Blake: the old friend of my sister. He had no experience at all and struggled the entire time.

The first session ended and I barely broke a sweat, but Blake could barely breathe. "I'm not used to this. I need to sit down," he panted as he staggered toward the crowded benches.

During the fifteen-minute rest, I decided walk around a little. I hoped to get information about Sonny and Nic. They were both Combatants and pretty good ones, too. Someone might have something to say.

However, there was a problem. I was a Nerd. They were Combatants. Normally, the tough guys don't like talking to us computer freaks.

I walked around and tried approaching some of the guys. They took one look and made the effort to ignore and avoid me. I heard a few of them talking about me as they left. Why? I don't know. I didn't do anything to them, and they didn't know anything about me. It was obnoxious.

Being rejected a fourth time, I began to get angry. I clenched my fists and grit my teeth. *I will show you all*, I thought. I've been pushed around too long. *You'll all be wishing you were me one day.* Frustrated, I stormed back to our spot on the field.

On the way, I caught a glimpse of a familiar red Mohawk. I looked over and saw Nic helping some girl Combatants carry heavy boxes into the warehouse. He wasn't trying to impress them like normal. No flirting or anything. He kept a straight face and carried the boxes inside.

My frustration dissipated and was replaced with confusion. *That's weird*, I thought. To my surprise, when he saw me, he waved his long arm in the air and yelled, "Hey, Mark!"

That was a shock. Whenever he was with his fellow Combatants, I became his victim. Today was different. Confused and not knowing what to do, I approached him. "How's it goin'," I responded, slowly.

Crossing his thick arms, he asked, "Where were you this morning? You left early."

"Yeah, sorry," I apologized, pushing my hair out of my eyes. "Had a lot on my mind and just needed to get busy."

"I hear ya," he replied. He looked over to my group and saw Thyme getting ready to blow the whistle. "Oh, you better hurry. They're going to start without you."

I thanked him and ran to begin my second session. *That was really weird,* I thought as I fought Blake again. My mind drifted the whole time we were sparring. My partner got a few attacks in and quietly celebrated one too many times before he realized I wasn't giving my all.

"Stop going easy on me," Blake complained, breathing heavily. "I need to learn how to do this."

"Sorry, man," I apologized. I looked closely at his face. His bright blue eyes were filled with determination as he tried to slice me with his fake knife. He was concentrating hard. With great effort, he lunged, but I quickly stepped out of the way. Before he could fall on his face, I pivoted and grabbed the back of his jacket.

Embarrassed, he jumped up and brushed himself off. "Thanks," he mumbled.

"No biggie. Just chill. You'll get it sooner or later," I told him, twirling the rubber knife in my hand.

He looked up at me and gave a little smile. "You're one of Aymie's brothers, right?"

I still wasn't used to the sound of that. "Yeah, I am. Mark Hodgins. I don't think we officially met." I held out my hand.

Shaking it, he replied, "Blake Bain. Aymie talks a lot about you guys."

"Really?" I said, confused. "We only see each other at free time. I feel like I barely know her." I tried to ask him a question, but the words wouldn't come out. Having a sister still felt unnatural. Clearing my throat, I tried again, "Can you tell me what she's like? I kind of know her back story, but not her."

His face lit up. "She's amazing, beautiful, caring, an amazing piano player, and—" he went on and rambled about everything great about my sister. His passion for her was enough for me to know how incredible she is. He probably would've kept going on if I hadn't been grinning. "Why are you smiling like that?" he asked, uncomfortable.

"Seems like you have a thing for my sister."

His face turned beet red. "N-no! It's not like that. She is my best friend."

"Relax, man, it's all right," I said, laughing. "Whatever it is, just take good care of her."

Embarrassed, he nodded. The whistle blew and it was time for the next period. Thanking me, Blake quickly ran off to shower before his next class.

I chuckled and said to myself, "He wasn't on my list of people to keep an eye on, but I guess I don't have a choice now."

Flinging a clean towel from the benches over my shoulder, I was about to move on when I heard a loud crash. People began shouting and screaming. I saw Nic storming out of the warehouse with Sonny, Zander, and Thyme following.

"Where do you think you're going?!" Thyme called.

The big guy growled over his shoulder and stomped away. I watched as they chased him towards the house. Curious, I went inside the warehouse to see what had happened.

There was equipment scattered everywhere. The ceiling high shelves were turned over and boxes were destroyed. Bullets littered the ground like shiny confetti. A tub of grenades had come crashing down and the deadly weapons lay about. Combatants scurried around me, carefully cleaning up the mess.

Holding my breath, I cautiously made my way around. I asked if they needed help, but only received dirty looks and was told to get lost. Thankfully, I found one friendly face.

"Mark! What are you doing here?" Shannon greeted. She poked her head out of a curtain that was blocking off the rest of the warehouse.

"I heard the commotion and came to check," I explained. I balanced on one leg, trying not to step on the pile of bullets at my feet. "What happened?"

She sighed, her body still hiding behind the curtain. "Nic lost it again. So far, he has had at least one outburst every day. Now, they are getting frequent and more violent. This was the worst."

I felt guilty. *I should've told them*, I thought gently taking another step towards her. "I'm sorry."

"It's okay, it's not your fault," she replied, pulling the curtain away. "Why don't you come in?" She looked around. Seeing all her Branch-mates still busy, she added, "Just don't tell anyone."

"Never thought the daughter of an esteemed detective to be a rule breaker," I teased.

She laughed. "I'm not 'breaking' the rules. I actually could use your help with something." Without saying anything else, she led me in.

Behind the curtain was a long wooden table covered in papers. Lying atop the mess of articles and reports was a recently used viola. On the wall behind the table was a large map of the world stabbed with pins. Stand-alone cork boards covered in newspaper clippings photographs, and notes stood to the left and the right.

"Whoa," I marveled at it all. "Impressive."

"Thanks," she said. "I really took over the place when Mr. Wyght assigned me back here." Leaning towards me, she whispered, "They are actually making progress now."

"Not bad, beautiful," I complimented. "Not bad. So, what did you want me to see?"

She threw her finger in the air and remembered why I was there in the first place. "I'm working on something that actually might be linked to Nic. You're his roommate so I figured I'd discuss it with you." She went over to a small box and pulled out a photograph. "I think *this* guy is responsible for Nic's 'issue' along with other things related to our current investigation." She handed me the picture. "We met him that night at the Junior Olympics and he was trying to sell Shane and Nic something. Has Nic ever mentioned anything about him? Appearance, name, anything?"

Taking a closer look, I saw the one she was pointing to. In the crowd of people I recognized the familiar face of a man with long, ratty hair. "I knew it," I whispered. I looked up at my confused friend and explained, "I worked for him. It's thanks to me that he does things like this."

"Well," she said, taken aback. "That wasn't the answer I was looking for, but it helps a lot. Care to explain?" She pulled a chair from under the table and motioned me to sit. "I know you've been hiding things." She sat across from me. "You have things on your mind. Care to let me in?"

I sat down and took a deep breath. *I barely know this girl, should I trust her?* I wondered. Yet, there was something in her kind, beautiful blue eyes that made me unlock the door and let her inside.

So, I told her everything, and I mean *everything*. All of the stuff I am relaying to you guys now, I told Shannon. She was the first person to hear the whole truth. I choked back tears because of the horrible memories I had: Brand leaving, my part in Mr. Mallory's schemes, my friends turning against me, and so on. I didn't want to look like a total weakling in front of her so I held it together as best I could.

Throughout it all, she listened intently. She leaned forward with her elbows on the table and hands folded. Her chin rested on her hands, and her blue eyes remained locked onto me with such interest and care. She was genuinely concerned with my well-being… unlike other people I knew.

An hour later, I finished my life story, and we sat in silence. She slumped back in her seat. "I suspected you lived a difficult life of thievery and lies, but this," she shook her head, "I never would have guessed."

"No one would have," I replied, rubbing my eyes with my black jacket sleeve. "They wouldn't understand. I was always afraid my story would change the way people feel about me." *Not that they feel anything at all*, I thought bitterly.

Shannon sighed. "I'm not going to lie to you. Your past *will* change the way others look at you."

"Thanks, sunshine. That makes me feel better," I said, coldly.

"You didn't let me finish." She crossed her arms. "Yes, people will look at you differently but there are only two possible outcomes." She held up one finger. "First outcome: they won't be able to look past your past and think lowly of you." She held up another finger. "Second outcome: they will take a look at your past *and* the person you are now. Comparing the two, they will realize how far you have come. How much you've changed. For that, they'll admire you, respect you, and look up to you."

Not knowing what to say, I sat there in quiet and reflected while Shannon stood up to work around me.

*Is she right? Would they accept me if they knew who I was?* I looked at her. She picked up her viola and played a soft tune, which she often did when she was thinking. *Does that mean she accepts me for who I am?* The thought of being cared for by a beautiful girl like her made my heart race. I didn't know why at the time…

All that aside, I still couldn't soak any of it in, but I couldn't sit there until it did. I stood up and stretched. I was about to say something to Shannon when my eyes noticed the clock above the map. "It's *two* already?" I gasped.

"Is it?" She stopped playing and turned to look herself. "Well, look at that. We missed lunch."

"I'm sorry," I apologized, "I didn't realize how long I was talking for."

"Don't be sorry. You needed it." She tilted her head back to look me in the eyes. "If you ever need to talk, I'll listen. I'm not a counselor like Johanna, but I've picked up things. If you are ready, you can also talk to Papa E. He's had the most experience and knows the right things to say." She smiled. "You have friends, Mark. Talk to them."

With that, she picked up her things and left me alone in the warehouse. I stood there for a moment and thought, *'Friends'… I like that.* I breathed in through my nose and out through my mouth. Spinning on my heel, I headed back out the now clean warehouse and made my way to the mansion.

Rather than looking for leftover lunch, I went right into the Nerd Headquarters to work on my virus. Everyone was already seated and working. I knew for sure Vandewater would hear me come in. In fact, he was waiting for me.

"Mark, there you are," he called, still facing his computer. "Come here please." The other Nerds turned to me and stared as I walked down the stairs to see him. "The rest of you, back to your work." Once he heard the clicking of keys, he whispered, "I know it has only been a day, but I was wondering if you made progress with Nic and Sonny? After today, we fear Nic will only get worse. Sonny has also continued to arouse suspicion. We want to put an end to it ASAP."

"Believe it or not, I have learned some things," I told him. "I have the entire explanation as to why Nic is the way he is."

Vandewater's eyebrows rose. "Write a detailed report and send it to me," he commanded. "I'll address Thyme afterwards." He grinned. "You are destined for great things, kid. Keep up the good work."

Telling him I would, I proudly went back to my seat and wrote him my report. *Thanks, Shannon,* I thought as I sent him my completed explanation. After that, I continued working on my virus. *If he is impressed by that, I hope he'll be impressed by this.*

# THE MAINLAND

# CHAPTER 32
## Shane: XII

Now that all of our stories are connected, I'll try to keep it as consistent and relevant as possible.

Two months passed after the day Mark just told you about, and we were into the New Year. The ground was covered in snow, the days freezing, and we Agricola *still* had to work on the farm. However, I preferred working in the snow over the rain. My Aquaphobia tends to forget that snow is just frozen water, but that didn't mean I didn't complain about it.

"The Combatants get to train inside," I whined as I put the chickens back in their coop one January afternoon. "Why can't we have indoor farming?"

I heard a chuckle from behind me. "Relax, Shane," Marian Best—the Royal Veteran Agricola—said. "You've only been here three months. You'll get used to it."

"How long did it take you?" I asked, latching the coop door.

She smirked. "Not long. I grew up on a farm before here. I thought you lived with farmers, too?"

Remembering that horrible day I lost Uncle Chuck and Aunt Monika, my face fell. "It was only the first six years of my life before my foster family was…you know."

Obviously embarrassed, she apologized and changed the subject. "At least we don't have to be out here as long as we would if the day was nice. To be honest, there isn't much for us to do. We get extra free time."

That wasn't the first time she told me that. "I know, but it's just us," I continued to complain. "Everyone else is still busy."

She spat in the snow. "I know you miss your many girlfriends, Mr. Popularity, but you can still hang out with us."

My face got red. "That's not what I meant." Then, what she said processed. "Wait, what do you mean *girlfriends*? I don't even have one."

The farm girl laughed. "That still surprises me. You just hang out with so many I can never tell which ones you actually care about."

She wasn't wrong. I was pretty popular among the students, but I never thought of all of them as my friends, let alone all the girls as my girlfriends. Yet, I could never get attention from the one girl I thought differently about. I grew so close to her and her friends before we came here. Now, I felt like we were all separating.

Marian shook her head. "You know, you are going to get in trouble one day. Those girls are going to gang up on you. Not only that, but you have *ruined* our period for meditation. You know we are supposed to be quiet, right?"

"I can't help it," I told her, "I'm impatient, and they all try to sit next to me in the library. I used to be good at it. Last place I lived, the family had us all do something super similar. I guess I lost it once their parents were taken from us." That last part was a lie. I just felt guilty because I knew I needed that time of quiet.

"That's still no excuse," she sighed. "Next time, you should sit in the chapel. Papa E would be happy to help you out." Looking around at the fields, Marian decided our work was done. "I think it's time." She pulled out her pocket watch. "Yup. Time to go. I'll ring the bell."

Before she could, I finally asked her something that bugged me every time she pulled out that silver watch. "Wait, Marian, can I ask you a question?"

Surprised, she turned and said, "Of course."

"That picture in your watch. Who are they?"

She pulled it back out and showed me. She pointed to each person in the faded photograph. "My mom, dad, me, and my baby sister, Marlene. Together, we are the Best family."

[Yes, you guys knew it! I thought her last name, Best, would've given it away. I told Marlene that she had a sister when I gave her the pocket watch… I know, we all miss Marlene.]

I peered closely at the picture. "You have a beautiful family," I complimented, "What happened?"

"Well," she took a shaky breath, "all I know is my parents were taken. I don't know what happened. One morning I woke up and they were gone. It was just Marlene and me. We had no other family to turn to and no one came looking for us. So, I took care of her myself. It wasn't hard," she smirked, "we grew our own food and our farmhouse barely had electricity to begin with." Smiling, she looked at the baby. "She was the happiest little thing. Not having a care in the world. She was supposed to come here with me, but…" Her eyes cast downward. "We were separated. I was out in the field when I heard a crash in our house. I ran inside and found the baby was gone. I saw a dark figure running out the door and into the woods. I chased them, but got lost. After hours of being stranded, I found my way to a highway and Mr. Wyght's Veteran Umbrella at the time—Virginia Michaelson—picked me up and brought me here." She bit her lip and shook her head. "I know my sister is still out there. When I'm strong enough, I'm going to find her and take her back. No matter what." Not saying another word, she picked up her shovel and headed to the barn.

I had no words to say. I was dumbfounded. That was a story I never forgot. I always hoped that someday her and Marlene would be reunited. *I'll help however I can*, I mentally promised, too stunned to actually tell her. I knew the feeling of being separated from siblings. I wanted to bring families together as much as I could. She was a start.

My thoughts were interrupted by Marian ringing the bell. I was finally saved from the awful frozen water. I pushed Marian's depressing story to the back of my mind for the rest of the day. There was nothing I could do at that moment; I figured I shouldn't dwell on it.

Once my things were away, I raced to the house. In a flash, I changed and was in the music room with my guitar. I tuned my stringed instrument and thought, *Maybe Mark will want to jam today. He said he was done with that assignment he was working on.*

Sitting on the cozy sofa, I played and sang to myself for a bit before others came in. My rough calloused fingers plucked the strings to create an original melody.

My new song reached the end when a few of my friends entered the vast white room. "Johanna, Blake, little girls, welcome," I greeted with a smile.

"Clarius!" four-year-old Rebecca greeted, running over to me. Agnes followed her sister, and Rachel tried to waddle along, but fell and sat on the floor giggling. It was amazing how much I watched them grow. Two years passed since I first met them. We all went through so much together.

"Does Mr. Popularity have time for us today?" Johanna teased as she picked up Rachel after she fell.

"What's that supposed to mean?" I asked, defensively. Rebecca and Agnes tackled me before she could respond. "Good to see you, too," I said as I held them.

I heard a shutter click. I looked up and saw Blake with his digital camera. "I am printing that one," he said.

"Can I see?" Peggy, who was nine now, asked. She was Blake's little girl companion for the day. All of my good friends had a Hollinger that would follow them around from time to time. Peggy was interested in photography, so she would follow Blake. After seeing the photo, she exclaimed, "This is awesome! Can I try taking a nice picture like this?"

The white haired teen looked at the girl. Peggy twirled her hair on her finger and smiled. He couldn't say no to those beautiful brown eyes. Cautiously, Blake took the camera from around his neck and gave it to her. "You can take a few, but be careful."

Clutching it tightly, she replied. "I promise!" She took

photographs immediately.

"Your memory is going to be full in about five minutes," Johanna told him as Peggy wandered off to capture the day's moments.

"It's fine. I put all the photos onto a drive every night," he replied. "Let her take all the pictures she wants."

I stood up with Rebecca and Agnes latching onto my legs. "How'd you guys get out of Branch work early?"

They looked at each other and laughed. "We Umbrellas don't have difficult things to do, farm boy," Johanna said. "We clean, cook, and keep order."

"Pretty much. Well, Johanna also counsels and takes care of these little ones," Blake added, taking Rachel from her arms. "Besides, Aymie and the Polymaths do the harder stuff that we 'can't' do."

"How are she and everyone doing?" I asked. "I feel like we haven't hung out since that first day we told Aymie we were related."

Johanna shrugged. "I think everyone's good. Your friend Nic is a mess though. Every day he gets into trouble, but doesn't understand why until he sees the mess he made. Two Royal Veterans are working with Mark to figure out how to help him, but they haven't made a move yet."

"I hope they do soon," I confessed. "I'm afraid he might burn the mansion down."

"I wouldn't go *that* far," a deep voice said. Nic stood in the doorway, his burly arms crossed. "So, you're talking about me?" he asked, walking towards us.

"What of it?" I replied, confidently.

"Talk about me all you want. Makes me almost as popular as you," he snickered. "So, what have you all been up to, other than obsessing over me?" He playfully rubbed his fingers through his red Mohawk.

Thankfully, Johanna was quick and sarcastic. "We were only obsessing over you, Nic. You are our pride and joy. The purpose of our very existence. We are up to nothing else."

The big guy laughed and said, "I would hope you would be doing nothing less." I noticed after a while that Johanna was one of the main reasons he hung out with us. Mark told me that there have been many nights where he would talk about nothing but her. He would mostly talk to himself, thinking Mark wasn't listening. If he knew the things he said aloud, he would be begging Mark not to tell anyone.

The four of us were chatting when other students filed into the music room. Someone claimed the piano and drum kit. Sighing, I mumbled, "I'll have to jam with my siblings another day…again."

"Why don't you just ask Myles for a separate room with extra equipment to practice in?" Johanna suggested.

"He's given me enough," I told her. "I don't want him to think that I'm using him."

"Good point," she responded. "Anyway, I told Shannon and Aymie we'd hang this afternoon. Care to join us, boys?"

Accepting her invite, we followed her out of the room, and Peggy came back, returning Blake's camera. "Thanks for letting me borrow it. I had fun." Without another word, she ran off to find her other sisters.

"How many do you think you need to get rid of?" Johanna whispered.

Blake shrugged. "I'll take a look later and only keep the good ones."

"If any," Nic added.

Before joining Peggy, Rebecca and Agnes snatched my guitar from my hands. Giggling, they galloped out of the room with my precious instrument. "Please be careful while practicing 'Thunder-duck'!" I called to them.

Blake and Nic were confused while Johanna laughed. "I almost began to miss that song," she said. "Now, I think I am going to start hating it again." She smiled and remembered the old days. "Ah memories. Not a day goes by where we don't miss them…" Her eyes became distant as she thought of her family. "I still can't believe they're gone sometimes," she mumbled as she became lost in thought.

Nic waved his big hand in front of her face. When she snapped out of her trance, he said, "Weren't we going somewhere?"

Johanna pulled herself together and led us out. As we walked, a flood of people wanting to hang with me rushed our way. They were mostly girls. Any of the guys that were there just wanted to just get with the females I had swarming me. I tried not to be rude when I repeatedly told them that I was spending time with old friends.

When they didn't listen, Nic gave the crowd a stare that scared them to death. His glare was cold and frightening. My swarm scattered and left us alone. "Hope you don't mind me freaking out your lady friends," Nic told me after another ran off.

"By all means, please do," I said, honestly. "I didn't realize being popular was so much work."

When we entered the dining hall, Blake pointed to a group ahead of us. "You aren't the only one who is popular." Shannon and Aymie were sitting with Mark, Sonny, my sister's gang, and a few others I didn't recognize.

"I thought popularity was Shane's thing," Johanna teased as we went over to them.

"It is," Shannon said. She kept her eyes locked on the paper she was writing. "We just have friends of friends of friends with us."

"What am I considered?" Mark asked, nervous. Something was off about him that day, and I couldn't put my finger on it. He glanced around the room like a dog on patrol. He wouldn't stop tapping his feet (which was really annoying). Shannon would be able to tell in an instant what was wrong with her amazing deduction skills.

Speaking of Shannon, she didn't seem herself either. As she wrote, her movements were harsh. Her expression was more angry than concentrated. Normally, when she worked, she was quick, elegant, and precise. In the moment, she looked rushed and not in her right mind. *What's going on?* I wondered.

Aymie interrupted my problem solving. "You don't count," she told Mark, poking his arm. She looked up at us and said, "Come, sit, and help us out."

"What are you doing?" Blake asked as he sat in an empty seat on her left.

Aymie pointed to a guy sitting next to Sonny who was on Shannon's right. He wore a clean button up with the sleeves rolled up.

His dark brown hair was clean and his face shaved. He looked ready for a fancy party or job interview.

"You remember Joshua Wolfrum; the guy who picked you up?" Aymie asked. "Well, there is an opening for a Royal Veteran Umbrella. We are trying to get him that."

"This means so much to me," Joshua told everyone, fiddling with a button on his sleeve. "You guys are the best."

"Don't thank us yet," Shannon said as she finished the letter. She passed it and the pen to Aymie. "Sign the back of it and then get everyone to do the same."

"Wait, that's all you have to do to become a Royal Veteran?" I asked. "Write a letter and get signatures?"

"It's not that simple," she replied, sharply; quite unlike her. "You have to have witnesses to your good works, determination, and a long list of reasons why you should be chosen. That's only to become a Royal. After that, you have to be handpicked and voted in by Mr. Wyght, Mr. Powell, and the other Veterans. This is the first step."

"Which I think will go well," Umbrella Dylan Cheatle stated after signing the paper. He held out his chubby hand and gave the letter to Roxanne. "You are an inspiration to us all, Joshua."

The young man smiled. "I try."

Groaning, Sonny tried to get up to leave, but Zander stopped him. "You know you can't go anywhere without me. It's my turn to pick what we do at free time."

"You guys still don't trust me?" his raspy voice whined.

"Once you make friends and start opening up, then we'll trust you," Roxanne said rudely.

Under his breath, Sonny said some probably not-so-nice things in Russian. Every time he complained about something it was always in a different language then the last time, and he complains a lot.

Once we all signed, Joshua snatched the letter and hopped over the table. "I'll see you all later. Wish me luck guys!" In no time, he was out of sight.

"I hope it all goes well," Aymie said, fixing her wig. Ever since Blake joined, she was never seen without it and she was always dolled up. I  thought she looked fine without the whole getup, but a brother's opinion probably never mattered, so I never told her. Once she was sure it was still on, she added, "He really is a great guy."

Zander put his hand on his chest, "Not as great as me, I hope," he teased.

"No one is as great as you, Zander," she replied sarcastically. "Except maybe Blake of course." She elbowed her best friend who was busy deleting the photos Peggy took to hear the compliment.

Zander turned green with envy. He was always jealous of Blake and Aymie's friendship. From time to time, he would mutter that he wish he'd never asked Joshua to get Blake from the orphanage. I think he was hoping to impress my sister, but it backfired.

*Speaking of impressing girls,* I thought, looking at Shannon. Her blue eyes seemed far away, and she was thinking hard. Before I could say anything, everyone started to stand up.

"Well, I think I'm going to go workout in the gym downstairs," Nic said. He stretched his unnaturally long, buff arms.

Johanna chuckled. "This is going to sound weird, but I think that's a good idea. I'll join you. I haven't exercised at *all* this week. I have to practice what I preach." Being a counselor, she would always have kids who would complain about being tired, sluggish, or feeling depressed. One thing she told them was to exercise and take vitamins. An old but surefire trick she learned from her medical expert parents.

At the sound of that, Nic's face lit up. "Awesome. Anyone else want to come?"

"I won't join you, but I will be there," Sonny told them as he started walking away.

Zander exhaled sharply and threw his arms in the air. "I guess I'll be there too," he said, following his responsibility.

Roxanne laughed at him. "Let's just go and make sure they don't beat each other up." With that, they left for the gym.

While the others that stayed behind were busy talking, I decided to try and start a conversation with Shannon. I sat down across from her and cleared my throat. "So, how's the detective work been?"

Without looking up from her notebook, she replied,

"Exceptional."

I nodded. When she didn't say anything else, I asked a follow up question, but still received a one word answer.

*Now I know something's up,* I thought. I mentally went through a list of things that usually got Shannon to talk. I crossed my arms and rested them on the table. I tried to show off my muscles through my tight long sleeve shirt. Being an Agricola was like working out every day. I didn't need to spend as much time in the gym for exercise. I also ran for miles no matter the weather and would practice my acrobatics. When I lived with the Hollinger's, Shannon and the girls would love to watch me do flips and such.

*That's it,* I realized. "So, I started working on my acrobatics again," I told her, subconsciously rubbing my arms. "I'm determined to be better at it than before; along with being faster on my feet."

"That's good. You're good at it," she said emotionless. I would have appreciated the comment if she wasn't so… bleh.

Before I could continue, a beeping went off on Mark's watch. "Shannon," he whispered, looking at her. His blue eyes seemed to shake as if his watch gave him horrendous news.

Shannon nodded, grabbed her things, and jumped up. Mark stood from his seat and they raced off together.

One of Aymie's friends—Alexandrea—looked at them leave and then at my shocked expression. "Ouch, that's rough," she said, fixing her blonde ponytail. She came and sat next to me and attempted to flirt. She smacked my back with her heavy fire proof work gloves. "She just doesn't appreciate you like some other girls do."

Not wanting to keep that conversation going, I decided to follow them. I quickly excused myself and ran off, ignoring Alexandrea and Aymie who called after me.

I ran into the crowded hallway and asked people where they went. Finding a likely answer, I headed down the hall past the music room, the gallery, and the chapel until I finally reached the computer room where the Nerds worked.

I opened the door and rushed in. I was blinded by red light. The large, dark room was illuminated by flashing crimson warning symbols that displayed on every monitor. Walking down the aisle, I glanced at each one and tried to understand what I was seeing. The screens were flashing red and code quickly scrolled down like ending movie credits.

I approached the front computer where the blind guy, Shannon, Mark and his two friends were standing. "What is going on?" I asked.

Mark turned to me and said, "Nothing, go back to your friends."

"What's that supposed to mean?" I snapped. "And yes there is something happening."

Just then, the computers simultaneously made a deafening beeping noise. "That was one," Mark told everyone, uncovering his ears.

"Will this actually work?" his short friend with almond eyes asked.

"It will, Derek," Shannon stated, confidently. "Mark knows what he is doing."

"Just what *is* he doing?" I begged. "And what is a Combatant doing in Nerd work?"

"Why do you care?" she retorted. There was a second loud beep. "That's two," she whispered.

Before I could answer her, Thyme barged in. "Is it almost finished, Vandewater?" he panted. His black face was covered in sweat.

"Eight more beeps," the blind guy responded.

Thyme groaned. "The suspense is killing me." He went down the aisle stairs and stood behind his Royal Veteran comrade. "And when Mr. Wyght and Mr. Powell catch up, they will *kill* me."

Mark turned pale. "What? How did they find out? I thought you were keeping them away from all electronics until it was over."

"I tried!" he bellowed. "It's not my fault Mr. Powell is an inventor of devices that are connected to the internet."

With his hands on his ginger hair, Mark's other friend—Clive—asked, "This won't damage the devices, will it?"

"It shouldn't," Mark responded. "I guess we'll find out." There was a third obnoxious beep.

After a few minutes, we heard the fourth… and then the fifth.

"It's getting faster," Mark pointed out as he chewed on his first finger.

Then, the door swung open and hit the wall with a loud *BAM*. Mr. Wyght loomed in the doorway and bellowed, "JUSTIN THYME!"

"No, it's too late!" Derek responded. He didn't understand. "There's no time to stop it."

"That's not what I said," the older man growled. Stomping over to the Royal Veteran Combatant, Mr. Wyght grabbed the young man's collar and began shaking him. "Justin, what is the meaning of this?!" he yelled.

All the computers beeped twice more.

"Don't be mad at him, sir," Vandewater said, kindly. He turned around in his leather seat. "This is none of his fault."

"Whose is it then?!" he barked, letting Thyme go.

Vandewater was about to take the blame when my brother spoke up: "It's mine. Don't punish anyone else. It was all me." Mr. Wyght opened his mouth to speak, but two more beeps interrupted him.

"One more," Shannon whispered. We all stood in silence and waited for the final beep.

After a minute of suspense, there was an ear piercing noise that lasted thirty seconds while the computers randomly flashed colors. Code fell from the top to the bottom of the screens like a waterfall.

Suddenly, it all stopped and the computers shut down simultaneously.

Everything was quiet.

# CHAPTER 33
## Shane: XIII

Isn't the suspense killing you all? Sorry we needed to stop. We are more than halfway to our destination though. Stalling? I'm not stalling, Aaron. Okay, okay fine! I'll tell you what happened.

Everyone froze. We stood still in the dark, quiet room. "If text pops up saying 'Shall we play a game' I will pee myself," Derek whispered, breaking the eerie silence.

After another moment, the screens flashed back on. The mother computer made some odd noises. A green text field appeared on the screen, asking for a login. Vandewater entered his information and unlocked the computer. It clicked and beeped. He typed again and got more weird sounds. "My computer is fine," he told us.

"Wait, how do you know?" I asked.

"His computer talks to him, stupid," Mark insulted. "Whatever coding appears on the screen, it beeps to him and he can understand what it's displaying."

"That's sick, Guy," Thyme complimented. "Reminds me of that movie with the hacker and the people living in the artificial computer reality. They were able to make pictures out of code. I guess they can do anything nowadays."

"That wasn't my inspiration when I programmed it, but I suppose that's a good analogy, Justin," Vandewater replied as he continued typing.

"Okay, before we go further into this conversation," I interrupted, "can I address something?" I turned to Shannon's superior. "I don't mean to sound rude, but is your name really Justin? Justin Thyme?"

"Yeah, that's me," he replied. He rubbed his dark crew cut hair. "I think that's one of the reasons my parents ditched me. They gave me a horrible name and were embarrassed."

"I find it intriguing," Shannon told him without looking back. She kept her arms crossed and stared at Vandewater's screen. "Is it all gone?"

Vandewater opened a browser in a display on the left so we could see what he was doing. He entered information into the search, but was denied. Tried again, same result. Then, he opened unfamiliar software. After a few more failed search attempts, he sat back in his chair and chuckled. "It's all gone. There is nothing," he said with disbelief. "Not on the regular internet, Darknet, nothing."

Shannon turned to my brother. "Mark, you did it," she said softly.

"I did it?" he whispered. He paused for a moment and shook his head, not believing it. To check for himself, he ran back up the stairs and sat at his own computer. He typed frantically for a few moments. His searches failed. "No…way…" he exclaimed, "I did it?!" He threw his head back and started laughing. "I did it! Oh, I can't believe it."

The Nerds and two Combatants began celebrating. Shannon ran up to Mark and wrapped her arms around him. His face turned bright red while mine turned green.

"What did he do?!" Mr. Wyght yelled, impatient.

Standing up, Vandewater went next to Thyme and explained, "Sir, you have just witnessed the greatest hacker in the world make an astounding achievement." Vandewater motioned his hand to Mark who still had his arms around Shannon. "As of this moment, the Order of Xenophon has been *completely* removed from the internet."

The older man's eyes widened. "What?"

"You heard him," Clive clarified. "OX's digital presence has been deleted. They cannot sell, promote, or even communicate via internet or Darknet. It will take years to get rid of Mark's virus that infected the entire world."

Mr. Wyght stood there dumbfounded. He tried to think of something to say, but couldn't fathom it. "This isn't possible…" he mumbled.

"Well, it is," Derek added with a smile.

Putting his hand on the shocked man's shoulder, Thyme said, "Sir, this is the opportunity we've been waiting for."

We stood in silence for a few moments, letting Mr. Wyght understand. It finally soaked in and Mr. Wyght began laughing. "This is insanity! How did you do it?" he asked, but immediately dismissed, "Oh, that doesn't matter. We must start planning immediately." He turned and danced up the stairs, humming a song of praise to his Creator. Before exiting, he looked back down at us and exclaimed, "This is a glorious day! Come, Thyme and Vandewater. We have much to do." When the two joined him, the older man looked at my brother and grinned. "Mark, I expect a new title for you in the near future." With that, the three happily left.

"No. Way," Clive said with his mouth open. "Does he mean?"

"I'm sure he does," Shannon beamed, elbowing Mark.

He pushed his long bang behind his ear and blushed. "I can't take all the credit, though. You were always there to support me. You should get something. It is your birthday after all."

I slapped my palm to my face. *Stupid, stupid, stupid*, I scolded myself. "It's January sixth, isn't it?" I muttered with my hand over my mouth.

"So, now you remember," she accused. "I thought you were too busy with the ladies to care."

"Are you mad at me?" I hissed. "I would've thought of your birthday sooner or later. And for the record, they hang out with me. I don't hang out with them."

"Sounds the same," she retorted with her arms crossed. "But that's not really why I'm upset with you."

"So you *are* mad." I glared down at her. Despite her height, she was still intimidating. Her brow was furrowed and she stared right back without flinching. Her fighting uniform didn't help.

"Okay, I am going to go spread the good news before this gets ugly," Derek said, inching away.

"Let me help you," Clive added. The two of them bolted, leaving the three of us alone.

"Tell me why you're 'upset' with me," I demanded with my fists clenched.

She never altered her gaze as she let it all out. "You've changed," she began. "You aren't the fun, kind, caring Shane we found in our backyard years ago. Ever since we've been here you haven't been happy as an Agricola and won't be until you get your way." She took a deep breath. "You're mad at us because we are content, so you stay away from us. You only hang out with us when *you* feel like it." She held her arm out in front of Mark. "You've been here three months and haven't spent any time with your brother or sister. You talk about starting a band, but that's just another popularity thing, isn't it?"

*I hate when she does that*, I thought bitterly. She always knew my true intentions, but I wasn't going to give her that satisfaction. Not wanting to admit defeat, I did something I regretted. "What would you know? You're just a stupid thirteen-year-old girl who thinks she's a detective and can solve every case. You know what? You know *nothing*." I leaned over her and growled, "This isn't like your stupid mystery stories. In ten years after you become a cop and earn the detective title, then talk to me."

She bit her lip and clenched her quaking fists, trying to contain her emotions. It was no use. Her blue eyes watered and tears dampened her freckled cheeks. She hung her head low. "I'm fourteen now," she choked. "Not that you'd care." Without saying another word, she calmly walked up the stairs and out of the room.

"What's your beef, dude?!" Mark exploded once she left. "How could you say something like that?"

"My 'beef'?" I responded. "My 'beef' is that my friends think I don't care about them." I looked at him up and down. "And since when did she start hanging out with a deadbeat like you?"

# SHANE: XIII

Taken aback, Mark's eyes widened. He put his lean hand on his chest. "'Deadbeat'? Is that what you think I am?" he scowled. "Out of all the insults, you choose deadbeat. I think of myself as a crook, a thief, and a liar. Unlike you, I have to work *hard* to achieve anything." He stormed toward me, leaving only an inch between us. He jabbed his bony finger into my chest. "Listen, circus boy," he sneered, "insulting me doesn't work. But you better listen carefully." His blue eyes became serious and sharp as he glared, cutting me deeply. "You ever make my best friend cry again, I will *destroy* you. I don't care if you claim to be my brother." He tore his finger away and left me alone in the computer room.

Full of rage and pride, I began cussing aloud and blaming Shannon and Mark. *How dare they? Why do they hate me so much?* I thought bitterly. Frustrated, I stomped up the stairs, down the hall, and out the back door. I didn't know what to do. So, I did what I was good at.

I ran.

I raced past the barn, across the training fields, behind the jet runway, and all the way to the base of the mountains. Without looking back, I hiked. I trekked up through snow until I reached the top. I skidded to a stop before falling off the edge of the cliff. White rocks plummeted to the abyss beneath my feet. The orange setting sun bounced off the bright ground, illuminating the hilltops.

The beautiful sight didn't calm my nerves. I tried to steady my breathing. Frustrated, my eyes squeezed shut and my fists clenched. I took a long breath. On the exhale, I screamed at the valleys and rivers below. I let my voice shake the trees and frighten the birds. I shouted and yelled until I felt my throat bleed.

When my voice was gone and my energy spent, I collapsed to the snowy ground. I crossed my legs and hid my face in my hands. The enraged emotions that swirled inside of me began to cease. My head was clearing, but I still couldn't understand. I looked up from my hands wet with tears and out at the view. The scenery was gorgeous, but I couldn't enjoy it.

*It looks like the first day my life changed.* I remembered the orange sunset and the fluffy purple clouds. *The first time I ran.* I glanced back down at my hands and saw the tears. Terrified, I wiped them away.

I tried to brush aside the memory of the last hiking trip I took with my aunt and uncle; the memory of them being plunged into a river immediately after. The night I became a scared runaway. That day still haunted me. My brave, happy façade masked who I truly was.

*But what does that have to do with anything today?* I thought, trying to understand my confusing, dramatic teenage feelings. Puberty does nasty things to you. I continued to wonder, *Why are things the way they are? Why am I even here?*

Suddenly, my mind flashed back to that first night with the Hollingers. The first time I tried to sit in silence. Shannon's words came flooding back. "*It's only in the silence that we can truly hear*", I remembered her saying.

"'Only in the silence will we find the truth'," I finished aloud.

I sat up straight and closed my eyes. I listened for the first time since we left the Hollinger home.

I never knew if I got a real answer, but I was given what I needed to get through the moment. It took a while, but I finally remembered the kind voices of Uncle Chuck and Aunt Monika, my friends at the circus, and the new family I had at WHYP. I felt like I was reliving my greatest memories with them. I recalled the day I became a believer in the Truth. I felt the peace I had that day. Unfortunately, everything faded in an instant.

*Everyone has done so much for me,* I realized. *I think I should give something back.*

I opened my eyes and let out the breath I was holding. I put my hands together and looked at the starry winter sky. "Thank you." Standing up, I wiped the snow off my pants and headed back. In the dark, I carefully descended the mountain, crossed the fields, and made it to the back door.

I shook the snow off my sneakers and went inside to find the house eerily quiet. No one was around. I peeked in all the rooms and found them vacant. "Hello?" I called, finally. My voice bounced off the walls and echoed throughout the mansion.

I wandered endlessly until a familiar voice shouted, "THERE YOU ARE!" Turning around, I saw Johanna coming out of the ballroom doorway and stomping towards me. She did *not* look happy.

"Whoa, what's wrong," I asked nervously. She wore a long emerald dress and her hair was pulled into an elegant bun, but her enraged expressions outshone her beauty. Her brow was furrowed, her teeth gritted, and her fist clenched. She was so tense I thought she was going to pop. Without warning, she pulled her arm back and drove her fist into my stomach.

Staggering backwards, I winced and gasped for air. "What… was," I panted, but couldn't finish. I wrapped my arms around my torso.

"If you ever make my best friend cry again you will need counseling even *I* can't provide!" she bellowed. She swung again, but thankfully I was quick. I grabbed her arm and threw her downward. She fell hard on her knees, almost tearing her maxi dress

"Hey, hold on!" Aymie shouted before Johanna could get up. "What are you doing?" She raced towards us and grabbed her friend. Looking at me she said, "What did you do?"

"She started it," I protested.

"Okay, sure," Aymie replied, rolling her eyes. My sister was also dressed formally in a bright pink frilly dress. I wondered what I was missing…

Johanna stood up and rubbed her legs. "No, he is right. I started it."

Surprised, my sister looked at her friend and said, "Seriously?"

She nodded and fixed her heart-key necklace. "I punched him." Thinking about it, she replied, "It actually felt good."

"Of course it did. Anger needs to go somewhere," a raspy voice spoke up. Sonny had heard the commotion and came out from the ballroom to see what was happening. He was wearing his Combatant uniform. "Is the fight over, though? I wanted to bet."

Zander, who was wearing a suit, came jogging out of the room and went up to Sonny. "Stop leaving! We are enjoying this celebration whether you want to or not."

He rolled his red eyes. "Make it entertaining. Then I'll enjoy it."

Zander pretended to strangle him. After some dirty looks, Zander shook his head and came over to us. "Aymie, you need help?" he asked, fixing his long slick hair.

Johanna answered for her. "No, we're okay. You take your son and go enjoy yourself."

"Oh please, my son would be much better behaved," Zander replied, pointing over his shoulder to the edgy teen.

Sonny scoffed. "You would be a terrible parent, but you are better than the demon I had as a father figure." Without saying anything else, he went back to the ballroom.

"I think he complimented you," Aymie said, still holding Johanna's arm. "That's a start."

Zander shook his head. "I should be so lucky." Before leaving, he asked Aymie, "You still interested in that dance?"

She smiled. "Blake hasn't asked me yet so why not?" Instead of being excited that she accepted, Zander was a little disappointed that he was her second choice. He simply nodded and went back.

"Wait, dance? What's going on?" I asked, rubbing my new bruises.

"Where have you been?" Johanna asked, snobby. "Joshua Wolfrum became a Royal so we are celebrating."

I was relieved. *Mark isn't a Royal, yet,* I thought, still jealous at what Mr. Wyght told him.

"Seriously, where have you been?" Aymie questioned, concerned. She took another look at me. "Why are you all wet?"

"I was thinking clearly," I responded, glancing down at myself. I tried not to freak out that water had soaked my clothes. "I wanted to apologize to Shannon, Mark, and all of you."

Aymie raised her drawn on eyebrows. "To us? For what?"

"Everything," I replied. I kept my eyes to the ground. "I wanted to say sorry for not being around and for taking you for granted. You are my sister and I know nothing about you. I never took the time, but I won't make that mistake anymore." I lifted my head and looked into her gray eyes. "Can I become your brother?"

"Don't you mean 'may I'?" Johanna interrupted the moment.

"You know what I meant," I retorted. "I am sorry for my bad English, Johanna. Also sorry for throwing you on the ground."

She thought and said, "I forgive you for both, but if I get knee problems, I am blaming you."

"I forgive you too," Aymie told me. "I want nothing more for you to be my brother." She wrapped her arms around me and hugged me close. I returned the gesture wholeheartedly.

After a moment, Johanna exclaimed, "Yay, family. Now can we get back to the party?"

"Yeah, I'm ready," Aymie said, "but I think Shane has two more apologies to make."

I followed them into the grand ballroom. Round tables covered by white cloths were uniformly placed across the large wooden dance floor. Balloons hung on the curtains of the stage in the front of the room where Mr. Wyght was about to give a speech about Joshua. The founder tapped the microphone and began to speak.

Being me, I didn't listen. I have no memory of what he said. I knew Joshua was awesome and that's all that mattered. Throughout the whole speech, I looked around for Mark and Shannon. I finally spotted them standing to the left of the stage.

While Mr. Wyght was still talking, I tiptoed my way forward. He finished his speech when I reached them. When the clapping ceased, I tapped Shannon on the shoulder. Without turning around, she said. "Enjoying the party, Shane?"

"Actually, nobody told me about it," I mumbled. I paused and collected my thoughts. Finally, I said the two words that wounded my ego the most: "I'm sorry."

"What was that?" she asked, still facing forward.

I took a deep breath. "You were right," I told her, crushing my pride. "I was upset because I was separated from you all, and I made it worse by blaming everyone else. Not to mention, my past still has a hold on my emotions. I hope you can forgive those terrible, untrue things I said."

She turned around. Her blue eyes were puffy, and her freckled cheeks were stained with tears. Her long curly hair wasn't at its best; even her purple dress was disheveled. *She still looks amazing*, I thought. Feeling awful that I caused that, I begged, "Please, please, forgive me."

"Only if you talk to Mark," she replied, subconsciously wiping her nose.

"I was planning on it," I told her.

She showed me that beautiful smile I adored. "Then of course I forgive you, Shane Hodgins," she said with sincerity.

I felt a weight lift off my shoulders. "Thank you," I replied. I looked up and searched for Mark. When I spotted him, I said, "Don't go anywhere, I'll be back."

She understood, and I went to my brother who was talking with Thyme… Justin Thyme. *I still can't get over his name,* I thought at an inappropriate…*Thyme*.

Sorry, bad pun.

Mark saw me coming, but acted like he didn't. When I went to him, he pretended to be surprised. "There you are," he greeted. "How many ladies have you danced with so far? Have you counted?"

Not wanting to get upset, I got to the point. "I'm sorry. Truly, I am. I didn't mean what I said, and—"

Mark put his hand up, stopping me. "I don't care. I've been treated worse. I was mad for Shannon." He put his hand over his heart and rubbed his chest. "Besides, I haven't told you everything. I feel like it's time we started being brothers. You know?"

I perked up. "Exactly what I was going to say." I held out my hand. "So, you forgive me?"

He shook it. "Of course, man, but before we do any 'brothering' let's enjoy ourselves."

Myles came over and joined us. "There you are!" he cried, looking up at me. "Everything okay?" His blue eyes were filled with worry.

"Never better," I reassured him, rubbing his blond head of hair.

The boy smiled as he felt my palm ruffle his locks. "Oh, good."

he said. "You are just in time. I'm so excited. The girls are going to sing."

As he said that, there was the sound of a microphone falling on the stage and crashing into a drum cymbal. Looking up, we saw Carol-Ann and Agnes trying to fix it as the sound of feedback rang through the hall. The piercing noise ceased and Rebecca came out carrying my guitar with Peggy and Lucy behind her.

Mark chuckled at the sight. "These chicks are the best."

Inside I was freaking out that they were swinging my guitar around. Outside I tried to remain calm. "What are they doing?" I asked as unruffled as possible.

Mark shrugged. "Something about a duck and happy birthday."

Standing on her tip toes, Rebecca yelled, "Is this on?!" After receiving more obnoxious feedback, she went on to say, "We are going to play a song on Clarius' guitar."

"Thunder-duck!" Agnes screamed.

Taking the guitar from Rebecca, Peggy whispered, "Not now; maybe later." She stood by the microphone with her sisters on both sides. She put the strap around her and began playing. Together, the five girls sang "Happy Birthday" for their big sister. Immediately after, they faded into their beautiful Gaelic Lullaby. It was adorable. They sang loud and strong, and the older ones tried harmonizing. What meant the most was that they did it because they loved Shannon.

When they finished, the girls received a standing ovation. Excited, they started dancing on stage.

Mark laughed at the sight. "I hope the three of us end up being as good of siblings as these girls."

"You will," Shannon said behind me.

"Thanks, beautiful," Mark replied, winking. "Happy birthday."

I wished her the same: "Happy Birthday, Shannon."

"Thanks guys," she replied. She glanced up at her sisters on the stage and then back at me. With a mischievous look, she said, "I know what you can do to make it up to me."

Before I knew it, I was shoved on the stage with the five little girls. I wasn't nervous and didn't feel awkward. To be honest, it wasn't the first time. I performed with the girls before and always had fun.

Taking my guitar back, I fixed the microphone and began, "Along with it being a day to celebrate Joshua's awesomeness, it's also the day one of my closest friends was born, as you probably could tell from their song. So if it's all right with Mr. Wyght, we'd like to sing another tune to celebrate both occasions."

From the crowd, Mr. Wyght nodded and shouted, "Let's see what you got."

"Are we playing 'Thunder-duck'?" Carol-Ann asked.

"'Thunder-Duck!' Yes!" Agnes yelled. "'*ABCD*!'"

Sighing, I gave in. Before striking the first chord, Mark jumped on stage and sat behind the drum kit. "I'm pretty sure this song needs these." He twirled his sticks and counted in.

Together, my brother, the girls, and I sang an acoustic version of their favorite song. I sang lead while the girls screamed "Thunder" in between. I have to say, we sounded awesome together. Mark's drumming brought the whole thing to life. We took turns having solos, and we ended strong. Everyone cheered.

I hopped off the stage and let the girls down. Once they were all off, Shannon ran up to me and gave me a hug. "That was an incredible birthday gift. Thank you."

My face turned bright red. "Anything for you," I replied, patting her back.

Stepping away, she looked at Mark and me and said, "You guys are becoming brothers fast."

"Yeah, I guess we are," Mark said, smirking. "Now, we just need Aymie and you to complete our band."

"I'm still thinking about it," Aymie yelled as she ran towards us. "That was surprisingly good. I was never a fan of that kind of music, but man," she turned to me and put her hands on her face. "Your voice. It's amazing. I can't." She couldn't get words out. "It sounds like it belongs in the era of swing and jazz, but it can pull off rock and probably anything."

Johanna chuckled. "You should've heard him before puberty. You wouldn't be saying such nice things."

I laughed sarcastically. "Ha. Very funny, Johanna." I loved Aymie's compliments, but tried to stay modest. "You think I'm good? You should hear Shannon and her mom. That's something to freak out over."

"Thank you," Shannon replied. "My mom would be grateful, I am sure." Her mind drifted for a moment. "My first birthday without them; what a peculiar feeling." She took a shaky breath and whispered, "I miss them so much." She sniffled and tried not to think of it. Turning the attention back to me, she added, "I've always loved the way you sing, though. It's classy. 'Crooner' I think it's called, but you give it a modern feel. I'm not the only fan. It's also Carol-Ann's favorite style."

I blushed again and couldn't find the words to say. Thankfully, Carol-Ann was eavesdropping and interrupted. "People say Clarius kinda sings like '*Michael Bubbles*' and '*Disco Panic*' who copy my jazzy guys."

"You were so close that time," I told her. "'Bubbles' was probably the most accurate."

"I want bubbles!" Rebecca said.

"Bubbles?! Where?!" Agnes shrieked as she ran around looking for them.

"Stop doing that," Johanna scolded. "I swear, one of these days their freak out sessions will get the better of us all."

"You'll miss it," Blake told her. He, Alexandrea, Dylan, and Roxanne came to join us. The three were pushing Blake who had an envelope in his frail hands. Holding it out, he said, "I actually have a gift for you, Shannon. Well, it's from all of us."

"I did all the hard work," Roxanne joked through a mouthful of cupcake. Alexandrea elbowed her.

Surprised, Shannon took the envelope. "That's very kind of you, Blake, but you didn't have to do anything."

He grinned. "I didn't do anything. I just saved the moments."

Opening it, Shannon slid out beautiful photographs of all of us. The captured moments each had a story to tell. "I'm not good with words, so these do it for me." Blake said, smiling.

"These are incredible," Shannon complimented with a grin on her face. "Thank you." She pulled out a picture of the day that started it all. The first time we all sat together.

"I love this one," Johanna whispered.

"What are we looking at?" Nic inquired, coming over with Zander and Sonny. Peering over Johanna's shoulder, he said, "I remember that."

"I would hope so, you were there," Johanna replied.

"I wished I wasn't," Sonny mumbled.

Myles rebuked him. "Don't be so negative. You're enjoying yourself here." Out of the corner of my eye, I saw Sonny smirk.

"Photo credits, me," Zander interjected. "Don't forget that." He tried to joke, but had a disappointed look in his eye. He wasn't in the picture. Not to mention Aymie had her arms around Blake and was hugging him tightly.

After gawking at the images for a while, the party was coming to a close and it was time for bed.

On the way to the boys' floor, I stopped to say one last goodnight to Shannon. She had let all of her sisters run ahead and was the last one to head for the stairs. She saw me coming and stopped before going up the second step. She turned to me and asked, "Something on your mind?"

"Yeah, uh," I hesitated. I wanted to apologize over and over for what I said to her earlier. I wanted to tell her how I *really* felt. However, I was afraid. I couldn't talk to her about it… Instead, I said, "Just wanted to tell you that you already earned the detective title by finding my family."

She blushed and played with her Celtic knot key necklace. I still wondered what was in the box it opened. "Thank you, but I understand," she confessed, interrupting my curiosity. "I have much to learn, but I will make my father proud one day."

I walked up to her. With her on the second step, she was a little taller than me. "You already have," I whispered.

Her eyes sparkled and a smile spread across her face. Before saying another word, she put her hand over my heart, leaned over, and gently kissed me on the cheek.

My eyes opened wide and I felt the blood rushing to my face. My heart pounded so fast and loud it was about to burst out of my chest. She must've put her hand on me to prevent that from happening. When she pulled her lips away, she looked at my shocked expression and giggled. "Thanks again for the birthday gift," she whispered and then went up for the night.

Not knowing how to react, I stood there for a while. My heart was racing, and I couldn't move. *Did she really just do that? I* wondered, amazed. I had been such a jerk to her and then she goes and does that… Then, a thought crossed my mind: *Does she already know how I feel? Does she feel the same?*

I would've been standing there all night if Myles hadn't come up to find me. "Shane," he whispered. "It's time for bed! What are you doing at the bottom of the girls' stairs?"

Not being able to respond, my best friend grabbed my hand and dragged me to our room. I didn't tell him anything. I changed into pajamas and plopped on my bed. Until I drifted off to sleep, I stared at the LED lights in the metal canopy above me. I watched as the colors changed, still in awe that I received my first "kiss".

# THE MAINLAND

# CHAPTER 34

## Aymie: XI

Once Shane starts talking, he can never stop; especially when it's about himself...or Shannon. I'm sorry! I just thought that last bit took a while. I may be impatient, but not as impatient as you.

After Joshua Wolfrum's Royal celebration and Shane's "fit", everything was looking up in our group of friends. However, there was one who started falling away.

Winter faded, spring came and went, and the summer was upon us once again. From June to August, we didn't take any Classical subjects. Instead, we focused more on our regular Branch work in the mornings and had afternoons off.

That summer, I couldn't believe how time flew. An entire year had passed since I left Saint Maria Goretti's and an eventful time it was. My brothers and I were another year older and wiser. Well… I was wiser. Sixteen-year-old boys still aren't mature.

One August afternoon after I had finished my daily seamstress quota, I sat on a supply crate out in the training fields. I was a spectator for an intense football game. As I watched the teams clash, my mind drifted back to the times I would play sports with the sisters at the orphanage. It was always exciting to see the sisters in full habit racing across the field, their veils flowing in the wind. I had so many wonderful memories with them and my friends there…especially Janelle

Thinking about her, I felt awful. Not only about what had happened, but how I didn't think of her as often as I should have. I always forgot about the sacrifice she made for me.

Blake interrupted my thoughts. "Aymie!" he called. "Check out this picture of Shane and Mark I just took." He ran over, rested his back against the crate, and held up his camera.

I leaned over and expected to see my brothers making a fool of themselves, but was surprised. It was a picture of them with their heads together preparing to tackle each other. The action shot was dramatic and made the two sweaty teens look attractive. Mark wore a green workout shirt and black shorts and was reaching for his brother. Shane was topless (again) with his combat pants and had his guard up. Their expressions were determined yet they were smiling.

"That's pretty good," I complimented. "What's the story?"

Blake chuckled. He always had a deep explanation for each photo he took. "It shows how much they've grown as brothers," he began. "To make it short, even though they still fight, argue, and compete, they still care about each other. Their smiles say it all. No matter what battles they're going through, whether it's with each other or something else, they will always be brothers."

I nodded. "I sure hope that's the case."

As Blake went through the other images, half time was called and the players took a break. I was by the water dispenser so everyone swarmed around me.

"Yo, Aymie, why aren't you playing?" Roxanne asked, pouring water on her curly hair. "You're missing out."

"I have my reasons," I said. I tapped my wig.

She scoffed. "Not a good one."

"She's got a very important job," Alexandrea said. Holding both arms out, she gestured to the water dispenser. "She is the Mighty $H_2O$ Guardian."

"That's a high honor," Zander joked. With wide eyes, he asked,

"Aymie, did you see that last play I made? It was pretty awesome."

"I'm sorry, Zander, I think I missed the last few minutes," I confessed. He looked at Blake then back at me. Disappointed, he nodded and continued drinking.

Dylan jogged over. Johanna followed and cheered him on. When he reached us, he put his hands on his knees and panted, "This…is… torture."

"What? Running is great!" Shane chimed in, avoiding everyone drinking water.

"It's only great for you, '*Zippy*'," Johanna mocked. She put her hands on her hips. "It's harder for the rest of us."

Roxanne snickered. "That is the worst stage name ever."

Sonny got in on the taunting. "I would rather keep the name of my demonic father figure than be called 'Zippy Presto'," he stated. He really opened up over the past couple months.

Shane rolled his head back. "I was, like, seven," he whined, "and they gave me that name."

Sonny put his long dark hair into a pony tail. "You agreed upon it, circus boy," he mocked.

"I was going to call him that," Roxanne complained. "You keep beating me to my insults."

While the three were bickering, Mark came over to me. He pushed his damp bang behind his ear. "Well, seems like I don't have to keep an eye on Sonny anymore," he said. "He fits right in."

Blake shook his head. "I don't know. I got a bad feeling recently."

"Did you have another dream?" I asked, concerned. When he nodded, I smacked his shoulder. "Why didn't you tell me?!"

"I can't yet," he whispered. He looked around to see if anyone else was listening. "I feel like someone is going to betray us… but I can't tell you now. Not in public."

"Whoa, man, you can't be alone with my sister," Mark joked, ignoring the comment about a betrayal.

Blake held his hands up. "Whatever you say, Royal Nerd Mark. You're the brother *and* the boss."

He chuckled. "I'm no Veteran, man. I still think the Branch title 'Nerd' is insulting but the 'Royal' part is nice. I still can't believe Shane wrote that letter and got practically everyone to sign. That isn't like him."

"Ever since the day you sent the virus, he's been coming around more," I stated.

"I knew he would," Blake said, smirking.

"What, did you have a dream?" Mark teased. Remembering the first time Blake told his friends about his premonitions, he added, "But seriously. These dreams of yours are dumb crazy. I still can't believe how you saw the towers fall in New York City."

"I couldn't believe when I saw it for the second time on television," Blake replied. His light blue eyes became far away and distant. It was as if he was watching the scene replay before him. A yell from a Combatant practicing on the field snapped him back into reality. "Nic mentioned that he was there that day," he added. "I wonder what that was like."

"Well, after he talked about it, he ran out of the room and started spazzing out again," Mark reminded. "That triggered something. Whenever that day is brought up, he goes out of control worse than ever. With the anniversary approaching soon, people have been mentioning it so he freaks out even more than normal." He scratched his sweaty head. "I have a theory that *that* is the main cause of all his problems. Something happened that day that he can't cope with and his 'issues' take over."

"'Theory'? You are hanging with Shannon too much," I teased. Ever since he started spending time with her, he began to change. He had theories for everything and always asked questions unlike his previous philosophy of "going with the flow". Not to mention he was always so happy when he was with her. *If this escalates, things might get complicated,* I thought, looking at Shane.

"Are you allowed to tell us why Nic acts like that yet?" Blake questioned.

Mark shook his head. "Not yet. If he has another mad crazy accident then we tell everyone." He flicked his silver hoop earrings. "I feel bad for him. He is such a nice guy and then he turns into a jerk."

As we were speaking, we heard a commotion on the field. I saw Thyme standing over Nic who was doubled over on the ground. He lay motionless on the green grass.

"Uh oh, speak of the Beast," Mark sighed.

"Is he going to have a fit?" Roxanne asked after she gave up arguing with Shane and Sonny. "Is that what he does?"

"It depends," Mark replied. "Sometimes he'll lay there for a while just making noise. Other times he jumps up and starts going nuts."

Thankfully, it was the first one. After confirming he was okay, Thyme announced to leave him be. I felt bad for the guy. It was embarrassing to be the biggest, strongest one of the group and be easily knocked down.

"I guess we won't be playing the game for a while," Zander remarked. "It's happened during combat training several times. The longest he stayed like that was four hours."

"That's what I don't understand," Mark began, "because wouldn't he—" quickly he stopped himself.

Before I could press him to finish the sentence, Shannon yelled from the warehouse. "Sonny, Zander, Mark! Time for the meeting!"

"We will settle this later, Zippy," I overheard Sonny say to Shane. He walked away with Zander quietly trudging behind.

*What's wrong with Zander?* I wondered.

Interrupting my worry, Mark said, "Duty calls. Shannon and I are presenting our evidence of an investigation we're working on. Wish us luck." With that, he took another swig of water and ran to the Combatant warehouse.

"I still don't find it fair he gets to skip classes and work with the Combatants," Shane grumbled.

"Stop whining," Roxanne scolded. "You were the one to make him a Royal in the first place."

Johanna chuckled. "He's more jealous because Mark is—" she was interrupted by Shannon calling her name. Surprised, she said, "What do you know. I get in on the secret meeting."

"Wait, Mark is *what*?!" Shane yelled as she ran away.

Dylan rested his forearms on a crate and asked, "Does anyone wonder what they do in there?"

"All the time!" Shane replied instantly. Mumbling, he added, "Shannon and Mark are always alone doing who knows what."

Not hearing him, Alexandrea said, "I heard from Flicks—our Veteran Drone—that they made a breakthrough with a project they were working on. Ever since Mark deleted OX from the internet, Mr. Wyght and Mr. Powell have been working the Royals and Shannon like crazy. Not to mention our RVs are on *constant* missions. They're never here. I know RV Agricola Marian has been gone for months."

"Yeah, that's true, but where does Shannon fit into all this?" Roxanne wondered, cleaning her ear out with her pinky.

"She is good at finding things," Alexandrea said. "Flicks says that thanks to her they've made progress. Now with her working with Mark and Sonny, they finally have what they need to do whatever they have planned."

"Shannon works closely with Sonny too?" Shane muttered, disappointed.

Dylan nodded. "Sonny was a former member of the Order of Xenophon. That's *obviously* what they are working on."

"Guys, Nic is gone," Blake interrupted.

As he said that, there was a metallic *BANG*. Nic stormed out of the meeting warehouse, smashing his fist against the wall as he left. He had a stolen black backpack on his back. He dropped on all fours and started galloping like an animal. He barged through the teens on the field.

Racing out behind him were Mr. Wyght, Thyme, and Sonny. While Thyme and Sonny went after Nic, Mr. Wyght dashed over to us. He abruptly stopped and tried to catch his breath. Something was clenched in his fist. He was covered in sweat and was breathing hard. Emotions of rage and concern shone in his eyes. He looked at my brother and said, "Shane. You're fast, right?"

"The fastest," my brother replied, confidently.

"Complete this task, and I'll make you a Royal," the older man declared, pointing to him.

That was an unexpected response, but it didn't matter. Surprised and excited, Shane's face lit up. "What do you need me to do?"

The older man gripped my brother's hand and placed something in it. I saw a large, filled syringe in Shane's grasp. "Catch him, tackle him, and inject him with this," Mr. Wyght commanded.

"Uh," Shane hesitated, staring at the needle. "What will this do?"

"It won't kill him if that's what you are worrying about," the man snapped. "Now go!" Not saying another word, Shane dashed off.

We saw Nic climbing to the top of one of the high watchtowers. He was rummaging through his backpack, but couldn't find what he was looking for. Before he knew it, Thyme and Sonny were at the top with him and Shane wasn't too far behind. I watched as my brother scaled the side of the tower like a monkey climbing a tree.

When Shane was up there with them, Nic started to feel threatened. At first he lunged at Sonny who quickly dodged but didn't attack. Nic turned to Shane. Flaring his nostrils, he growled and charged.

Unafraid, Shane ran straight for him, jumped, and *flipped* over the tall teen. Nic stood there confused while Thyme and Sonny were impressed.

Nic snapped out of it and started mindlessly swinging his long arms at the three. When Nic was himself, he was an incredible fighter. When he was this Beast he lost the all reasoning and strategy. Thyme, Sonny, and Shane were able to stand their ground and take several blows, surprisingly.

Nic was losing his energy and Shane was about to make a move, but Nic did something that shocked us all.

Nic staggered backwards towards the edge of the tower. Looking over his shoulder, he studied the ground below.

With a grunt, he jumped.

Nic bounded off the tall tower and landed hard on his feet below, leaving a crater in the dirt. Once he regained his balance, he kept running.

*His legs should have broken*, I thought, amazed and horrified.

*What is he?*

"You all get inside and round up the rest of the kids," Mr. Wyght commanded. "Do not come out. Understand?" Once we affirmed, he turned and raced to help.

We went around ordering everyone to get inside. While I was counting the Hollinger sisters, Flicks and Adeline—my superior— came to me. "Aymie, we need your help," Adeline cried.

"You need to stop Shannon and Johanna," Flicks finished, fixing the goggles on his full blond hair.

"What's going on?" I asked.

"They're going to approach Nic by themselves," Adeline told me. "They can't. Nic is armed and unstable."

Gasping, I began to panic. "What am I supposed to do? I'm just a Polymath!" I cried, afraid. I pointed over my shoulder. "Roxanne is a Combatant, have her go."

Adeline shook her head. "We need you to talk them out of it before they get too close. They won't listen to Roxanne or anyone else."

"We tried to stop them, but they ignored us," Flicks explained.

I looked at the two of them. They had such desperation in their eyes. *Why do they trust me?* I wondered. Then, my mind recalled the words of Abigail Quartermane: *"A true princess is obedient..."* Wanting to keep my promise to her, I agreed and dashed off to find them.

I didn't know where I was going, what I was doing, or what I was going to say. I ran across the training field, frantically calling their names. "Shannon! Johanna!" Looking around, I saw our obstacles were destroyed and injured Combatants lay on the ground. *Please, where are you girls.*

I ran for what seemed like an eternity until I saw two girls out of the corner of my eye. They were trekking up the mountain. Immediately, I chased after them.

*Dylan was right,* I thought as I continued my quick ascent. *Running is torture.*

Finally, I caught up. They were stopped behind a tree at the top of the mountain and peering into a clearing that overlooked the valleys below. Shannon clutched a messenger bag that hung over her shoulder.

"Girls!" I shouted as I fixed my sideways wig. "What are you doing?" They ignored me and continued to stare. I went over and stooped behind them. "What are you doing?" I asked.

Holding her hand up, Shannon hushed me. A minute of painful waiting went by until I realized. Nic came huffing and puffing up the mountain and collapsed in the clearing. On his knees, he dropped the pistol he was holding and bent over. He was groaning and growling as he dug his nails into the dirt. After a minute, he abruptly pulled his head up and roared at the sky. His frightening scream was inhuman and it echoed off the mountains below. He put his hands on his head and began to speak. "Please, stop. Please, stop," he begged.

Finally, Shannon and Johanna stepped out of hiding. "No, wait!" I called after them.

"Nic, are you there?" Johanna said aloud. "It's us. It's your friends."

Nic looked up at them. His violet eyes were dilated and had a crazed look. His red Mohawk was a mess and his crimson t-shirt was torn.

"Nic, please, answer us," Johanna begged, deeply concerned for her friend.

He shook his head and looked up again. His pupils shrunk. He stared at the two girls for a moment and then whispered, "No… you can't." He glanced at the pistol on the ground and remembered why he had it. He snatched it and begged, "You have to go, now! Please!"

"No," Johanna told him. She held her hands out. "Put the gun down and then we will go."

Tears began to fall from the big guy's eyes. "Please, you don't understand." He cocked the gun and… put it to his forehead. "Please."

I couldn't believe what I was seeing. *No*, I thought, *Please, don't.* I dug my nails into the tree I leaned against. Behind us, I heard the shouts of Combatants racing up the mountain.

"Get away from me!" he bellowed, baring his sharp teeth. He gripped the pistol tighter until his knuckles turned white. "Leave.

Now."

When the others caught up, they hung back by me when they saw Nic had a weapon. Together we watched as the girls walked closer. Ignoring Mark's and Shane's cries, Shannon and Johanna were five feet from Nic.

Shannon reached into her bag and pulled out another pistol. She cocked it and pressed it to her own forehead. "If you pull yours, I pull mine."

"Shannon, stop!" Shane cried. Mark stood beside him with wide eyes. Sonny and Zander also were shocked at her bravery.

Nic couldn't believe what he was seeing. He twitched as if he was going to change back into the Beast again. Thankfully, he was able to control it for a few seconds. "No. I don't want to hurt anyone anymore. Let me do this."

Johanna crossed her arms and kept her determined gaze locked on our unstable friend. "If you pull it, Shannon pulls it. Then, *I* take it and do the same," she threatened.

Nic inhaled sharply. "No," he whispered. "Please, Johanna, don't. I-I," he tried to say more but nothing would come out. He began twitching and growling. He dropped the gun and shakily put his hands on his head. "I need it to stop, but I can't hurt you," he fell to the ground, "I can't, I can't."

Seeing an opportunity, Shane ran up to Nic with the syringe. As he was about to inject him, the Beast came back. With a snarl, Nic's hand shot up and Shane's arm. Thankfully, my brother was quick. He tossed the needle into the air, grabbed it with the other hand, and plunged it into our friend's neck.

Roaring inhumanly, Nic threw Shane against a tree and stood to his feet. He tried to run, but he staggered and fell to the ground. He convulsed and then lay still. I thought something terrible happened until I heard a low snoring sound.

I let out the breath I was holding and wobbled to a tree for support. Zander came over and put his hand on my shoulder. "You okay?" he asked.

"I'll be fine," I told him. "You should probably go with the others and help them." I waved him away with my hand.

Zander sighed and didn't protest. "Guess you don't want my help, oh wait that's normal," I overheard him mutter. At the moment, I was too shocked to care or wonder what was wrong with him.

I leaned against the tree and watched as Thyme, Zander, and the older Combatants carefully carried Nic down the mountain. It wasn't easy but they did it. My brothers, Sonny, Johanna, and Shannon stayed behind.

"What were you thinking?!" Mark yelled to the girls. "That was dumb crazy. You could have *died*."

"So could've Nic!" Johanna shouted back.

Frustrated, Mark shook his fists in the air. He went over to Shannon and said, "I thought we had a plan. You can't go scaring me like that, beautiful."

"You knew," Sonny interrupted, looking at her. "You knew he was going to try sooner or later."

"Yes," Shannon whispered. "Ever since Mark told me why he acts like that, I began paying even closer attention than before. Every time Nic has a serious incident like this it is always triggered by related things. Like when someone insults his strength and appearance, when someone mentions firefighters, and when—"

"The New York City terrorist attack is mentioned," Mark finished. "I think that's when he became an orphan. I think his parents died in that attack."

"Good observation," she commented. "I absolutely agree. My theory is whenever he gets really depressed or horrible memories come back, the Beast takes over and he has no control."

"I can't believe it," Mark whispered. "He mentioned bits and pieces about that day, why he went to juvenile, and then why he accepted the illegal 'steroids'."

"What steroids do *that*?" I snapped.

Rubbing his bruised head, Shane began to remember something. "Wait, Nic and I were approached by a scientist at the Junior Olympics. He said he had a way of giving us super strength and speed. Nic compared them to steroids, because we weren't sure what he was getting at."

"No one really knows what Mr. Mallory—I mean, the scientist uses," Mark slipped. He immediately regretted using a name.

"Wait that was Mr. Mallory?" Shane said. Mark had told my brother and me a few months ago that he smuggled things for a Carl Mallory that used them in horrific experiments.

"Are you saying Nic is a Mutant experiment?" I questioned.

Mark nodded. "I'm almost positive." He cast his eyes downward. "It's my fault. I helped him get what he needed."

Sonny scoffed. "It isn't your fault. Trust me. Guys like him are manipulative and abusive. You had no control."

"How would you know?" Mark snapped. "I *wanted* to do it."

"You knew nothing else!" Sonny sharply replied. "Trust me. The things I've done and regret are ten times worse than you smuggling drugs for a psycho."

"Although, you did that too," Johanna remarked. "One day you are going to tell us the full story."

Rolling his eyes, Sonny began mumbling something in Korean.

"If you are going to curse in a different language, just pick one," Shane complained. "These different languages are hurting my head."

"Whatever, let's just go," Sonny retorted, walking back. We followed him down the mountain and back into the mansion. It was on lockdown so everyone was in their rooms waiting for further instructions.

"We should probably do the same," Johanna said once we were in the hallway.

We agreed and went our separate ways. I followed Shannon and Johanna up the stairs. Before they went into their room, I asked, "Why did you do that for him?"

They looked at each other and back at me. "Isn't that what friends do?" Johanna asked. "Sure it was crazy, but Nic is also crazy."

"There's a method to our madness," Shannon joked. In an instant, her tone became solemn. "Nic needed to see that people cared for him enough to die for him. It's an extreme, but you know just as well as we do that it's the ultimate sacrifice."

With that, the two friends went in their room to the young Hollinger girls. Quietly, I went into my big pink bedroom where my Polymath peers were waiting for me.

"There you are," Adeline cried, racing down the loft stairs. "We were so worried. What happened?"

"I…don't know if I should tell you yet," I hesitantly responded. "Things happened but everyone's okay."

Adeline nodded and gave me a hug. "I'm happy you're all right."

"Yeah, me too," I replied. Then, the events started to sink in and I became overwhelmed. "I think I need to lie down."

Going up to my bed, I plopped myself on the edge and thought, *He wanted to kill himself? Was it to protect us? Was it to protect himself?* My mind tried to wrap around it for hours until I decided to sleep on it.

# THE MAINLAND

# CHAPTER 35

## Aymie: XII

A month passed before we heard any news of Nic. They took him to a secret holding place that only a select few knew about. Mark wouldn't tell us where he was or about what he was experimented with or if he could be helped.

"Wait for Mr. Wyght to tell you," Mark said one afternoon during free time. He and our usual gang sat around one of the long tables in the dining area. We were going to play cards, but we got sidetracked.

Carol-Ann stood braiding Sonny's long black hair. "Why do we have to wait for the old guy? We were Nic's friends first," the young Hollinger girl asked.

"You met him one time," Roxanne reminded.

"So what?" Carol-Ann retorted, tugging too tightly on Sonny's hair.

After Shannon told her sister to let go of his hair, Sonny said, "This is nothing. I've undergone worse torture than this."

"At least you're a good sport," Dylan chimed in. He rubbed cookie crumbs off his chubby cheeks. "Agnes tried to braid Zander's hair, and he ended up making her cry."

"That was *you*?" Shane exclaimed to the long haired Combatant.

"She was so upset I let her play with my hair to make her feel better." He ran his fingers through his thick, layered locks. "Takes me a while in the morning to make it stick up just right."

Zander kept his dark eyes locked on the deck of cards he shuffled for the fifteenth time. "Girls are too emotional."

"Right now you seem like the emotional one," Alexandrea teased. She smacked her work gloves on the table and almost knocked over our drinks.

Before that fight could begin, Mark, Shannon, and Johanna were called over the intercom. Mark stood up. "We'll let you know if we hear anything."

Shannon handed Rachel to Shane. "Hopefully it will be good news," she added. With that, the three of them left.

*I hope so too*, I thought. Once they were gone, I turned to Blake and asked, "Have you had any dreams about Nic?"

Shocked by the question, he spat out his milk all over Dylan. The baby faced Umbrella sat there, eyes opened wide as milk dripped from his eyebrows.  "Excuse me?!" Blake choked, wiping his mouth with his gray sleeve.

Roxanne smacked her tan forehead. "You idiot! Your stupid 'vision' dreams."

"Oh...I figured that," he muttered. He handed Dylan a napkin. "That just sounded weird." He thought for a moment and shuddered. "To answer your question, no. The last precognitive dream I had was months ago."

"Did it come true?" Dylan wondered, wiping his face clean.

Hesitantly, Blake looked around at us and shook his head. "Not yet. I'm hoping it was nothing, but I have a weird feeling."

I was about to ask what the dream was when the loud doorbell rang. Everyone turned to look at me. "What?" I asked.

"You're the Polymath," Roxanne stated, leaning back in her chair. "You go get the door."

I sighed. "Fine." Standing up, I looked at Shane and commanded, "Come on, you're coming too."

Tearing Rachel's hands from his hair, he replied, "Why? I have the baby."

"She isn't a baby anymore," Carol-Ann corrected. "She's two now."

Rachel continued to smack Shane in the face. "She sure is acting like a baby," he mumbled. He grabbed her hand and told her no. Giggling, the little girl threw her arms around his neck. Shane rubbed her beautiful light curly hair.

I urged him to hurry up and we raced to the door. Before opening it, I fixed my nametag and my outfit. Shane didn't care. He wore his uncle's brown jacket over a blue flannel that was half tucked into his grass stained jeans. He looked like he was a filthy, smelly farm boy. (Thankfully, he actually didn't smell.) *At least he's cute enough to pull it off,* I thought, quickly glancing at my brother.

When I was sure Rachel wouldn't make a fuss, I took a deep breath, opened the door, and found two men on the other side. The man on the left was slim, pale, and had dark intimidating eyes. His hair was neatly trimmed and he had a mustache growing above his lip. He wore a white collared shirt adorned with a lime green tie and gray pants.

The other man had a rougher look. His features were sharp and his posture straight. He wore a new leather jacket over a white shirt and jeans. His crew cut hair was blond and complimented his light gray eyes that looked out through small round glasses.

"Welcome to Wyght's Home for Young People," I greeted, "where the youth of today transform the future of tomorrow. How may we help you?"

The dark haired man slightly bowed. "Hello, my dear," he said in a thick Russian accent. "My name is Nikita Patya and this is my comrade, Walter Jarvis." Walter jerked his chin up slightly as a greeting.

[Yes, mind blown! Mr. Wyght told you before that he knew them. It shouldn't be too much of a surprise. I understand you don't even want to hear their names, but you all wanted to know why they hate the Hodgins' family so much…]

"Pleased to meet you," I replied. "I'm Aymie Hodgins and this is my brother, Shane." Shane smiled and waved Rachel's hand.

At the sound of our names, Nikita's eyes widened. He peered closely at the both of us and slowly responded, "The pleasure is all ours." He shook his head and brought his attention back to why he was there. "We are old military friends of Stanley Wyght. Is he available to meet?"

When Shane didn't say anything, I told them, "I'm not sure. He is currently in a meeting with some of the students. We can give you a tour while we wait, if that's okay."

Smiling, Nikita replied, "That would be wonderful."

We brought the two men inside and showed them around. Shane and I described our schedules, how the Branches worked, who did what, and basically all the ins–and–outs of WHYP.

Throughout it all, Nikita was making notes in a little book while Walter made jokes with Shane.

The long tour ended when we finally found Mr. Wyght. He was conversing with some of our instructors in the arithmetic classroom. Before Shane or I could say anything, Nikita and Walter went over to him.

"Stanley Wyght," the Russian started, "long time no see."

Mr. Wyght turned and stared at the two. After processing it for a few moments, he began to laugh. "Patya, Jarvis! Look at you." He gave them each a tight hug. "How've you been?"

Walter fixed his glasses. "Pretty good," he said in a thick German accent, "considering everything that's happened. Ve have a lot to tell you."

"You must tell me everything," Mr. Wyght exclaimed, but quickly changed his tone. "In a little while, though. I have some things to take care of."

"Any way we could help?" the dark haired man offered.

Mr. Wyght thought it over. "I guess you can join us. If things get out of hand I will need extra manpower." He turned to Shane and added, "No offense."

"None taken," Shane replied, rubbing Rachel's back as she slept. "I'm the one holding the little girl. I won't be of much use."

Mr. Wyght smiled. "You're still of a lot of use especially with that speed of yours. Remember, a month ago we made that deal that if you stopped Nic you would become a Royal. Once he is recovered, that can be arranged."

"I appreciate it, but I didn't stop him," Shane reminded. "Shannon and Johanna did. They should be Royals."

I was shocked. *Where did that humility come from?* The biggest egomaniac turned down one of the highest honors.

Mr. Wyght was also surprised. However, he left the offer on the table. "Well, you've shown great progress in character. I'm still seeing a Royal in your near future."

Shane was ecstatic, but didn't want to show it. He nodded and remained quiet. With a smile, Mr. Wyght turned back to his old friends. "Well, let me finish a few things then I will meet you in the hall. We have someone to attend to." Before leaving, he looked at my brother and me and added, "You two may also join us, but keep it quiet." He left and we went out to the hall wait for him.

When Mr. Wyght returned, we followed him outside, across the field, and into the hangar. Behind the massive jet and several fighter planes was a section for supplies. Hidden behind the boxes was a chrome sliding door.

Mr. Wyght turned to Shane and me and ordered, "Keep quiet and only speak when spoken to. Understood?"

When we agreed, he led us through a large metal door and into a dim back room. In front of us several Royals sat at a table that lined a long glass window.

Nic was on the other side. His arms were outstretched and suspended in the air by chains that attached to the walls on each side. He knelt on the concrete ground and his head hung low. His shirt and jeans were torn and dark hair poked through the rips.

"Mr. Wyght," Thyme greeted, jumping up out of his seat. He looked at Nikita and Walter and asked rudely, "Who are they and why are they here?"

The older man held up his hand. "Relax, Justin. They are old friends of mine. We fought side by side overseas. You should remember them, my boy. Isn't that right gentlemen?"

They were too busy gawking at Nic to hear him. Walter took off his glasses and muttered in German. Nikita took out his notebook and jotted some things down. "Carl was right," I heard him whisper.

"Was Papa E or Johanna able to get through to him again today?" Mr. Wyght inquired.

"Yes, we've made great progress," Thyme informed. "He is more responsive than ever. It's been practically two weeks without an outburst. We are thinking he is okay to be set free."

"Why is he chained like that?" Shane asked, speaking out of turn. I elbowed him. "What?" he whispered.

"Is…that…Shane?" I heard Nic pant over a speaker system. Looking up, I saw our friend tilt his head up and look around. He was breathing heavily and sweating.

"Oops," one said. It was Joshua Wolfrum, the Royal Umbrella. "Forgot to turn off the microphone." He pressed a few buttons on the control panel and put his hands on his dark hair. "Mark needs to write everything down for me."

"Mark?" Nikita questioned.

"Our brother," Shane clarified. "Looks just like me but with a weird half-shaved haircut."

Nikita and Walter looked at each other, but said nothing.

Clearing his throat, Mr. Wyght said, "Let Shane in to see him. Monitor Nic's heartbeat and responses."

Joshua turned the speaker back on and opened the door to our left. Handing me sleeping Rachel, Shane went in and sat in the chair across from his friend. They began conversing as if their situation was normal. Nic's responses were as they should be and his heartbeat was steady. Well, when they brought up Johanna his heartbeat increased slightly, but that was usual.

While they were talking, Joshua looked at Mr. Wyght with hope in his brown eyes. "I think the Beast is gone." Mr. Wyght said nothing, but continued to stare at the two teens.

I tip-toed over and stood next to Adeline who was writing data down. "What *was* the Beast?" I whispered.

Overhearing me, Mr. Wyght explained, "Nic was one of many failed experiments done by a sadistic scientist. This man experimented with genetic mutation by Splicing a human's genes with an animal's. It worked in a sense…" he paused and looked at Nic, "but it had side effects other than appearance."

I looked closer at our chained friend. The more I thought about it, the more abnormal his features were. His arms were longer than normal and his height was high above average. He was unnaturally brawny and covered in dark hair. His eyes were violet, and his hair had bright red highlights.

As I was staring, Gregory Flicks came over to the seat next to Adeline who blushed when he sat down. He fixed the goggles on his head and said, "We are thinking he was Mutated with a gorilla."

"Seriously?" I scoffed.

Joshua left the microphone on. "That's right, Aymie," Nic said aloud. "It sounded like a good idea at the time."

"My bad," Joshua apologized.

"No keep it on," Nic pleaded. "I think it's time I told these guys the truth, too." Taking a deep breath, he knelt as straight up as he could. "I already told a few people in private," he began, "but I think I can tell you all now.

"I wasn't always an orphan. I grew up with two incredible parents who loved me, but never had much time for me. My mom was a business woman, and my dad was a city fire fighter." He smiled. "My dad was a hero. I wanted to be just like him when I grew up. He was always saving and protecting people." His grin faded and he looked downcast. "He did his job until the moment of his death.

"It was several months after we moved to the city where my mom got a great job offer. My dad was able to join the fire department, and I enrolled in school. I don't remember much, but I remember hating every day. Not because of classes, but because of how the students behaved. Kids ganged up on other kids, teachers ignored it, and there was no sense of justice.

"One day I begged my dad to take me with him to the firehouse. I wanted to get away from all that and see if I could learn a thing or two about protecting people. I had no idea that *that* day I would learn the greatest thing anyone could do for someone." He took a shaky breath. "The greatest thing was sacrificing your life for another.

"I remember sitting in the firehouse kitchen when the alarm blared. My dad let me hop on the fire truck with him and we went to the scene," he shook his head, "I couldn't believe my eyes. Two enormous skyscrapers were on fire and beginning to crumble." He paused and collected his thoughts. "'She's up there!' I heard my dad scream to another firefighter. When he was given permission, he grabbed his equipment and raced inside the first building." Nic choked back tears. "Looking up, I watched in horror as people jumped from the windows and plummeted to their deaths. I saw every gory detail." His eyes shook. "I watched the towers fall.

"As they were crumbling, I was in shock. One of my dad's friends grabbed me and told me to run, but I wouldn't listen. Both of my parents were in there, and I did nothing." Nic growled and gritted his teeth. "I did *nothing*," he repeated. It looked like he was about to blow again. Joshua hovered his hand over an emergency button, ready to push at any moment.

Nick took a deep breath and calmed down. "The firefighter rushed me to safety, and my aunt picked me up. My parents were dead. I was an orphan."

With a sigh, Nic went on to how he became a Mutant Gorilla: "My aunt wasn't really the nicest person. She saw me as a burden and used me to make money any way she could. Illegally was her favorite, and I was usually caught. Thankfully, the longest I spent in juvenile was a year." He chuckled. "That was fun. Nobody messed with me, and it felt good. I was always the biggest and took advantage. The smaller trouble makers hung with me; I protected them from the *real* baddies." He looked up at Shane and then at us behind the one way glass. "That's why I needed to be stronger. I was never enough. Someone still got hurt. I could never forgive myself.

"To top it all off, after failing in the Junior Olympics, my aunt ditched me. She said I was useless and told me to basically…" the words got caught in his throat. "She practically told me to go die," he croaked. This time, he couldn't stop the tears. They dripped down his dirty, unshaven face. "That's why I took Carl Mallory's offer," he said through his cries, "I didn't care if I lived or died after the experiment. It was worth a shot."

Telling us his story took its toll. He hunched over and sobbed hysterically for a few moments. He calmed his breathing and whispered, "Thank you for not giving up on me like I did." He clenched his eyes shut. "Until today, I always thought about giving up. Even though my time here has been amazing, I still hurt someone in some way. Last month I got *so* close to ending it all." He opened his eyes. "I promise not to let you down any more."

When he finished, we stood in silence. Even Nikita stopped writing in his notebook. Nic's past was so pitiful I couldn't help but cry. My mascara dripped down my face as I held Rachel tightly. Everyone else remained quiet.

The only one to say anything was the little girl who had awoken during his sorrowful tale. She leaned over and pressed her tiny hand against the glass. She looked at Nic with her brown eyes and babbled, "Ni-Ni-Ni."

Hearing the noise, Nic looked up and smiled, "Do you have Rachel Hollinger? What's she saying?"

"I think she's saying your name," I whispered, wiping the tears from my eyes.

She said it again with a big smile on her face. "Ni! Ni! Ni!"

Nic tilted his head back and laughed. "Yes! Ni, Ni."

Mr. Wyght gave Joshua a look who in turn pressed a few buttons. The chains released and fell to the ground with a crash. Struggling to his feet, Nic stretched and rubbed his wrists. The door opened and I went inside to see him and my brother.

Nic looked at the little girl and asked, "Can I hold her?"

Carefully, I placed her into the big guy's hairy arms. The Rachel looked up at him and patted his face. "Ni," she said.

He smiled and stroked her cheek. "Yes, Ni."

"I think you made a wise choice, Mr. Eerkens," Nikita said over the speaker. "You were already strong and had a caring heart before your experiment. Now, those both increased tenfold. Male gorillas' main goal in life is to protect those they care about. I think you are going to do that just fine."

"Thank you sir," Nic replied, bouncing Rachel up and down. He leaned over and asked, "Who's the Russian?"

"We heard that," Joshua said. "Now get out of here you guys and get some food."

With that, the three of us and Rachel left the Royals and two men alone. As we were walking back, whoever was around stared at Nic carrying Rachel. They couldn't believe what they were seeing. Only a month before the big guy was wrecking the place and then about to cap himself. Now, he was tenderly playing with a toddler.

When we were back in the main hall, Roxanne, Dylan, Blake, and Alexandrea ran up to us. "There you guys are!" Alexandrea yelled. Her face was covered in soot and she had her gloves on. "Someone told me they saw you heading this way so we came as fast as we could."

"Yeah," Dylan confirmed. He was covered with flour and wearing an apron too small for him. "We were in the middle of making dinner and heard a big fuss."

"Sorry," I apologized. "Look who's back though?" I motioned to Nic who was standing a safe distance away.

"Dude, you're not going to bite," Shane reminded him. "Get over here."

"He might punch and kick, though," Roxanne said with her arms crossed. "How do we know he isn't going to go all psycho again?"

"He's fine," Blake interjected. "Otherwise he wouldn't be holding Rachel."

Roxanne was about to comment, but just shrugged her shoulders. "Well, that settles it. Welcome back, Nic." With that, she turned and left to go back to training."

"Insensitive," Dylan muttered. Looking up at Nic, he said, "We are glad you are okay though. That was scary."

Alexandrea nodded. "Flicks said you tried to *kill* yourself? What was that about?"

Nic's face got as red as his highlights. "Sorry, I thought I couldn't get better, but I was wrong."

"I'm glad you were wrong." Alexandrea said. "Who else is going to get stuff off high shelves for us?" Chuckling, she took off her glove and whacked his arm. "I'll see you later." Then she left.

To change the subject, Blake leaned back and snapped a photo of Nic and Rachel with his camera. He looked down at it and smiled. "Definitely a keeper."

"You'll have to print that one out for me," Nic said peering over his shoulder. "This is a day I don't want to forget." Blake nodded and ran off to fulfill the request.

Nic held up his giant hand and Rachel high-fived it. "The day Nic can finally start protecting people again," he said.

Shane punched him in the arm. "Good. I need help with the Hollinger girls. I'll take half and you take half."

"Why not?" Nic replied. "I'm taking this one though." With that he ran off to find the other Hollinger girls.

"Hey!" Shane yelled. "You can't outrun me." Then, he dashed after him, leaving me in the hallway alone.

I shook my head and began to walk towards the stairs when Flicks called from the hall. "Aymie! Wait up." The RV Drone was panting. Sweat dripped from his forehead. "Can I ask you something?"

"I don't know where Adeline is," I replied instantly. "I thought she was with you in the hangar." Every time he came looking for me it was to see her… and every time he would get embarrassed.

Once again, his face turned red. "Uh, no, t-that's not what it was about," he stammered. He cleared his throat. "Have you been noticing Zander's been acting kind of," he looked over his shoulder, "weird?"

After thinking for a moment, I nodded. "A little bit. He's more moody now, and he doesn't want to talk to me about anything."

"Me either," Flicks told me as he wiped his damp hands on his gray jumpsuit. "I keep asking him what's wrong, and I have no idea. I'm worried for him."

"Me too," I agreed. "Maybe he should talk to Papa E or Johanna."

Flicks shook his head. "He is avoiding them more than ever. He and Papa E used to be pretty tight. Now, something is up. I have a bad feeling."

Then, it hit me. *Blake said he had a bad dream*, I thought, *could Zander be involved?* Not bringing it up, I said, "Let's hope it's only a feeling and nothing else."

"Let's hope," Flicks ended. He said his thanks and went back to his work.

Heading up the stairs, I kept pondering the thought that Zander could be involved in something terrible. I finally reached my room and stood in the doorway. I thought it over more and laughed to myself. *What could Zander possibly think of? I'm sure he's just moody.* With that, I pushed it aside and got ready for the evening.

# CHAPTER 36

## Mark: XI

So, that happened. Crazy to think I was right all along and how it was partially my fault that Nic has Gorilla DNA flowing through him. That's something I try not to think about.

Anyway, so I am sorry but I am going to skip ahead again to the following year. Keep up guys! Once again, we all grew in skill, wisdom, and age.

It was May, and we just had an eighteenth birthday and Royal celebration for Nic. He finally proved that being a Mutant didn't affect who he really was. At first, they were all terrified and confused. Nic lost a lot of friends… but he never lost us. We helped him get through the difficult times.

It all worked out fine. He showed everyone that he was an incredible fighter and protector when faced with danger. He saved the little Hollinger girls and some other students from a bear during a hiking-trip-gone-wrong. Not only did he receive a Royal title after that, but people began to see him through different eyes. They looked past the animal blood that flowed through his veins and focused more on the human heart he had.

The party had ended, and I was packing up the drum set on the stage. My siblings, Shannon, and I were able to start that band we talked about. We called ourselves *Left Lane Only* after a near-death driving experience.

[Yes, yes, Aymie, I know that was my fault. I wasn't used to those roads, man. Now let me get back to my story without you nagging me.]

We played at every event and even did side gigs outside of WHYP. Our group of friends usually helped with setup and break down, but this time they were all gone and in bed already.

As I put the last cymbal away in its torn, black case, Shane came up to me with his acoustic guitar slung on his back. "Hey brother, got everything?" he asked, glancing at my pile of cymbals. After he made Shannon cry that previous year, he changed. He was more mature. I wasn't sure the reason. Was it that incident? Did him becoming a Royal change his tune? Or was it because we were turning seventeen the next month? I'll never know for sure, but despite his maturity, the two of us bickered and fought over almost everything.

[Yes we do, Shane. No denying it.]

"Nah, I got it," I said. Looking around, I saw everything was off the stage and packed away. "Man, you're fast."

"When was I not?" he smirked.

I rolled my eyes and fixed my long bang. It had been three years, and I still had that stupid haircut. I hated how I looked anyway, so I didn't think my hair mattered. Also, it and my earrings reminded me of Big Daddy and Fallout.

Thinking about it all, I instantly made myself depressed. There were days that I wished I could go back with all the knowledge I obtained. Being a Royal really pushed me to ask questions and to learn. Because I was mission control for the Combatants' field missions, I had to solve problems and find out the truth about everything. That was exactly what my Fallout family—especially Brand—told me *not* to do…

*Brand,* I thought, my mind branching off. I had loved him like a brother and yet he abandoned me. *Then again, it was my fault,* I quickly told myself (even though it wasn't true).

My depressed thoughts were interrupted when I heard Shannon laugh at something Aymie said. I looked over and saw her beautiful smile as she giggled at my sister's joke. After working with her every day and listening to her advice and wisdom, she kind of took a hold of me. Every time I was down, she would say something to pick me up. I admired her more and more every day and eventually…I fell for her.

"Yo, Mark!" Shane shouted, waving his hand in front of my face. I snapped back into reality, and he laughed. "I think you need to get some sleep."

"That sounds like a great idea," Aymie said. "I am exhausted." Her makeup was smeared and her wig was crooked, but she was still pretty. Then again, both of my siblings always looked nice without even trying. Shane's hair was always perfect and his skin was clear and smooth. His eyes were bright, and he had a great smile. Not to mention became stronger and his muscles were more defined.

I looked at my siblings as they compared reasons as to why they were tired. *Why'd I get the ugly genes?* I thought bitterly. I looked down at my own appearance. I was as tall as Shane but not as fit. He always looked good in his flannel and denim while I looked dumpy in my green t-shirt, ripped skinny jeans, and dirty black high tops. It's who I was.

I sighed and went back to packing up my things. Shannon noticed my distressed expression. "Hey, you okay?" she asked.

My heart raced when she came over. Every so often I would get nervous like that. "I'm good, thanks." There was something else I needed to say, but no words would come out.

She crossed her arms. "I know you're lying, but when you want to talk, you go right ahead."

*I wish we could talk now*, I thought.

I felt Shane glaring behind me. Quickly, he jumped in and changed the subject. "So the Russian and German guys are coming again in a few days. Do you want to join Aymie and me on our routine tour?"

"I think you two are doing just fine with Nikita and Walter," Shannon said.

Aymie rolled her eyes. "Oh, please. All they do is come, walk around, ask a billion questions, write stuff down, and then go home. They don't want to do the tour with anyone else but us."

"That's not true," Shane disagreed. "They talk to Zander too. Other than that, just us."

"Really?" Shannon asked, surprised. "I didn't know that. What do they talk about?"

"Stuff that happened outside WHYP I guess," Shane explained. "I think Zander is trying to have them find his uncle or somebody."

"Which is weird, because he got Joshua Wolfrum to find Blake for me," Aymie reminded as she played with a silver ring on her dog tag chain. "Why not have him look for his uncle?"

"Joshua is training for a top secret field mission," Shannon informed. "They have him working overtime ever since he became the Royal Veteran Umbrella."

"What's the mission?" Shane inquired.

She stared at him with her blue eyes as if to say, "*Seriously*?"

"What? I'm curious!" he replied.

She scoffed and picked up her viola. "Anyway, we should probably head to bed. Mark and I have a lot of preparations to make before Joshua leaves." Turning to me, she smiled and said, "Isn't that right?"

"Right," I mechanically replied. To be honest, I totally forgot we had to see him off. Shannon and I grew close to Joshua over the year. We worked with him on his mission equipment and set up ways for him to communicate back to us. Shannon is going to be his primary contact, and we set up a way for us to secretly send letters back and forth. A bit old fashioned, but our way is not easy to track and trace.

Obviously jealous that I got to spend more time with Shannon, Shane ended the conversation: "Well, then we should get going." Hopping off the front of the stage, he made his way out. "See you all tomorrow," he called without looking back.

"See you," Aymie yawned. "All right, let's go Shannon. Good night, Mark." With that, the two of them left me alone on the stage.

"Night," I whispered after they were gone. I grabbed my drum sticks and made my way back to my room. When I opened the door, I found the birthday boy sprawled out on top of his bed. Nic was fast asleep on his stomach and still in his suit. I tiptoed to my side, changed, and quietly hopped in my bed.

Unfortunately, he heard the creaking of my box spring. His eyes popped open and he grunted. He lifted his head and sleepily asked, "Did you do it?"

*Ugh, he remembered,* I thought, pulling the blankets over me. "No," I growled.

He chuckled. "You're gonna have to ask her soon. Shane's been telling me he's been prepping to talk to her, too." Out of all our friends, Nic was the only one who knew I had deep feelings for Shannon. I tried not to tell him, but he was being irritating one day and it kind of slipped out. As for Shane, every guy in WHYP knows he's head over heels for her. Because of that, he thinks no one would try and get in his way.

Man, was he wrong.

"I know he is," I replied. "I don't want to talk about it." Abruptly, I rolled over.

"You're going to have to talk to someone else about it soon," he replied. "You and your brother will have some hard fights ahead of you if you don't." Not saying anything else, he flipped over and fell back asleep. I tried not to think about that last part and forced myself to rest.

The next morning, I got ready as fast as I could and dashed upstairs. Papa E was saying a farewell Mass for Joshua. I wanted to be early… only because I knew Shannon would be there already. If she ever had a free moment, she was usually in the Chapel.

I was about to pass the gallery when Mr. Wyght and his two friends came out. Not wanting to be seen, I ran back and ducked into the music room, hiding by the door. They walked a little bit and stopped outside my hiding spot.

I overheard Mr. Wyght say to his friends, "I don't think that's such a good idea. Things could get out of hand."

"What are you talking about?" the Russian one said. "We have already built the facilities and have men appointed to each one. With your curriculum and lifestyle, we could create the ultimate home for children and adults alike. It would be a safe haven for everyone."

"Safe haven from what?" Mr. Wyght asked.

"The war," the third man replied. "I have foreseen it, Stanley. Ve are going to have another vorld war. The bombings, the abductions, the attacks, everything. This is a repeat of what ve had before. Only this time, people are denying the signs. Everything is an accident."

"So when will this 'Accident' take place?" Mr. Wyght inquired.

"Before we know it," the Russian replied with a stern tone. After that, they continued walking and I heard no more. *Wonder what that was about,* I pondered as I poked my head out the doorway. Once I knew they were gone, I ran to the chapel.

I opened the doors a crack and looked inside. Shannon and all the Veteran Royals were already there. I cursed under my breath and sat down in the back. After a few moments, Papa E came out and began the Celebration.

Patiently, I participated for the hour as I always did. To be honest, I didn't mind it even though I couldn't understand too much. One thing's for sure, the things that the faithful did to better humanity always amazed me. The stories Papa E told us of his ministry work were humbling. He truly inspired me. Thanks to Shannon, I started talking to Papa E more and entrusted him with most of my secrets. He would always give me great advice and help me with my questions. He wasn't super preachy like I thought he'd be.

Secretly, I began to develop an admiration for what they believed in, but I felt…unworthy to become one of them. I knew my brother and sister adopted their beliefs, but I felt undeserving. That was something I never shared. I had so many questions about myself and if I could be accepted… but wasn't strong enough to ask them.

Before I knew it, the Celebration was over and it was time to say farewell. We followed Papa E out to the hallway where the rest of the students were gathered. The priest walked through the sea of people and stood before the door with Joshua.

Papa E placed his hands on the boy's shoulders and said aloud, "My son. You have taken on a great burden for the sake of us all.

Know that we will be praying for you every day until your safe return." With that, he blessed him and gave him a tight hug.

Pulling away, Joshua wiped the tears from his brown eyes. "Thank you," he said, his voice cracking. He took a deep breath and turned to us. "Thank you everyone."

He was about to leave when all of Shannon's sisters ran up and gave him a group hug. They were crying hysterically, and it didn't help his nerves. One by one he hugged them. Shannon then came over and wrapped her arms around him. "Be safe," she whispered, squeezing him tightly.

He held her back and promised he would. After hugging Mr. Wyght, Joshua finally walked toward the door and slowly opened it. He stood up straight and looked out at the black van that was waiting for him below. Clutching his backpack, he stepped down and closed the door, leaving us all behind.

Joshua Wolfrum was gone. He was out to join the Order of Xenophon.

[Yes, yes, that was the secret mission. Sorry, that's all I can tell you about it right now; it's too dangerous to speak of here. Joshua's mission could be jeopardized. It's bad enough we just told you that. OX has ears everywhere…]

After that, we silently went back to our classes. The day went by and free time finally rolled around, but no one wanted to do anything. I sat with a few friends around one of the dining tables.

"I can't believe he's gone," Johanna mumbled.

"It's always the Umbrellas to go first," Dylan choked, wiping the tears off his chubby cheeks. "First Virginia, now him."

"He'll be fine," Sonny said coldly. "I've prepped him for all the possible scenarios, who he should watch out for, and things like that."

"You said yourself the Order of Xenophon is hell on earth," Dylan cried. "Joshua is timid and never good under pressure. Why did Mr. Wyght pick him anyway?"

"Because he is an actor or something I heard," Roxanne replied, picking her teeth. "He can stay in character and not give away his real identity."

Dylan and she were bickering about Joshua's acting skills for a few minutes before Aymie came running into the dining hall. "Roxanne! Roxanne! Have you seen Zander?"

Confused, she turned and looked at her panting friend. "Uh, no. I'm not in charge of him." She looked at Sonny. "Usually, he's with you."

"He's been leaving me alone lately," he replied. "I haven't seen him in days."

"No one has," Aymie cried. "Flicks and I can't find him anywhere."

Concerned, Shannon jumped up from her seat and commanded, "Take me to Flicks and let's figure this out."

My sister nodded and the two ran out of the room. Not thinking, I raced after them with Sonny following close behind. We chased them outside to the meeting warehouse. All the Veteran Royals were there with Mr. Wyght.

"How long has he been missing?!" I heard the older man shout.

"I'm not sure, sir," Thyme replied. "We only noticed this morning."

Mr. Wyght slammed his fists on the table. "Someone must know something." Looking around, his eyes fell on Shannon. He let out a deep breath. "Good, there you are. We need your help," he told the fifteen-year-old.

"Do we have any leads?" she asked, grabbing a notebook.

"None," he replied, flatly. "All we know is he's gone."

"That's not true," Aymie spoke up. "He's been acting really weird lately."

Flicks agreed. "Zander hasn't been himself. He's been…moody. Depressed, I think."

"He wasn't putting his all in combat practice recently," Thyme added. Looking to Sonny, he asked, "Did he say anything to you?"

He shook his head, his long black hair bounced back and forth. "No. He purposely avoids me now even though he still has orders to keep an eye on me."

Then, I remembered something. "Aymie, didn't you say that he was talking to Nikita and Walter about his uncle?"

She slapped her forehead. "Yes. Thank you, Mark. He would talk to them in private."

Mr. Wyght's eyes widened. "What would they talk about?"

She thought for a moment but couldn't think of anything. Mr. Wyght groaned and sat down at the head of the table. He leaned back and thought. Then, he looked up at me and said, "Mark. Is there any way you can contact Fallout?"

At the sound of my old gang, my face paled. Everyone turned to look at me, making me uncomfortable. They didn't know about my past, and I still didn't want them to. "Uh, I'm sure I can get a message to Mason Couch," I replied hesitantly. "I don't think it's a good idea though."

"I don't care," he snapped. "Nikita and Walter told me they had some business with Carl Mallory, the one you smuggled drugs for. Zander could be with them for whatever reason. If Couch has a number or something we can find them."

Before anyone else could say anything, I nodded and left the warehouse. I raced back to the mansion and made my way to my Branch's headquarters. I heard my two Nerd friends shouting after me.

"Mark! There you are," Derek yelled. Ignoring him, I went right to my desk and started typing away.

Clive and Derek ran in after me. "Mark! What happened?" Clive asked. His Nerd outfit untucked and sloppy. "Why are all the Veteran Royals having a meeting? Did Joshua screw up already?"

"No," I replied, not looking away from my screen. "Zander has been missing for a while. We think he could be in danger." I went to Fallout's corner of the Darknet and hacked into *Couch's Concoction* site. I sent a message: *We need to meet*.

"Wait, when did he go missing?" Derek asked. "I thought he was going on a mission with Mr. Wyght's friends."

Abruptly, I stopped typing and turned to look at him. "What mission?"

Derek shrugged. "I don't know. I found him the other day on your computer printing some stuff out. I asked him what he was doing and he said that the German and Russian guys needed his help stopping 'history from repeating itself'."

"That's what I overheard the German guy, Walter, say this morning," I replied. "Wait, if they were here this morning, shouldn't he still have been here?"

Clive shook his head. "He got into a van with the two of them and some other guys last week."

"What did they look like?" I asked, hoping I could recognize one.

"I only saw one guy. Some twenty-something year old with light brown skin and dark curly hair on his head and face. His eyes were dark and serious and he had three earrings on his right ear." Thinking for a moment, Clive looked up at me and added, "Exactly like yours."

My heart stopped. *Could it be?* I wondered. *After all these years?* "Do we have any security footage of the front driveway?"

"You're the Royal," Derek said. "You have access to it. They're on the external drive."

Immediately, I searched for the date and times they told me. I opened the footage. It glitched a few times as if it'd been tampered with, but I could make out figures in the black and white scene. Zander was hopping into the back of a van with Nikita and Walter and another man behind them. The last one poked his head out of the back to close the two doors. Before he shut them, I stopped the footage and zoomed in. I gasped. It was a face I could never forget.

"No. Way," I said, my mouth open. "*Brand*?!"

# Chapter 37

## Mark: XII

"He's been with Nikita and Walter this whole time?" I exclaimed, sitting back in my chair and throwing my hands up.

"Wait, is that *Brand* Brand?" Clive asked. "Your partner in the gang?"

"I can't believe it. After all these years…" I replied. I looked longingly at the pixelated image of my old friend. "I'm happy he's alive." Suddenly, my computer began to malfunction. The screen turned black and blue code appeared, shaking back and forth.

"Whoa, whoa, wait," Derek said, backing away. "Are we being hacked?"

I rubbed the earrings on my ear. "No, Couch responded," I told him. That was a classical Fallout communication technique. We coded a harmless virus to disguise our messages. Every time the police got close to cracking it, we'd send them a malevolent bug to destroy their computers, making us untouchable.

Clive stared intently at the screen. Unable to understand, he groaned and asked, "What does it say, O Master Hacker?"

I looked over it one more time to make sure I got the message right. "He said 'We'll be waiting' and gave an address." I wrote down the message on a sticky note and printed out the picture of Brand, Zander, and the men in the van. I took my data and went back to the warehouse.

I found Mr. Wyght barking orders to the Royals while Shannon and Sonny sat at the table, conversing in French. *I hate when they do that,* I thought, not being able to eavesdrop.

They stopped when they saw me coming. Shannon stood up and asked, "Did you get a response?"

I shook the papers in my hand. "Even better. We know for a fact Nikita and Walter took him. They also had an accomplice." I placed the papers on the table and tapped Brand's face. "That's my old friend from Fallout. The one who ended up hating me because I was branded before him."

"Brand," Shannon whispered, carefully looking at the picture.

Peeking over at the image, Sonny's eyes widened when they fell upon the other men. He snatched the photo from Shannon and looked closer at it. After a moment, he slammed it on the table and began mumbling in Russian. He stomped over to Mr. Wyght and interrupted him. "Sir, I request you send me to go after Zander and those two men you call 'friends'."

Shocked at his sudden outburst, the man stopped yelling at Thyme and looked at the red-eyed Combatant. "That's fine… any reason in particular?"

"I want to kill them both," he sneered.

Stunned, everyone stopped and stared at Sonny. "Absolutely not," Mr. Wyght declared. "How dare you ask to execute an order such as that?"

Through gritted teeth, Sonny replied, "I've done it before and I'll do it again. Nikita Patya is a spawn of Satan himself." He took a deep breath, stood up straight, and put his hands behind his back. "I lied to you when we first met. I do know Nikita Patya. To him, I am known as Erik Patya, his son."

Mr. Wyght thought for a moment, trying to process his claims. He pointed to the boy and stared at him with wide eyes. "You… really are Erik?" He paused. "Nikita spoke highly of you. He said how strong, intelligent, and incredible you were." He looked the boy in the eyes and stated, "He thinks you are dead."

"Good. I hope he blames himself," Sonny growled. "He let his friends in the Order of Xenophon kill my mother and take me away after he betrayed them. OX made me their drug smuggler. That's when I decided to get myself thrown in jail."

Mr. Wyght put his hand up. "Wait, Order of Xenophon? Are you saying he was part of OX?"

"Yes," Sonny confirmed. "Remember when you attended the meeting between the armies of the Americas and Europe over twenty years ago? Nikita and Walter joined OX during that time. They started out as spies, feeding OX Russian and German intel. When they entirely betrayed their countries, Nikita and Walter rose to power in OX, becoming true Xenophonians."

The war veteran paused for a moment and thought it over. Mr. Wyght shakily grabbed the back of his chair and steadied himself. He couldn't believe what he was hearing. "No, that can't be true. When we met, we were all fighting together. We were fighting for peace. The Order of Xenophon hadn't even made themselves known yet. Why, they helped my search team when we found—" he stopped himself. "When we found an OX base." Slowly and carefully, he sat down in his chair. "They took a great interest in everything they found whereas I found it disgusting and immoral. OX was running experiments on civilians thinking they could reconfigure their minds to accept their will."

"And Nikita and Walter have helped them finally succeed," Sonny finished. "They got one of the higher Xenophonians the intel that he needed to make it all work."

Mr. Wyght covered his mouth with his hand and rested his elbow on the table. Distress and shock filled his eyes. These men whom he called his friends betrayed their countries, their families… they betrayed him. He looked up at Nikita's so-called son and asked, "So where do you fit into all this? Did Nikita have you when he was with OX?"

Those words were repulsive to the teen. They were a poison that stung and pained his entire being. Utterly disgusted that the thought was even presented, Sonny slammed his fist on the table and pointed at the man. "He did not have me!" He exhaled sharply as if the poison began to dissipate. "Seventeen years ago, Nikita was doing his final raid in Russia for intel to bring to OX when he saw my mother and a man walking home one night. As soon as he laid his eyes on my mother, lust filled his heart." Gritting his teeth, he continued, "That disgusting pig followed them home and broke into the house in the middle of the night." He clenched his fists. The poison that Mr. Wyght stabbed him with returned once more.

With a growl, Sonny added, "Nikita murdered the man with her–my *real* father–with his bare hands. He strangled him and threw his body out their bedroom window. Then, he went after my mother, grabbed her, and—" it took all of his strength to pause and find the appropriate words to say. Recollecting his thoughts, he calmed down and continued solemnly, "He forced himself upon her. After that, he abducted her and took her as his prize back to OX where she became his mistress."

For the first time, Sonny showed the emotion of sadness. Tears streaked down his pale face and onto the cold ground below. He grabbed his long hair and pulled it out of frustration. "He defiled my mother! He hurt her. He abused her." He couldn't control his emotions. The stone cold teen showed us all how fragile his heart was. Clearly, he had never told this story to anyone. It pained him to relive it. He began to sob uncontrollably. Mr. Wyght and all the Royal Veterans stood in silence. His tear ducts had emptied before he pulled himself together.

Taking deep breaths, he looked up at Mr. Wyght. "He must pay for what he has done," he spat. "For murdering my father, violating my mother, and turning me into the cold-hearted, perfect Xenophonian soldier he always wanted."

Everyone around remained quiet, not answering his request. *I thought my life of crime was bad.* I felt guilty. No one knew what to say. Mr. Wyght sat staring at Sonny with a blank expression on his face, unsure of whether to believe the story or not.

Inhaling sharply, Sonny broke the silence. "If you want proof, I have written accounts as they occurred. My mother always told me to keep a journal to help me think. Nikita thought it was a good idea and let me keep it. Normally, anything I cared for or wanted he took from me." He scoffed. "He probably figured it would help me get my feelings out rather than taking them out on other OX kids like I usually did." Smirking, he wiped his pale wet face. "The only friend I didn't kill was PH. He and I were tight and rose high in OX for our ages. If he stuck around, he is probably one of the lead Xenophonians by now."

"Wait, back to Nikita," Mr. Wyght interrupted, holding his hand up. "I will speak with you about OX later." He leaned forward and pressed his forearms against the table. He spoke no more about Sonny's episode and offered no sympathies. I thought he believed it to be best to not dwell on that matter…for Sonny's sake. "So, Nik is no longer a part of OX? You said he betrayed them."

"After I was taken, apparently he opened his eyes and didn't like the way OX planned to dominate the world," Sonny replied. He was back to his cynical self. "He thought abducting adults and leaving children to die was a ridiculous tactic. Apparently, he had some sort of love for me that made him pity the children, but that's only part of his MO. He is creating safe havens for the youth abandoned by OX."

"Because he knows children can be more easily manipulated," Shannon put in.

"Yes," he replied. "That is what I've come to believe. Walter says that they need to prepare for the war with OX. They know it's going to happen, because they helped plan it. Now, they regret it. They have to hide until the first stage dies out."

"They're calling it the Accident, right?" Mr. Wyght asked.

"Yes," Sonny said. "Do you remember the event when Russia 'accidentally' bombed all of the Hawaiian Islands years ago; killing a million people?"

Remembering that tragic day, Mr. Wyght sighed. "Yes. They said it was a malfunction."

"Which is impossible," Sonny snapped. "The world is blind.

These aren't 'accidents'. That was OX. I know. I was there when Nikita received the order to betray his country that final time. That was when he first betrayed OX as well. He reduced the damage of the bombs to make sure the islands were still inhabitable. *That* is where he is building his safe havens."

"That's why he wanted Zander," Mr. Wyght said, softly. "He mentioned that he needed some of our soldiers to help him train the kids in his safe haven and assist him with other plans."

Wondering where Brand fit into all this, I butted in and asked, "He wouldn't want to turn children into monsters, would he?"

Mr. Wyght looked up at me and then back at the table. "I overheard the term 'Mutants' being used."

My face fell. "No, no, no," I repeated. "That's where he is going. Carl Mallory. He is going to hire him." Thinking over my past, I remembered that Brand went to volunteer himself to be a test subject for Mallory. "No, Nikita and Walter must have met him already. That's why Brand is with them." I pulled on my long bang. "I should never have helped him. More kids are going to become mindless Mutants thanks to me."

I kept rambling and blaming myself until Mr. Wyght shut me up. "Mark, relax," he commanded. "We have time. Let's get started now. What did Couch say?"

Totally forgetting he responded, I grabbed the note and handed it to him. "He knows we are coming and will be waiting for us."

Taking it, he replied. "Good. We prepare today and leave tomorrow." With a deep breath, he looked up at the students with him. "Royal Veterans, you are dismissed. Return to your duties, we will speak tomorrow."

Confused, they all stood there staring. "Um, sir? Don't you want us to prepare for dispatch?" Thyme asked on behalf of them all.

"No," Mr. Wyght replied, standing up. "I need my Royal Veterans with me in case Nikita and Walter return. I am afraid that they will come back with an army to take the children away." He looked up at all their faces. "If it's children he wants, this is where he will get them. I am entrusting Shannon Hollinger and Mark Hodgins to command this operation under the supervision of Nicolas Eerkens, our newest Royal."

I couldn't believe what I was hearing and neither could the others. "Are you serious? They haven't had any field missions yet," Thyme reminded. "Nic is the oldest and he just turned 18. They're still kids."

Agreeing, Flicks said, "No offense, sir, but that would be a suicide mission."

"They can handle it," Mr. Wyght told them. "Nicolas and Mark have a history with Mallory, and Shannon can strategize the whole thing. They will choose their other officers accordingly. Any questions?" When no one said anything, he dismissed us.

Shannon, Sonny, and I walked out of the warehouse together. "What just happened?" I asked, still in shock.

"I think we are leading a mission," Shannon replied, slowly.

"Amateurs," Sonny muttered. "This won't be nearly as bad as what I had to endure. So let's hurry up and get it done." With that, the three of us went to pick our officers. We searched for Nic first. We found him bench pressing in the mansion's gym. Luckily, half of the students we were going to choose were there.

"Hey, Shannon," Shane greeted. He was shirtless (again) and practicing his acrobatics on the pull up bars. "Care to join us?"

"Not this time, Zippy," Sonny replied, harshly.

"Again with the Zippy," he complained. He did a front flip off the bars and landing a foot away from him. He stood up straight and glared into Sonny's red eyes about to pick a fight.

"Before an argument can ensue, let's explain what's going on," Shannon interrupted. She put her hand on Shane's sweaty chest and pushed him backwards. "We need help."

"With what?" Roxanne asked. She wiped her curly brown hair with a towel. She looked at Sonny's serious expression and asked, "What's got Sunshine here so upset?"

"That is a perfect comeback name," Shane exclaimed.

"Too bad you're too stupid to come up with it yourself," Roxanne retorted. "Anyway, back to my question."

"Zander has gotten himself into terrible trouble," Shannon explained, "and Nic, Mark, and I are in charge of getting a team together to bring him back."

"Whoa, what now?" Nic asked as he put the weights down. "Who's leading the mission?"

"Yeah, run those by me again," Shane asked, cleaning his ear with his pinky. "I could've sworn you said Nic, Mark, and you."

I crossed my arms. "You heard right," I stated.

My brother looked at me dumbfounded. Throwing his hands up, he said, "Okay, I believe you. I won't argue."

"So, what do we have to do?" Nic asked.

"We are meeting up with some old friends of ours," I told him. "We are going to see if we can stop something before it starts."

Understanding who I was referring to, Nic nodded. "Let's do this. You can brief us all before we leave. Who are we bringing with us? Do we have a limit?"

Shannon shook her head. "He didn't say a limit and I have some people in mind."

"I'll let you choose then," Nic said. "If that's all right with you, Mark. You are also leading this mission." He spoke so calm as if we were picking friends to go to the movies. No, this was serious. The three of us were about to be in charge of people on a field mission. People could die.

Inside I was panicking, but I tried not to show it. "Fine with me," I replied, calmly. "You pick, beautiful."

"Shane, Sonny, Roxanne, Alexandrea, and Aymie," she said. "We should have a pretty balanced team."

"Wait, why Aymie?" Shane asked. "No offense to my sister or anything, but her job is to sew clothes for everyone and answer the door."

"Why are we bringing you? You're a farmer," Roxanne retorted.

"Got me there," he quietly replied, obviously defeated.

"She's a Polymath so she does everything. She also has a photographic memory if you've forgotten," Shannon said. "Trust me, it comes in handy."

"You're the boss," Shane replied. He put his arm around her and pulled her close. He meant it in a friendly way, but my face still turned bright red and I involuntarily glared. When my brother looked over at me, his expression became confused and he let go.

"Okay," Nic exclaimed, clapping his big hands together. "Let's tell the others and start packing." He threw his bag over his shoulder and went out of the room.

"This will be interesting," Sonny muttered.

"I agree with you, Sunshine," Roxanne added. She turned to Shannon and said, "I'm excited though. First field mission before even becoming a Royal. You guys have nice privileges." She winked and left.

"I wouldn't call this 'nice'," I mumbled. I dreaded going back to Fallout. Part of me didn't want to see Couch or Mallory ever again. The other part longed to see Brand and Big Daddy. I was torn and didn't want everyone to see the group I had belonged to.

I hadn't noticed I zoned out again until Shannon spoke up. "Hey, Mark," she said. She moved the bang out of my face and looked up at me. "It'll be okay. You and I make a great team, don't you think? And you know Nic best. The three of us will be fine." She smiled and her bright blue eyes had a look of care and sincerity.

My heart started beating faster again. *Stop that*, I scolded it. "Yeah, we'll be good. You should go get ready, sweetheart," I said.

"You guys will be fine, but, we should go, Shannon," Shane interrupted, grabbing her arm. "Let's tell Johanna and your sisters what's going on before they start panicking." As he took her away, he glared at me over his shoulder.

Rather than getting upset, I let out a sigh and went out to pack my own things and rest. I knew the next couple of nights would be sleepless.

# THE MAINLAND

# CHAPTER 38
## Shane: XIV

I was excited the next morning. It was our first mission, and I loved the thrill of adventure. I jumped off my bed and grabbed my things. I tried to be quiet and not wake Myles up. I failed. I banged my head against the glass table trying to grab my combat boots that I had carelessly thrown underneath.

Groaning, Myles sat up in his bed and rubbed his eyes. "Shane? Where are you going? It's four am."

Unsure if the mission was a secret or not, I decided not to tell him. "Morning run," I lied, but a reasonable excuse.

Unfortunately, I couldn't fool the child prodigy…not because he was a prodigy, but because I wasn't very discreet. "You're packing weapons and your combat uniform," he stated.

I tried to make up a better reason. "Uh…it's a combat training run?"

"How stupid do you think I am?" he said, sliding out of bed. He went over to his closet and pulled out his uniform. "As the son of the co-founder, do you really think I wouldn't know what was going on?"

"Wait, man, you can't come with us," I told him as he changed. "It's way too dangerous. You could get hurt."

"Hey, I fight Lucy every day," he reminded, zipping his jeans. "If I can handle her and the other Hollinger girls, I can handle anything."

"You aren't wrong," I agreed. I remembered the many bruises I received from that Hollinger girl. She was tiny but as strong as an ox. The other girls were tough too, especially when they tackled you all at once… I know from experience. Getting back to the subject, I replied, "This is different."

He chuckled. "You'll need me. What Drones do you have on your team?"

I thought for a moment and replied, "Only Alexandrea."

"Not bad, but you'll need another," he told me, flinging his big bag over his shoulder. "Now, let's go. Don't wanna be late."

The two of us went outside and met everyone in the driveway in front of the mansion. Waiting for us was our team, Mr. Wyght, and the other Royal Veterans. It was still dark and the outside lights were on. In the driveway was a long white van that had "Gracie's Nursing Home" painted on all sides.

"Nice cover," Roxanne said sarcastically as she tapped the side of the van.

"Wait, how's my acting?" Alexandrea asked. She mimed using a walker to climb into the back.

"Needs work, but it'll do," Flicks told her. He checked over his list. "It seems like everything is here. They should be good to go." Looking up at Alexandrea, he said, "Don't get into too much trouble."

"Can't help that," she replied, putting her fireproof gloves on. She never went anywhere without them. Saluting her Royal Veteran, she hopped into the back of the van.

"I don't like this," Marian, the Royal Veteran Agricola, muttered. She came over to me and said, "Are you sure you guys'll be okay?"

I put my hand on her shoulder. "We will be fine. We've been through worse. Besides," I looked around and continued in a quieter tone, "we have the Beast to back us up." I gestured towards Nic who was speaking with Mr. Wyght and Thyme.

She shook her head. "I don't know… I finally get back from a mission and now everyone is leaving for an even more dangerous one."

"We'll be back in a few days," I told her. "I promise."

She sighed and wrapped her arms around me, giving me a big hug. "Please be safe," she whispered.

I was shocked at her gesture, but I hugged her back anyway. After I pulled away and my friends said their goodbyes to their superiors, we all climbed into the van and prepared to leave.

"Bring Zander back in one piece," Thyme said as he grabbed the handles. "If things play out as Mr. Wyght and Sonny say, then we will need all the help we can get." With that, he shut the doors and left us in the dark.

After a few moments, the lights flickered on. We sat in seats against the right side and faced a work bench covered in computers and maps. Underneath was a weapon rack and to the right were bins full of supplies.

"Wait, who is driving?" Roxanne asked, counting us.

Myles then spoke over the loudspeaker. "Fasten your seatbelts. Our first stop: Brooklyn, New York!"

"Wait, Myles is driving?" Aymie exclaimed.

"He sure is," Nic replied over the sound system. When it clicked off, the van began moving and we were on our way. We all held on to our seats and prepared for the worst. To our surprise, Myles was a very smooth driver. Being an eleven year old kid, you would think he would kill us all. Then again, he can build a car out of scraps; I would think he would know how to drive them.

We went for ten hours straight only stopping a few times to use the bathroom and gas up. The rest stops were tough. We had to park far away and make sure no one was watching us get out. We were a bunch of kids jumping out of a nursing home van. Talk about suspicious.

*They should've made it a Geek Squad van or something,* I thought, carefully climbing back in after our final stop. That time, I made a final effort to sit next to Shannon. She sat furthest back so she could talk to Nic and Myles through the window. There was only one seat open next to her. Mark always beat me to it which was aggravating because I was so much faster than him.

I pushed my way back and sat down next to her. Mark glared and plopped next to me. "What's your beef, man?" he whispered. "Shouldn't I talk to the people who are leading the mission with me?"

He was right, but lucky for me, Nic was snoring away. You could hear him over the speaker when Myles told us we were on our way again. I had an excuse. "One of your partners is asleep. What's there to talk about?"

Grumbling, my brother took out his laptop and began typing away some Nerd stuff. Shannon pulled out a book and began to read. I peered over her shoulder to see what it was: her favorite detective stories which I expected. I watched as she became engrossed in her book. Her beautiful eyes scanned the delicate pages, and she played with the Celtic key around her neck. Her long curly hair was draped over her purple t-shirt. Even in casual street clothes, she still looked amazing.

"May I help you, Shane?" she whispered.

"Help with what?" I asked, clueless.

"You're staring at me again," she said.

Embarrassed, I faced forward and tugged on my blue shirt. "Sorry, lost in thought I guess."

"Something on your mind?"

*You; like always*, I thought but didn't say. Clearing my throat, I said, "Same old. Same old."

"Okay, but when you want to talk, I'm here," she replied, then went back to her mysteries.

I was going to say something else when I felt something sharp jabbing me in the side. I whispered to Mark, "What's your problem?"

Taking out an earbud, he said, "Huh?" He tried to act like he didn't know what happened, but it was obviously him. "Don't interrupt me, I'm busy."

I threw my hands up and back down again out of disbelief. I crossed my arms and tried to sit still for the final stretch of the trip. Thankfully, I made it the last hour.

The van jerked to a stop, and I heard Myles' little voice call over the intercom, "Ladies and gentlemen, we have arrived at our destination."

Time for the mission to begin.

Nic opened the back and let us all out. We were in the parking lot of a run down, abandoned warehouse. Looking around, Mark gasped. "This is where we stored our food for Theo…" he said.

"Sure is," Nic said. "I only met the Shrew and Slow loris once. Nice guys. Well, if they weren't being forced to do messed up stuff."

"Wait, what?" Roxanne asked.

"Oh, yeah forgot to tell you," Nic said. "Being leader is tough. Anyway, I'm not the only Mutant. There are many others, but Mark's friends are leading them all. They are the ones with the most power and…free will."

"How many more has he created?" Mark asked as he clutched his backpack.

"Every boy of Fallout has become one," a voice called from the brick warehouse. Coming forward was a pasty guy covered in tattoos and scars. He had three earrings on each ear and two on his right eyebrow. His eyes were crazed and I got the feeling he had the capability to kill us all on the spot. He stopped a few feet in front of my brother. "Everyone except you, Mark." He held out his hand, "Welcome back."

Mark shook it. "Mason Couch. It's been a while." Thinking for a moment, he asked, "What do you mean 'everyone'?"

"Don't be so worried," he replied. His lips turned up into a mischievous grin, revealing stained teeth. "They paid us handsomely and… most of the boys are sane." He looked up and down at Mark. "You've grown stronger." He pointed to my brother's hair and snickered. "Haircut is the same and you kept the earrings, though. Love it."

Mark rubbed the shaved part of his head. "Reminders of home."

"Glad to hear it. Your accent is fading though; such a shame," Couch replied, clicking his tongue. "Now, to business. Who are your friends and what do you want?"

"These friends are simply my friends," Mark lied. "We are looking for another friend of ours, Zander Grath. We heard a rumor that he is traveling with people who are Mallory's customers. D'ya know where he is?"

Couch shook his head. "Heard of him. Never seen him."

"He's traveling with Brand," Mark added.

Couch's eyes widened. "Really? Now, what would a coward and a traitor like him be doing with your friend?"

Mark shrugged. "Who knows? Brand ran off to prove himself. He thought being experimented on would do the trick. Maybe Zander wanted to do the same."

"Yeah, well Brand's experiment failed," Couch said harshly. "He was too afraid to go through with it and begged to help in a different way. He nearly cost me four million bucks. We didn't want him back, so he stayed with Mallory and his comrades." He shook his head. "Brand was lucky Mallory accepted him. He was useless to us so he would've been Shrew food."

Mark seemed repulsed by his statement, but said nothing of it. "Is there anything you can do to help us then?"

Thinking for a moment, Couch finally said, "Yeah, I think so. Mallory is picking up more of my Concoction here tonight. You could wait and talk to him."

Mark looked over his shoulder. When Nic and Shannon nodded, he turned back and replied, "Okay, we'll wait then."

"Fine by me," Couch said with an eerie smile. "Oh, and I told Victor you were here. He's come to visit if you don't mind."

As he said that, a tall man with black skin came running towards us out of the warehouse. When Mark saw him, he began to laugh and put his bag on the ground.

The man skidded to a stop before Mark. He was breathing heavily and coughing hard, but he still had a smile on his face. "My boy," he said, weakly. Coughing a few more times into his sleeve, he finally steadied himself. He looked my brother up and down and then flung his arms around him. "We've missed you."

"Missed you too, Big Daddy," Mark replied, hugging him back.

Big Daddy put his hand on Mark's face. "Look at you; all grown up." He stared at him with a smile and experienced a feeling of nostalgia. A moment passed and his smile faded. Worry fell across his face. "What happened to you that night? Theo and Jordan said something spooked you and you ran off. The men you were meeting with said the same."

"Really? That's what they told you?" Mark scoffed. He glanced over Big Daddy's shoulder and saw something in Couch's eye that made him change the subject. "Anyway, how are things here?"

"Business is great, but things are getting lonely," Big Daddy quickly replied. "I would love to talk more, but I have to check up on some things. Will you be here later?" Mark nodded. Big Daddy smiled and patted Mark's face one more time. He turned and slowly walked back to the warehouse with Couch, coughing most of the way.

"Things don't seem right," Alexandrea whispered after they left.

"They never are with Fallout," Mark said, glancing at Big Daddy. Shaking off whatever he was thinking, he turned back to us. "Last time I was here, I was betrayed by my friends and handed to the guys who have been after my family for years. I think we should prepare for the worst."

The whole rest of the afternoon, we sat in the van readying weapons, equipment, and escape plans. We changed into our black combat uniforms and stuffed our pockets with ammunition. We weren't sure what to expect. If Mallory really was coming, he would most likely have plenty of Mutants with him. If it was Couch trying to get the jump on us… we could probably handle him.

Finally, the sun disappeared behind the cityscape and the street lights flickered on. This part of the city was quiet, which I was not expecting.

Creeping out of the van, we raced across the parking lot and up to the warehouse entrance. We pressed our backs against the walls, waiting for a signal. As Nic made his way towards the entrance, I gripped my pistol tightly. Nic took a deep breath, wrapped his fingers around the handles, and pulled the massive doors open with ease. We carefully shuffled inside the dark building.

Prowling around for a while, we found no one. I shined my flashlight on full crates of supplies, weapon racks, shelves of books, and piles of useless junk. Dust floated through my light beam like a thick fog, obstructing my vision. I took a deep breath and got a whiff of an unfamiliar drug.

"What is all this?" Myles whispered, plugging his nose and rummaging through the crates. He picked up an automatic, metal crossbow. He examined it and scoffed. Apparently there were a million things wrong with its design. He called Alexandrea over and the two Drones criticized it mercilessly. What caught Myles' eye was the ammunition. They were thin, glass arrows with green liquid in the shaft. "What's this inside?" He looked closely and read the label aloud: "'*Mark's Menacing Mixture*'." He looked at my brother. "You have a poison named after you?"

"It *is* my fault he has all these weird Concoctions, mixtures, and Mutant serums," Mark said. "Speaking of that psycho, where is Couch?"

"He could be hiding somewhere," Aymie replied as she memorized a fire escape map on the wall. There was one spot she really paid attention to. "This place has so many nooks and crannies."

I agreed and ventured down a corridor by myself. Not a smart move, but I was so pumped I didn't care. Thrill and suspense tingled throughout my entire body. I loved it. I crept down the long hall and peeked into all the different rooms. "This place is bigger than I thought," I said aloud.

"It's not as big as the warehouses back home," a voice called behind me.

Startled, I turned around and shined my light on a familiar face. I gasped. "*Zander*?"

"What do you know? Mr. Popularity found me first," he replied, crossing his tan arms that were now covered in scars. He had bags under his eyes and looked unwell. "I'm surprised you even remembered my name. Must be hard to keep track with all the friends you have."

"What's that supposed to mean?" I replied defensive as I looked at him up and down. He was in his combat uniform but it was tattered, torn, and covered in blood. His once long black hair was chopped off above his ears and uneven. His sharp dark eyes glowered at me. He had a look about him that gave me an uneasy feeling… the kind of feeling I got when I lost my aunt and uncle, when I was attacked at the circus, and when Mr. and Mrs. Hollinger were taken.

Remembering those horrible events, I looked up at Zander and demanded, "What have you done?"

Confused, he scoffed, "What do you mean? How about 'Hey, Zander! Sorry we were all such jerks for ignoring you and treating you like dirt. Please forgive us'?" He laughed. "Like you could crush your pride enough to say that. You had such a hard time apologizing to your girlfriend. I wonder how hard it would be to say to me?"

"What are you talking about?" I asked. "When did we ever treat you like that?"

"Ask your sister!" he bellowed. "I've done everything for her and it blew up in my face. I had a chance to find my family, but I chose to find her friend instead." He gritted his teeth and stomped over to me. "Not only that, she's got you now. What does she need me for?"

Thinking he was overreacting, I pushed him away. "Get ahold of yourself. You're our friend, man. She is worried about you!"

"Yeah, whatever," he replied, fixing his white tank top. "Besides, I found my family without anyone's help. As much as I hate his guts, he's still family."

"Hate your guts too, Zander," a terrifyingly familiar voice said from behind me.

That uneasy feeling washed over me like a tsunami. It irked me so much I began shaking. I was losing a grip on my pistol as I turned to see the figure. He was a man with olive skin and neatly trimmed black hair. His piercing eyes stared right into mine. Behind him a larger, bald man with inked, dark skin came into the light. I recognized that double edged sword tattoo anywhere.

"No…" I whispered as I looked at the two.

"Finally, Gerrior; we have a Hodgins," he said to his friend, grinning mischievously. "Good job, Zander. Your Uncle Masdit is very proud."

# THE MAINLAND

# CHAPTER 39

## Shane: XV

I couldn't believe it. The men I had been running from my entire life had found me again… scratch that, they found all the Hodginses again.

My mouth gaped open as I stared unbelieving at the two men before me. Their glowing eyes I knew too well. "How did you—" I started, but the rest was caught in my throat. Turning to Zander, I blurted, "*He* is your uncle?"

"Can't pick your family," Zander said, walking over to Masdit. "We hate each other, but we have to stick together."

Dumbfounded, I slowly replied, "No… you don't. You had a real family at Wyght's. Why are you betraying us all?"

"Bah!" Masdit scoffed. "Spare me the sap. Besides, what does an orphan know about a family?" He leaned over and grabbed a container from a crate next to him. "Or do I need to remind you." He unscrewed the cap with his lanky finger. With a devilish look, he threw its contents all over me, soaking my entire head in water.

Unfortunately, I had a mini panic attack, proving his point. I tried to swat the water away as if it were a living creature. I felt like liquid was filling my lungs and I was choking. My mind remembered when he and Gerrior plunged the heads of my loved ones into the river. I rewatched their arms flail and their lifeless bodies drift away. The pain was unbearable.

I backed against a crate and sank to the floor, trying to stop my hyperventilating.

Laughing, Masdit patted Zander on the back. "You were right. He is such a baby. Well, this one is as good as ours." I was still on the floor when Gerrior reached for me with a rope and gag.

Thankfully, I recovered sooner than they anticipated. I rolled to one side, jumped up, and dashed past him. Masdit and Zander tried to block my exit, but I jumped over them. I was running away from my attackers… again.

*No, not this time,* I told myself as I raced out of the hall. *Getting help first and then stopping them.* Going out into the main floor, I found no one. The crates were destroyed, shelves were pushed over, and it looked as if all hell broke loose. *I didn't hear a fight,* I thought. Before I had time to look around, I heard the shouts and footsteps of my pursuers. I raced up the stairs.

After going up a few flights, I found my friends. They were ducking in a hallway on the third floor, facing doors they barricaded. They had piled shelves, crates, and whatever they could find in front of it, trapping their attackers. I cautiously went over to join them.

Shannon was the first to notice I returned. She let out a sigh of relief and ran to me. "What happened?" she whispered. "Why are you all wet?"

I had no words to say. I bent over, threw my arms around her torso, and held her close. I feared the worst. I feared I would never see her again if we failed. *No,* I thought, squeezing her. *I am not going to run away again.*

After a moment, she stood on her tip toes, wrapped her arms around my neck, and rested her chin on my shoulder. "What happened?" she asked again.

Without letting go, I whispered, "They're here. They've found us again, Shannon. Masdit. Gerrior. They're here for my siblings and me. They're probably here for you too. I'm tired of running. I've run away my whole life. Now, Zander is Masdit's nephew, and—" I rambled for a few moments and barely made any sense. The feeling of adventure was gone. I was filled with fear. I was afraid for the lives of my friends and family.

She didn't know what to say, so she hugged me tighter. I held Shannon for a few more moments until Mark came over and tore her off of me, which I was not happy about. "Enough of that," he scolded, glaring at me. "We need to focus. Brand, Theo, and Jordan could be back at any minute."

"Mark, Masdit and Gerrior are here with Zander," she told him, a worried expression on her pale face. "Masdit is Zander's uncle."

His stared wide eyed and jaw dropped. He didn't know what to say.

Aymie jumped up from her post. "Wait, wait, wait," she said. "Zander is Masdit's nephew?" She thought for a moment. "Zander said he had an uncle that he never liked talking about… and whenever we mentioned Masdit's name, he got uncomfortable." After a second, she put her hand over her mouth, "Blake! Months ago, he said he had a terrible dream about a bad event that was going to happen. I was too stupid to ask him for more details. From what I know, someone in our group of friends betrayed us."

"Zander says that we treated him like trash," I told her. "He wanted a real family, and I guess we pushed him away…somehow."

Roxanne was eavesdropping and put in her two cents: "Well, Aymie ignored him all the time."

"That's not true," Aymie denied. "He always hung out with us."

"Yeah, but you are always with Blake," Roxanne reminded her, still carefully watching the door. She wrapped her hands tighter around her pistol and tried to shake her curly hair out of her face. "Every time he tried to get a moment with you, Blake would either come up in the conversation or join in physically."

Aymie was about to protest, but then she thought for a moment. Her face fell as she realized Roxanne was right. "I never meant it… I was just so happy to have my best friend back."

"It's been years, Aymie," Mark said. "Zander was mad in love with you. We know you didn't mean it, but he took it the wrong way."

"I think he's overreacting," I added. "Why would he betray us all because someone stole his girl?"

"I can relate," I heard Mark mutter.

Before I could think about that, Aymie protested, "I am not his girl! I am no one's girl." She groaned and went back to her post.

"Enough," Sonny snapped. His eyes still locked on his target. He paused and we all were silent. Jerking to the door with his gun, he said quietly, "They've started moving around again."

I listened and heard what he was talking about. Slow footsteps came from behind the barricaded doors. Feet shuffled back and forth as if they were pacing.

"Wait," Shannon whispered, "there are only two. Where's the third?"

"Here," a voice called from behind. Quickly turning around, we saw Mark's old partner Brand gripping a knife in one hand. He lunged for Mark, but my brother was too quick. He grabbed Brand's arm and threw him to the ground.

"I wish we didn't have to meet like this," Mark said, pressing his foot against his old partner's back.

Brand laughed. "We will have plenty of time to catch up when I take you with me and your friends are dead." Suddenly, the shelves in front of the door were knocked over and the doors flew off their hinges.

Everyone scurried backward, trying not to get hit by the barricade. Mark and Aymie grabbed Brand and dove into the next room while I grabbed Shannon and shielded her behind a crate. Once everything stopped flying, Shannon pushed herself away from me, peeked out from behind the box, and gasped. When I looked, I understood why.

Theo the Shrew and Jordan the Slow loris were leading an army of Mutant boys. Instead of rushing at us head on, they halted in their positions and stared. Theo had this crazed look in his brown eyes. Jordan's brow was furrowed and he was sucking venom from his inner elbows, preparing for a poisonous bite.

"What are they waiting for?" Alexandrea whispered, aiming her pistol at them.

Nic pressed his hand on her arm and motioned for her to put it down. "They're waiting for orders," he told her. Standing up straight, he slowly walked towards them. He placed his gun on the ground and held up his hands. "We are willing to negotiate," the big guy announced. "There must be something you all desire. We can give it to you."

Theo shook his head. "You'll do just fine, Nic. I'm starving." He bared his teeth, spit dripping from his mouth. "They haven't fed me all day. Besides, I've never tried a Man-Gorilla before." He paused to think. "I've eaten Man and Gorilla but never both together."

"Is that what they are feeding you with now?" Nic asked, horrified.

Theo nodded. "The day you abandoned us was the last time I ate normal food. Now, any boy that misbehaves…" He growled, bit the air, and cackled.

I was absolutely disgusted. I couldn't believe what monsters these guys had become. Having enough of the conversation, Nic challenged, "Well, what are you waiting for then?" He banged his chest twice with his fists. "Come get me."

Jordan shook his head as he took his final suck of poison. "You're lucky. You have Brand." He looked past Nic and saw my siblings with Brand tied up on the ground. "We are forbidden to attack when one of us is taken. Because once these guys get let go," he motioned to the army behind him, "there is no going back."

"I say you let them go anyway," a girl's voice called from behind the two. Emerging from the sea of monsters was a pretty girl a few years older than me. Her appearance didn't resemble a Mutant's. She had smooth black skin that was covered in scratches and long, thick, dark hair. Her serious eyes were brown, but one was covered in a milky white cataract.

After a moment, I heard my sister gasp from behind me. "J-Janelle?" she stuttered, looking at the young woman. It was the same girl who sacrificed herself for my sister back at St. Maria

Gorretti's. "What happened to you?" Aymie thought for a moment and remembered. "Masdit took you. What has that monster done?"

Cocking her head to the side, the lady looked at my sister. "Who are you? And how *dare* you speak of my father that way," she spat. She ripped out a gun and aimed it for my sister. Before she could pull the trigger, the ground shook beneath us.

We had a window. Mark dragged Brand back to the staircase. Shannon grabbed Aymie and they and the other girls followed him down. Myles, Sonny, Nic, and I stayed behind to make sure they got down safely.

Once Brand was down the stairs with the others, Janelle ordered, "Jordan, Theo, come with me to cut them off and meet up with my dad and Gerrior." She turned to the others and said in a low voice, "It's safe to kill them now."

The Mutants yelled and charged.

We had no choice but to fight back. I whipped out my pistol, aimed, and prepared to fire. The first few Mutants went for Sonny and Nic who were up front. Those two kept most of the fighting to themselves. Nic didn't need a weapon; he knocked our enemies out in one effortless punch. Sonny shot them down left and right without even flinching. He did his best to aim for their limbs so they couldn't fight but were still alive. A courtesy you wouldn't expect from a member of the Order of Xenophon.

Lucky for me, a few slipped past our friends so I got in on the action. Bad news was Myles had to fight too. Gripping his gun, he dropped into a stance and prepared to engage. "Ready?" he asked as they got closer.

"Always am," I replied with confidence. I was horrified and dreading what we had to do… and yet, I felt the rush of excitement again. The pain and terror of Masdit and Gerrior dissipated and I was ready for the adrenaline rush.

The lights flickered on and off in the eerie building as we watched the monstrous boys race towards us. They appeared as shadows afraid to disappear in the sunlight. Their empty and lifeless glowing eyes were locked on us. They growled and ran on all fours; no human decency left within them.

In an instant they were within range. We tried to follow Sonny's lead and aim for the limbs, leaving them writhing in pain on the ground. Myles and I shouted simultaneously as we fired our pistols. The brass littered the ground beneath us as the bullets left their chambers and found their marks. One by one, the Mutants collapsed to the ground, heaving and clutching their wounds.

In a flash, they were all down and we were still standing. I looked around at their faces and began to feel guilty. Most of them were little kids. They were turned into mindless monsters for a scientist's crazy experiments and another man's greed. "I can't believe Mark took part in this evil," I muttered.

"It's not entirely his fault," Nic reminded me. He gently carried a little Mutant boy to lay his back against the wall, careful not to let his fingers get bitten off. "Mark was just a kid; he couldn't have known better."

I knew that, but it was still hard to push past. Most of Mark's life was dedicated to helping Couch and his crazy Concoctions. For crying out loud, Mark has a poison named in his honor. He played a big part.

Shaking my head, I glanced again at the unconscious boys in the flickering light and said, "I can't believe we did this."

"Yeah... The worst...part is that it...was easy," Myles panted.

"Too easy," Sonny stated. "Something is wrong."

Then, we heard a girl screaming and the ring of gunshots. As fast as lightning, I ran down to see what had happened. *No, no, no, Shannon,* I worried as I ran. I came back to the main hall and was horrified at what I saw.

Zander had his empty, smoking pistol pointed towards Roxanne in the center of the room. She was on her knees and clutching her chest. Blood spurted out of her mouth as she tried to speak.

"Zander," she struggled to say, "you were once a… strong Combatant; almost as good… as me." She took a shaky breath. "Now… you've become lower than dirt." With that, her eyes rolled back in her head and she fell to the ground.

I watched in horror, unable to move. To my right, Mark, Aymie,

Shannon, and Alexandrea stood with tied up Brand; their eyes locked on the horrific scene before them. Alexandrea was screaming and the others were in shock. Emerging from the shadows to my left were Masdit, Gerrior, and Janelle. No sign of Theo and Jordan… which worried me.

"Now, have you learned your lesson?" Masdit asked, walking to his nephew's side. "Every time you piss me off, a friend dies." He took a deep breath. "Let's try again. Aymie, do you agree? Mark, will you help us?"

Confused, I asked, "Agree to what? Help you with what?"

Masdit rolled his eyes. "I hate when people show up late. Then I have to explain myself all over again." The hatred in his dark eyes pierced my soul like a dagger. "We want Aymie to come with us for… personal pleasure. As for Mark, he sent a virus throughout the world to destroy our online presence? Ring a bell?"

"*Our*?" I interrupted. "*You're* Order of Xenophon?"

"Be patient!" he yelled back. "You can't even wait five seconds for me to finish. You really are the most like your father."

At the sound of that, my jaw dropped and I was dumbfounded. *My father?* I thought, amazed. I stared at the villain and tried to ask what he meant.

My face was explanation enough. "Yes, of course we know your father," Masdit said, rolling his eyes. "He was Order of Xenophon with us. We were instructed to keep it a secret, but…" He shrugged.

"But what?" I asked through gritted teeth.

"Uncle, we should hurry," Zander reminded. "We only have so long."

Before he could respond, the ground shook again. Mark saw an opportunity. He tried to run up and tackle him, but wasn't fast enough. Masdit saw him coming, grabbed him, and threw him down. Luckily, it gave me an opening. I dashed up to Masdit, grabbed his forearms, and threw him down. I slammed his head hard against the cold floor, knocking him out.

Shouting, Zander picked up his pistol again, but Sonny was quicker. Purposely, he shot low, grazing the sides of Zander's legs. It was enough for Zander to buckle to the ground, screaming in pain. Gerrior and Janelle ran to their help but were blocked off by Nic and Sonny. In no time, my friends knocked the two out, and we were safe for a few moments.

I grabbed some rope from my bag, tied Masdit, and dragged him over to our other pile of secured prisoners. Sonny and Nic watched them while Aymie bandaged Zander's legs so he wouldn't bleed out. As she worked, she kept her eyes low while he looked at her with hatred, lust, and disgust. Myles kept Zander's hands back so he wouldn't reach for my sister.

Trembling, Alexandrea went to Roxanne's body and fell to her knees, unsure of what to do. Roxanne was Alexandrea's best friend. Now, she was gone in an instant.

While all this was happening, I stormed over to my brother. I yanked him to his feet and shook him by the shirt. "What were you thinking?!" I yelled in his face. "You could've gotten yourself killed. You couldn't have knocked him out if he gave you a free shot."

Tearing himself away, he exclaimed, "What's your beef? I could have done it if you gave me a chance. Sorry I'm not as perfect as you."

"What's that supposed to mean?" I asked, throwing my arms out.

"Sorry I have to work hard," he replied. "Sorry I have to make mistakes before I get things right. Sorry I have to compete with you over everything."

Now I was convinced he was just rambling. "All I said is you were going to get yourself killed."

"Immediately followed by an insult," Mark added. "I know I'm not perfect and am probably responsible for all of this—"

"Yeah, you are," I interrupted, jabbing my finger into his chest. I glared into his blue eyes and said, "Those boys lying upstairs. Whatever is running through their veins is a result of *your* thievery. *Your* hacking. *Your* screw ups."

"Of course I know that!" he yelled back. "Thanks for reminding me." He smacked my hand away. "Go back to your perfect life, and I'll go back to my 'evil' one."

"Guys, enough of this," Shannon cried, pushing the two of us away from each other. "Shame on both of you. I can't believe this. You're bickering because Mark tried to help and made a mistake. You find out your attackers are here to take you back with them and you don't care. Your dad is Order of Xenophon and you don't care. Roxanne was just *murdered* by our friend and neither of you care!" She motioned to her body that was laid on Alexandrea's lap.

I looked over and immediately felt guilty. Tears dripped down Alexandrea's cheeks and onto her cold, lifeless friend beneath her. She sniffled and looked up at Mark and me with hatred and rage. If she wasn't so stricken by sorrow she would've pulled out her pistol and shot us where we stood.

I didn't want to show sadness so I turned back to Shannon. She looked at Mark and me. Her blues eyes were puffy and her cheeks stained with tears. Shannon took a deep breath. "Shame. On. You," she said, her voice cracking. "Both of you need to crush your pride and start caring about someone else for once."

"I do care," I protested.

"Wow, he cares for someone other than himself," Mark said, clapping sarcastically. He looked at Shannon and added, "You know I care for you, beautiful, along with everyone else here."

"He's not the only one who cares for you," I said without thinking. Embarrassed, I quickly added, "And everyone else."

Before she could respond to that, she saw something behind me and gasped. Within seconds, she dug her nails into my arm and threw me on top of Mark so we both crashed to the ground. As we fell, I heard her exhale sharply and my sister screamed. Quickly, I rolled off my brother and looked up. My face fell.

Before me, Shannon was struggling to stand as she gripped the arrow that stuck out of her chest. Blood dripped from the wound. Slowly, the green liquid in the arrow's shaft began to disappear as it leaked inside her. She was shaking and staggering backward.

Mark and I were too shocked to do anything. We sat there staring like idiots while our friend was dying. Sonny ran up and grabbed Shannon as she fell backwards. Behind them, I saw the Mutants, Theo and Jordan, standing at the bottom of the stairwell. Jordan was clutching the crossbow Myles found earlier. His white fangs shown in the dark as he smiled menacingly. Before he could fire again, I watched as Nic hurled a crate towards the two, causing them to scurry back up the stairs before the entrance was blocked.

Realizing what was going on, I snapped out of it and jumped to my feet. I went over to Sonny who had Shannon in his arms. She was conscious but quickly fading. "We need to get her to a hospital!" I shouted.

"There is no time," Sonny replied, cradling her head. Shannon's eyes were fluttering and her skin was paling. "She won't make it there."

"Fallout isn't too far away," Mark put in. "It's our only option."

"Hurry up and let's go," Aymie shouted as she jumped up. Zander managed to get released from Myles' grip and latched onto her leg, causing her to come crashing down. With a shout, Aymie kicked him in the face, knocking him out. She stood to her feet and shuddered. "Get him away from me!" she ordered Myles. The boy nodded and dragged him to Nic.

Once again, the warehouse shook, causing us all to stagger. "You go!" Nic yelled, regaining his balance. "Myles, Alexandrea, and I will finish things here."

Within seconds, we were at the van. Once Aymie, Sonny, and Shannon were in the back, Mark and I hopped in the front. Before I knew it, Mark had it started and we were on our way.

Still trying to process it all as we drove, I looked at my brother and asked, "What have we done?"

# CHAPTER 40
## Aymie: XIII

Fine, I'll finish this part of the story. You boys should be ashamed, I won't sugar coat it. That entire time you both were insensitive. You shouldn't be apologizing to me. The ones you should apologize to the most aren't here anymore.

That five minute drive to Mark's old hangout felt like an eternity. I sat in the back of the van with Sonny, cradling Shannon's head. Her face paled and her eyes were distant. I was in shock and didn't know what to do. *I couldn't save Roxanne…but please let me save you.* I watched her struggle to breathe with the long, thin arrow sticking out of her chest. The fragile shaft continued to dispense the contents into my friend's weak lungs. It was more than half empty now.

Mark jerked the van sharply, and we screeched to a halt. Sonny stopped Shannon and I before we slid off the bench. My brothers flung upon the back doors. Sonny gently took Shannon into his arms, and we exited the van.

Carefully, we followed Mark down many dark corridors until we reached an alleyway lined with garbage dumpsters. Mark ran up to the wall and searched for something. Finding a hidden keypad, he entered the code and a dumpster slid away, revealing a hidden staircase below.

We cautiously descended, careful not to shake Shannon and stir the poison filling her lungs.

At the bottom, we found ourselves in a dark, damp, disgusting kitchen. One lightbulb hung above an island. The paint was peeling off the walls and the machinery was rusty. Not to mention the entire place smelled like bad body odor and decay. I didn't have time to comment on Mark's old home. Shannon was dying and we needed to do something. We threw everything off the island counter and placed her down.

Hearing the crash of glass, Mark's foster father, Big Daddy, came out to see what was going on. When he saw us and the arrow in Shannon's chest, his jaw dropped and he froze. He was speechless. He pointed to our friend, looked at my brother, and made a horrified face.

"Big Daddy, we need your help," Mark begged. "Do we still have the first aid kit?"

"Yeah, but you'll need more than that kit," he remarked as he ran to fetch it.

"It's all we'll need for the wound," Sonny said. He took off his combat jacket and threw it on the couch in the next room. "Not sure about the poison, though." He thought for a moment and ordered, "Get me a bowl of water, a needle, string, and two towels." He quickly washed his hands and a knife that was nearby. With the utensil in his grip, he leaned over Shannon and began to cut her shirt off.

Shane turned bright red. "Whoa, what do you think you're doing?" He didn't want his friend to be violated.

"Saving her life!" Sonny bellowed. He couldn't finish cutting because the knife was too dull. He stopped and went to get a new one, but his belt got snagged on something. Shannon's beautiful long hair flowed across the island. Sighing, he bunched all her hair up in one hand and slightly pulled. With the other, he chopped it off up to her ears.

I gasped. *No, not her hair,* I thought. I was always jealous of her brown curls. I would never want it to be treated like that. When you have alopecia, seeing that was depressing.

"Dude!" Mark yelled.

"Enough!" Sonny tossed her cut hair onto the counter behind him. Then, he noticed another obstacle: her Celtic knot necklace.

He was about to cut that too when Shane grabbed his arm. "Don't you dare," he threatened. Not wanting Shannon's prized possession to be destroyed, my brother took the initiative and removed the jewelry and put it in his pocket.

Sonny glared. "Go get me that stuff." When my brothers ran off, he looked at me and said, "You're a seamstress right?"

I knew where that was going. "I've never sewed a person before."

"It's not that different, trust me," Sonny told me as he pulled his long dark hair back into a low ponytail. "You can do it; just stay as close to the edge as possible without it bleeding and releasing the stitch."

"Why don't you do it?" I asked. "Seems like you have experience."

"Enough arguing," he commanded. "You truly are a Hodgins. I can't do it because I will be removing the arrow as you stitch. I have to make sure it doesn't get caught on her lung. Otherwise..." He didn't finish, and I didn't need him to.

I closed my eyes and took a deep breath. Then, the words of my foster sister Abigail came flooding back. "*A true princess puts others before herself...*" Looking at Sonny, I stated, "I'll do it."

Sonny nodded and turned his attention back to Shannon.

Mark, Shane, and Big Daddy returned with the supplies. Following them in was Mason Couch. He was more shocked than Big Daddy when he saw one of his weapons sticking out of our friend's chest.

"Whoa," he said in amazement. He examined it while Sonny put latex gloves on. "The crossbow actually works." He pressed his hand against Shannon's forehead and then her chest. "And *Mark's Menacing Mixture* is working effectively."

"That isn't sometime to be proud of," Mark shouted. "Why did you name it after me?"

"It was named in your honor after you raided that science facility and saved Theo and Jordan; when you received your brand," Couch told him, poking Mark's chest. "We never had it in someone this long so I'm not sure if it's fatal or not."

"What does it do and is there an antidote?" Sonny asked as he removed Shannon's shirt. Blushing, my brothers turned away out of respect and embarrassment.

"Of course, there's an antidote," Couch exclaimed. "I always have one, because the boys are my test subjects. What sucks is it isn't permanent." He scratched his pierced eyebrow and went on, "As for what the poison does: it's meant to pierce the lungs and fill them with a painful toxin that suffocates them. The toxin attaches to the sides of the lungs and gets stirred when she breathes. Oh, and she is also temporarily paralyzed."

"Then go get the antidote," Sonny growled through gritted teeth. Intimidated, the tattooed man ran. Our friend looked back down at Shannon and his face fell. Her chest was barely moving and her pulse was fading. The arrow shaft was empty of its green poison. Taking a towel, he wet it and began cleaning the blood off her chest. "We need to get this out of her."

I put on gloves, fixed my bandana, and threaded a needle, shaking with every movement.

Couch came back with another arrow filled with clear liquid. "Here it is," he said, handing it to Sonny. "You need to put this *exactly* where the hole is in her lung. Once it's in there, it'll close up the hole in seconds and distribute some of the antidote. The rest has to be breathed in."

Sonny nodded and took the antidote arrow in one hand. He wrapped his fingers around the other in Shannon. "Aymie, I need you to pull her skin away as I do the switch."

I nodded. I placed my fingers on other side of her wound and gently tugged. Ever so carefully, he pulled one arrow out and slid the other in its place. His sharp red eyes were locked on his task. A bead of sweat trickled down his pale forehead. Nothing could break his focus. Despite the pain it must've inflicted, Shannon didn't flinch.

The antidote was in.

"In the hole," Sonny told us as the liquid disappeared from the shaft.

"How do you know?" Shane asked; his back still towards us. "I bet you couldn't even see inside."

"I never need to," Sonny replied, confidently. We watched as the liquid decanted rather quickly. "Ready Aymie? It's up to you now."

I was not ready, but I had to be. Shannon needed me. I wasn't able to save Roxanne from Zander or Zander from himself. I *had* to be able to save Shannon. I took a deep breath and said, "Ready." Slowly, Sonny removed the arrow, and I stitched what I could. He was stable and calm as if he'd done this a million times. As for me, I was trembling with every stitch.

"Steady, my dear," Big Daddy told me as I tugged the needle out of her skin.

After an agonizing minute, the arrow was out and I did the final stitch. I tied it off and cleaned up her wound. I looked at Shannon, hoping for her to wake up instantly. It was worse; she wasn't breathing. "What's wrong?" I cried.

"I told you, she needs to breathe in the rest," Couch reminded. He had a handheld pump. "She needs to take this inhaler."

"How can she take it if she's not breathing?" I panicked.

Swiping it from Couch's bony hand, Sonny tore off his gloves and began shaking it. "I'll breathe it for her."

"Wait, what are you gonna do?" Mark asked, still facing the opposite way.

Letting out a few breaths, Sonny inhaled the antidote, put his fingers against Shannon's lips, bent over, and breathed into her mouth. After a breath, he inhaled the medicine and did it again. He repeated the process until the pump was empty.

When Sonny pulled away for the last time, Shannon inhaled and coughed. She gasped for air. It took her several tries, but she was able to steady her breathing a bit. She was struggling, but she was alive.

With his hands still on her cheeks, Sonny chuckled and said, "I think she's going to be okay." He carefully lifted her head and helped her to sit up. He stood behind her and let her recline on his chest.

Everyone let out sighs of relief. Shane took off his combat jacket, reached his arm back, and shook it. "Aymie, please put this on her so Mark and I can turn around."

Shannon smiled. She wanted to say something but no words would come out. "Don't speak. Just breathe," I told her as Sonny and I dressed her.

Once they heard the zip, the boys turned around. Looks of regret and guilt fell over their faces. They stared at Shannon and tried to find the words to say.

Shane grabbed her hand. Meeting her eyes, he shook his head and whispered, "I am so sorry." He thought over everything he had done and his green eyes began to well up with tears. "I'm sorry," he said with his head down.

Before Shannon could attempt to say anything, the ground shook again. "What is going on?" I asked. "The warehouse kept shaking like this."

"Probably another bombing somewhere in the city," Couch said nonchalantly.

"'Another'?" Mark asked.

"Yeah, where have you been?" Couch asked, his pale arms crossed. "The bombings have been more frequent. Not just in New York, though." He went to a kitchen drawer and pulled out several newspapers from all over the world. "Don't you keep up with the news?"

"We never think about it," Mark told him, pushing his brown bang behind his ear.

"You should start now," Bid Daddy chimed in. Before he could continue, he had a coughing fit. He denied that there was anything wrong with him and went on, "The world is collapsing and you need to know why."

"Nah, we'll be fine," Couch said. "First off, we live in a bomb shelter. We're safe from those. Second, all these attacks are mostly accidents anyway. They're caused by the mentally insane or misunderstood. Once those people are under control, things will go back to normal."

When he mentioned the word "accidents", Mark's face fell and he became nervous. *He must know more,* I thought, looking at my brother.

"Oth…ers," Shannon interrupted as best she could. She was still resting against Sonny's strong chest and holding Shane's hand.

"Right, you should probably get back," Couch advised. "Those guys who I was trading with said they would pay me ten million to blow up my warehouse. So…yeah… that's probably why the floor shook."

We all stared at him. Even Big Daddy was shocked at his words. "What 'guys'?" Mark asked through gritted teeth.

"The bosses of the guys who did this to you," he told us. "Some Russian and German dudes."

My face paled, and I was shaking again. *It can't be…* I thought. *They were so kind to us.*

Shannon shakily touched my arm with her free hand. She knew what was going through my mind. "So..rry," she croaked.

"I knew they were behind this," Sonny growled, getting stiff. "Although I wasn't expecting they were working with the Hodgins' attackers."

"Then again, they all were a part of the Order of Xenophon," Shane put in.

"Like dad, apparently," Mark muttered.

"We don't know that for sure," Shane reminded him. "We have Masdit and Gerrior in custody. We'll find the truth."

We had been waiting too long and needed to get back. Sonny carefully lifted Shannon off the table, releasing her from Shane's grasp. He wasn't happy, but he understood.

"We have to go," Sonny said. Looking at my brother, he ordered, "Mark, get a year's worth of antidote. She won't survive without it." He said nothing else and carried Shannon away without saying goodbye. Peeking over his shoulder, she weakly waved to Big Daddy and Couch.

"He's right," Couch said, slightly surprised. "She isn't really cured and never will be. The antidote just makes the poison dormant.

Once she starts moving and gets the slightest out of breath, it will wake up and try to take over." He didn't wait for a reply and left to get it.

We were all too shocked for words. *How will she ever be the same if it will kill her to breathe?* I wondered.

Thankfully, Big Daddy interrupted my thinking. "Yes, you must take as much as possible and hurry back." He went over to Mark and gave him a manly hug goodbye. He whispered something into his ear. Nodding, Mark patted his foster father's back who in turn started a coughing fit. "No...I'm fine," he reassured, covering his mouth.

Couch returned with a tattered shoebox of inhalers. He handed it to Mark along with a piece of paper. "This is my recipe if you have someone smart enough to replicate it," he said. "Good luck."

Tearing the items from him, Mark glowered at Couch and dashed up the stairs with Shane and me close behind.

In no time, we were back in the van and speeding to the warehouse. Sonny was now in the front with Mark, and Shane stayed with Shannon and me. We laid her down across the seats with her head resting on my lap. Shane sat on the floor next to us so he could hold her hand.

The van jerked to a stop. After regaining my balance, I placed my hands on Shannon's shoulders to steady her. "I wonder what had happened," I thought aloud.

"Why don't you check it out with the others? I'll stay with Shannon," Shane offered, fixing his brown, layered hair.

I looked to Shannon for an answer. She slowly nodded. Carefully lifting her head, Shane and I traded places. I grabbed a weapon and hopped out the back. When I looked up, I couldn't believe what I saw.

There was nothing. The morning sun peaked over a pile of rubble that was once the warehouse. Dust snowed from the sky and the street lights flickered, eerily illuminating the debris. What scared me the most was no one was around.

Mark rushed over and asked as calmly as possible, "Aymie, do you remember what the map looked like? You stared at it on the wall."

"Of course."

"Were there any rooms that they might have stayed in?"

Envisioning the map in my head, I went over each section. From what I could tell, each room was destroyed. Then, I decided to remember what each room looked like individually. I remembered there was one nook in the wall that could've been a possible safe space. "There is one part in the northwest corner on the main floor; close to where we were when…everything happened."

"Let's go," Mark ordered. He yelled to Sonny, who was scrutinizing the wreckage for signs of life. Cautiously, the three of us went to what used to be the corner of the room. We examined each section, moving away bricks and scraps.

"Guys, over there!" Mark shouted. He pointed to a large, metal shelf lying across the bricks. It was dented, melted, but still intact. Rushing over, we all grabbed an edge. "On the count of three we lift," Mark said. "One, two…" Before he could finish, the shelf rose on its own.

I looked underneath and saw Nic, covered in bruises and bleeding. He was pushing the shelf up with his upper back. We all stepped away as he stood upright. Grabbing the shelf, he roared inhumanly and threw it over his head.

Filled with adrenaline, he rapidly scooped up the bricks and threw them away, revealing Myles, Alexandrea, and our prisoners underneath; all conscious and alive.

Mark was amazed. "You…saved them all."

"Of course I did," Nic said, laughing. His adrenaline faded and exhaustion began to take him over. He moved enough bricks for everyone to escape. "Hurry up and get them out," he ordered as he wobbled back to the van. We obeyed and carefully helped Myles and Alexandrea up. Once they were safe, we violently yanked our prisoners out and dragged them back to the van.

Looking back, Mark mumbled, "I hope Theo and Jordan made it out…so I can kill them myself."

While the boys piled our prisoners in, I stood outside and tended to Alexandrea's and Myles' bumps and bruises.

Alexandrea's blond hair was caked in blood and tears fell from her blue eyes, staining her dusty cheeks. Her combat uniform was torn and she was missing a fireproof glove. "Roxanne..." she mumbled as I cleaned her up. "I couldn't even give her a proper burial."

"It's not your fault," I told her.

"You're right." She looked up. Hatred in her light eyes. "It's yours and Mark's," she spat. "It's your guys' fault she's dead." She snatched my hand and squeezed it as tight as she could. I squealed as my bones cracked in her grasp. "It's your fault Zander betrayed us. You should've done us all a favor and went with him."

Taken aback, I tore my hand away. I stared at her blankly with my mouth gaped open. I didn't know what to say… I felt like she was right.

"No it's not!" Myles yelled. He ruffled his bright blond hair and wiped the dirt off his pale face. He looked Alexandrea dead in the eye and said with his little voice, "Zander made an offer Aymie had to refuse. He has become a disgusting animal like his uncle. Aymie should never be expected to go *anywhere* with him. " The thought of it made the mature eleven-year-old shudder. He changed the subject. "Mark did his job. There is nothing that can change that. Don't forget, they were after all the Hodginses. They wanted Shane too."

"Seems to me like Shane didn't do anything wrong. They didn't say anything," she remarked. Although we knew her admiration for Shane was the only reason she didn't blame him as well. "As for Mark doing his 'job'," she made air quotes with her fingers, "that's the only time that deadbeat has done anything worth noticing. Other than that he's useless. If I can remember right, he is the one who knew these people. His connections did this."

Overhearing this, Mark kept his head down; obviously taking it all to heart. I wanted to reprimand her for talking about my brother like that, but I tried to be understanding. We did just watch our friend die right before our eyes. However, I regretted not speaking up. The fact that no one stood up for Mark made those awful words stir inside him.

"Guys, we have to get moving," Nic told us, still breathing heavily. "We tranquilized our prisoners for now, but they'll wake up soon."

We all piled into the van. Sonny sat to the back and kept his weapon pointed at our sleeping guests. Alexandrea sat next to him, and I next to her. Shane had Shannon who fell asleep in his arms. He tried not to smile but couldn't help it.

Seeing the two, Mark was obviously filled with jealousy; not to mention he was still upset from Alexandrea's words. He sat on the end aloof from the rest of us.

As we started moving, I reflected on everything that happened. The ghostly quiet of the van left room for me to think. I thought about the men who had been after my family for years and if what they said about our dad was true. I thought about my friends and what Alexandrea said. *If I really went with Zander, would Roxanne have lived?* I wondered. Then again, the thought of being abused and violated in such a way disgusted me. *"A true princess is virtuous in all things,"* I remembered Abigail say.

Then, a horrifying thought came to my mind. I glanced at my old friend, Janelle. I couldn't believe her condition. She was blind in one eye, covered in scratches, and not her fun loving self. *What awful things did they do to you?*

Not wanting to think, I decided to rest. I laid my head on Shane who smiled and wrapped his arm around me. My brother's embrace soothed my worried spirit. Not to mention he was a comfortable pillow. I needed rest and for my brain to stop thinking. So much had happened in a short amount of time. I was overwhelmed and exhausted. I fell right to sleep.

Hours later, I was awoken when Myles jerked the van to a stop. Thankfully, Shane was still holding me so I didn't go flying like Mark and Alexandrea. Cursing like a sailor, Mark rubbed his newly bruised forehead. He abruptly jumped up and flung open the van doors.

What we found on the other side left us speechless.

The driveway was covered in rubble and ash. The trees around us were on fire and the air covered in thick black smoke. The smell of gas, electrical, and explosives polluted the air. Directly ahead of us was a gaping hole in the front of Wyght's Home for Young People.

Our home was attacked.

# CHAPTER 41

## Aymie: XIV

"No, no, no," Mark repeated, jumping out the back of the van. Alexandrea and I quickly followed behind. "Who did this?!" he screamed.

"Whoever they are, I'll kill them," Alexandrea growled. The three of us ran up to the hole in the front of the mansion. Climbing over the rubble, we went inside the destroyed foyer. The stairs to the girls' dormitory had crumbled and the entrance to the classrooms straight ahead was barricaded with stones.

"Hello?" I shouted. "Blake? Johanna? Dylan?"

"Lady Clarius!" a familiar little voice called. Racing out of the door leading to the boys' dorms was five-year-old Agnes. Her reddish-blonde hair was matted and her freckled face was covered in dirt. She smashed into me and wrapped her arms around my legs. "You're okay." She looked up at me with big blue eyes and cried, "I can't find people."

Kneeling down, I shakily put my hands on her shoulders. My heart was racing. I knew something was wrong. "Who can't you find?"

Before she could say, two people raced up the dorm stairs. I let out a sigh of relief. It was Blake and Johanna. "Aymie," they said simultaneously. They looked terrible. Blake's white hair was black with soot and his gray sweater was torn. Johanna's pale face was scratched and her dirty-blond hair was untamable.

Blake ran up first and flung his arms around me. I smelled gun powder on his sweater. "Thank God you're safe," he whispered.

"Yeah, I'm safe too, guys. Thanks for caring," I overheard Mark mutter. He shoved his hands deep into his pockets and headed over to the hall that led to the Nerd headquarters.

When Blake pulled away, I saw sadness in his bright eyes. "It came true."

My heart sank. *I knew it...* I had no words. Knowing something was coming and not being able to do anything about it was a horrible burden he was bearing. And...I did nothing to aid him. After Blake had told me he had a dream, I thought immediately about Zander. A piece of me knew he would be responsible for this, but I remained silent.

Johanna snapped me out of it. "Hey, Aymie."

"What?" I replied, startled.

"Where's Shannon?" she pleaded. Her green eyes filled with worry. I hadn't noticed the other five Hollinger girls came over. They were a mess and desperately looked around for their sister. Despite the horror they must've endured, the little girls were brave and calm.

Thankfully, Shane came into the foyer carrying their sister before I could respond. Shannon was awake. She leaned her head on Shane and clutched his chest for support. Even after sleeping for ten hours straight, she was still tense, exhausted, and couldn't walk. When she saw her sisters, her eyes lit up and her body relaxed.

The girls and Johanna rushed over to her and Shane, asking a million questions at once. They were worried sick. Of course the first thing the little ones noticed was their big sister's haircut.

Shane carefully sat down on a rock with Shannon perched on his lap. Shannon still couldn't speak so he did it for her. Looking at them all, I couldn't help but smile. They were the cutest little family ever.

*Family*, I thought, remembering that our dad is supposedly OX.

"So what happened?" Alexandrea interrupted, growing impatient.

"We were attacked a few days ago," a man's voice said. It was

Papa E. His gray robes were ripped and he was missing the beads that hung from his belt. "Those two men that were Wyght's friends did this." He rubbed his beard. "They tricked us. They sent in a child as a decoy to make a ruckus on the inside. While many of us were distracted, Nikita and Walter's men abducted many children. Once they were done, they blew up the front of the house so we couldn't chase after them."

"Was anyone…killed?" I asked, slowly. Papa E shook his head, and I let out a sigh of relief. "So everyone's okay?"

"More or less," he replied. "We are banged up a bit, but still breathing. However, many children were taken and who knows what torture they will undergo. We have to pray and work hard to get them back."

"Who was taken?" Alexandrea asked, sternly.

The older man's eyes filled with sadness. "At least ten from each Branch. They were strategic with their choosing. Among them were close friends of yours: Dylan Cheatle, Clive Foxwood, and Adeline Zarra."

I couldn't believe my ears. I didn't want to. I wobbled over to Shane, Shannon, and Johanna and sat next to them. I needed to reflect. *That explains why they were asking so many questions*, I thought. *Nikita and Walter wanted to do this from the first beginning.*

Seeing my distressed face, Shannon shakily reached out and placed her hand on my head. I looked up at her through tears and managed a smile. Sweetly, she rubbed my cheek. She rested her face on Shane's chest and mumbled slowly, "Not…your…fault."

"It is," I replied, gently putting her hand down. "I let Nikita and Walter in that first day and every day after. I knew something bad was going to happen. I knew Zander would betray us…" I was going to continue but the tears fell from my face. The dam had burst and the waters rushed forth. I sobbed and couldn't control it. Blake came over and wrapped his arm around me in a failed attempt to console my bitter weeping. I threw my hands on my face and cried, "Now Roxanne is gone, Dylan is gone, and Adeline is gone."

"So is Clive but who cares about my friends," Mark sharply

added. He was back from his search. I looked up at him and was about to apologize, but he held his hand up. He saw Shane holding Shannon on his lap and scoffed. "I hate to interrupt your 'family' circle but one of our prisoners agreed to talk." With that he began to walk away and called back, "Meet us in the hangar."

"Well, we better follow Mr. Cranky Pants," Johanna said, trying to keep the mood light. Turning to the little Hollinger girls, she told them Peggy was in charge and to go look for food in the kitchen. Once the six were gone, Johanna jumped up and fixed her disheveled attire. She tightened the knot in the leather cord around her neck that held the heart shaped key.

Eyeing her necklace, Shannon noticed her own was missing. Panicking, she shakily rubbed her fingers across her neck to feel for hers.

"Don't worry, I have it," Shane told her. He reached into his pocket with his free hand and pulled it out. "All intact with the key and all the rings." Shannon let out a deep hoarse breath, smiled, and stroked his face to say thanks. He blushed and cleared his throat when she removed her hand. Examining the key, Shane chuckled and said, "One day you are going to show me what's in the box it opens." She shrugged and motioned for Johanna to put it on her.

"I didn't know it opened something," I asked, standing up and wiping the tears from my face. I wanted to keep my mind busy.

Johanna nodded when it was secure around her friend's neck. "They sure do. 'Box of Secrets' we call it. For one person's eyes only."

"Who is that person?" Shane asked, interested. Johanna ignored him, grabbed Blake's and my hand, and dragged us away. "Hey!" he called after us.

Still being pulled by Johanna, we made our way out of the destroyed house, across the burnt fields, past the runway, and into the safe hangar. "I'm glad this place is okay," I said when she let go.

"They didn't need to come this way," Johanna replied. "All the kids were in the house."

Finally, we were in the confinement room that was Nic's prison cell when he went crazy. Inside were Mr. Wyght, Sonny, Nic, Myles, and Mark. Only one of our prisoners was behind the glass: Gerrior. Handcuffs were secured around his thick wrists. He sat in a chair behind a plastic table.

When Nic saw Johanna, he let out a deep breath and ran over to her. "You're alive," he said, relieved.

"No, really?" she replied, sarcastically. Chuckling, he threw his giant arms around her and pulled her close, not caring what she said. Not being able to wriggle her way out, she hugged him back. As much as she denied it, she did care for him.

I left the two alone and went to stand by Mark. "What's happening?" I asked my brother.

"He is finally going to explain why he has been after us since we were born," Mark said flatly, not taking his eyes off the large tattooed man in our custody.

"Everyone there?" Gerrior asked through the speaker. Shane shuffled in and placed Shannon in an empty seat Sonny set up for her. Mark rolled his eyes when they entered. He hated the sight.

"Shane is back with Shannon. There are nine in here with me," Mr. Wyght said, crossing his arms. He looked in bad shape too. His dress shirt was ripped and his pants littered with holes. Stress and sorrow grayed his hair, and his eyes were sad. His veteran's cap was crushed and laid neatly on the counter top. "Now, tell me. Why are you giving us information so quickly?"

"I've wanted to tell someone ever since I was ordered to take the Hodgins' children," Gerrior explained.

"Who ordered you?"

Taking a deep breath, he answered, "Nikita Patya and Walter Jarvis."

My face fell and I stared blankly at him. His words seemed foreign, yet I understood it perfectly. *Everything really is our fault...*

"Impossible!" Mr. Wyght denied, interrupting my self-loathing. "You have been chasing them for seventeen years. Nikita and Walter were practically boys then."

"Boys old enough to serve in the military," Gerrior told him. "Didn't you meet them overseas?"

"Yes? And?"

"They joined the Order of Xenophon while they were there," he explained. "You said you already know how they rose to the top. Well, they had a superior who kept an eye on them." He took a deep breath and leaned back in his chair. "It was one of the head Xenophonians—called Titans—known to us as Marcellus Hodgins: the triplets' father."

Everyone was quiet and turned to us. We were once again too stunned for words. For the first time, we heard our father's name. "Marcellus?" I asked.

"We don't know if that was his godly OX name or his real one," Gerrior clarified.

"Mark…" Shannon spoke up as best she could. "Marcellus."

Mark understood and thought for a moment. "If that's his real name…I'm named after Dad." His blue eyes danced excitedly. "I'm named after Dad!"

"We should probably hear what he did first before you get too excited," Shane said, placing his hand on our brother's shoulder. Jealousy glinted in his green eyes that he didn't receive that honor.

Thinking, Sonny rubbed the OX brand on the back of his neck. "If he was a head, I should've known him. Nikita was promoted not too long after he abducted my mother and me."

"You're the same age as the triplets," Gerrior reminded. "We've been after them since they were born which means Marcellus ruined everything before you came."

"What do you mean?" I asked, nervously.

Finally, Gerrior told us the truth:

"Marcellus joined the Order of Xenophon at fifteen. Even at that age, he was a favorite among the higher Xenophonians. He excelled at everything he tried. He was part of the Hermes Division which meant he would travel from base to base doing deliveries and scouting. It's the toughest Division to be a part of. You need a wide skill set or you won't last. You have to be quick and shrewd." He smirked. "Your father had all that. He was the fastest and sneakiest one of the entire English Pandemonium—which is everyone in OX with English as a first language. He also had an amazing memory and a knack for computers.

"He was twenty when he trained to lead our Pandemonium as the Titan of the Hermes Division. Several weeks later, he went on a solo mission where he met your mother: a lonely street musician in California. He fell in love immediately. We're taught to abduct, but he's a little old fashioned. He courted her, respecting her dignity. He would visit whenever possible and eventually asked her to marry him. She said yes and became Amelia Hodgins."

Hearing my mother's name, Johanna gasped and smacked my arm repeatedly. "Aymie!"

I ignored the pain and stood dumbfounded. Her name was sweet and its feeling was kind. *Mom...* I thought, trying to remember her.

"Wait, where did my name come from then?" Shane asked, slightly disappointed.

Gerrior shrugged. "Someone's middle name maybe? Marcellus never talked to anyone about his personal life…because he and Amelia would've been killed if they found out."

"Why? What was so wrong?" I asked.

"One of the main purposes of marriage procreation," Sonny interjected. "You can't do that at OX without special permission and a specific mate. That's what the Eros Division is for. Those who belong to those are designated a partner. Everyone else can abduct their own if they choose and as long as no children are born."

Gerrior nodded. "Marcellus never took her back with him. She never knew about OX. She thought he was a business man always on trips. She didn't find out until after they had you triplets. Unfortunately," he sighed, "she had to find out the hard way. When Masdit and I were sent to kill Marcellus and take you all."

"What did he do that made you hunt him?" Nic asked, deeply interested in the entire story.

"He betrayed us," Gerrior said, flatly. "One day Marcellus decided he didn't want to be an OX member anymore. He hated lying to his wife, and he needed to provide for his children. He was tired of stealing money to support them. He was tired of tearing other families apart and struggling to keep his together. He needed to get away. But," he shrugged, "it's OX or death. So, he betrayed everyone." He leaned his forearms on the table, his cuffs clanking against the plastic. "He leaked thousands of documents to the police, setting OX back years from their next phase."

"Which is?" Mr. Wyght asked.

His dark eyes glared through the one way glass and somehow found Mr. Wyght. "The Cleanse," he stated. "We are living right in the middle of it. The attacks, the 'accidents', are because of them. They are cleansing the world of the lesser beings."

"Okay, I can see why they'd be pissed," Sonny interjected. "Betrayal is the biggest offense and they've been working on that phase for over twenty years, but you said that Nikita and Walter hired you. They betrayed OX, too."

"They did. Marcellus was the one who ratted them out, setting *them* back years as well," Gerrior explained. "They sent Masdit and me to kill him and his wife to stop them from talking. They also wanted us to take the children to assist them in their new plans. After all, they are the offspring of the greatest OX member in the Hermes Division. From what I can tell stalking them for seventeen years, they each have a third of their father's talent. Together, they could match, and even surpass, Marcellus. Now that they're older, they have an even better chance.

"And so, we went after the Hodginses. Amelia escaped and separated the triplets before we found her again. Marcellus gave us one hell of a fight."

I held my breath. I dared not to ask, so Blake did it for me: "What happened to their parents?"

Gerrior cast his eyes downward. "When Amelia ran off with the kids, Masdit and I had to separate. I was the one who went after Marcellus. I chased him through the woods and to the edge of a cliff. He had nowhere to go. I cocked my pistol and pointed it towards him." He paused for a moment and lifted his head back up. With a smirk, he said, "I didn't pull the trigger."

"So, he's alive?" Shane asked hopefully.

"Not sure," the prisoner responded. "He thanked me and ran off to find Amelia. I never knew if he saved her or not. Now," he held up his hands, "here we are. Seventeen years later. I've been hunting you your entire lives. Now you know why."

I needed years to process all this, but Sonny didn't even give me a second. Immediately after, he asked, "Why didn't you kill him? Judging by all your tattoos you were in the Ares Division." He pointed to the double edged sword that crawled from behind Gerrior's left ear and disappeared beneath his shirt. "You also have the Mark of Ares which means you are unmistakably an assassin. Killing their father should've been easy."

"I always hated our violence," Gerrior spat. "Every kill I made I regretted. These tattoos are all reminders. I'm sure you have your share. You would've gotten this if you stayed," he patted the sword on his neck. "You were Ares too, weren't you?" Sonny subconsciously rubbed his right side and didn't grace him with an answer. "Despite all these markings, I hated the entire ideology of OX. I only followed orders because…" Gerrior cleared his throat. "I'm afraid of death."

Sonny scoffed. "You never had it in you to be a part of OX."

"Why do you think I'm here now telling you all this?" he stated, defensively. "I've been following orders from Nikita and Walter to get away from OX. It's my only option. They protect me from OX, I do their bidding."

"If you hate violence why did you plunge my aunt and uncle into the river?" Shane asked, bitterly. His face reddened and his eyes watered. "Why did you murder the entire Regal Circus?"

"Masdit gives the orders," he replied, harshly. "He would kill me in an instant for disobeying him." He let out a deep breath. "I'm sorry about your friends, especially Robert. I know he betrayed you, but we shouldn't have had to kill him. He did help us after all."

Shane's face fell. He never knew what happened to the teen trapeze artist that turned him in. He slowly staggered back and leaned against the wall, taking a deep breath. He shook his head and thought for a moment. All those deaths and now he knew another life was lost…because of him. Shane shielded his eyes with his right hand and looked down. I watched as he wet the floor below him with his tears.

Shakily, Shannon reached out and grabbed his other hand in an attempt to comfort him.

"I can't believe this," Mr. Wyght said, pressing his palms against the table in front of him. "What about the other children we took as prisoners? What happened to the Hollingers and Wattersons?"

Quickly, he explained, "Janelle is now Masdit's adopted daughter whose brain was tampered with by some of Nikita's men; he calls them Keepers for some reason. She forgot who she was and just does whatever Masdit says. Brand actually works for a scientist, Carl Mallory, but we are borrowing him for this mission." He paused and thought for a moment. "You know, I don't remember going after the kids' parents. I only remember knocking out Quinn Hollinger to get the kids who ran off. We got out of there when we heard trucks coming."

"Trucks?" Johanna asked. Remembering that awful day, she said, "There were no trucks."

"We heard them and fled," Gerrior repeated.

"The Order of Xenophon uses trucks when they go on raids," Sonny put in. "I bet they took your parents."

"Probably," Gerrior said. Standing up, he stepped away from the table and went over to the door. "We have spoken enough. You need to put me back and prepare."

"Prepare for what?" Mr. Wyght asked.

"The next raid," Gerrior stated. "Nikita will return."

Mr. Wyght ordered for Gerrior to be put back and he ran off to make preparations. I let Nic and Sonny take care of that. My siblings and I needed to take a minute. The three of us went off into the corner and stared at each other. We had no tears to cry and no words to say.

After a moment, Shane put an arm around each of us and pulled us together for a group hug. I embraced my brothers and prayed the worst was behind us. "Let's never leave each other," I begged. "I think our family has been separated and broken enough."

Agreeing, the two pulled me closer. "We will be stronger than Nikita and Walter could ever imagine," Mark said, confidently.

"Yeah," Shane agreed, "They will never see us coming."

# CHAPTER 42
## Mark: XIII

After Gerrior told us about our parents, everything changed for my siblings, me, and all of WHYP. Not only were we on constant alert, but we started a separate operation designed to take OX and Nikita head on. It took an entire year to prepare. During that time, things grew interesting.

It was the Christmas after the attack and no one was happy, despite the joyful holiday. Papa E celebrated a beautiful Mass and we were throwing a party, which should have been enough, but everyone was glum. It was another holiday without our friends.

I was depressed for many reasons:

First off, I felt like everyone hated my guts. Thanks to Alexandrea's big mouth, everyone thought that it was only *my* fault that Roxanne was killed, we were attacked, and Shannon was injured. People ignored me. Avoided me. Every other sentence was a bash against me. My good image was tainted and distorted by my past and these new rumors.

Despite my siblings and me promising that we would be together no matter what, we were still apart. They were never there for me. I felt like they didn't want me around what happened. As a result, I remained aloof. No sense hanging with people who don't want you, right?

Christmas day I sat alone at my desk in the Nerd Headquarters, working on the backend of our new operation. Together, Myles and I brainstormed several ideas that could protect our digital footprint.

Normally, Derek would help, but he was too depressed. Clive was his best friend since they arrived at WHYP together. Now, it was the first Christmas without him. Even though I was there, Derek still felt alone. That was a stab through the heart. Of course losing Clive was tragic, but was I not enough?

"I guess I never am enough for anyone", I muttered as I entered more code.

"What's that supposed to mean?" a familiar voice said behind me.

My heart jumped. Not only was I startled, but I knew who it was. Turning around, I found Shannon standing at the top of the stairs. She wore a purple homemade Santa hat over her short, curly hair. It hadn't grown back after Sonny cut it. Honestly, I liked it. Something was tucked under her arm.

My face reddened when I saw her. I hadn't talked to her while she was in the final stretch of physical therapy. She was the only one who never gave into the lies that were told about me…

That's why I loved her. She was the only one who accepted me for who I was.

"Uh, it doesn't mean anything, sweetheart," I lied. I fixed my long bang and quickly made myself look presentable.

She hopped down the stairs and sat down next to me. The coloring returned to her freckled face, and her blue eyes were bright again. Because of the paralysis, she was bedridden until the beginning of December. During that time, Shane took care of her, which I was not happy about. She stayed in Shane's bed while he catered to her every need.

The two grew closer and Shane was always glued to her side. Whenever she had trouble, he was always there and wouldn't let anyone else help her. *He must've told her…* I thought. I regretted not expressing how I felt after Nic's celebration the year before.

"Are you okay?" she asked kindly.

"Yeah, why?" I lied again. I returned to my computer and continued to enter code. "Just a little stressed with this new operation and all."

"Uh, huh," she replied. She took the Santa hat that was tucked under her arm and placed it on the desk. It was my favorite shade of green. "You know I know when you're lying, right?"

I felt the blood rushing to my cheeks. "How can you be sure?"

She smiled. "You gave yourself away. You're all red."

"Well," I cleared my throat, "forget about it. I'm crazy busy and life is weird."

She sighed. "Fine. Don't tell me." Changing the subject, she added, "So, you know you're up for the Royal Veteran Nerd of the new operation, right?" My fingers abruptly stopped their typing, hovering over the next string of numbers. I stared at her. "You heard me," she stated.

"Why me, though?"

"You're the best of the best," she complimented, punching my arm.

I couldn't help but grin. "Thanks, beautiful. Are you up for anything?"

"Nic is taking the position of the Royal Veteran Combatant. I will be in charge of combat strategies and things like that."

"Who are getting the others?"

"Mr. Wyght only chose the ones who heard Gerrior's testimony about your father," she explained. She counted on her fingers. "Johanna will lead the Umbrellas, Myles the Drones, Aymie the Polymaths, and Shane the Agricolae."

*Of course Shane is…* I thought. *I can't be better than him at anything.*

My sour expression gave my feelings away. Shannon commented, "Hey, I think that's awesome that you *and* your siblings are going to be RVs." When I didn't respond, she said, "What do you have against them?"

I looked down at my lap. "I don't have anything against them. I just…" I trailed off.

"Feel like you're not as good as them?" she finished. "I've noticed that, Mark," she said. She inhaled deeply and exhaled slowly, trying not to arouse the poison in her lungs. Her eyes looked into mine and she stated, "You've hated yourself your entire life. Now, you hate yourself more and feel small compared to your family. Why?"

My face paled and my mouth dried. She put my life story into words and asked the question I've been struggling to answer. "I dunno," I replied, flatly. "I've always felt unworthy. Unworthy of my family, unworthy of their Faith, unworthy of my friends..." Casting my eyes downward, I muttered, "Unworthy of you."

I felt a finger under my chin. Gently, Shannon lifted up my head. "Never say that," she ordered. "You can't even fathom your own worth. All of us here care about you. Sometimes we fight, but we are human. You are not unworthy of anyone. Understand?"

I didn't know what to say. Her eyes sparkled with something I never saw before. Her smile was kind, and she made my heart race. Honestly, I wanted to lean in and kiss her…but Shane would probably kill me. So, I simply replied, "Yeah."

Pressing her soft hand to my cheek, she said, "Good. Don't ever forget it." She pulled away, leaned back in the seat, and crossed her arms. "Now, explain what you meant by you are 'unworthy' of me?"

Nervousness rushed through me like a river. *I knew I shouldn't have said that, stupid, stupid,* I scolded myself. "Uh… well," I started. "I…kinda. I mean, I think you're..." I fumbled and made a complete fool of myself. No words would come out.

After watching me struggle, she pressed her fingers to my lips to shut me up. She laughed. "I always knew you did. You make it so obvious. I'm honored you feel that way."

My eyes widened. *What does that mean? Is that good?* I put my hand on hers and pulled it away. "So, uh, would you wanna…I dunno," I asked.

Her hand still in mine, she replied, "I'm sorry, I can't."

My heart fell into my shoes. *My brother took her from me.*

"We are in the middle of a war," she explained. "The OX attacks are happening more frequently across the world. We need to focus on stopping it. Besides," she rubbed the key that hung around her neck, "I'm only fifteen and not ready for that kind of commitment yet. I don't think you are either. If I am giving my love to anyone, we are going all the way."

Frankly, I was relieved. *There's still hope.* "I understand. I think that's the best way to do it." I paused. "This doesn't make anything weird between us, does it?"

She pulled her hand away and smiled. "It better not. If you stop hanging out with me, I'll have my sisters beat you up. You wouldn't want that? Especially when they made you this present." She held up the green Santa hat like it was a prized possession. Red glittery letters spelled *MARK* on the front. It was dripping with glue, rhinestones, and sequence.

I put it on. "I definitely don't want to get on their bad side." I untucked my long hair and let it cover the side of my face. I paused for a moment and asked the hardest question: "So… uhm, do you feel the same about me?"

Before she could say anything, Shane burst through the doors. "Shannon! There you are." He had tinsel draped over his shoulders and was wearing a homemade blue Santa hat. Seeing me, he smiled (surprisingly). "Good, you found the party pooper." He jumped down the stairs and stood behind Shannon. "You've been missing out, man," he told me.

"How many girls have kissed you under the mistletoe?" I asked, smirking. I tried not to show I was frustrated that he barged in before I could get an answer from Shannon.

"Six. Hoping for the seventh." He subtly tilted his head towards Shannon when she wasn't looking. Shocked at his answer, she whipped around in her chair to glare at him. He laughed at her reaction. "Your sisters, Shannon. You have six sisters," he told her, ignoring the part about the seventh. "They each attacked me when I went under the archway and kissed my cheeks." He rubbed his face. "Some of them hurt."

She punched his arm while he laughed. She rose and said, "Let's go see what they're up to." She looked at me and smirked. "You have to show them you're wearing it."

Wanting to be with her, I agreed and prepared to interact with people. I shut down the monitor on my screen and stood up to follow them.

As we walked up the stairs, the computers began to beep loudly. I recognized that dreadful noise. I ran back and turned my monitor on. As I read the message, my face fell. "Oh no," I whispered. I quickly entered codes and set off an alarm that blared through the mansion. Without saying anything, I ran past my friends and went to find Mr. Wyght.

Dashing through the long hallway, I frantically watched the students run about. They understood what the alarm was for and began to prepare. I found Mr. Wyght in the foyer with Mr. Powell—Myles' father—shouting orders to the kids. "Mr. Wyght!" I yelled.

"Mark. What's going on?" he asked as he pushed along some younger students.

"Something tripped our censors at the bottom of the mountain," I explained. "Something is coming and fast."

"What part of the mountain? The base of the driveway?"

"Past the runway and hangar. Something is coming up the side of the cliff."

"Our prisoners are in the hangar," Mr. Wyght said. "They may be trying to release them."

"Wait, Mr. Wyght," Shannon called, her voice cracking. She bent over and rested her hands on her knees, trying to catch her breath. She was wheezing and coughing. Shane was right there with her…of course. "It…could," she tried to say.

"She thinks it could be a distraction," Shane finished for her.

"It very well could be," Mr. Powell said. "My son says that the new defense weapons he was working on are ready. Create a perimeter and send a small team to scope out the hangar."

"Sounds like a plan," Mr. Wyght agreed. "I will have my Royal Veterans take groups to surround the mansion and warehouse. I've instructed Nic to take a handful of people to see what triggered the alarm." He turned to my brother and me. "You two go with him. Grab whoever else you need."

"Let me go too," Shannon croaked, standing upright.

Mr. Wyght shook his head. "No, Shannon. You are in no condition to fight. Stay back here and play defensive."

"Sir, please, they may need me."

"You are remaining behind and that's an order!" he bellowed. "You are sick and can barely breathe. If you get too worked up, the dormant poison could spread and kill you." He let out a deep breath. "Myles is working on something to help you, but the defenses had to come first. For now, you will cease from fighting."

She understood and backed down. Shane wrapped his arm around her waist to comfort her. I went over and tore his hand off her. I didn't need to see that. "He's right, beautiful," I said. "It's too dangerous."

Before she or Shane could say anything, Myles came running over. "Intruders have been spotted," he panted. "We need to hurry." Shane and I went with Myles to the warehouse to grab our backpacks and weapons. Once we were armed, we hurried to meet up with Nic outside.

We ran back out of the warehouse, across the field, and all the way to the hangar. Nic and Sonny were waiting for us.

"What took you so long?" Nic complained. "We've got company."

I saw two dark shadows running towards us down the side of the snowy mountain. They wove between the bare trees and made inhuman noises. Their bright eyes glowed in the dark. "No…" I said distressed. "Theo and Jordan are alive."

# THE MAINLAND

# CHAPTER 43

## Mark: XIV

"Yeup, that's them," Nic said, unsurprised. "I'd recognize their beady eyes anywhere."

"How did they survive?" Shane asked. He removed his blue Santa hat, revealing a mess of thick brown hair.

"You'd be surprised what they can handle," I told him.

Sonny cocked his gun. His long slick hair was pulled back into a ponytail and his menacing red eyes glowed in the dark. "They can't handle us," he stated confidently. "Let's go."

Gripping our weapons, we followed Sonny towards the base of the mountain. We stood in a line before the first row of trees. My heart thumped in my chest as I heard the familiar growls and snarls of my Mutant friends.

The shadowy figures emerged from the trees, running as fast as they could. They were upon us. We dropped in our stances, but there was no need. Digging their heels into the snow, they stopped themselves before ramming through us. They hunched over and were panting heavily.

"Well…if it isn't Mark," Jordan sneered. His brown eyes locked on me. "Surprised to see us?"

"I'm happy you're here," I told him. "Now I can kill you myself to get back at what you've done."

Jordan laughed, showing his white fangs. "You don't have the guts."

Rage stirred inside of me. Every bad thing that had happened throughout my life was surfacing. He was a painful reminder of my criminal life at Fallout. He was a reminder of what my actions did to Shannon. A reminder of what a worthless thief I was (despite the things Shannon said to me). My blood boiled and it took every ounce of me not to put a bullet in each of their skulls.

Thankfully, Nic interrupted. "I wouldn't test him. Now, what do you want?"

Theo answered for Jordan. "Bosses, bodies, food," he quickly said and repeated three times. His moves were anxious and he was getting antsy. He had a crazed look in his yellow eyes and he kept gnawing at his fingers. The Shrew didn't eat…he was looking for his next meal.

Jordan tilted his head toward his friend. "What he said. Let us get our guys now or we kill you."

"Not a chance," Shane state. He aimed his gun at the Slow loris. "Shannon will never be the same because of you. You aren't leaving here with anyone."

Jordan cackled. "How cute, you love her, too? That must get complicated." He looked at me and raised his hairy eyebrows. "I still can't believe she is Detective Hollinger's kid. He was a good cop and came close to busting us. A shame he had a daughter as weak and pathetic as your Shannon."

That was it. That pushed me over the edge. Yelling, I aimed my gun and fired it at him and Theo. Shane did the same, not that it surprised me. Unfortunately, we both missed. They leapt off the ground and hid in the trees, unable to be seen.

"What did you do?" Sonny scolded. "I had him right where I wanted him. You blew it."

"I could've gotten him if Mark didn't fire first," Shane yelled, blaming me again.

Myles was about to say something—possibly in my defense, but I cut him off. "Yeah, right," I sneered. "You have hardly any experience with a gun." It was my turn to be insulting. He stood up straight, ready to get the first word in, but I was quicker. "You act perfect, but inside you're a coward. You've spent your entire life running." I jabbed my finger into his strong chest. I looked right into his green eyes. "What do you know about fighting back?"

I saw anger and bitterness build up inside of Shane. His brow furrowed and he gritted his teeth. He was about to defend himself, but Nic grabbed our arms and tore us away from each other. "Enough!" he bellowed. "You two are acting like children. If you want to avenge Shannon, let's go get them." With that, he ran into the woods with Sonny. Shane and I looked at each other for a moment then ran after them.

We chased their shadows up and down the mountain. We followed them back and forth, firing into the tree tops. They knew how to stay hidden. They always did. If you weren't stealthy, you were no use in Fallout, which meant I could be just as sly. Instead of firing randomly, I went back to the hangar and waited. I knew Theo and Jordan wanted to tire us out. We used that tactic when we broke into the science facilities.

Nobody noticed I had left (which was typical). I waited a half an hour before the Mutants finally slipped out of the darkness. They left my friends lost in the woods. They had a few minutes to make their move.

Jordan led. He hunched over and sucked the poison out of his elbow glands, ready to attack. Theo scurried behind, trying to control himself as his stomach growled. I watched as they came closer and closer. They were out in the open…I had a perfect shot.

As much as I wanted to and even with all the tough talk… I couldn't kill them. I had known them my entire life. They and Brand were like brothers to me. *Better brothers than Shane.* I let them walk past me and into the hangar.

I followed close behind. I crept along with my gun in hand. I made sure they didn't know they were being tailed, but I needed to stop them. I had to knock them out somehow. We had no tranquilizers in the hangar and shots to the legs were too loud. Unfortunately, I was running out of time. They sniffed out the wall where the hidden containment area was. Jordan quickly worked to get in. He hacked the keypad and the doors flung open.

On the other side were five occupied cells. When our prisoners saw them, they jumped up from the floor. "What took you so long?" Janelle complained. She frantically tried to fix her thick black hair. She had a nervous look in her good eye and was experiencing anxiety. "I need to get out of here."

"Relax," Jordan told her.  "We're professionals." In no time, the two Mutants freed our captives. Theo and Jordan led Gerrior and Masdit out while Brand helped Zander hobble along, his legs still sore from when Sonny shot at them. For some reason, Janelle hung behind. She looked around in her cell and had to be yelled at by her "father". Something was going through her mind.

I had to do something. Still no sign of my friends, I needed to act. I waited until they walked past me to make a move. I tip-toed behind them, grabbed Janelle, and yanked her backwards. I wrapped an arm around her torso and held a gun to her head. "Stop or she dies!" I bellowed.

They froze and turned around. All hands raised in surrender except Masdit's. "We're on a tight schedule," he told me. "We need to take you and your siblings and get out of here."

"Father," Janelle cried as she tried to pry herself from my grasp. I was stronger than I looked. She couldn't get free.

"Mark, you can kill her if it makes you feel better," Masdit said, "but remember it will just prolong the inevitable. Get your siblings, come with us, and this can all be over."

I couldn't believe what he was saying. "You would have me kill your own daughter?"

"I have a nephew to replace her," he said, coldly. "Zander is blood, she is not. I no longer have use for that worthless girl."

When Janelle heard this, it took her a second to process it. She stopped struggling and stared at Masdit. "Father…"

"I'm sorry, darling," he lied. "You've served your purpose." He looked me in the face. His dark eyes as cold as ice. "Kill her, Mark."

Before I could respond, there were gunshots and Masdit screamed. He buckled to the ground and grabbed the back of his left leg. Blood pooled on the ground below him, and everyone backed away. Behind him, I saw Sonny and Nic. Sonny's smoking gun pointed at Masdit. Nic hunched over and growled. His brown and red hair was a mess and his purple eyes glowed. He didn't look sane.

Theo and Jordan screeched and charged. Jordan sucked more poison while Theo bared his teeth. Nic roared in response and ran straight for them, ready for a collision. While I watched, I hadn't noticed that Brand, Zander, and Gerrior disappeared. With Janelle still in my arms, I frantically looked around. They were nowhere in sight.

I wasn't paying attention to the fight as I searched. Thankfully, Janelle was. "Watch out!" she screamed as she pulled me to the ground with her. Jordan was thrown across the hangar, right over our heads. He sprawled on the cold floor, motionless.

Lying on top of Janelle, I slowly picked my head up and saw Nic holding Theo in the air by his shirt. He was sweating and panting but didn't let go no matter how much Theo squirmed. Sonny, Shane, and Myles returned from wherever they were, sedated the Mutants, and tied them up tightly. Once they were secure, they dragged the two back into the cells.

I jumped to my feet and pulled Janelle up with me. I followed them to the cells and saw all the prisoners were back. Zander and Brand were crammed in a cell with Theo and Jordan. Thankfully, Myles threw Theo some hero sandwiches so he wouldn't eat his inmates.

Once they were settled, Sonny put his hand on the door handle and stared at them. "Merry Christmas, you filthy animals," he growled as he slammed their cell shut.

"Did you just quote a movie line?" Shane said with a chuckle. "I didn't know you had a sense of humor."

Sonny rolled his eyes and went over to guard Masdit. Aymie and Blake who came out during the confusion were bandaging Masdit's leg (despite his protests). When Aymie saw her friend in my arms, she stopped what she was doing, jumped up, and cried, "Janelle!"

"You again," she snarled, tearing herself from my grip. "What do you want?"

Aymie threw her arms around her friend. "You're okay."

"Why do you care?" she retorted, trying to get free, but my sister was taller. "My own father doesn't care? Why should you?"

Aymie pulled away, put her hands on Janelle's shoulders, and looked her into her eyes. "He is not your father. He doesn't care about anyone. You are not who he says you are. You are my friend," Aymie shook her gently, "Janelle Arends."

"Wait!" Masdit cried, but it was too late. Aymie had said it. The magic word.

When Janelle heard her last name, her head took a moment to process. Her muscles relaxed and her face was blank. She stared expressionless at Aymie as if in a trance. Neurons fired rapidly in her brain, and the veil that covered her memories slipped away. Moments passed then her eyes widened and her jaw dropped. She looked up at my sister and laughed. "Hello, love," she said smiling. Tears ran down her cheeks as she wrapped her arms around Aymie. "It's been so long."

"I know," Aymie said, hugging her back.

"Uh, what just happened?" Shane asked as the girls began sobbing together.

"She just unlocked her memories," Sonny answered. "Names, places, or certain events are trigger words for releasing memories after someone goes through the Process." He glowered at Masdit. "Isn't that right?"

Through gritted teeth, he responded, "Yes. She was the first test subject of the new Process done by Nikita and his men which still uses trigger words. Just as a failsafe, apparently." He shook his head. "I think it's ridiculous, but they are convinced no one will figure it out. OX is developing a newer Process to keep the memories locked away forever." When Blake finished bandaging his leg, Masdit rubbed the wound and went on, "Nikita is almost fully operational. He plans to take on OX, but he needs to know something from you all."

"What's that?" Nic asked, crossing his thick, hairy arms.

Masdit locked eyes with the Mutant Gorilla and said, "Whether you will join him or not. You can finish this endless chase. Just work with him."

"What's the catch?"

Masdit smirked. The look of insanity in his eyes. "You do things his way," he declared.

Hearing enough, Nic grabbed Masdit by the back of the shirt and threw him into his cell, not caring about his wounded leg. "We'll think about it." He slammed the metal door tight. With his big hand pressed against it, he sighed and said, "We have to finish everything. Tonight."

"What're you talking about?" I asked.

"Shannon explained you were up for RV Nerd, right?" he replied.

"Yeah, but that was it."

"Mr. Powell, Mr. Wyght, and I have finished the ins and outs of our new operation," he explained. "With everything that's going on, I think it's time to launch it. The next step of OX's plan has started. Cities all over the world are being invaded, raided, and destroyed. Now, we have these guys to worry about," he tilted his head towards the cell door he leaned against. "We need to get out of our safe bubble and do what we've been training for." Standing upright, he said nothing else and led us back to the mansion.

We followed behind in silence, even Janelle was quiet. After her memories returned, she hadn't made a peep.

Returning to the mansion, we found it still. We went through the front door and found no one. "Hello?" Shane called. "Shannon? Johanna?"

"Quiet, stupid," a voice snapped. Johanna came down the newly built stairs to the girls' dorms. In her arms was the restless toddler, Rachel. "Once we knew we were safe, Mr. Wyght sent everyone to bed early."

"Why? What's going on?" Shane asked as he took the little girl from Johanna's arms. Rachel nuzzled her little round face in Shane's shoulder and began snoring immediately.

Johanna looked at the girl asleep in his arms. "I'll never

understand how you do that," she said, exasperated. Rachel gave her such a fuss about bedtime, but she always listened to Shane. Johanna shook her head and returned to the subject. "Bad things are happening in the real world. Come look." We went into the dining hall where Mr. Wyght, Mr. Powell, Shannon, and the other Royal Veterans were. They sat at a long table, huddled around a laptop.

"Dad. What's wrong?" Myles called to his father.

"The world is collapsing," Mr. Powell replied solemnly. We watched as different news stories flashed across the screen: Bombings in Europe, deadly poison spreading across the Middle East, raids in Asia, sieges in Africa, and so much destruction happening at once. "They haven't reached our hemisphere yet. We are okay for now but we need to act."

"What should we do?" Blake asked as he nervously fixed the beanie on his head of white hair.

"Put our operation into effect. Right now," Mr. Wyght answered. He went over to Nic who stood at attention. "Nicolas Eerkens," he started, "do you accept your position as Royal Veteran Combatant and Co-Director of this operation?"

Understanding the responsibilities and dangers, Nic nodded. "Yes, sir."

The older man smiled. "Thank you. You will do your part well."

Thyme went over and held out his hand. When Nic shook it, the RV smiled and said, "I wish you best of luck." He reached into his pocket and pulled out a small patch embroidered with a crowned Combatant emblem. "Wear it with pride."

Nic thanked him, took the rectangular patch, and stepped back.

When they finished, Mr. Wyght called all of us to attention and continued, "Myles, Shane, Mark, Aymie, and Johanna. Do you all accept your positions as Royal Veterans of your Branches for this new operation?"

I was hesitant to answer. Everyone else accepted at once, but I was a little nervous. *Why would they listen to me? They all hate me*, I thought, bitterly. However, my time was limited. All the eyes were on me. Taking a deep breath, I stood up straight and answered, "Yes, sir."

With a smile, Mr. Wyght motioned for us to go to our superiors and receive patches.

I went to Vandewater and saw tears well up in his milky white eyes. "Mark," he croaked, "I am honored to give this to you." He took my hand, placed the patch on my palm, and folded my fingers over it. "I have faith in you."

"That makes one of us," I muttered. Realizing that wasn't the greatest response, I quickly added, "Thank you, Guy. It means a lot."

He smiled and patted my hands. "You'll learn to trust yourself. I promise."

After everyone finished, Mr. Wyght cleared his throat and announced, "Welcome, newest Royal Veterans. I know you will oversee your Branches justly. Now," he took a deep breath, "when Mr. Myles Powell and I rescued you all and sheltered you here, we didn't ask for much in return. You obey our rules and understand why we do what we do. At this moment, I am asking for so much more. I am asking for you to dedicate your lives for the better of humanity." He looked at each of our faces. "If anyone wants to back out speak up now."

No one said anything.

Mr. Wyght sighed. "We aren't starting a war," he took a deep breath, the happiness drained from his face. "It has begun."

# THE MAINLAND

# Chapter 44

## Shane: XVI

Six months went by since I received the position of Royal Veteran Agricola, and I still had no idea how it was going to work. I wasn't sure what use a farming branch would have in an operation that constantly moved from place to place.

With this mentality, I didn't take my chores seriously. Marian was still the RV at WHYP so I felt like I didn't need to do anything.

It was the beginning of June and the operation was going to be officially launched in a few weeks (around my siblings' and my eighteenth birthday). I was supposed to be in a meeting, but I fell asleep in an apple tree on the farm…again.

Thankfully, Marian found me before I could get into any serious trouble. "Shane," she whispered as she pulled on my dangling leg. "Shane!"

Startled, I almost fell out of the tree. I grabbed onto the branches and steadied myself. "Marian! Don't scare me like that."

"You know you have somewhere to be, right?" she told me. She pulled her prized pocket watch out of her overalls and checked the time. "You're twenty minutes late."

I groaned. "Ugh, that's right." Hopping down, I said, "Thanks for watching out for me."

She smiled. "You've become an annoying little brother to me. I've got your back."

"Little?" I bent over to try and even out our height differences. I playfully rubbed her head of dirty blond hair and said, "Younger seems more appropriate."

She rolled her blue eyes and pulled my hand away. "Whatever. You better get going, but first," she picked up the basket of produce she was carrying and shoved it into my chest. "Run this back to the barn and then head to your meeting." She pointed a dirty finger at me. "Just because you're the RV of this new op doesn't mean you can slack off under my supervision."

I jokingly saluted her. "Yes ma'am. I'll do it under one condition." I clutched the basket tightly. "Time me." I dashed out of the orchard and to the barn in no time. I dropped it and ran back to the warehouse where the meeting was being held, all without breaking a sweat.

I skidded to a stop before the building. Taking a deep breath, I went in and made my way to the back where the curtain was drawn. I could hear muffled voices coming from the other side. I peeled the curtain aside and tip-toed into the meeting.

The other RVs were seated at the table while Mr. Wyght was going over some final details. He was so engrossed in his damaged map covered in Xs and pins that he didn't notice me coming in. I snuck over to the empty seat next to Mark and sat down.

My brother leaned over and whispered, "Where've you been, man?"

"Sleeping."

Mark couldn't help but chuckle. "You'll need to come up with something better than that."

Mr. Wyght turned around and saw me. "Shane," he called. "Do you have a valid reason for your tardiness?"

"Sorry, sir," I replied. I sat up straight and fixed my overalls. I hesitated for a moment to try and think of a better excuse. Not finding one, I told him the truth: "I fell asleep doing my Branch work."

Johanna rolled her eyes. "Of course you did."

"Now, Johanna, an Agricola does have to get up at four in the morning," Mr. Wyght told her. He looked at me and smiled. "As long as you finished your chores, I will accept your excuse. Just set an alarm next time."

I was surprised at his response, I expected a worse reprimand. Apparently, so did Mark. When Mr. Wyght went back to explaining, my brother crossed his arms, leaned back in his chair, and had a pout on his face. Even then I never really understood why Mark hated me so much. I loved him like a brother, but he never understood. Sure we fought sometimes, but it was always over little things. He hated me for something, but I never realized what it was until it was too late…

Finally, the boring meeting ended. I was not paying attention. Johanna was just going to re-explain it to me later. When we were dismissed, instead of going back to the barn, I decided to try to spend time with my brother for the rest of the day.

"Mark, wait up!" I called as he went back towards the mansion. "Forget something?"

"No, I was wondering if you wanted to hang out this afternoon?" He arched an eyebrow. "What're you playing?"

"I'm not 'playing' anything," I told him. "I feel like we haven't hung in a while. If we are going to stick together, don't you think we should get to know each other?"

Blowing the long bang out of his face, he replied, "I guess so. I have some stuff to finish this afternoon for the new op, though. It won't take long."

"I could watch you and then we can do whatever afterwards," I suggested.

Mark laughed. "You'll fall asleep again, but sure."

"We'll see about that," I replied and followed him back to the Nerd headquarters.

Reaching the spacious computer room, we went down the stairs and to Mark's desk. The place was practically empty. In the blue glow of the screens, I made out three Nerds and Vandewater at his master computer.

"Where is everyone?" I wondered aloud.

"Probably done for the day," Mark said. He plopped himself in his swivel chair and turned his computer on. "There isn't too much they can do until we are operational." He typed in his password almost as fast as I could run. While I was quick on my feet, he was quick with his fingers.

I sat down next to him. "So, what do you have left to work on?"

"Coding for our op's new firewall." His blue eyes locked on the colorful words that flashed on the screen. "Vandewater and I are going to make it so no one can get into our systems."

"That's for sure," Guy called from his desk.

"Man, he has better hearing than a dog," I mumbled.

"He has to," Mark replied. "When you're missing one sense, you have to make up for it somehow. Besides, he needs to be able to hear his computer."

"I still will never understand that," I said. "It's awesome what you guys do, though. You know the Nerds are really the first ones to make a move against OX."

Mark gasped, sarcastically of course. "Whoa, a compliment. Didn't know you could praise something other than your reflection."

"Ha. Ha," I replied, jokingly. "Don't forget, in a way you are my reflection."

"Sucks the mirror is distorted then," he muttered.

Not wanting to continue on that subject, I leaned back in my chair and said, "So, what do you want to do after this? Anything in mind?"

He shrugged. "To be honest, lately I've just been hanging out here. I'll get a little visitor now and then, but I haven't seen her in a bit. Normally, Shannon would invite me to chill with her and her friends, but she's been busy."

"Yeah, I've heard," I replied, "but that doesn't mean you can't come hang with me and Myles."

He snickered. "You haven't been with all the ladies lately?"

I laughed sarcastically. "No, I've been helping Myles in the warehouse with his new inventions."

"I didn't know you were a science guy," Mark replied.

"More of a test subject," I said, subconsciously rubbing my back. "Whatever he makes, I test."

"Sounds fun," he replied with a smirk. A beeping noise came from his speakers. "Seems like I'm done for the day."

"Awe, all done?" a little voice said from behind us. Turning around, I saw Rachel holding Rebecca's hand at the top of the steps.

Mark smiled. "Sorry, baby girl, all done."

The two of them hopped down the stairs. It was amazing how much they've grown. I've known Rachel since she was born five years prior to that day. Rebecca was the one who woke me when we met and she was seven now. The little Hollinger girls saw me as an older brother. It made me happy.

"These are your visitors?" I asked, smiling as the girls came up to us.

"Usually just Rachel," he said. He placed her on his lap. He rubbed her curly, dirty blond hair and said, "We've grown pretty close these past few months."

"Yeah, she only talks about you," Rebecca put in, leaning on my arm.

"More than you talk about Shane?" Mark teased.

"Shut up," she yelled as she pulled herself away from me, her face bright red.

I laughed and rubbed the little girl's back. "Hey, what's this about?"

"N-nothing," she denied, swatting my hand away.

"Yeah, right, Rebecca," another female voice said. "You know you love him." Carol-Ann was leading Agnes by the hand. "Come on, Shannon is waiting for us. We have to finish packing."

Sighing, Rebecca said, "O-okay…come on, Rachel." Rachel whined a minute in protest, but Mark told her to listen. After giving him a long hug, she hopped off my brother's lap, hugged my legs, and then ran up the stairs to meet with her sisters.

When they left, I said, "They are the cutest things ever."

Mark agreed. "All the Hollinger girls are, but why are they

packing?"

"You're leaving, tonight. The girls are going with you," Vandewater interjected. "Weren't you paying attention at the meeting?"

"No," my brother and I responded simultaneously.

"You Hodgins boys," Vandewater replied. "You better go pack your things. You relocate tonight. You won't return here for quite some time."

My brother and I looked at Vandewater then at each other. We both jumped up and ran to our dorms.

"Meet me in the warehouse when you're done," Mark told me before ducking into his room.

I went to the back of the hall and into my bright white suite. I looked around and saw Myles had packed his things already. His blueprints were gone, his drawers were empty, and his uniforms weren't hanging in the closet. On my bed was a large, black suitcase with my first initial and last name on the tag. On top was a note from Myles: *Pack only what's necessary. We need to travel light.*

"Thanks for the heads up," I mumbled as I shoved the letter into the front pocket of my overalls. As fast as possible, I rummaged through my things and grabbed a few outfits, my uniforms, and some toiletries. I shoved it into my suitcase and struggled to zip it shut. Of course I didn't fold anything to save space, but I was able to close it.

I smacked the top of it to make sure it stayed secure. My eyes then were drawn above my suitcase to the pictures Blake had taken. My favorite was when Shannon fell asleep on me when she was still sick.

I took the picture, folded it, and put it in my wallet. The others I shoved in the front pocket of my suitcase. I looked around at the room and double checked to make sure I had what I needed. I heaved my suitcase off my high bed and grabbed my guitar that was resting against the wall.

I lugged my things out the door and up to the foyer where I found other suitcases lined up. I brought mine over, placed it with my guitar resting behind, and went to meet Mark in the warehouse.

I found him in the back of the cold building with Sonny and Myles. He and Sonny talked while Myles worked on a small black triangle at his work bench. "What's that, buddy?" I asked.

"The answer to Shannon's problem," Myles replied, tampering with it for the final time. "There." He held it up and examined it, fascinated by his own work. While he was in awe, Sonny came over and snatched it from him. "Hey! Be careful."

"Relax, kid," Sonny retorted. Examining it, he said, "Not bad. This should do the trick. Did you put that special voice feature I suggested?"

The kid genius nodded. "Yeah, I don't know what she would use it for."

"Trust me, it will come in handy," he reassured. "If OX has the same systems, she will be our ticket in." Before he could return it, the Secretary called for those departing for the new op to meet in the gallery. "We'll bring it to her there," Sonny decided, holding up the small triangle. With that, he left with the device.

"I'll never understand him," Mark said, shaking his head.

"Seems like you two hit it off, though," Myles pointed out. "You, Shannon, and he get along just fine.

"Only because we're forced to cooperate," Mark reminded him. "Whenever we talk it's usually work stuff."

"At least he's talking to someone about something," I put in. "If we are going to all be leading this new operation together we should try to bond."

"I agree," Myles exclaimed, hopping down from his tall stool. "But first, we should go see what my dad and Mr. Wyght want."

We made our way to the gallery where we found fifty students. They sat on the floor facing Mr. Wyght, Mr. Powell, Papa E, and the Royal Veterans.

Seeing us, Mr. Powell said, "Junior, you and your friends come sit down. We have to discuss a few things before we leave."

Myles nodded and the three of us sat down. Immediately, Rachel jumped up from her spot, ran over, and sat on Mark's lap. Rebecca followed and sat with me. I looked around and saw Shannon and

Johanna sitting with Aymie and Janelle—Masdit's adopted daughter. She had now devoted herself to helping us and undoing all of Masdit's evils.

Once everyone was settled, Mr. Wyght began: "I apologize for doing this to you all last minute, but I'm afraid we are out of time. OX's strikes have become frequent. Some nations are still calling them accidents; others are finally accepting them as terrorist attacks. One thing is for sure we have to stop this from happening. You are the chosen few who we deemed fit for this operation, which we have finally named Resist Rescue Protect Retake or RRPR for short." He paced back and forth, looking at each of us individually. "You will *Resist* whatever the Order of Xenophon throws at you. Accept no bribes, fall for no tricks, and do not let them in. You will *Rescue* whoever needs our help regardless of who they are. You will *Protect* them and your comrades at all costs. And finally," he stopped and stood up tall, "we will *Retake* the world. We will eliminate the Order of Xenophon once and for all."

This was a lot for us to take in. We knew the day was coming, but no one wanted it. The room was filled with an eerie quiet. I wondered what went through their heads.

As for me, mixed emotions swirled inside. Nervous as I was, I was also excited. I was a risk taker and had a love for thrills. Putting myself in danger for a noble cause? That sounded awesome. However, I looked at the others and became nervous. I knew I could hold my own, but…could they?

Mr. Wyght interrupted my worrying. "I am asking much of you right now but I need your word." Mr. Powell motioned for all of us to stand up.

Clearing his throat, Papa E pulled a paper that was tucked in his rope belt. "Only respond 'I will' if you truly mean it," he said, rubbing his long gray beard. "If you don't wish to be a part of this, you may exit silently." A few members quietly left the gallery with their heads hung low. The rest of us rose and stood at attention. Our chins up, our arms behind our backs, ready to answer the call. Even Rachel, Agnes, and Rebecca stood uniformly.

Finally, Papa E began the oath: "Will you resist the evils of the Order of Xenophon and those who share in their ways and actions?"

"I will," we responded unanimously.

"Will you rescue anyone in need and never leave a man behind?"

"I will."

"Will you protect the life of every human being; born and unborn, sick and healthy, rich and poor, man and woman?"

"I will."

"Will you, until your last breath, do all you can to retake the world in the name of justice and all that is good?"

"I will."

Papa E tucked the paper under his arm, held up his right hand and declared, "With God as your witness, may you obey this oath and fulfill it with every breath you take. May the Creator bless you." He signed a cross over us and I did so on myself. Out of the corner of my eye, I saw Rachel showing Mark how to do it. I couldn't help but smile.

Papa E stepped back and Mr. Wyght gave his final orders. "Go prepare yourselves now. We leave in twenty minutes."

One by one, everyone left the room to say their final goodbyes to the friends they were leaving behind. I hung back and let the others rush ahead. I was about to follow when I heard my name. "Shane. Come here."

Turning around, I saw Marian waving me over to the corner of the gallery. She stood beneath her portrait with her hands shoved into the pockets of her overalls. Her hair was a mess and her blue eyes were distressed. Her face had aged and she seemed pale and sickly. Something was wrong with her health, but she would always refuse to admit it.

"What's wrong?" I asked. Without warning, she stood on her tiptoes and flung her arms around my neck. I was shocked and stood there for a moment before I hugged her back. Her breathing was shaky, and my shoulder was dampened with her tears. I squeezed her tightly and said, "Marian, it's okay."

"No," she cried. "Please don't go. You won't survive out there."

"You don't know that. I survived the last mission and I have grown in my skills since then."

She pulled away and looked up at me. Tears streaked down her face. "You haven't been on real missions yet. Trust me. The things I've seen…" Her eyes became distant as she remembered the many times she went away.

"I've survived people trying to kill me for 18 years," I told her. "Not to mention I've watched horrible things happen to people I've loved…I couldn't do anything about it then but now I can. Please," I put my hands on her shoulders, "trust me."

Taking a few short breaths, she nodded and wiped her nose with her sleeve. "Fine. But you have to promise me two things."

"Anything."

She held up one finger. "First, please be safe. Second," she reached into her pocket and pulled out the Best family heirloom: Her beloved pocket watch. She dangled it delicately by the chain between her thumb and forefinger. The shiny brass gleamed in the light. She looked me in the eye and ordered, "You are going to find my sister Marlene Best and give this to her."

I was amazed at her request. "No, I can't." I backed away from the pocket watch as if it were cursed. "You should be able to give it to her yourself."

"I won't be able to," she stated, clicking it open. "Mr. Wyght and Mr. Powell are leaving. We Royal Veterans and Mrs. Powell are in charge of all of WHYP." She took a shaky breath. "Besides, I've tried. Every mission I went on I tried to find some trace of her. I got nothing. All I know is she was taken by a short, round, black man in overalls. Please," she took one final look at the picture and choked back her tears. Snapping it shut, she shoved it against my chest. I felt the ticks against my heart. "Find her."

Finally, I agreed. I wrapped my hands around hers and said, "I promise."

Her eyes welled up with tears again. "Thank you." She placed the watch in my hand and let go. She stood on her tip toes and kissed my cheek. "Be safe."

I couldn't help but smile. "I will." With that, I put the watch in my pocket, said my final goodbye, and left the gallery.

As I walked down the hall, I didn't realize I was being shadowed. "Clarius!" a little voice called when I was almost into the foyer. I turned around and saw Rebecca following me. "Is Marian your girlfriend?" she asked.

I laughed. "No. More of a big sister."

She gasped. "Are you replacing us?"

"Never." I squatted down to meet her eye level. "No one could replace you girls."

She smiled. "Good. Because we would *not* be happy; especially Shannon, because—" she quickly clasped her hand over her mouth, stopping herself. I asked her what she was going to say, but she wasn't listening. Her eyes were glued on something behind me. Her big brown eyes shook and she kept her hand on her mouth. She wasn't stopping herself from spilling a secret…she was trying not to scream.

Before I could ask, I heard an explosion go off behind us. It shook the tile floor, and I fell off balance. I grabbed Rebecca and shielded her from whatever it was. Crashes and ringing filled my ears. Finally, it ceased and I turned around.

Once again, our home was being attacked.

# THE MAINLAND

# CHAPTER 45
## Shane: XVII

I sprawled on the floor, shielding Rebecca with my body. I lifted my head to look. I was in shock. I watched as a flood of people marched through the gaping hole of our newly repaired home. The electricity shut off, and the setting sun let in blood orange light, casting long ghostly shadows on the walls. Without hesitation, they began their raid. They ran upstairs to the girls' dormitory and headed to their right to the boys'. I watched as my friends scurried about and fought back. Unfortunately, our opponents were armed, and we were outnumbered.

"I need to get in there and help," I told Rebecca as I stood up and put her down.

"No!" she cried. She latched onto my leg.

I tried to shake her off, but she was clutching tightly. I saw Marian and Thyme rush out of the gallery. "Shane, what are you doing?" Marian cried.

"I have to go help!" I yelled.

"No! You have to leave, *now*," she ordered. Skidding to a stop, she panted and said, "Take Rebecca, get on the jet, and go."

"I can't leave you all like this," I protested.

"No time," Thyme told me. "We can handle this. Go." He picked up Rebecca and put her in my arms. Before I could say anything, the two ran off into the chaos. Gunshots and piercing screams echoed off the walls, but that didn't scare them.

The two stood side by side, weapons in hand. They aimed at enemies I couldn't see. The two of them shouted until a shot rang out… but my friends didn't fire.

I watched in horror as my superior, Marian Best, dropped to her knees. Her blue overalls became stained with red. Her fair hair draped around her sweating face as she spat blood on the ground. Out of the corner of her eye, she looked at me. Then, she exhaled and fell on her face.

Enraged, Thyme clenched his fists, screamed, and charged at the unknown enemy. I stared, frozen in fear with Rebecca crying on my chest.

I wanted to go help, but I didn't know what I could do… especially with Rebecca. Fearing for the little girl's life, I held back my tears and clutched her tightly. I ran as fast as I could, leaving my friends behind.

Going outside, I saw large helicopters landed on our training fields. I watched in horror as they dragged my friends away, throwing them on board. Once again, I was helpless. I couldn't do anything. I clutched Rebecca tighter and ran as fast as I could across the field, ignoring everything behind me.

As I approached the runway, I saw the others climb on board the jet. Nic urged everyone to get on as quickly as possible. When he saw me, he yelled, "Where's Shannon?"

I screeched to a halt before smashing in to him. "What?"

He took the girl from my hands and handed her to Sonny. "She ran back looking for Rebecca and you!"

"Why would you let her do that?!" I screamed. I spun and raced back towards the mansion. I didn't have to go very far. Shannon headed right for me. She ran as fast as she could…and she wasn't passing out. From afar, I saw she had a black, glowing machine covering her mouth, nose, and jaw.

She waved at me to head back to the plane. I ignored her and ran forward. When we met, I grabbed her hand and dragged her along, quickening her pace. My heart raced. I felt like we were being followed, but I dared not to look back.

We were almost there when Shannon lost her footing. I snatched her up and carried her. I pumped my legs as hard as I could and held on tight. She buried her face in my shoulder and wrapped her arms tightly around my neck.

We reached the jet as it was taking off. I saw Sonny standing on the hatch as the plane began to slowly roll away. With my last bit of energy, I ran faster than ever before to the back of the jet. Just in time, I jumped up into the plane. Sonny yanked Shannon and me off the door, and we crashed to the floor.

Sonny went over to the chrome control panel and shut the hatch. He let out a deep breath and pressed his forehead against the wall. Shannon and I stayed down, gasping for air. I felt the plane gaining altitude.

We left. We left all of them alone to die. I closed my eyes and tried not to think.

After a few moments, I opened them and saw Sonny leaning over us. His red eyes filled with concern. "You two good?" He held out his hands and helped us sit up. We rested our backs on a cargo box filled with weapons.

"I think so," I replied with my hand on my chest. I looked over at Shannon who was still trying to catch her breath. She had an easier time than normal because of the weird triangle on her mouth. She looked at me out of the corner of her eye and nodded.

"Good," Sonny said. He took his dark hair out of the ponytail. "It looks like Myles' machine is working, Shannon. Otherwise you would be dead."

"Thanks…" she mumbled. The contraption muffled her voice.

He chuckled. "I'll leave you two alone then." Without another word, he left us in the bay of the plane.

I rubbed my fingers through my thick brown hair and exhaled. "That was crazy."

"Yes, it was," Shannon agreed. With her thumb and forefinger, she pressed two buttons on either side of her face and the machine clicked. She pulled it off and it retracted into a small, metal triangle.

"I'm happy you're okay," I told her honestly, wiping my sweaty face with my shirt. "I don't know if I could live with myself if something happened to you again…" Thinking about the horrifying events, I began to choke up. It was finally sinking in. I pressed my hand over my chest where Marian's pocket watch was. I looked over at Shannon and said seriously, "I can't lose you now too."

She took a shaky breath. She didn't know what happened, but I feel she didn't need to. To console me, she looked up, pressed her hand over my heart and kissed my cheek tenderly. She wrapped her arms around my torso and rested her head on me.

I couldn't believe it. My heart was racing so fast it was about to pop out of my chest (again). Blood rushed to my face, and I couldn't move. I felt exactly as I did when she kissed my cheek the first time. I wrapped my arms around her, leaned back, and closed my eyes. I was able to forget about all the terror and pain for a few moments and rest in her embrace. After a little while, I fell into a sound sleep.

I was awoken the next morning to a crash. My eyes popped open and I looked around. I saw a figure dashing out of the room. Nervous that we might get in trouble, I gently shook Shannon awake. "Hey, we should probably get up."

Shannon stirred and her eyes fluttered open. She yawned and asked, "What time is it?"

I was about to tell her I didn't know when I remembered…I had Marian's watch. Reaching into my pocket, I carefully took it out and examined it. After yesterday, I hoped it hadn't broken. I clicked it open. It was still ticking. I let out a sigh of relief and looked at the picture above the face. Seeing little Marian, I began to cry. *I can't believe it… she's gone…* I pressed the back of my hand to my eyes and turned away.

Shannon understood entirely now. "I am so sorry, Shane."

"She knew," I sniffled. "She knew she wouldn't make it. That's why she asked me to…" I broke down again.

"I'll do whatever I can to help you find this little girl," She tapped the picture. "For Marian."

I pulled myself together and managed a smile. Clicking the watch closed, I tucked it back into my pocket. "As much as that would mean to her, I can't ask you to do that."

Taken aback, she stared at me with an offended look. I pushed her curly hair out of her eyes. "Don't take it personally, but I can't ask you to. You've done so much for me. You have your brother Pietro to find, and I am going to do everything I can to help you."

Her look faded and she said softly, "Thank you, but if you need help, I am here." Slowly standing up, she tried to lighten the mood. "Now, I think I'm going to go shower and change. I feel disgusting."

"Don't worry, you don't smell that bad," I replied, jokingly. She punched my arm, and we both went out of the bay and to our rooms.

When I entered mine and shut the door, Mark came out of the shower wearing only boxers. *His hard work is paying off,* I thought with a chuckle. It was apparent that he started working out a few months before. He looked stronger and wasn't as lanky.

I was about to make a joke when I caught his gaze. He glared at me through his wet bangs, the water dripping off his shoulders and over the Fallout mark branded into his chest. Those small, pure droplets of water frightened me. Horrible thoughts about him drowning flooded into my mind.

I shook off the thought. "Uh, hey, man." He gave me a dirty look out of the corner of his eye and proceeded to get dressed. "Fine, don't talk to me," I said crossly. I went over to my bed, removed my dirty clothes, and grabbed my stuff to speed shower. The entire time, Mark and I ignored each other. *What is wrong with him?*

Although, I shouldn't have judged him for his mood. I don't know who else was lost during that attack…

In no time, I was clean, dressed, and ready to start the new day. I went to the dining area to meet the others. I grabbed some food and went to sit down by my brother, hoping to clear up whatever was going on. Unfortunately, every time I tried to say something he would ignore me.

I was about to yell at him when Mr. Wyght stood up and addressed us: "Everyone, we are reaching our destination sooner than we expected. Everything was rushed on us at once…" he sighed. "Our operation still has two years left of preparation work."

I almost choked on my eggs. *Two years?* Without raising my hand, I firmly asked, "Then why did we leave?"

Surprised at my interjection, Mr. Wyght stopped for a moment and looked at me. He seemed to have aged since I saw him yesterday. His hair was becoming white and more wrinkles appeared on his face. "Excuse me?" he asked. He leaned forward and pressed his hands against the table.

"Why did we leave everyone alone to fend for themselves?"

"They can handle it," he replied.

"No, they can't!" I cried. "I watched Marian Best, our RV Agricola, die defending WHYP. Who knows who else was killed after we abandoned them?"

Mr. Wyght held his hand up, and I held my emotions back momentarily. "Shane, I feel tremendous loss more than you can imagine. I knew every student personally, Marian included. Losing one feels like…" he paused, "losing my own child." Taking a deep breath, he changed the subject: "Besides, we couldn't afford to have this operation destroyed. We may be the only hope humanity has left." He pointed towards the window.

I stared at him, then at the window, and back again. Slowly, I stood up from my chair and went over to it. I looked below and gasped.

The ground billowed with smoke. The cities appeared as black smudges on a gray canvas. From what I could make out, there were crashed planes on streets, collapsed buildings, and debris covered the landscape like a blanket. The Mainland looked ruined and lifeless.

I stared at the scene with my mouth gaped open. "Do you understand now, Shane Thomas Hodgins?" Mr. Wyght said from behind me. I slowly wobbled to my seat unable to grasp what was happening. Mr. Wyght sighed and went on, "It will take two years before we can really save anyone. We need to build a base, recruit soldiers, and gather supplies. For right now, we will have small missions to begin rescuing people. Understand?"

I nodded and sat there quietly until it was time to get ready. Once the bell went off, I stood up from my chair and went back to my room.

I flopped on my bed, burying my face in the new sheets. I went over all that was happening and couldn't wrap my mind around it. A few moments passed by before I heard a rapping on the door. "Come in," I said, my voice muffled by the pillows.

Ducking through the doorway was Nic. He was dressed in his black combat uniform, his new RV Combatant patch stitched over his heart. "Ready for bed already?" he said with a chuckle. "You practically just woke up."

I sat up and replied, "Yeah…I just can't believe what happened to the world. We barely had any idea."

"Well, we actually did." He came and plopped himself next to me. He rubbed his Mohawk and explained, "Sonny, Shannon, and I have been monitoring OX's actions for years. We had the RVs do recon missions, but they only came back with bad news. We kept it a secret. We realized it was a bad idea. Now, you're all thrown into this blind."

"Hey, don't worry. We'll get through it," I told him. "We made a vow. We will take back this world even if it kills us."

The big guy smiled and his violet eyes lit up. "Thanks, Shane." Standing, he stretched and said, "Get your uniform on. We land at the destination of our new home in thirty minutes." With that, he left me alone.

I took a deep breath and exhaled. Before doing anything, I sat in the silence. I knew that once I dressed and left the plane, nothing would be the same.

# THE MAINLAND

# CHAPTER 46
## Aymie: XV

I don't know about my brothers, but the launch of RRPR was a blur. From the moment we stepped off that plane until we finished building our base, I can barely recall anything. There was so much to do and I was thrown in charge of more than I anticipated. Mr. Wyght put a lot on my shoulders. I didn't like it, but I was obedient as I should be.

After working through a brutal North Dakota winter, we finished the base in the following spring. I swear time flies by when you're suffering. Also, again sorry for the timeline jumps. I don't think you want to hear me rant about building a base in freezing weather. I finally got used to winters at WHYP, which was in Maine, but this was ridiculous.

[I know you guys don't know where that is, that's why I didn't bother telling you before. Just know that Maine and North Dakota are up north and get cold.]

Finally, the base was operational. The Branches had their designated sections, dorms, and other recreational areas. We also built over five different buildings for the people we rescued. We had our hands full.

I didn't realize how much I would be responsible for when I agreed to be the RV Polymath. I wasn't even nineteen at that time, and I helped oversee the entire operation when Mr. Wyght and Nic were away. Thankfully, even with my clueless leadership, our teams managed to stop many OX attacks and rescue over 100 people in less than a year. Things were looking up.

But when we thought we were safe, everything began falling apart.

It was a chilly spring morning, and I sat in the RV lounge, reading over the checklist Mr. Wyght gave me. He was out for over a week with Nic, Shannon, and Sonny. I was deathly afraid something had happened to them. Not wanting to think about it, I sipped my tea and went over the list again.

"Mornin', love," a voice called from behind me. Turning around, I saw Janelle entering the lounge with Blake, Johanna, and Peggy. "Why are ya up so early?"

"Hey, guys," I replied. I put my tea down on the glass coffee table. "Couldn't sleep."

"Still worried about the others?" Blake asked as he sat next to me.

"Yeah, they usually aren't gone this long."

He grabbed my hand. "Don't worry. They can handle themselves."

"Yuck, don't you kiss her," Johanna complained when she saw we were holding hands. "I'm fine that you're together, but don't start doing stuff like that. Especially in front of the little Hollingers."

"I'm thirteen, now. Not so little anymore," Peggy replied, putting her short brown hair into a ponytail. "But, yeah don't do it in front of my sisters. It's bad enough some of them are crushing on Aymie's brothers."

"We won't, I promise," I laughed. Blake blushed.

"Yeah, well I just think you're jealous that the gorilla guy hasn't asked you out yet," Janelle teased Johanna.

"Nic and I are too busy for a relationship right now," she replied. "Besides, he'll wait for me. He's good like that."

"Yeah, well he won't be waiting as long as some other guy we know," I said. "Do you know why Shane hasn't said anything to Shannon?"

Johanna shrugged. "She knows. Shannon shared with me what happened when we left WHYP, but then she told him to wait, too. Besides, I think there are some complications that Shane doesn't know about."

"What kind of complications?" Blake asked, interested in the gossip.

Johanna was about to explain when she looked above me and stopped herself. Turning around, I saw that Mark entered the lounge and was making himself coffee at the kitchenette. He obviously heard the conversation, but ignored it. I knew about his obsessive feelings for Shannon and how he hated Shane for "taking her" from him. I never understood what happened between the three of them.

Interrupting the awkward silence, Peggy said, "Good morning, Mark."

"Sup, Peg?" he replied, sipping his drink.

"Talking with the girls…plus Blake," she told him, stealing my boyfriend's camera.

"Nice," he responded mechanically. "Just so you guys know, Myles and I got the defense systems up and running for real this time. No more false alarms." He took another sip of his coffee. Nonchalantly, he added, "Also, Theo ate Masdit last night because someone forgot to feed him. Johanna, you're going to need to give the others therapy." Without any further explanation, he left us in the lounge.

We sat with horrified expressions on our faces. He says that like it's no big deal and then walks away. He was so insensitive…

Johanna was the most disgusted. "Sometimes, I wished I didn't become a psychologist…"

"Why did we even bring them with us?" Janelle complained, her hand over her mouth. "I joined you guys to get away from them."

"Well, if Theo just ate your dad, I think it was a good thing we kept him from our friends back home," Peggy told her.

"That's true," Johanna said. Thinking about it, she shuddered. "Well, I'm not eating breakfast. I guess I'll see you all later. C'mon, Peggy. Let's go wake your sisters." The younger girl nodded, and they both left.

"Ya'know she left with your camera, Blake," Janelle pointed out, staying away from the topic of her late "father".

"She does that," he said, smiling.

"Ever since she was little," I added. "Okay, I'm going to try and not think about Theo's disgusting act." I almost gagged but stopped myself. "That's so messed up," I muttered. "So, I'm going to get going and distract myself. I have to let everyone know what they're doing for the day anyway." My friends understood, and I left to go to the control room.

I scanned my card and the metallic doors slid open. I went inside and strained to see. The Nerds never used the lights on the ceiling and only saw by the lights of their computers. There was only one monitor on, but it covered the entire back wall.

Slowly, I went down the aisle to the lonely Nerd that sat at the master console. "Mark, I need to do an announcement."

Leaning back in his chair, he motioned with his right hand over to the intercom controls. "You know what to do," he said, spinning his blue tie around like a propeller blade.

I rolled my eyes, but he didn't see. Quick and clear, I spoke into the microphone and relayed my instructions to all those at the base. When I finished, I decided to approach Mark about some things that had been bothering me. I pulled up a swivel chair and sat next to him. Slightly taken aback, Mark leaned away as I brought myself closer. "Uh, you okay, sis?"

"No," I stated, flatly. "What's wrong with you?"

Confusion fell across his face. "Uh, what are you talking about?"

"Why are you acting so weird?" I blurted. "You've been acting like this for almost a year and it's driving me crazy."

"This is how I act," he motioned to himself. "If you don't like it, you'll have to deal." He turned back to his computer and started typing.

I grew impatient and tried not to slap him. "If you want us to deal with you, you should try coming around more," I growled.

He held his hands up. "Hey, you've got Blake. What do you need a useless brother for?" He sighed. Resting his elbows on the desk, he put his head in his hands. "Look, I'll survive. I'm trying to figure stuff out," he confessed. "Also, my old friend just *ate* one of the men that have been after us all our lives. After practically nineteen years and now he's gone like that. " He snapped his fingers, his face still resting in his other palm. "Plus, he was one of our only connections to dad." Without lifting his head, he pointed to the wall of monitors above us.

There were news stories, police reports, security footage, and photographs of a shadow of a man. From what I could see, he had thick brown hair and light skin. In most of the images, he wore dark clothing and a hat...I couldn't make out his face.

I was speechless. *Is this...really him?* I wondered, trying to take in all the screens at once.

"I've been looking for him ever since Gerrior and Masdit told us," Mark went on. "Neither you nor Shane even dared to think about finding him. One moment we're all like 'Nik won't know what hit him...we're gonna be strong' blah blah..." He looked up at me. From behind his long bang, I could see sadness and disappointment in his blue eyes. "When you actually start to care about your blood family, then come back. For now, just go to Blake."

I couldn't believe what I was hearing. It broke my heart that that's how he felt. Frustrated and upset, I abruptly stood up from my chair which startled Mark. I locked eyes with him for a moment and then stormed off.

I marched through the hallways of the base, trying to hold back my tears. I couldn't let the other members or those we rescued see me so fragile. I needed to be strong. I was the face of RRPR after all.

But I still couldn't get over Mark. I loved my brothers...both of them. The fact that he didn't love me tore me in half. *Why doesn't he care? God, make him care*...I prayed. Not wanting to think about it anymore, I shook off those thoughts and repeated aloud what my foster sister Abigail would always say to me: "A true princess puts others before herself… a true princess puts others before herself." Frankly, my routine mantra only made it worse as I recalled the childhood I had with Abigail.

I pushed everything into the back of my mind and decided to go outside and check on the Agricolae.

Heading out the front door of the base, I went down the mountainside to the crop fields below. It was a long walk but the view was worth it. The base looked upon the empty valleys of the state. It was the beginning of spring and everything was blooming, creating a sea of bright colors. Up there, everything was peaceful. *I wish the rest of the world was like this,* I thought, instantly making myself depressed again.

I reached the red barn where I found Shane instructing some of the people we rescued. I was grateful that they agreed to help us with work around the base. We would never be able to keep up otherwise. I leaned against the rustic barn doorway and watched. Shane was dressed in his ripped overalls over his favorite blue shirt. Despite working outside all day, he managed to keep his hair perfect and styled just right. My brother was adorable and I have no shame in admitting it (because he probably got it from me).

I didn't realize I was still staring when he dismissed his helpers. "Aymie?" He waved to me.

Shaking my head, I went over and said, "Sorry, Shane. Lost in thought."

He laughed. "You're starting to sound like me. What can I help you with?" He looked at me with such kindness…and love. Whatever I saw in his green eyes broke me inside.

I lost it. The feelings surfaced, and I sobbed. I buried my face in my hands and let the tears fall, dampening the ground below. I felt my makeup running, but I couldn't stop.

Shane wrapped his arms around me and pulled me close. "Shh… I'm here; it's okay."

I shook my head against his strong chest. "Shane...we're… falling…apart," I managed to say through my sobs.

"We're still rebuilding, everything will work out."

"No," I looked up at him, my gray eyes filled with tears. "Our family. Mark…I feel like he hates us and thinks we hate him. He's… looking for dad."

"I know," he said, not surprised. "He works on it every night. I've asked if he wanted help, but he says he'd rather do it alone. He said I have 'too many people' to find already."

I sniffled. "But, he said that you didn't even think about finding him."

"He's not wrong," Shane replied with a sigh. "I never thought of looking for dad on my own… with Shannon trying to find her brother and me in charge of finding Marian's sister." He put his hands on my shoulders and reminded, "Mark doesn't hate us. He has a lot on his plate and is working through some things I guess. He'll be fine."

"Do you even know what those 'things' are?"

He shook his head. "No. Shannon knows, though. You should ask her when she gets back."

As he said that, we heard the clamor of trucks trekking up the side of the mountain. I wiped my tears and watched as a dozen Combatant vehicles parked in front of the garages. My brother and I looked at each other and raced off to see who it was.

Mr. Wyght and his team finally returned from their mission. They were banged up, bruised, and exhausted. Nic and Sonny hopped out of the high black truck and helped Shannon get down. Shane ran up to see if she was all right. He wanted to embrace her, but she pushed him away. He wasn't upset; he understood.

"What happened out there?" I asked.

"It's total chaos," Shannon said in a deep voice that wasn't her own. It freaked me out a bit. I never knew her mask could do that. Frustrated, she smacked the side of the machine and spoke again. This time in her normal voice. "Sorry, I've used the copier so many times. The voices are being left behind. As I was saying, everything is getting worse."

"Much worse," Sonny added, fixing his slick hair. "We are coming back with fewer rescues every time. People are taking them from us."

"What?" Shane asked, confused. "How is that possible?"

"Ask the guy we got in the back," Sonny replied firmly. Nic and Mr. Wyght carried an unconscious man out from the bed of their truck. They hurried him inside so I only caught a glimpse. From what I could tell, he was wearing a navy combat uniform similar to ours in style.

"We are going to question him as soon as he wakes up," Sonny added once they left. "Director Wyght wants all the RVs to be informed once we get answers."

"'Director?'" Shane said. "What, is this a movie set now?" Shannon and Sonny rolled their eyes simultaneously. Shane shrugged. "Eh, it was worth a shot."

"Next time, don't try," Sonny retorted. Turning to me, he said, "Aymie, I'll make the announcement to the RVs when it's done so you can look over Shannon and clean up her wounds."

"I'm fine," Shannon stated, taking the mask off.

"I think that's a good idea," I told her. Secretly, I wanted to get to the bottom of why Mark is acting so weird. What "things" were he dealing with?

Against her will, I took her into the base to get cleaned up. I brought her into the infirmary and had her sit on the examination table; her short legs dangling in the air.  Even though she never grew in height, Shannon had matured. Her solid stature had become stronger and her mind, wiser. She kept her curly hair cut short and pulled back. That day she looked older than she really was. The seventeen year old girl carried a lot of weight on her shoulders.

Worried, I bandaged her up and asked kindly, "Shannon, are you okay? Really?"

She kept her blue eyes down. "Everything that's happening…I can't believe it. What I see out there I don't wish anyone else to see."

"What's it like?"

Taking a deep breath, she remembered the awful sights. "The cities are in ruins; burned down, destroyed, and lifeless. Bodies of people litter the streets like trash. Those who survived were taken from our grasp, to be slaves for OX for as long as they lived. All those faces etched into my memory." She paused for a moment. I was bandaging her arm when I saw a tear roll down her freckled cheek. "I miss my parents," she croaked. "They would know what to do. They would know what to say." She took a shaky breath. "I don't know what to tell my sisters. They shouldn't have to grow up in a world like this. No one should."

"You're right. That's what we're here for. We're going to fix this."

"I don't know if we can," she said flatly. "I've gone over the figures dozens of times and—"

"Forget the figures!" I snapped. I tugged too tightly on the gauze wrapped around her forearm. "No detective work. No science. You of all people should know the importance of trust."

She didn't say anything more. I finished cleaning her up in silence. As I bandaged her final cut, I asked, "What's wrong with Mark?"

"I'm sure I don't know what you mean," she replied. She was always a good actress, so I almost fell for that.

"Does Mark actually hate Shane and me?"

She shook her head. "No. He feels unworthy of everyone. He's felt that way all his life." She sighed. "No matter what I do, how much I try to help, he doesn't see it."

"You do so much for him," I exclaimed. "Why doesn't he understand?"

"I think it's because of his deeper feelings for me," she explained. "I don't think he will accept what I have to say until I admit I feel the same way for him."

My eyes widened. "*Still*? It's been years and I thought he would've gotten the hint by now."

She laughed. "Both of your brothers don't know how to take hints. Shane still has no idea. That's why Mark's been so distant. He thinks Shane and I are officially together."

I was surprised. "Aren't you?"

"Not exactly." She subconsciously grabbed the key around her neck. "I'm still not ready. I told Shane to wait; he said he would and understands. I never got to tell Mark the truth when he confessed that

Christmas. Mark is still waiting for me too."

"Oh man," I replied. "This is making my head hurt. No wonder Mark is so upset."

"I know. I don't want your family to fall apart because of me," she said, honestly. "That's another reason why I haven't said anything. The boys need to figure this out before it goes too far." She hopped off the examination table. She pointed her finger at me. "You also need to straighten things out. Prove to Mark that you will be there for him. He needs to be reminded he isn't the only Hodgins here."

I promised I would. Before we could say another word, Sonny called to us from over the PA. We hastily made our way to the lounge. Inside, we found the Director, Royal Veterans, and a select others.

"Hurry, we have a lot to prepare for," Director Wyght started. "We interrogated the spy. He cooperated easily, surprisingly. He isn't OX."

"He's with Nikita and Walter," Sonny finished. "Their operation is up and running. Apparently, half the people we have been facing out there aren't even OX."

"Exactly," the Director confirmed. "Three organizations are fighting over the survivors of this catastrophe known to the Order of Xenophon as 'The Cleanse', but Nikita is calling it 'The Accident'." He rested his hands on the table. "Our prisoner was sent to spy on us and OX. The oddest part is he doesn't remember who he was. He only knew what he was sent to do. He wants to know if we could be possible allies. He even offered an incentive."

"Which is?" Johanna asked as she chewed on her sweatshirt string.

"He offered us information about the next OX strike," Sonny told her. "We know where they will be next and can cut off a head of one of their Divisions."

That sounded too good to be true. I had a feeling that this couldn't have been right. I wasn't the only one. "Seems more like a trap," Mark put in, leaning against the wall. "C'mon, after all Nikita has put us through, do you really think we can trust him?"

"If the spy is telling the truth, think of how many lives we can save," Shane told our brother.

"Yes, but we have to look at it at all angles," Mark replied. "The Director wants to send all his RVs in. If it is a trap, you lose the leaders of all the Branches."

"But if it's not, we have a better chance of defeating that section of OX," Shane reminded.

The two bickered for a few minutes until the Director finally made the decision. He held up his hand and silenced my brothers. "Mark, you are making sense, but logic can't help us right now. I say we go for it. Sonny and I have known Nikita for years. We both think he is telling the truth. He wants you Hodginses desperately; I think he will do anything to get you on his side."

Frustrated, Mark tensed and shook his fists at his sides. "If it is a trap and he does get us, then it's on you," he snarled through gritted teeth.

"Yes, I know," Director Wyght said. "We have a few months to prepare. You won't have to worry about it yet; let me do that. I will give you further details when it is time. For now, go back to your duties." Ending the meeting, he blew his new silver whistle. We all stood at attention. As he walked past, we saluted him as we were recently told to do.

When he left, we tried to understand what was going on. "What happens now?" Johanna asked, removing the wet sweatshirt string from her mouth.

"We anticipate our deaths," Mark muttered as he pushed past Shane and exited the room. Shannon wanted to go after him to talk, but Shane stopped her.

Giving in, Shannon let him leave. "We'll be able to handle this," she said, pulling away from Shane. "The spy gave us enough information to be prepared. Not only that, Gerrior is still alive and Masdit is no longer a threat to him." Thinking about what had happened to that man, she tried not to gag. "He will be able to give us more information about who we will be facing."

"I have a pretty good idea of who the leader of this attack will be," Sonny said, crossing his bruised arms. "It's been a while since

I've fought with my childhood best friend."

"Wait, are you sure it will be his group?" Nic asked. His violet eyes filled with curiosity. "If so, Joshua Wolfrum might be there."

"If he is in the correct Division," Sonny replied. "I can't believe it's been two years since he left."

"Well," Nic shook his head and chuckled, "we have a few months before we see him. Let's get to work."

# CHAPTER 47
## Aymie: XVI

The day of the OX attack snuck up on us. The time flew and I felt unprepared. Things kept getting worse. Every time we sent out groups to rescue survivors, they would come back with less and less…if they came back at all. Whenever our teams went out, there was an attack. But it wasn't always OX. Nikita wasn't going to lighten up his forces until he got an answer.

"They will never stop until we help them," Shannon said. It was a few days before the known OX attack and we ladies went over the plan for the upcoming battle. "Nikita and Walter will keep playing tag with us until we give in."

"I don't understand why they are telling the people that *we're* the bad guys," Johanna complained as she sat on the polished mahogany table.

Picking up her viola, Shannon explained, "They want to be seen as the heroes. Builds trust." She began to play the tune to the Gaelic lullaby her parents always sang to her.

"Obviously." Johanna rolled her eyes. "I just can't believe what they do to their own people. I fear what happens to the ones they rescue." She was referring to the last spy we captured. When we had one of Nikita's men in custody, he suddenly died before we could ask him any questions. We examined him and found an electronic tracker in the back of his neck that released a fatal, quick acting poison, killing him instantly.

"What monsters," I muttered. "They steal our blueprints, survivors, machinery then kill our men and their own."

"Just like the Order of Xenophon," a raspy voice said from behind us. Sonny entered with Nic and Mark. "Sorry ladies, we need to have an emergency meeting."

Johanna threw her hands up and jumped off the table. "All yours." She patted Nic on the arm as she passed. "Coming Aymie?" she called.

"Yeah," I said, tightening my bandana. "Good luck guys."

"Thanks," Shannon replied still playing her viola. "Can you make sure everything is ready in case we have to leave sooner?"

I nodded and went out with Johanna. I wrapped my pink shawl around my shoulders as the autumn wind whipped against us. The colorful leaves danced across the pavement at our feet, putting on a show. As I watched, I was reminded of the beautiful tree arches that shaded WHYP's driveway.

I couldn't believe a year had passed since we were there. My heart missed it. "Wonder what's going on back home," I said as we were away from the warehouse.

Johanna shoved her hands into the pockets of the oversized sweatshirt Nic gave her. "Yeah, me too. Myles contacts his family every now and then. They say it's all okay. Thyme is running the place, and I don't think there's been another attack."

Remembering all those we left, I began to tear up. I remember the screams and cries of our friends below as our plane ascended. I recalled when we were first contacted after we left them… how many lives were lost.

"I heard that they're trying to move out of Maine," Johanna added, interrupting my tragic flashbacks. "They have connections elsewhere and believe they'll be safer at this new place."

"Where are they thinking of going?"

Before Johanna could answer, an alarm sounded throughout the base. We looked at each other and understood immediately. We had to depart much sooner than we thought. Without saying another word, we left to prepare.

I went to my room and got ready. Throughout it all, I was more frustrated than nervous. We had to rush into another fight with more death and pain. I just recollected the deaths of former friends and now it was time to experience more…

I wasn't ready for it… not physically, not mentally, and especially not emotionally. I hated the way life was now. We had taken everything for granted, rushed through it all, and never took time to appreciate what we had. Even us telling you our story seems too quick for my taste.

I took a deep breath, closed my eyes, and tilted my head back. "'A true princess is obedient'," I repeated to myself. After a moment, I calmed down, grabbed my backpack, and headed out.

I met everyone by the garages. They loaded weapons and equipment into military quads. I went to Director Wyght. "Sir, what's going on? I thought it wasn't for a few days?"

"We thought so, too, but our outside men reported that they saw OX trucks on their way already," he zipped up his jacket, "We need to get their first."

I understood and headed to my designated all-terrain vehicle. I was to travel with Shannon, Sonny, and Mark.

When I got there, I heard a little voice shouting behind me. "We come too! We come too!" I turned around and saw Rachel, Rebecca, and Agnes running towards me. "Lady Clarius. We're coming too," Rachel said. She crossed her little arms and looked up at me with determination.

"No, Rachel. You have to stay here with Peggy." I took the oversized backpack from her. "It's too dangerous for you little ones."

She shook her head. "No! I'm six now. Agnes is seven and Rebecca is eight. We are big girls."

Mark came over and knelt down. "Rachel, we've talked about this. In five years you can come with us."

Tears filled the little girl's eyes. "No! I wanna come now." She flung her arms around Mark's neck.

He sighed and hugged her back. "I know, but we won't be long. This one is short and boring. I'll take you on a fun one, okay?"

She sniffled. "Promise?"

He put his hands on her shoulders. "Promise," he replied, looking into her dark eyes. She nodded and kept quiet.

Mark rubbed her golden hair and told her to run along. With a grunt, he stood up and went into the vehicle. I waved goodbye to the girls and hopped in the backseat next to him.

Shannon slid into the passenger side. "You guys ready?"

Sonny sat down and turned the key in the ignition. "Born and raised ready." With that, we took off.

For most of the ride, we sat in silence. I stared out the window and watched the autumn trees zip by. I tried again to wrap my mind around the reality we were living in, but it was no use. I couldn't comprehend what the world was suffering.

Breaking the quiet, Sonny finally said, "We'll be there in twenty. If OX arrived already, do not engage. We are only going to scout and report back to the others."

"I still think this is a trap," Mark muttered.

"It may seem like it, but we have to try and think otherwise," she said.

He scoffed. "Look, beautiful, you said it yourself. These things don't add up. They interrupt our missions, steal our stuff and our people, and then they decide to give us the location of a high ranking Xenophonian?" He pushed his long bang behind his ear, finally showing both of his blue eyes. They shone with determination and frustration. "My theory is that they used this as bait to lure us in. I *know* OX will be there but I have a feeling that so will they. When our numbers are decreased, then Nik will strike."

"Don't think so negatively," I scolded. "I don't believe they would do that."

"Whether Mark's right or not we have to be ready for that," Sonny concluded. "Frankly, I don't doubt his theory. I think he's right."

I prayed he wasn't.

Finally, we arrived. We drove through the remains of the city of Fargo. This time, I kept my eyes in the car. I wasn't ready to see what was out there. Sonny made several turns until the vehicle came to a jerking stop. He looked in the rearview at Mark and me. "This is it," Sonny said. With a smirk, he grabbed his bag and hopped out.

I took a deep breath and gripped the silver door handle, my hands trembling. I forced myself to push open the door and step onto cracked sidewalk.

I looked around and saw a sad vacant city longing to be filled again. The sky was dreary; the sun trapped in a dark prison. Trash and debris littered the streets, and there wasn't a soul in sight. Many of the buildings were reduced to dusty piles of rubble. The crisp wind stirred up the ash and dust that covered the city in its gray blanket.

"I hate to see what the rest of it looks like," I thought aloud. I grabbed our supplies from the trunk. Warily, the four of us made our way down the cluttered streets. That was my first time being outside the base since we arrived, and I didn't like what I experienced.

I breathed in the fetid air. I plugged my nose with my forefinger and thumb. I wondered why it smelled so putrid until I brought my eyes to the ground.

Strewn across the streets were those who never escaped. I didn't want to look down at them, but looking up was worse. On the sides of the buildings were large OX symbols—an overlapping *O* and *X*—painted in blood. Red handprints tainted the sides of the structures as if civilians were desperately attempting to climb up. Above the prints, I realized what they were reaching for. I clasped my hand over my mouth, trying not to scream.

Inside every OX symbol was a body pierced by a sword to keep it in place. I shook my head in terror as I examined the bleeding weapons lodged in the center of each dead person's chest. The final looks of terror and pain still remained on their faces.

I couldn't bear looking at it anymore and kept my eyes locked on the ground in front of me. At that moment, I was so scared I couldn't move.

"Aymie, we have to keep going," Mark commanded, averting his eyes from the heinous sight. I didn't want to go anymore. I kept my hand on my mouth and shook my head. My eyes filled with tears and I tried not to scream. My brother came over and grabbed my hand. "You can close your eyes. I'll guide you."

"Thank you," I whispered as I squeezed his hand. Together we walked through the destroyed city. That was the first time Mark really showed he cared about me.

"This is PH's doing," Sonny admitted finally after we passed more horrific displays. "This is one of his signatures."

"Why does he do this?" Shannon asked. She tried not to cry as she looked away from another pierced body.

"To make himself seem intimidating," Sonny told her. "He is also a diehard Xenophonian. He and I grew up together, but thankfully I had my mother to keep me on the right track. He was taken from his family and raised by one of our leaders. There is no good in him."

"What was your mother like?" Shannon asked. She wanted to draw our attention away from OX's disgusting deeds.

"She was a remarkable woman and we will leave it at that," Sonny replied, crossly.

Embarrassed, Shannon quickly apologized. "I'm sorry, I didn't mean to—"

"It's fine, I understand," Sonny interrupted. "I would share more with you, but now is not an appropriate time for me to lose focus." Without saying another word, we made it to the destination.

We were too late.

There was an OX camp set up in the city plaza. Heavy automatic artillery lined the perimeter. A hundred OX soldiers walked about their duties. Small tents circled a large one that had three emblems embroidered above its entrance. The first design was a circle with two wings inside, the second was the OX symbol, and the third was another circle with two snakes woven around a sword in its center.

"Why are they so early?" I asked quietly.

"I think Nikita sold us out," Mark added.

"Wouldn't surprise me." Sonny pulled a tablet out of his backpack. He typed a message on it and sent it to Nic. "We are going to need a backup plan and some extra help."

"Why?" I questioned.

"PH is here," Sonny confirmed. He put the device back in his bag and pointed to the tent. "That third sword emblem is his. He's officially the head of the Hermes Division." He chuckled. "Always knew he would be."

"Wait, isn't that what our dad was?" Mark asked.

"Yes, and apparently, he was the leader of the entire English Pandemonium. If PH is leading this Division, it's a good possibility he holds the same position your father did."

"If we kill him then everyone with English as their first language at OX will be leaderless?" Shannon inquired.

"It would seem."

I tried to take that all in. We kill one person, tens of thousands will be thrown into chaos. *It can't be that simple.*

"If you stayed, would you have been a leader like PH?" Mark asked.

"Oh yeah, for sure," Sonny replied. He subconsciously rubbed his right side. "No one could match PH and me. We were always told we would lead someday. That's why we trained the hardest and can speak every major language. We never knew which Division we would be in charge of, though. For him, Hermes makes sense."

"What would you've been?" my brother questioned.

Thinking for a moment, Sonny replied, "Probably Ares like Gerrior, but in the Russian Pandemonium. Killing was what they usually made me do even though I am well rounded. PH can do everything also, but they assigned him to strategy and tactics. He planned the missions, I carried them out. The two of us are evenly matched."

"We were hoping you were better," I mumbled.

Before an argument could start, we saw a few Xenophians approaching. We ducked into an alley. Sonny and Mark kept watch while Shannon and I hid behind them. I didn't dare look.

When they were gone, Sonny scoffed and mumbled, "Wonder where he is…"

"What do we do now?" I asked, trying not to sound afraid.

Sonny jerked his thumb over his shoulder. I unzipped his backpack and checked the tablet's messages. My heart sank. "'Ran into some trouble; be there tomorrow. Make camp and keep an eye out,'" I read aloud.

Mark cursed under his breath. "Great. I knew it was a trap."

"Trouble doesn't necessarily mean what you think, Mark," Shannon stated, trying to stay positive.

"Regardless of what it means, we have to get ready for the night," Sonny concluded. Tightening the straps on his backpack, he walked along the side of the building until he came across a rusted fire escape. Not knowing what else to do, we went to the top.

The roof was clear and we set up camp. I looked out at the army of OX below and tried to wrap my mind around the organization as a whole. It made no sense to me. I couldn't think anymore. It was hurting my head. I let out a deep breath, dropped my bag to the floor, and sat down. "This is crazy," I mumbled.

"Tell me about it." Mark plopped down next to me. He rubbed his hands through his long brown bang and rested his elbows on his knees. I closely watched his movements and remembered the moment I first met him. A stinky, weird yet cute kid whom Thyme rescued from abduction. I couldn't help but smile.

Out of the corner of his eye, he saw me staring. "Uh oh, now what's wrong?"

I shook my head. "Nothing. Just remembering."

He smiled, scooted himself closer to me, and put an arm around my shoulders. He kissed my head and said. "Never saw you smile at me like that, Sis. Nice to see you care."

Thankfully, I was in a good mood. I took that as a compliment. My brother cared even though he had a hard time showing it. Saying nothing, I rested my head on his shoulder. The moment the sun disappeared, I fell into a deep sleep in Mark's arms.

# CHAPTER 48
## Mark: XV

Ugh, Aymie can't you just keep going? You know how much I hate that day we encountered OX. I don't care if you want to know my side of the story.

Hmph, fine. So, picking up where my sister left off…

That morning I woke up to Sonny kicking my side. Groaning, I grabbed my ribs while Sonny gently shook the girls awake. He always had a deep respect for women and wouldn't hurt them in any way. That's great; chivalry isn't dead. But that's no excuse to knock the wind out of me while I'm sleeping.

I struggled to my feet, hissing from the pain. Looking around, I saw the sun wasn't up, and Sonny had packed our things. "What's going on?"

"The others are here," he said, tying his long black hair into a ponytail. He had a disturbing look in his red eyes and a smile I'd never seen before. It wasn't friendly… "Time to get some revenge," he stated, maliciously.

We cautiously descended the fire escape and were back into the alley. Rather than going out through the streets, Sonny ordered me to pick the lock of the adjacent building. I granted us entry easily. We stealthily made our way through and exited through the other side as not to be seen via roadway. We repeated the process several times until we found Director Wyght's camp on the outskirts of Fargo.

Nic was the first to see us approaching. "Hurry, we have things to discuss." We followed him into the Director's tent where we found all the other RVs as well as a handful of the best members.

As we walked in, I felt someone watching me. I looked over my shoulder and saw Alexandrea standing by the door. Her lip curled at the sight of me. Her golden hair was a mess. Her nose and cheeks were red. She kept her glare fixed on me. All the while she was sweating and breathing heavily.

She was drunk…again.

Two years had passed and she still hadn't gotten over Roxanne's murder. Worst of all, she blamed me for it and encouraged others to as well.

Trying to ignore her, I stood up straight and went to my place at the table.

Once we were settled, the Director began: "All right, no small talk today. We have a serious situation on our hands. At first, I thought things were going okay, but Blake had a dream." A few kids around began chuckling. Blake turned red. I forgot that not everyone was informed of Blake's precognitive dreams. "Enough," Director Wyght scolded. The students immediately hushed their ridicules and gave their full attention. "God granted him this gift for a reason and—as much as I hate to admit it—I believe him. After all, he informed of us the stowaways in our caravan."

"Stowaways?" Aymie questioned.

The Director nodded. "A portion of Blake's dream involved the Hollinger girls in the battle. Sure enough, we found Agnes and Rebecca hiding in the weapons truck. That's why we were delayed. We had someone run the two girls back."

Shannon shook her head. "Thank God for your dreams, Blake."

The white haired teen kept his eyes locked on the ground… there was something else he wasn't telling us.

"Anyway, that's beside the point." The Director turned to the diagram behind him. He pointed to the OX encampment Sonny had mapped out. "Wilcox has informed me that this is the Hermes Division," he circled their position on the rough paper with his finger, "which means they aren't here to fight. Their leader happens to be in charge of the entire English Pandemonium. He is known as PH. There is a chance Joshua Wolfrum may be with them." He looked at each of us in turn. His eyes serious. "If he is, do not blow his cover. He needs to carry out his mission no matter the cost. We will proceed with the plan as normal." Then, he relayed everything out in full.

I'd be here talking for an hour if I went over it, so you'll just have to wait and hear what happens. What I will tell you is that an important part fell upon my shoulders. Normally, I was collected on these missions, but this time I was anxious. Not to mention Alexandrea made everyone lose faith in me at that moment.

"Ha," she mocked after Director Wyght complimented me on my computer and lock picking skills. "You think…that is going to make this successful?" She wobbled forward, slammed her hand on the table, and loomed over me. I smelled the vodka on her breath. "You're going to kill us all," she spat, her tone cold and hateful. "Whatever happens in Blake's dream is because of you."

"McCracken, that is enough," Director Wyght commanded.

Throwing her hands up, she stepped back. "Just saying a lot of the crap that has happened is his fault." She turned to the other members. "Those Mutant beasts we have in custody, our home being attacked twice, practically everything." She motioned to me with her fireproof glove. "That Hodgins is responsible for it."

Shane was about to say something, but the Director stopped him. I hoped he was going to stick up for me, but I would never know for sure.

Finally, it was time to act. The Director blew his silver whistle, and we all stood at attention. He gave us our commands and we went to prepare.

Being ready immediately, I went out to sulk for a little while. I weaved through the swarm of busy bees and reached a building on the perimeter. Leaning against it, I closed my eyes and thought about what

I needed to do.

A few minutes before we had to leave, I thought I heard a strange voice to my right. I ignored it the first time until I heard it again. I looked over, but didn't see anyone. I didn't realize I was staring until Shannon interrupted me.

"Mark, you okay?" she asked. Her short hair was pulled back by a black headband, and her freckled face had been washed from yesterday's dirt and grime. Her blue eyes watched me with concern.

I couldn't help but smile when I saw her. All my troubles left when I was with Shannon. "Hey, sweetheart. I'm good." I reached for her face and pushed a stray hair behind her ear. She didn't flinch.

Instead, she grabbed my hand and sighed. "Mark, when this is over we need to talk." My heart pounded in my chest. I wanted to ask what about when Shane interrupted us…again.

Seeing her hand on mine, Shane had a confused look on his face. "We have to go…" he said, slowly. He stared for another moment. "What did I miss?"

Shannon rolled her eyes and let go of me. "Nothing, relax." Without another word, she patted my arm and went towards Shane. I quietly followed her and pushed past my brother without looking up.

Finally, the dreaded moment was upon us. Sonny led the RVs and Shannon up to a rooftop while our comrades stayed on the ground.

Crawling towards the edges of the building, we peered out at the enemies below. Nic pointed to sections of the camp. "Mark and my team will head in through the west side and see if we can reach the main tent," he explained. "If Sonny's OX knowledge is still accurate, the main computers should be in there. If they are, Mark can encode his virus into it. Hopefully, the chips embedded into the Xenophonians' necks are connected and will be destroyed with the virus."

"What if PH is in there?" Shane asked.

"We capture him and bring him back for questioning," Shannon told him as she put her mask on.

"If we get that opportunity, let me handle it," Sonny ordered. "PH won't come easy."

Saying nothing else, we jumped up and hastily slid down the fire escape. We stealthily ran towards our entry point. On the infiltration team were Nic, Shannon, Shane, Sonny, and me. The rest were to secure the outskirts. Even though it was only supposed to be the five of us, I felt like we were being followed.

*This is a trap*, I know it, I thought to myself.

Finally, we reached our destination. We hid behind a turned over eighteen-wheeler. Peeking over its cab, I saw the heavy automatic artillery that blocked our entrance. OX members could walk past no problem, but Sonny said it shoots at any foreign life. Thankfully, we solved that problem months ago. Whenever the Combatants went on a mission, they brought back OX chips from the unfortunate Xenophonians that challenged them.

I patted the pocket that the tracker was in and took a deep breath. Nic motioned for us to follow him and went around the back of the truck. We crept about and hid behind whatever debris we came across. The horrid scent of BO and decay blew past us on a gust of wind.

I held my breath and tried not to gag. *Man, OX is disgusting*, I thought, repulsed.

The wind died and I could concentrate again. Taking a deep breath, I pulled out the tablet in my backpack as we walked. Nic gave the word, and I tapped the screen. Within seconds, an explosion went off behind us.

A dozen alarmed Xenophonians ran to the source. In the chaos, we took the long way around and went into the encampment. Once inside, I didn't stop to sight see. We stayed low and kept hiding. The others weren't supposed to take action for another five minutes.

The clock was ticking and our time was short.

Dodging the other Xenophonians was easier than we thought. A few times I could've sworn they saw us, but they didn't care. *What's wrong with them?* I thought after making eye contact with an older OX member as he cleaned his rifle.

"These ones are in the worst condition I've seen," Sonny whispered. "Their Entrance Rituals are becoming more severe. They are less human now."

We didn't have time to discuss what he meant. Our five minutes were up. Our friends wreaked havoc on every side. The Xenophonians jumped to their feet and ran about like mad. It looked like chaos...but an organized chaos. They knew what they had to do but bickered and argued with each other, invigorating their anger and panic. Exactly what I saw in the videos I had erased from the internet years ago.

While this was going on, we continued with our portion of the mission. We reached the main tent without a scratch. Sonny cautiously peeled away the heavy pine green curtain and looked inside. When he decided it was safe, we went in.

The interior was impressive. To our left was an enclosed sleeping chamber; parallel was a personal kitchenette and bathroom. Straight ahead was a large, white marble table with the Hermes logo etched into it: two wings enclosed in a circle. Behind it was what we were looking for: the master computer.

"This seems too easy," Shannon stated. "I didn't need to use my voice copier to get in like previous times."

"PH has always been different. He may have another way of telling we are in here," Sonny warned, holding his hand up. No one took another step forward.

"Yeah, like laser beams," Shane joked. He bent over, grabbed some dirt off the ground, and flung it as a joke. Nothing. "Eh, I tried."

"Throw it higher," Sonny commanded. Baffled, Shane took more dust and did as he said. This time, red beams of light appeared, blocking our way to the computer. They started at the center of my chest and went up to the ceiling.

"Wait, what use is that?" Shane asked confused.

Sonny chuckled. "He always hated alarm systems but the other Titans made him put them in anyway. He did it his own way."

"Wait, is PH short? Like, Shannon short?" Shane said. He pushed his hand towards the floor to indicate height.

"Not too sure," Sonny replied, loading his pistol. "Last I saw him we were fourteen. He hadn't hit puberty yet so I wouldn't know."

Ending that conversation, Nic urged us to get on with it. We ducked and went over to the computer...well, Shannon didn't need to duck.

I sat down in the cold marble seat. "Whoa," I said, falling backwards. "This is weird…and inconvenient." I tried reaching some buttons on the far end of the console. "It doesn't move or swivel."

"How does PH reach if he is so short?" Shane asked.

"Shut up and get going!" Nic snapped. His patience was growing thin and we were afraid the Beast would take his place. I hopped to it and began my hacking.

It was harder than I anticipated. The other OX firewalls were simpler. It took me fifteen minutes to break down the first wall. "Whoever coded this is almost as good as me," I said aloud. "I didn't know you had computer Nerds in OX."

"We only had a few," Sonny explained. "Only the Titans and a select few members had experience with computers. They kept the rest as far away from technology as possible. It is how they control 80% of their populace. Can't let it fall into the wrong hands."

I wanted to ask what he meant by "Titans" but kept quiet. Finally, I was into the system. I took the USB out of my pocket, kissed it, and inserted it into the console. "Okay, baby, let's do this," I whispered. When it was in, I let it do its job.

I was about to tell them how much time was left when I was interrupted by an ear-piercing scream. Unfortunately, I recognized it all too well. My heart sank into my shoes, and my face fell.

Shannon gasped and ran out of the tent without thinking.

"Shannon, wait!" Shane called and raced after her. Jumping up, I ran out with the others.

The fighting had ceased and I couldn't believe what caused the chaos to stop. In the middle of the encampment was a large Xenophonian covered in tattoos. He was lifting a little girl into the air by gripping her throat. "No…" I whispered. I realized why I felt like we were being followed.

It was Rachel.

The little Hollinger girl was gripping onto the man's arms to keep herself from falling. Her curly golden hair was caked in blood that dripped down her face. Tears fell to the floor as she cried…for me.

"Mark…Mark! Help!" she screamed when she saw me.

All heads turned. I could see our friends hiding behind the debris watching me. They couldn't fight back because Rachel was taken hostage. I never felt so small. I didn't know what to say.

The man holding Rachel glared at me and laughed. "Look who we have here?" He brought Rachel's face closer to his own. "This who you're looking for, little girl?" She didn't answer. He repeated his question, but this time screamed it in her ear.

Frightened, she began to cry. "Yes! Yes!"

He cackled. "Well, what's he doing in our Titan's tent?" When she didn't reply, he squeezed her neck harder. Her face turned purple and she was struggling to breathe.

Just then, a rock hit him in the back of the head. Unfazed, he turned and saw who threw it. Emerging from the crowd was someone I didn't expect to see: Joshua Wolfrum.

He had changed. He was stronger and his face had aged. His dark eyes glared at the giant through the glasses we gave him for the mission. His dark hair was long at the top and shaved from the middle of his ears down. Like the other Xenophonians, he wore a black combat uniform adorned with the three Hermes emblem patches to set him apart from us.

Rubbing the back of his head with his free hand, the man laughed. He loosened his grip and said, "What're you trying to do, Wolf?"

"Take your prize from you," Joshua sneered as he gripped another stone. "Why should you get all the spoils, huh?" Around him, the other members yelled in agreement. The big guy wasn't too well liked.

Before he could say anything, all the members became quiet. Their eyes were focused on something to my left. Looking over, I saw the sea of Xenophonians part. I heard light footsteps and a man singing an old English ballad: Scarborough Fair. Whoever it was had a melodic voice, but we weren't interested in a show.

He walked out into the clearing and up to the brute and Rachel. He was a shorter man in a long black trench coat. He had pale skin and curly brown hair. Around his neck and over his mouth was a long green scarf that flapped behind him in the wind. On his back was a thick sword as long as he was tall. When he reached the two in the center, his song ended. He kept his eyes locked on the ground and pulled his scarf down. "Goliath, what're you doin'?" he said in a thick, rustic English accent.

The giant nervously staggered back a few steps and let go of the girl. The short man caught her. Rachel struggled to breathe and held her throat. "What 'ave I told you about takin' hostages?" the man growled. He looked up at Goliath who scurried back into place. "That's what I thought."

He put Rachel down and gently held her hand. He looked around at his half destroyed camp and said aloud, "What is goin' on 'ere? I leave for twenty minutes and you've all shown me nothing but weakness."

He paused for a moment and an eerie quiet swept through the camp. The Xenophonians kept their eyes locked on their leader. Our RRPR members remained motionless. One wrong move and the man could kill Rachel.

Finally, someone did something unexpected. Sonny shouted commands in Greek (yes, Greek) and the crowd of Xenophonians that were in front of us scurried to the sides. Unafraid, he marched to the center with us following close behind.

Surprised, the man turned to look at him. His eyes, which were both different colors, widened and his mouth dropped. "Well, look who we 'ave 'ere!" he exclaimed, still holding Rachel's hand.

"Long time no see, PH," Sonny replied, crossing his arms. "Seems like you've been doing good. You're a Titan already. You're not even twenty yet."

PH shrugged. "Wasn't hard. You would've been a Titan, too, Mars...although," he thought for a moment and scratched his head of curly hair, "I don't think I can call you that anymore. Erik Patya is your Mortal name, ain't it? Still can't believe they knocked you off though. I honestly think it was your fraternal connection that did it."

Sonny gritted his teeth. "I wished they'd never stopped searching for Patya. He deserves to die."

"Ah right. He's not your dad, is he, Erik?" PH asked mockingly. "What's your *real* Mortal name? Aren't you your mum's 'little ray of sunshine'?"

"That doesn't matter!" he snapped. "Give her to us and we will be on our way."

Scoffing, PH said, "Now why would I do that? She seems like a nice girl." He stroked her face.

Sonny dropped into a stance and reached for his gun. "Let her go, PH."

Sighing, the British man reached over his shoulder and pulled out the long sword with his left hand. He raised it with ease and pointed it towards Sonny. "Tell me what you were doin' or else the little one gets it."

Not thinking, I ran up to him. "Enough! It was me." Unafraid, I stood before the short Xenophonian. I stared at his freckled face. "I tried messing with your computer, but it was no use," I lied. "Our mission failed. Let her go."

PH studied my features for a moment, as if remembering something. Scoffing, he replied, "I almost believed ya. What's your name, Yank?"

"Mark. Now let her go," I sneered.

He thought about it and looked down at Rachel. She was still crying. He shook his head. "Eh, I don't want her, but I deserve an incentive." Forcefully, he grabbed the girl's shoulder. A maniacal look crossed his face as he rammed his foot into the side of her leg with all his might.

She wailed in agony as she buckled to the ground. She screamed, cried, and clutched her leg to stop the excruciating pain. Shannon screamed her name in an unknown voice through her mask. She wanted to run towards her, but Shane held her back so they were hidden from view.

Then, the fighting started up again. RRPR fired at the Xenophonians and charged into the camp. The OX members grabbed their weapons and rushed to meet them.

I was still face to face with PH who had his long sword in his grip. He glared at me with hatred in his brown and blue eyes. "I've 'eard about you," he growled as he walked towards me. "You set us back. We could've won by now, but you set hundreds of thousands of our men free." He raised his sword and pointed it at my chest. "I 'ave every right to plunge this through your heart right now."

Unintimidated, I stared down at the short Titan and challenged him. "I'd like to see you try."

He pulled his elbow back and was about to thrust it through my heart when another bomb went off to my left.

I looked over and saw something I didn't like…but liked more than being stabbed. It was a stampede of Mutants. A blonde haired man led them in a small black vehicle.

"Oh, bugger. This guy again," PH muttered when he took a closer look. The Xenophonian began shouting in Greek and his men turned their attention away from RRPR and towards the stampede.

While they were distracted, I scooped up Rachel. She needed a doctor. I screamed for an RRPR member to come take her.

Unfortunately, Alexandrea found me first. She was covered in blood and full of rage. She ran up to me and began screaming and swearing. "This is all your fault!" I heard her say in the middle of it. She snatched Rachel away, not caring about the little girl's searing pain. "I hope all our friends you turned into monsters kill you." She spat in my face and ran off to get help.

Wiping saliva from my eyes, I looked over to see what she was talking about. I spotted familiar faces amongst the Mutants. I gasped when I recognized Dylan Cheatle and Adeline Zarra. Dylan had been Spliced with a bear. The chubby boy had grown 4 times in size and was covered in hair. He had sharp teeth, black eyes, and long nails that slashed at Xenophonians until they could no longer stand.

Beautiful Adeline had been turned into a hideous fruit bat. Her slender arms were now wrinkled and enveloped in grotesque wings. Her ears became pointed, her face hairy, and her eyes large and black. She swooped down from the air and grabbed her victims, carrying them away to their deaths.

My sister ran up and tried to get Adeline's and Dylan's attention, but it was no use. They were gone. I needed to rush in and help but I thought I should finish the mission in the midst of the chaos. I turned and ran back to the tent, but was cut off by another familiar face.

Blocking my way was a tall thin boy covered in orange and white fur. He hunched over and stared at me with glowing yellow eyes. When he recognized me, his long bushy tail wagged behind him. A sharp smile spread across his face…a smile I remembered all too well.

"Where do you think you're going, Mark?" he asked, drool dripping from his mouth. "We need you."

"Clive, you don't need me," I told him with my hands out. "Grab Dylan and Adeline and help us end this."

He cackled. "You joking? Go back and be stuck behind a computer all day? Never." He shook his arms out and cracked his neck. "This was my destiny. For crying out loud, my last name is Foxwood. This was meant to be." Slightly bowing, he said, "I thank you, Mark. You are partially responsible for these creations."

As much as I didn't want to admit it, he was right. If I had never helped Mallory, these kids wouldn't have been turned into animals. "I wish I wasn't."

"Well, too bad. Now, come with us or they all die," he commanded.

I looked over my shoulder at the chaos. Three different groups all fighting head on. I watched many RRPR members fall and couldn't bear watching any more. I took a deep breath and looked at my old friend. "If I agree, will you fight on our side against OX?"

Clive reached out for a handshake. "Fox's honor."

Taking a deep breath, I reached for him. I was about to shake his hand when I was surprised once again. Something in PH's tent had exploded, knocking Clive and I off our feet.

My ears were ringing and I couldn't stand. The smell of gunpowder filled my nostrils. Everyone stopped and stared at the commotion. Rolling over, I watched the Mutants scurry back—including Clive—behind Mallory in his buggy.

For some reason, a third of the Xenophonians weren't moving. They froze where they stood and trembled. Taking advantage, all the

RRPR members fell back and raced towards the camp, leaving me behind.

When my hearing returned, I heard a voice I wished I could forget. "Thanks, Mark!" Mallory yelled through a megaphone. "If you and your siblings want to come with me now, that's fine. If not, I'll be back or you come find me. Don't forget my promise!" With that, he turned and drove away with all the Mutants behind him.

"Get back 'ere!" PH bellowed as he slew another Mutant with his sword. He was going to chase after him, but needed to tend to his soldiers. After a few moments, the men who were stationary began to scream in pain. They pressed their palms to their heads and ran about frantically. I watched as blood dripped from their ears and noses. Frustrated, PH shouted something in Greek and the sane soldiers started attacking and *killing* the panicking ones.

I couldn't comprehend all the chaos and confusion. I struggled to crawl towards PH's tent to see what happened. Staggering to my feet, I walked over and studied the debris. Everything was destroyed.

*Who did this?* I wondered.

"You!" I heard a voice scream behind me. I turned and saw PH charging at me, his large sword in hand. He raised it above his shoulder, ready to slice it through my body.

I was too tired to move and I didn't care what he did to me. I closed my eyes and waited for him to come.

I anticipated his sword through my flesh when I heard an engine to my left. The next thing I knew, a hand had grabbed my arm and I was flung onto the back of a truck. With the wind knocked out of me, I lay there watching the sky fly by and listening to the voices fade away.

After an hour, the truck finally came to a stop. Sitting up too fast, I got dizzy and held my head. I needed to see who saved me. I turned around just to catch a glimpse of a figure scaling the side of a building. He was wearing all black and had a dark hat. A similar depiction of the man in all the news stories I was keeping track of...

*Could it be?* I thought. "Dad!" I yelled. The man ignored me and kept climbing. I tried another name. "Marcellus!"

For a moment, I could've sworn he hesitated, but I was so dizzy I couldn't tell.

Overwhelmed, exhausted, and in pain, I lay back down in the bed of the truck and passed out.

# CHAPTER 49

## Mark: XVI

When I woke up, I was staring at the ceiling of our lounge room. I thought my friends would've been nice enough to put me in the infirmary, but I guess more important people had to go there.

As I lay on the couch trying to regain my senses, I heard arguing behind me. I was conscious enough to know who they were and what they were arguing about.

"This is all his fault! Every last bit of it," Alexandrea screamed. "Didn't you see our friends? They were monsters. We lost so many soldiers. He was right; it was a trap. He's only right because *he* set us up."

"That's ridiculous! Mark would never do that," Shannon yelled back in my defense. "You're not making any sense."

"Despite what he has done, I don't think he would do this," Sonny agreed.

"Why should we listen to you?" Alexandrea argued. "You are the son of one of the worst Xenophonians who happens to continuously attack us for Mark and his good-for-nothing family. Might I also remind you that you are OX."

Trying not to blow his top, Sonny replied, "I am not Nikita's son nor am I OX. If I was, would I volunteer to go on this new mission to help you all get away from Mallory and his Splicing projects?" He paused for a moment. "If we can either shut him down or convince him to be allies with us, this all can be over. I'm willing to risk my life to go to these Isles for however long it takes. I want to end part of our suffering. I took the oath as an RRPR member just like you did."

*What's this new mission they're talking about?* I wondered as I eavesdropped. *Is it those Isles that Nikita Patya and Walter Jarvis mentioned back at WHYP?*

"I never wanted to be an RRPR member," Alexandrea bellowed. "I wanted to be able to leave WHYP and have a normal life. Now, none of us may get that chance. All our friends who died or were Spliced will never get that chance." She took a deep breath. "I hope that you and Mark know the pain and suffering you both brought upon all of us." With that, I heard her storm out of the room.

Groaning, I rubbed my face and mumbled, "I thought she'd never leave."

"Oh, you're awake," Shannon said, leaning over the couch. Her hair dangled around her face and she smiled at me. "How do you feel?"

"Like crap," I admitted. "How are you doing, beautiful?"

She took a deep breath. "I'm okay… really worried about Rachel though."

Remembering what had happened, I sat up so quickly that I bashed heads with Shannon. She yelped. "Gah! Sorry," I turned around on the couch, leaned over, and rubbed her face.

She pushed my hand away. "It's fine and Rachel is okay."

"By okay, she means may never be able to walk without aid again," Sonny chimed in, crossing his scarred arms.

I couldn't believe my ears. "Wh-what?"

Shannon bit her lip and tried not to cry. "PH fractured her knee in such a way that it may not heal correctly. She is going to need a brace for a long time."

I sat on the couch in shock. Saying nothing, I stood up and went over to Shannon. I wrapped my arms around her and rested my face on her head. "I'm so sorry…this is my fault," I whispered.

She hugged me back and replied, "It's not your fault."

I held her for a few moments until Shane came in and cleared his throat. He had that same confused face when he walked in on Shannon and me before the battle. "Director is going to make a choice tonight about who will take the mission," he said, slowly.

Shannon gently pushed me away and wiped the tears from her eyes. "Okay, thanks for the update, Shane."

Sonny couldn't help but chuckle. "I think I'll leave you three alone." He pushed past Shane and closed the lounge door behind him.

"Okay, now I am really confused," Shane said. He looked at the locked exit and back at us. "What are you two doing?"

"Mark was consoling me, nothing more," Shannon told him.

I shook my head. This was it. I couldn't take it anymore. I hated keeping secrets, I needed to tell him. "No. There was always more," I said, crossly.

Surprised, Shane stared at me. "What?"

I groaned. "Are you serious, dude? For a guy who is fast on his feet you sure are slow." Trying to find the words to say, I added, "I have the same feelings for Shannon as you do."

Shannon's face turned bright red and she stepped back. Shane tried to understand what he was hearing. He cleaned out his ear with his pinky and told me to say that again.

"You heard me," I repeated. "You're not the only one who deeply cares for Shannon."

He put his hand up for me to stop. "That's what this has always been about? You've put distance between *our* relationship because we both had the same crush?"

"There was always more, Shane," I corrected. "Shall I name them all?"

"Please do," my brother replied, crossly.

"Hmm, where should I begin?" I tapped the side of my face. "Okay, how about you constantly insulting me; reminding me how incompetent I am; making everyone think you are the 'perfect' brother and that I am a 'deadbeat'; the way you've treated Shannon and your other friends; never thinking of family first and only yourself—"

"Whoa, whoa, hold up," he cut me off, "First off, when have I made you feel like that? Second, I ditched all that 'Mr. Popular' stuff and got better. We are 19 now, Mark, I would've thought you'd have grown up too."

I laughed sarcastically. "Seriously? How about when I became a Royal? You were always jealous. Or how about when I tried to tackle Masdit when Shannon was shot? You did nothing but insult me and remind me how *evil* I am."

"I never meant it," he replied, getting tense. "In case you forgot, *I* was the one to write the letter for you to become a Royal or is that one of my many flaws?"

"What 'flaws', I thought you were perfect?" I sneered.

"Enough!" Shane bellowed. His green eyes were filled with anger and disappointment. "I am not perfect. I never was. My past was tough, too, Mark or did you forget that?"

"Ooh, living with families that doted on your every whim and loved you," I mocked. "So hard. I was a liar and a thief. I went to bed every night hoping that no one would try and kill me. You were worthy enough of all that love and attention. You get the fame, popularity, *and* the girl."

He thought for a moment. His eyes met mine. "So that's really what this is all about," he said finally. He tried to come closer, but I backed away. He stared me dead in the face and stated, "Why do you feel no one cares for you?"

He caught me.

Not wanting to admit defeat, I stood up straight and looked him in the eye. "Haven't you seen everything I've done? Why anyone would think otherwise is beyond me."

"Now you are being overdramatic," Shane complained. "This is crazy, Mark! You are being a childish brat because you're jealous of my hard work."

"What hard work?!" I yelled. "You do the bare *minimum* around here and still get what you want. The highest respect, the greatest rank, everything. You also took the only girl who could ever care for me away." I went closer to him and stared right into his green eyes. "Life is never easy, but somehow yours is. You take everything for granted and have treated me like dirt ever since we met. I think you try to look out for me but are doing a horrible job." I sneered and breathed in his face. "You are *not* my brother despite what these dog tags say. Jordan, Theo, Brand, they are my brothers. You are far from it. I am disgusted that we even share the same last name." Backing away, I spat in Shane's face.

Shannon stood in shock, a hand over her mouth. Wiping the spit from his eyes, Shane retorted, "That makes two of us." He went to Shannon and took her by the hand. That infuriated me even more. With a glare, he led her out. Together, they left me alone in the lounge without looking back.

At that moment, I hated everything about my brother. Finally, I found a home, a family, and a girl who accepted me for who I was. *Now, they all turned on me,* I thought. Shane and Aymie were just as much culprits of Masdit and Gerrior's attacks as I was and yet they escaped the reprimands unscathed. Everyone needed a scapegoat and they agreed on me.

At that moment, I understood something. I thought of everything that had happened…I thought of the people I hurt. I hurt Clive, Adeline, Dylan, Alexandrea, Shannon, and…especially, Rachel.

That's when I truly realized it wasn't everyone else I hated…

I hated myself.

All those feelings I had buried deep down surfaced. I staggered back and sat on the arm of the couch. A lump caught in my throat, and my heart thumped in my chest.

I realized then what I had to do.

Remembering the mission Sonny and Alexandrea were talking about, I left the lounge and went to find Director Wyght. He was alone in the kitchen making a sandwich.

When he saw me, he smiled and said, "Well, if it isn't Mark. How are you doing, son?"

Because I was full of hatred and repulsion, his gentle smile and kind words disgusted me. That was always part of my problem. People were good to me, but I never accepted it.

"Send me on the mission to the Isles," I demanded.

The old man's grin faded, and he stopped squirting mustard onto his bologna. He looked up at me with such concern. "I'm sorry, Mark but that isn't your field. You are to stay here with us and work with Myles and Shannon in the control room." He took a deep breath. "I'm still deciding to pick Sonny or Shane for the mission." He paused and then made a final decision: "Shane most likely because Sonny has his Brand and tattoos that would give him away."

*He even stole this opportunity,* I thought bitterly. "I don't care; you should send me. I'd be the best for the job. I've never met Nikita or Walter. It's perfect."

The older man shook his head. "I'm sorry, Mark. My decision is final. You are staying here. Besides, you are still recovering. You were out for a week."

Frustrated, I said nothing more and stormed out of the kitchen. I didn't care what the man said.

I was going, and I was leaving that night.

I went to my desk in the control room and plopped hard in my chair. Swiveling around, I began doing some research. I hacked into Director Wyght's files and read over the mission a hundred times.

*I'll be gone a while,* I thought. *Perfect. Let's hope I don't come back at all.* I dug deeper and discovered that the depart time wasn't scheduled for another two months and then on a boat for seven. *I can't wait that long.* So, I did something I couldn't believe.

I contacted Carl Mallory.

While I was finishing up my own details for the mission, I received a reply from him:

*Glad to hear you are coming! Your timing couldn't be more perfect. Walter Jarvis has one final rescue mission in North Dakota. He arrives and departs tomorrow at 0200. That will be his final journey to the US; lucky you. I will coordinate it so that you are already on his list when he arrives at the Isles, but you will have to remain out of sight until you get here. Your foster father, Victor (Big Daddy), has been taken by Walter and is on that copter right now. He can help you stay hidden. He has cancer, though. Poor guy. I could probably Splice him to make him better, but that's up to Dr. Damian.*

*Anyhoo, one final note, just so we are clear. I cannot help you. This is the extent of my assistance. However, I will never rat you out. I will do what I can to defend you. You've always been good to me, and I promised to return the favor. Just don't destroy my life's work too much, okay? Good luck, Mark Timothy Hodgins.*

*Sincerely,*

*Carl Mallory*

After reading the message a few times, I sat there trying to take it all in. I couldn't believe what I was doing. I couldn't believe that Big Daddy was taken by Walter. Frankly, I couldn't believe a lot of things.

"Huh, never thought you'd have the guts do to what I would've done," a low raspy voice said behind me.

Startled, I jumped and turned around to see Sonny standing in the doorway. "What?"

He snickered. "Like you don't know." He walked down the stairs and sat in a swivel chair next to me. He looked at me with his red eyes and stated, "I was going to do the same thing, but not for the same reason. I was going to do it to kill Patya, but you want to do it to kill yourself, am I right?"

My face paled. "How did you—"

"Please, I've been there and tried it. It's not going to work." The pale teen smirked. "Besides, you're tougher than you think. You won't give up so easily." He looked back at the door to make sure no one was listening. "I'm going to help you pull this off on one condition."

"What's that?"

A mischievous grin spread across his face. "Make Patya's life a living hell."

"Deal," I agreed without hesitation.

Sonny chuckled. "Good. Now, let's get to work." He jumped up from the chair and rubbed his calloused hands together. "First, you need to delete all the information about this mission from the systems so they can't follow you. I'll pack your bags." He ran off and left me to the computer.

*Thank God for Sonny,* I thought, shaking my head. If anyone was there for me from time to time it was him. He taught me to be tougher and would take my side in a fight. *I'll make sure Patya's life is worse than hell for him.*

While I was deleting the files, I thought I should inform my family about who saved me from PH back at the OX encampment. I hesitantly unlocked all the information I had on the man in the black hat (Dad, I believed).

As I finished, Sonny returned with a towel draped over his shoulder. He had a small box in one hand and a razor in the other. "Now, we have to get rid of your signature look."

I sat up straight in the chair as he put the towel around my neck. I closed my eyes, ready to lose the appearance I had for ten years. Turning the razor on with a vibrating buzz, he shaved my entire head. No more long hair on one side. It was all gone. I felt my hair as it brushed against the back of my neck, gently falling to the floor.

Sonny clicked off the razor and I rubbed my peach fuzz. After all those years… it felt so strange. My head was lighter and colder.

"Now to get rid of Fallout's visible presence," Sonny said, pointing to my ear. Hesitantly, I reached up and removed the three hoop earrings I had earned for my crimes. I gingerly rubbed them between my thumb and forefinger, taking one last look before they were away for good. At last, I placed them to rest in the little box in Sonny's pale hands.

"You're doing the right thing," Sonny told me, placing the lid atop. When he was cleaning up the mess, I turned off the computer monitor, my reflection appearing on the black screen. I was surprised to see myself. I looked…normal I guess. Unfortunately, I resembled my brother more. Not wanting to see that, I stood up and turned away.

Disposing of the evidence, Sonny said, "It's time for you to go. Everyone is asleep and Walter is scheduled to leave soon." He gave me a black hoodie to wear. "Your bags are out in the barn. There is a pistol in there just in case, but you will have to ditch it if they search you."

I took a deep breath and pulled the jacket on. "Man, this is ridiculous." I put my hands on my neck and tilted my head backwards. After a moment, I felt my chain. Unlatching it, I removed my dog tag; my one connection to my family. I looked tenderly at the Hodgins' signature *H* etched into the metal. I stared at it and was flooded with memories: from Fallout to that moment. Good and bad. I wanted to smile, but I would've made things worse for myself.

Shaking my head, I quickly said, "I think this should go in that box, too."

Sonny took my dog tag and gently tucked it away. "They'll be safe," he told me. He looked up and held out his hand. "Best of luck, Mark."

I shook it firmly. "Thanks, Sonny. For everything."

"You're welcome," he replied with a kind smile—a rare sight. "Just come back to us. You have to make it up to Rachel somehow."

I couldn't even bear to think about it. It pained me too much. "Yeah, sure," I replied, brushing it off. Saying nothing else, I pulled the dark hood over my head and rushed out the door.

I snuck through the base. I knew all the door codes so escaping was easy. If anyone saw me leaving, I figured they wouldn't care, but I shut down all the security cameras for a limited time just in case. I went about unseen until I was almost at the barn.

"Mark?" a female voice called from behind me. I stopped dead in my tracks and turned around to see Shannon. She was in her white pajamas and had her viola in her hand. "What are you doing?"

I cleared my throat and walked over to her, careful not to let my hood fall off. "Hey, beautiful. I needed some fresh air."

"Me too," she said, quietly. She looked at me, her blue eyes filled with concern. "You know, Shane really does care about you."

I didn't want to hear his name at that moment. "No, Shannon. He cares about you… like me." I sighed. "Look, Shane and I are different. Face it. We'll never see eye to eye."

"You're brothers," she reminded. "You think my sisters and I agree on everything?"

"I know, but this is different," I replied flatly. "We never started off on the right foot and it has only gotten worse." I looked up at her and stroked her freckled face. "But he doesn't mean that much to me."

This time, she pulled back. "Mark, I'm sorry," her voice cracked, "Please. I feel awful that I may have accidentally led you on all these years. I never had time to tell you…"

"I always knew he would end up getting you," I said coldly. "I've loved you from the beginning, and he has repeatedly hurt you. Yet, you still let him come back."

She took a deep breath. "We are *all* broken, Mark. Yet, we still pull ourselves together and stand back up. If one person can rise and stand for what's true, the rest will follow. I believe in second chances and forgiveness. I would do anything to let you see that."

"If you would do anything, care for me like I care for you," I asked desperately. "You're the only one who has seen me for who I am. You gave me a purpose in life and showed me I could be better. I am worthless and yet you showed me value." Without thinking, I grabbed her torso, pulled her close, and kissed her cheek and neck. She was too stunned to move. I put my lips to her ear and whispered, "Why can't you love me like you love Shane?"

She became flustered and shoved me away. She grabbed the Celtic key around her neck, which she always did when romance was mentioned. "H-how am I supposed to give my love to a man who doesn't love himself?" Backing away, she gripped her viola in her other hand and said, "I'll see you tomorrow, Mark." Then, she ran back to the base.

Frustrated, I began cursing and swearing to myself. That was the last time I might ever see Shannon and that was the note I left on. I knew it was coming, but never wanted to hear it.

She was right. I didn't love myself.

I needed to get out of there immediately. I ran to the barn, grabbed the bag, and headed to the vehicles. After hotwiring one, I slammed my foot on the gas and drove as fast as I could to the site, not daring to look back at the base.

I drove hard and fast until I reached my destination. Parking a safe distance away, I stealthily made my way to the spot.

I arrived just in time. I snuck along the rocky perimeter where the helicopters were and studied the movements of Walter and his men. They were busy counting the rescues and checking off the names on their lists. It wasn't long before I spotted a familiar face: Big Daddy. Warily, I made my way to where he was standing. As I got there, Walter began shouting at his men for them to round up everyone on board. The German went inside one and waited for the rest to file in behind.

I needed to get on the other somehow.

I tried to get Big Daddy's attention to see if he could distract them for me. It took me a few tries, but I eventually was able to hit him with a tiny rock. He subtly looked over and saw me in the bushes. Thankfully, he had a great poker face. I pointed to the copter and he immediately knew what I meant. He forced himself into a coughing frenzy and fell to his knees as they were shoving him up the ramp.

"Ugh, not again," a worker complained as he ran to help him. Not wanting the assistance, Big Daddy flung his head back and hit the prisoners behind him, causing a domino effect. During the confusion, I dashed onto the platform and pushed Big Daddy inside the helicopter labelled "Knight #2".

After placing him down, I sat on the bench in the corner. The others were still outside struggling and I heard Wally yelling to the men in the cockpit to get moving. The workers on the helicopter decided to leave a few of the rescued and their men behind. They pulled those on the ramp inside and sealed it shut while the others screamed to be let in.

In no time, we were all seated and airborne. One man came around to check us off his list, but was getting agitated because a few were missing. When he got to me, he couldn't match me up with the information he had. Not wanting to get in trouble, he checked me off as one of the men they had left behind.

I was in.

Looking over at Big Daddy, I smiled. He shook his head and mouthed, "*You shouldn't have come.*"

I shrugged and sat back in my seat. Frankly, I didn't know what to expect and I didn't care. All I knew was I was getting away from everything. Was I going to miss it? Maybe, but I figured they wouldn't miss me, so what was the point? Why have an anchor tied to your ankles when you're trying to stay afloat?

And so, that's *my* story. I think you Isle Members know the rest from there.

# CHAPTER 50
## Aymie: XVII

I'm still in shock at your side of the story, Mark…I can't believe *that's* how you really felt. I'm sorry I've been a terrible sister.

But let me tell you our side so you know we really do care. If you can't tell, Shane is a little emotional after hearing that so I'm going to take my turn first.

The next morning, I had no idea about my brothers' fight. I woke up before dawn, got dressed, and ran to the infirmary to visit our wounded. Inside the cold building, I checked on each individual. By the grace of God, they were all recovering. Slowly but surely.

Finishing my rounds, I walked to the end of the sterile hall and found Johanna fast asleep in a chair next to Rachel's bed. Her arms were crossed and her neck was in an unnatural position. Her golden hair was a mess, and she smelled of coffee that failed to do its job.

Tip-toeing, I made my way over and poked her shoulder. "Johanna," I whispered.

She shifted in her chair. I gently shook her and called again. Moaning, she popped an eye open and groaned, "Morning, Aymie."

"How long have you been here?" I asked, pulling up a seat next to her.

"Past few nights," she said, yawning. "Rachel is still a bit shaken up, so I'm here to calm her down. Shannon was going to come, but she had a rough day yesterday so I forced her to stay away."

"Why, what happened?"

She cocked her head to the side. "You didn't hear? Mark and Shane got into a huge fight. Mark basically told Shane how he was in love with Shannon and also how incompetent he feels compared to everyone else."

"Oh, geez," I replied, shaking my head. "I'm guessing that didn't go well."

"Nope," she rubbed her temples, wishing away her headache. "Mark said he was disgusted that they share the same last name and then spat in Shane's face. After that, Mark disappeared to his computers."

I sat for a moment, trying to take that all in. I was offended. "Is he disgusted…that I share the same last name?" I asked.

"Don't know, honestly," she replied. "He was just whining and being a big baby."

I couldn't help but chuckle. "For a psychologist you sure come to great conclusions."

She shrugged. "Eh, I try."

We sat there talking for about an hour when Nic came in with a plateful of food. "Oh, there you are, Aymie," the big guy greeted with a smile. "Blake was looking for you desperately."

"Oh, no did he have another dream again?" I asked as he sat down and handed Johanna and me the toast that was on his tray.

"No, he just wanted to see you. No dream, thank goodness. The last one he had was about that fight last week. Unfortunately, it came true, didn't it?" He looked at all our wounded friends.

I nodded. "He foresaw that we would lose many soldiers and that a Hollinger would get hurt. He also knew about the computer being the connection to the OX soldiers."

"Does anyone know what happened to the computer and why it exploded?" Johanna asked, tying her messy hair up into a bun.

"I thought Mark panicked and blew it up," I said.

Nic shook his head. "No, it wasn't him. That's what is so strange. We don't know what it was."

Before we could say anything more, there was an announcement from Director Wyght over the PA. His voice was harsh this morning. "Will all my Royals and Royal Veterans please report to my conference room ASAP."

The obnoxiously loud message woke up Rachel. She slowly propper herself up and started crying. "It hurts, it hurts," she moaned as she put her hand on the brace on her knee.

"It's okay, Rachel, it will get better," Johanna comforted as she stood up to leave.

"No! Don't go!" the girl cried.

Not having time to argue, Nic ran to the back of the infirmary and returned with a wheelchair. He gently placed her in it, careful to prop her feet up. I was about to protest, but her uncontrollable sobbing was enough to wake up the entire base. She spent a week in the infirmary, a few hours out would be okay. Pushing Rachel along, Nic led Johanna and I out into the bright day and across the fields. The warm sunshine was the medicine she needed to calm her down. After soaking in the golden rays, we went to the Director's conference room.

Everyone was around a long wooden table covered in the newspapers we collected from each city. Nic stood in the corner behind Rachel while Johanna and I went to our places.

After sitting down, my eyes scanned the papers in front of me. One particularly caught my attention. "*Mysterious Terrorist Strikes Again*" was the headline. I looked closely at the picture and saw a beautiful and happy family: the Alexuses. My eyes followed to the next image and saw the shop they were standing in front of had been burned down. *I pray they are okay*, I thought to myself.

My reading was interrupted by Director Wyght bursting through the doors. Everyone became silent and sat at attention. Marching to the head of the table, he shoved the standing map out of the way, revealing a large flat screen. He snatched the remote from Myles' hand and turned it on. Displayed was the desktop of his computer.

"Last night, all of our details about the mission to the Isles have been erased," he informed us. Anger reflected in his voice. He opened several secret, encrypted folders to find they were empty.

Gasps and murmurs fell from the lips of the Royals. Director tried opening the backup files on his hard drive. He came up dry.

"Also, our suspect left the base undetected," he went on. He gripped the remote so tightly his knuckles turned white. "Our security cameras were shut off for a certain period of time." He thought for a moment and then slammed his fist on the table, causing us to jump. "There is only one who could've done this!" he bellowed.

He didn't say the name, but we already knew who he was talking about. "Sir, are you saying?" I asked, shakily.

"Yes," he said abruptly. "Mark is gone and erased all information we had on the Isles and Nikita's men."

I couldn't believe my ears and neither could my brother. I watched as his face fell and he shook his head. "No, it couldn't have been him," he said in disbelief. "Why would he do something like that? He's going to get himself killed."

"Good riddance," Alexandrea said, biting her nails.

Frustrated, Shane jumped up from his seat and yelled in our brother's defense. "How dare you say that! Aymie and I are just as guilty for Roxanne's death. Stop holding a grudge against Mark."

Unfazed, she held her hands up. "I'm just saying what everyone was thinking."

"He's not going to die, McCracken," Sonny stated, leaning back in his chair. "He made me a promise." Everyone turned to look at him. "Yeah, I knew he was going. I helped him and told him to erase the files."

Director Wyght's eyes widened. "You…what?"

"You heard me," he replied flatly as he put his slick hair up into a ponytail. "He wanted to go on the mission; you said no. He was a better fit and would survive longer than Shane would. Also, I was going to try to take Shane's place, but Mark beat me to it."

"Why were you going to take my place?" Shane asked, sitting back down.

"You would've blown the whole mission," Sonny said flatly.

"With everything that's going on, we all forgot the little detail that Patya has *seen* your face." He pointed his pale finger. "He has only heard of Mark. Also, Mark can get us information from all the computers that Shane can't. He will let us know if there is absolutely any way that we could have Patya and Jarvis as allies. I doubt it though." He slumped back in his leather chair. He rolled up the sleeves of his jacket and crossed his arms, revealing his white scars. "As for me," he added, "I wanted to go just to kill Nikita."

"This is treason!" Director Wyght bellowed, stomping over to Sonny. "I gave an order; you and Mark disobeyed." He slammed his hand on the table and loomed over Sonny who wasn't fazed. "Not only that, you destroyed *everything* we had collected on Nikita and his connection to the Hodginses."

"Most of us remember that stuff anyway," Sonny reminded, staring up at our Director. "Mark left you guys some info in its place." He motioned with his hand to the file in the corner of the screen.

Director Wyght looked closely. He missed that file. Swiping the remote from Myles again, he selected it. In a flash, all of Mark's information on Marcellus appeared. He picked one and the screen went black. To anyone else, they would've thought it was a virus. To us, we knew it was important. A message in green writing appeared:

*To everyone:*

*At this point, I'm probably on my way around the globe in a helicopter by now. When I am on the Isles, I will do my best to send you all information that I obtain. I will be gone a while, which is for the best. I won't be around to screw things up anymore; you're welcome. Also, I wanted to tell Shane and Aymie that I believe that the man who blew up PH's computer was Marcellus. He is still out there. Find him for me.*

*Farewell,*

*Mark T. Hodgins*

I slumped back in my chair. I wrapped my long fingers around the cushy arm rests and squeezed tightly. I couldn't believe it. I didn't want to believe it. Mark was gone and he thought it was for the best.

He left without saying goodbye.

*He really hates us, doesn't he?* I thought bitterly, digging my nails into the clean leather.

"I'm sorry, I wish I'd known," I heard Shannon whisper. When the Director asked her what she meant, she took a deep breath. "I saw Mark last night when I was playing my viola outside. He came up to me…and seemed distressed." Tears burned in her eyes. "I should've stopped him… now he's gone."

"This isn't your fault," Sonny told her. He rested his forearms on the table. "Mark was determined to do this. Besides, we would've shipped Shane off in a few months anyway."

"That's different," Nic stated, rubbing little Rachel's head in front of him. "We would've done things the right way."

"So, Mark is gone?" Rachel said through tears. "He never said goodbye." She shook her head and sobbed. "He doesn't love us anymore!" She put her hands over her face and cried. She loved Mark just as much as we did. He was one of the little girl's best friends.

"I'm sure that's not true, Rachel," Myles said, going over to her. The child prodigy gave her a hug and said, "He is just lost. He will come back."

"He better," Director Wyght demanded. He took a deep breath and shook his head. "I just wish he hadn't left with such a sour taste in his mouth."

"He'll find himself, Stanley," Sonny told him. Reaching into his pocket, he pulled out a little white box and slid it across the table until it stopped by Shane and me. Shane removed the lid and took out the contents. In his hand he held three small silver hoop earrings and Mark's dog tag. Shane looked at the things and shook his head repeatedly. He couldn't believe it.

"If you want to know the truth," Sonny went on, "he really wanted to go on the mission with a hope of getting killed. He has too much pride and fear to do it himself."

*No…Mark, please no*, I thought, distressed. I looked at Sonny and saw the truth behind his eyes.

Mark wanted to kill himself.

That tore my heart in two. I couldn't hold back my tears anymore. I broke down. Embarrassed, I jumped up from my seat and ran out of the room. *It can't be true.* I made my way outside, still not believing it. I wasn't dressed for the cold weather, but I didn't care. I kept going until I skidded to a stop before the garages. I looked around and my eyes fell upon an empty parking spot. A quad was stolen.

Seeing it, I fell to the ground and sobbed. *He's gone, he's gone.*

"Aymie!" a voice called from behind me. I didn't look to see who it was until he was sitting on the frosted ground next to me. "Aymie, please," Blake said, grabbing my face with his hands.

I shook my head. "Mark's g-gone," I sobbed.

"Shh, he's going to be okay, I promise." He pulled my bald head to his chest and wrapped his arms around me. I loosened up and let him hold me. "I had another dream," he began to explain. His voice was cheerful and he smiled as he spoke. "I saw all of us on a ship. We were older and stronger. We were meeting with 17 kids. As we were introducing ourselves, Mark stepped out of a hiding spot in the corner of the room. He had matured and missed you just the same."

I clutched Blake harder and cried. "I hope this dream is real…" I begged.

Blake rubbed my head and sighed. "Unfortunately, my dreams have been, but this one is a good one."

I wiped my tears. "How frequent have your dreams become?" I asked, wanting to change the subject for a moment.

He looked at the ground. "Every time I close my eyes. I haven't told you all of them…I'm sorry."

"What are they about?"

"Mostly OX," he replied. "So far, every location I've dreamt of has been accurate. Director wants to start using my dreams as his main leads. We have no time to think about Mark's absence now. I'm so sorry. Our next mission is in 3 days. OX is going to attack a thriving city filled with civilians in France. We have to get there and stop it."

I couldn't believe what I was hearing. Once again, we had no time to care or to mourn. My brother went on a mission just to *kill* himself. I couldn't believe the Director's audacity.

I was about to protest when Blake put his pale hand under my chin and gently kissed my lips, shutting me up. After a moment, he pulled away and whispered, "I'm sorry, Princess. We made an oath; we have to keep fighting." He rubbed the sides of my face and looked at me. His gorgeous light blue eyes shone in the cold sunlight. "There are cities filled with people that are living as if nothing is wrong," he continued, seriously. "We have to wake them up and get them to fight back. These aren't accidents, this is a war. OX has grown powerful and has conquered almost every nation. We have to let Mark go for a time."

I took a deep breath. As much as I didn't like it, I had to.

I let my brother go.

After kissing me again, Blake stood up and pulled me to my feet. I looked into my boyfriend's eyes again and felt comforted. I fixed the gray beanie that covered his white hair and smiled. "Thanks for always being there for me, Blake."

"You know I always will be, Princess, but right now, I think you have to go be there for somebody else." He pointed to fields.

Understanding what he meant, I left to find my brother.

I spotted long legs dangling from a tall apple tree. I looked up and saw Shane sitting with his back against the trunk of the tree. I reached up and tugged on overall pant.

Surprised, he almost fell. His arms shot out to grab nearby branches. "Geez! Don't scare me like that."

I stood on my tip toes, grabbed a branch, and threw my legs over. I sat up and struggled to balance.

"Careful, Ayms," he said, grabbing my arm to steady me. "I spent years with the circus, I've had plenty of practice."

"I guess I have some training to do," I joked. Clearing my throat, I went on to the reason why I was there. "How are you doing with all this?"

Shane shook his head. I noticed he was clutching Mark's dog tag. "I feel so guilty. I feel like it's my fault. He thought I was so mean to him. He thought I was perfect and…" he paused for a minute. "He thought I stole the only girl who could ever love him."

"Are you serious?" I said in disbelief. "Was that why he was mostly upset?"

"Well… thinking about it more, I understand why he was upset." He twirled Mark's dog tag between his fingers. "Mark was convinced everyone hated him except for Shannon. I think… he was afraid."

"Afraid?"

"Afraid that," he paused, "Afraid that I would take Shannon away from him and that there would be no one left to accept him."

I sat in silence, pondering his words. *It makes sense now…* "Shannon was always there for him… when we weren't."

Looking downcast, Shane added, "Exactly. I feel so guilty, and so does Shannon. I hope she isn't blaming herself. She hasn't even looked at me today. I have a feeling whatever we had is over before it could even begin."

"Stop that," I said, slapping his leg. "That's the last thing you should be worried about. Shannon cares about you and Mark differently, Shane. Mark didn't get a chance to see that, but you do. Also, Mark was just getting all his feelings out during that fight. I'm sure he didn't mean half those things he said."

"It's annoying though," he admitted. He went over the fight in his head. "I feel like he forgot how *our* lives have been hard too. He forgot that every time I lived with a family, I would watch someone die or be seriously hurt. I always ran away…not to mention I'm afraid of water." He thought for a moment, shook his head, and threw his hands in the air. "Water! Who has *that* fear?"

"You can't help it," I reminded. I let out a deep breath. "I guess we are just going to have to accept that the three of us are very different, but we are still family and that's the truth." I grabbed Shane's hand that held Mark's dog tag. "We are Hodginses. Together we are going to fix this. We will stop OX and Nikita together. We made that promise years ago when we learned about dad. Now, we have to fulfill it."

He squeezed my hand and said, "Okay, sis. This time, we'll do it for real."

# THE MAINLAND

# Chapter 51
## Aymie: XVIII

Years passed after Mark left us. Occasionally, we would get brief transmissions from him, but nothing too great. In his absence, we continued to grow RRPR and save many lives.

Almost five years had gone by and we had over 3,000 members in different sections of the country with North Dakota as our home base. We were successful in every mission. God was good to us. Blake's dreams had continued to be frequent and gave us important information about OX.

He was our secret weapon.

We grew to rely on his dreams. At curfew, Director Wyght made sure that the entire base was silent so Blake could get his rest. He was treated better than any of the other members. He almost never saw battle and remained behind with Myles and Shannon in the control center. My boyfriend was one of the most important people of RRPR. Thanks to him, we were unstoppable.

OX was diminishing. We were winning.

However, one fateful day something unforeseen happened. When you have it good, you often forget it can be taken from you in an instant.

It was a quiet snowy April afternoon (yes, April) and I was waiting in the lounge for Shane. Like every day, we continued our research to find Marcellus, Shannon's brother, and Marian's sister Marlene. I sat on the couch with Mark's old laptop.

[Yes, Mark, I used your laptop. No, I didn't break anything! Of course I went through your files. No, I won't tell them what I found.]

I was working on a new lead we had on Marcellus. Shane came to join me, carrying a bag of chips. "Yo, sis," he said with his mouthful. "How are things looking today?"

Without taking my eyes off the screen, I replied, "Pretty good. That OX tail we were worried about is taken care of. They don't know we are looking for Marcellus."

Hopping on the couch, he swallowed his food and said, "Good. We really are making progress." He thought for a moment. "I wish we actually worked together when Mark was here…" he added solemnly.

"Shane, we've talked about this. We have to live with our regret, but it shouldn't stop us from pushing forward." I held up two fingers and poked him in the face. "Two Hodginses are better than one. OX won't know what hit them."

"Yeah, but what about Nikita?" he asked, his green eyes filled with sadness. "Frankly, he is the worst threat and Mark has been taking him on by himself. It's been almost a year since we've heard from him. What if something happened?"

"Nothing happened," I replied firmly. "Mark can hold his own. You have to stop worrying about him. He's almost twenty five, not fifteen. He spent the beginnings of his life on the streets of New York City, hiding from the entire world. He knows what he is doing."

He sighed and rolled up the bag of chips, the crumbs falling to his lap. "Yeah, yeah, okay." He leaned back and rubbed his hand through his thick brown hair. "How are the other searches going?"

"Shannon's brother is still a mystery," I replied with a sigh. "We need her help to continue looking. She has been so busy with missions that she hasn't had time to look."

"I know. Thankfully, they are back for a bit before their next one. I feel like I hadn't spent time with my girlfriend in months," Shane said, fiddling with his fingers. He cleared his throat and slunk back into insecurity and worry again. "Hey, if Mark comes back soon…you don't think he'd kill me because Shannon and I are…you know."

I couldn't help but laugh. "You've loved Shannon since you were fourteen and you are still worried about that?"

He shrugged. "Well, we've only been officially dating for two years. Besides, that's the reason why he left. I don't want him to feel betrayed."

Before I could argue, Mark's laptop made a beeping noise. My heart jumped. I entered the code that Mark gave us and a message appeared. A smile crept across my face. "Speaking of," I whispered.

Shane's jaw dropped. "Is it really him? What's it say?!"

After reading the message to myself, I began well up with tears. "He's alive. He's okay," I told him.

Shane was sitting on the edge of the seat. "Does this mean he can come home?"

I read on and sighed, the tears gone. Slumping back onto the couch, I replied, "No. He says he has no real proof. He doesn't want us to wreak havoc until we know 100% that Nik's intentions are just as bad or worse than…" I had to peer at the screen to make sure I read it correctly, " 'the Invaders'," I said finally. "Oh, OX. I guess that's what they call them."

"He really is one of the Isle members now," Shane said. "Picking up their lingo and everything."

"Sure has…and Shannon's too," I added, pointing to the message. "He used 'theories' about twelve times in this transmission." The computer beeped again. Opening the next message, I slowly read it. I had to go over it three times before I could grasp it. Finally understanding what it said, I clasped my hand over my mouth and gasped.

"What? What is it?" Shane asked, leaning over my shoulder.

"He thinks he found Marlene," I said, slowly.

Shane's eyes widened. He shook his head and laughed. "No… are you serious?"

I tapped a few things on the computer and opened up a

photograph Mark sent.

There she was, working in the fields. It was a close up and she posed dramatically as if it was used for an advertisement. She was a beautiful girl with light brown hair and pale skin. Her kind eyes were exactly the same as her big sister, Marian Best.

Shane patted his overall pockets until he found the watch. He clicked it and put it next to the screen. Looking back and forth a few times, he whispered, "It's her. It *has* to be her." He scoffed. "I can't believe it. How did he find her?"

I finished reading the message: "He said that his 'Keepers' are planning an annual Isle meeting with a sort of competition in mind. He hacked the computers to see what was going on. He saw her on the team of one of his friends, so he swapped her to be on his team. He says he isn't certain if it's her because he doesn't know their last names, but he will find out for us."

Shane's eyes began to well up with tears. "Dangit, Mark. Now I owe you a big one."

"I think you owe him a lot more than that," I teased. "So, one down, two to go."

Shane shook his head in disbelief. "This is crazy. I can't believe he found her."

"You better keep that watch intact until we can get it to her," I told him, poking his chest.

"Get what to who?" a boy's voice asked. Turning around, I saw Myles and Lucy entering the lounge. I still couldn't believe how they've grown. Myles the boy prodigy was now nineteen years old and the smartest man in RRPR…perhaps the world.

Lucy had grown into a remarkable young lady. Her long dark hair was in French braids and she wore her black combat uniform.  She was still such a brat to Myles, but he didn't mind. He loved having her around even though she always bullied him.

Jumping up, Shane greeted his best friend. "We found Marian's sister, Marlene," he said immediately without explaining.

"Wait, what?" Myles said, almost dropping the tablet in his hand.

"He found his ex-girlfriend's sister, dummy," Lucy retorted, slapping his back.

"First of all, I thought of Marian as a big sister. Never a girlfriend," Shane clarified.

"That's not what Rebecca said," Lucy replied, crossing her arms.

"Rebecca was just jealous because she had a crush on you," Myles said, laughing.

"N-no I didn't!" a girl cried. Rebecca pushed past Myles and Lucy and ran into Shane. Backing away, she blushed. "That's not true! Don't listen to them, Shane."

"You're too young anyway," Lucy said. "You just turned fourteen."

"Geez, that's how old you are now?" Shane said, crossing his strong arms. "To me, you're still two."

"Ugh! We're not little girls anymore, Shane," she protested. Waving her hand, she said, "I'm not going to argue. I came here with an important message."

"Dinner is ready?" Lucy asked.

"No!" she yelled. "Just let me speak!"

Before she could finish, the building rattled. Everyone paused. "Rebecca, what's going on," Shane asked firmly.

"They're here early…" she whispered. Fear filled her face.

Slowly, I closed Mark's laptop and stood up. "Who is here, Rebecca?"

She looked at me, her face paler than normal. "PH. He found us."

The computer almost slipped from my grasp. "What? How?"

"One of us must have slipped on the last mission," she said, looking over her shoulder.

"It wasn't me!" Lucy yelled, defensive. "It wasn't Myles either."

"Thanks, Lucy," Myles said, surprised.

"He's too afraid to go on missions so how could he have messed up?" she added.

"Thanks, Lucy…"

"Enough!" I shouted, startling them. I shoved Mark's laptop into its bag and said, "Let's go and prepare."

Rebecca shook her head. "You and Shane need to get out of

here."

Taken aback, Shane asked, "Wait, why?"

She took a deep breath and looked at us desperately. "PH is here for you two."

The building rattled again and an alarm blared. The shouts and footsteps of soldiers could be heard throughout the base.

Shannon spoke over the loud speaker: "Code Septum. All members need to wear full uniforms along with face masks. No real names; code names only. Speak minimally and listen carefully. This will not end well. Get to your posts except for the Hodginses and Bain. Grab your things and evacuate immediately. No questions asked."

"What?!" Shane bellowed as the message stopped.

"She said no questions!" Lucy yelled back.

"I am not letting her go into this fight by herself," Shane growled as he marched towards the door, but Lucy stepped in. "Lucy, get out of my way. I am going to see your sister," he growled.

"Sorry, Zippy. Not today," she replied, crossing her arms.

"I hate how *that's* being used for my code name," he mumbled. "Well, you have to move so we can evacuate." When she let down her guard, Shane threw her out of the way. She hit her back on the kitchenette counter while my brother ran down the hall.

"Shane, wait!" Myles called, chasing after him.

I couldn't believe what was happening. "Why is PH here for us? What did we do to him? Why is he here for Blake?"

"Well, the blondie with all the answers just left so you should go ask him," Lucy said, rubbing her back.

"Aymie," Rebecca had tears in her eyes, "you have to go."

I didn't like it, but I obeyed. I threw Mark's backpack over my shoulder and ran out of the room. I raced to my quarters and prepared to leave. As I pulled on my dark face mask, Blake burst through the doors. He was dressed and ready to go.

"There you are," he said, pulling the mask off his mouth. "Where's Shane?"

"He went after Shannon," I told him, grabbing my bags. "What's going on?"

"PH knows you and Shane are Marcellus' children," he explained. "He told OX and now you have a big price on your heads. Marcellus is wanted for treason after all. You are the next best thing."

"Now we have Nikita *and* OX after us because of our dad…" I mumbled.

"They know how amazing you three are, Princess," he said. "We aren't going to let them take that away from you."

I tried to smile, but I couldn't. It was impossible to comprehend. Thinking for a moment, I remembered. "Wait, you are supposed to evacuate too. How come?"

Blake put dark glasses over his light eyes. He tucked away any loose white hairs that were escaping from his mask. He was the easiest to recognize out of us all. "They know that I'm the one giving away their location. I don't know how, but they know it's me."

Before I could say another word, Alexandrea stopped short in my doorway. Her combat uniform was disheveled and her boots untied. "Get out of here, lovebirds!" she yelled through her mask. "You two and that irritating but attractive brother of yours are going to get us killed."

We followed her out of the base. Our mission was to get to the vehicles and escape before any real damage could occur. Unfortunately, that wasn't the case.

The moment we walked out of the door we were in danger. Heavy gunfire and yelling sounded from all directions. Enemy forces advanced and engaged those who met them on the perimeter. I heard the screams and cries of my friends. I kept my head down while Blake—who was following Alexandrea—led me by the hand.

We ducked behind a crate of weapons. "What do we do now?" Blake asked, raising his arms above his head to shield himself. "There's no way to get out safely."

"We don't even know where Shane is," I added, peeking around the corner of the box. I couldn't bear to look at the carnage. Bodies lay strewn across the snowy ground, staining the white with their blood. My friends were falling left and right. I watched as OX members mercilessly charged, firing all they had. Their faces were disfigured by their anger and rage. I didn't recognize them as human beings anymore.

PH had it out for us. He found our base and was planning to take the whole thing down.

Growling, Alexandrea grabbed her fireproof gloves and jumped up. "Get out of here, Aymie. Keep the Weapon safe," she said, referring to Blake. Pulling a pistol out of her holster, she screamed and jumped into the heat of the battle with our other friends.

I wanted to yell for her, but it was too late. She only made it a few feet. She was a Drone and never the best fighter. Within seconds, the OX members filled her with holes. I watched as the bullets shot through her uniform and out through the back. The blood stained the ground beneath her as she dropped to her knees. Despite the pain, she shot a few more times. With whatever strength she had left, she turned to us and mouthed to go. Then, her eyes rolled back and she collapsed.

Blake clasped his hand over my mouth to prevent me from screaming. I watched Roxanne go the same way and now Alexandrea followed in her footsteps.

Again, it was my fault.

Once more, we had no time to mourn. Blake grabbed my hand and pulled me away while the enemy was distracted with Alexandrea. We needed to get out of there. I kept my eyes closed and let him lead me. We dove behind crates, hid behind bodies, and did whatever we had to stay alive while our friends were falling left and right.

They were dying because of us… again.

Then, through the chaos and death, a familiar voice sang over a loud speaker. We were almost to the vehicles when we realized what the song was: Scarborough Fair. While he was singing, the OX members ceased their fire. They scurried back and hid. Seeing it as an opportunity, the RRPR members did their best to recoup.

The moment the voice started singing, I stopped dead in my tracks. My heart sank to my shoes and I couldn't breathe. Frozen with fear, I sat with my back against the metal garage. I mustered enough courage to peek and see why everyone stopped.

I saw PH with his sword in hand standing on top of a Challenger

II; a British tank with the OX symbol spray painted red on its side. PH had his green scarf over his mouth, but you could hear his singing as clear as day.

Behind his massive weapon, I saw a group creeping up on him. They were dressed in full uniform with masks covering their faces, but they had two members I could distinguish easily. The biggest, strongest one was Nic and the smallest was Shannon. She was wearing her metal mask to help her breathe and disguise her voice.

"We have to help them," Blake whispered.

"What are we going to do?" I asked with a panicked tone. I gripped the sides of the cold garage. "PH is almost done with his song."

Just then, I heard Nic growl. He got on all fours and dug his hands and feet into the ground. With a grunt, he leapt into the air and landed with an enormous amount of force on the tank, tilting it backwards.

PH's singing stopped abruptly. He lost his footing, rolling backwards off the machine and onto the ground below. Nic climbed on top, roared, and began slamming his fists into the metal beast.

The OX members below watched in awe and terror as he inhumanely beat the machine. Coming to their senses, the Xenophonians concentrated their fire at Nic. Struck multiple times, Nic stood up, roared, and jumped off the tank into the barricade of Xenophonians. Shannon and the other two went to help.

However, PH was to his feet and grabbed Shannon by the back of her shirt. With all his might he threw her towards the vehicles. She slammed into the side and collapsed to the ground.

Turning around, one of the soldiers saw her and shouted, "Detective!"

It was Shane.

Afraid for her life, he wanted to run to her, but the other member stopped him. Shane bickered with his companion in the middle of the field.

Taking advantage of the argument, PH charged the two of them with his sword ready. As he lunged, Shane leapt over the short

Xenophonian while the other dodged effortlessly.

"Mars! I am going to get Detective. Don't stop me," Shane yelled as he ran to Shannon.

Sonny (Mars) had no time to argue because PH was back to his feet and lunged for him. Sonny dodged and kicked PH in the side, knocking him to his knees.

Laughing, PH stood up straight, placed his sword in the sheath on his back, and put his hands on his hips. "Well, Mars. Good to see you're using that name again even though ya don't deserve it." He tugged his scarf down to hang around his neck. "You betrayed us all just like Marcellus. You, he, and his children must pay," he sneered. "Tell me which ones are the triplets and I'll let the rest of your soldiers go."

"Not a chance," Sonny growled as he dropped into a stance.

PH laughed. "Want a fight? Let's do it. I've missed sparring you, mate." Without warning, he threw a punch at Sonny blocked it with his forearm. Sonny returned the favor with a kick but PH was just as skilled. He jumped to the side and threw another attack. The two of them fought like I'd never seen before. Their attacks were so fast, I couldn't see what was happening. They were conversing as they sparred, but I couldn't understand them. They slipped into different languages. Greek, mostly.

While they were distracted, Blake grabbed my arm and dragged me to where Shane had taken Shannon for cover. They were hiding behind the nearest quad.

When we met up with them, Blake said, "Zippy, we have to go."

"No, REM," Shane said firmly as he rubbed Shannon's face. "I'm going to make PH pay first."

Shannon, who was sitting with her back to the vehicle, shook her head. "No, you're not," she panted in a deep, electronic voice that crackled with every consonant. Taking a deep breath, she added, "I am." Saying nothing else, she jumped up and ran out from behind the vehicle towards Sonny and PH.

"*NO!*" Shane screamed as he tried to chase after her, but Blake grabbed him.

"We have to go," he reminded as he gripped his arm.

While my boyfriend and brother were arguing, all I could do was watch. I felt so helpless.

Shannon ran towards PH while he was still fighting Sonny. She charged right into him, knocking him over. He slid across the snow and into the tank. Taken aback, Sonny stared at her and did nothing. While he was distracted, another Xenophonian picked a fight with him. He left Shannon alone with PH.

Struggling to his feet, PH shook the snow out of his curly brown hair and turned to look at Shannon. He studied her for a moment as if trying to figure out who she was. It was impossible to tell. She wore thick armor so no one could see her feminine figure. Her head and eyes were covered by a black mask and she wore the breathing machine over her mouth.

Wiping the blood off his freckled face, PH looked at her and spat, "You are goin' to pay for that, *Detective*."

"You are going to pay for a lot of things. That little girl you hurt especially," she retorted in the same electronic voice. She raised her guard and threw a punch at his face. He dodged it and threw one back. She blocked it and the fight ensued. The two fought for a while. They mostly used their hands to fight as if they were boxing.

Shannon put up a good fight until time was up. PH threw a left hook to her side and swept her legs, knocking her to the floor. Leaning over her as she struggled to breathe, he said, "Not bad, Detective. I hope to fight you again someday." He stood upright and took a few steps backwards, closer to the tank. Clearing his throat, he shouted some orders in Greek, causing his soldiers to retreat...no, take cover.

He was going to fire the tank.

We needed to get out of there. The shockwaves alone were dangerous enough. I watched as all the RRPR members scrambled about, trying to get somewhere safe. I turned to Blake and Shane to tell them, but they were gone.

I stood up and frantically looked around. I saw Blake prepping the vehicle. When it was started, he waved for me to join him. I looked over and saw Shane running towards PH and screaming. He wasn't thinking. He was going to get himself killed.

PH was about to sing the final verse of his song when he heard Shane coming. He turned, drew his sword, and aimed it towards Shane's chest. Shane didn't slow down. He clenched his fists and jumped, leaping right over. This time, he grabbed the sides of the tank and scrambled up.

PH tried to climb up after him, but was too short. Shane saw him struggling and took advantage. He grabbed PH by his curly hair and smashed the Titan's head into the tank, knocking him back to the ground. While Shane was enraged, he hadn't noticed that the turret—that was facing the base—had spun around quickly.

Shane turned too late. In seconds, the barrel of the tank smashed into my brother's back and sent him flying. He crashed to the ground a few feet from Shannon. Screaming in pain, he clutched his side and struggled to stand.

Now, I had to do something. I jumped up and Blake and I ran to help. Together we got Shane to his feet. He was staggering and about to pass out. Through his agony, he yelled, "Get Detective!" I let Blake drag him to the quad and I went to get Shannon.

She was still lying in the snow, struggling to breathe. I prayed she wasn't paralyzed again. Going over to her, I grabbed her under her arms and dragged her away. I needed to hurry. PH was getting to his feet.

I got Shannon to the vehicle and Blake helped me put her in the backseat with Shane who tended to her caringly despite his own injuries. Jumping into the front, I waited for Blake to get in and take off. Once he was in, he slammed his foot on the gas and we were on our way.

I turned back to watch the scene in the distance. PH was nowhere to be seen and the tank's turret faced the base once more. Then, it fired. I watched the bright explosion as the round shot out of the barrel and struck the front of our base, leaving a gaping hole. The glass of the nearby vehicles had shattered and the warehouses shook. I covered my ears as it fired high explosive rounds into our new home, reducing it to nothing. I watched it come crashing down, my friends dying with it.

# AYMIE: XVIII

I looked forward and didn't turn back again. I closed my eyes and prayed for mercy. I prayed that not everyone was gone. I prayed we weren't the only ones left. Unfortunately, my prayers were continuously interrupted by one haunting thought.

Once again, the Hodgins Family was responsible for the deaths of so many.

# Chapter 52
## Shane: XVIII

Okay, my turn to finish our tale off? Yes, yes, Aymie. I will do my best to keep it together.

After our base was destroyed, the four of us were on our own for two months. Blake drove hard and fast every day and didn't look back. We stopped through cities for breaks and supplies, but found no comfort in them. Every place we went to had been hit and destroyed by OX.

We were always too late.

Shannon figured that OX didn't just attack us to get my sister, Blake, and me. We all knew that they wanted RRPR dead. We thought they succeeded. In our absence, they destroyed many cities and killed and kidnapped more people than we would ever know.

It was the middle of June, and we still failed to contact to anyone. So, we did things our own way. Our plan was to get to an American military station in Tacoma, Washington. We wondered if it was actually abandoned like we were told. It was repeatedly said that the military forces of every major country in the world were destroyed. We never believed that.

It was about a week before Aymie, Mark, and my birthday and

we were still alone. The only good news was we finally made it to our destination. The beating sun was finally setting. We made camp in the ruined city of Tacoma. We planned to search for survivors, but were too exhausted on our first day.

My friends unpacked the vehicle and settled us into an old hotel. They brought everything into the ash covered lobby as I wobbled over to a tattered couch and sat down. I felt so useless because of my broken ribs. Aymie said that it would be another week or so to fully heal. It wouldn't have taken so long if I hadn't repeatedly fallen on top of them when we had to escape OX Hermes scouts.

Shannon came over with a roll of medical tape. At first, I refused her help, but she was as obstinate as I was. Carefully, I removed my shirt and let her wrap my bare, bruised, and cut torso.

"Stop being so stubborn," Shannon mumbled.

"I don't need it. I'm fine," I stated firmly. I hated her seeing me so weak. As she finished the final wrap, I grabbed her hand and asked, "How are you holding up?"

She didn't look me in the eye. Right after the incident, she was strong. She never shed a tear; always held it together. The other day… she snapped. At night, she would normally watch the stars with curiosity and admiration. Now, she'd run off and scream to the top of her lungs. She shouted the names of her sisters, Johanna, all our friends. She shouted at our Creator and begged Him to bring them back.

I didn't know how to help her. I wanted to show her affection and tell her that I was there, but she was in such distress that she didn't want it.

"Shannon, we found something," Blake called.

Saying nothing, Shannon pushed me away, stood up, and went over. I pulled on my shirt and joined them. "What is it?" I asked.

"An old military walkie-talkie," Shannon concluded. Her voice was hoarse from her screaming fit the previous night. She turned the device over in her hand. Looking closely, her eyes widened. "This hasn't been here very long."

"Is that good or bad?" Aymie asked, tying a piece of cloth over her bald head.

"Depends." Shannon cracked open the back of the walkie-talkie. "We don't know who it belongs to."

"Do you think it could be tracked?" Blake asked, yawning. As much as he loved to sleep, he hated what he saw at night so he forced himself to stay awake. His dreams continued to be precognitive and reveal the location of the next OX strike, but right now, he'd rather not know.

"It could be tracked, it could not," Shannon explained.

"Very helpful answer, Detective," I teased, trying to make her smile. It just made her mad.

"I don't know all the answers," she replied harshly. "I'm just making observations. Frankly, this could be our only shot." She put the walkie-talkie under her arm, grabbed her bag, and went to find a room for her and Aymie.

Sighing, I shoved my hands into my combat pants' pockets and went out of the hotel. I wanted to see if there were any abandoned food carts around. As I walked outside, I was disgusted at the sight of the city. It was in ruin and decomposing bodies littered every street.

I pulled a scarf out of my pocket and covered my nose and mouth. I wasn't hungry anymore. I didn't dare look at the horrified expressions left on the dead's faces. *OX and Nikita will pay for this.*

"Shane, wait!" Blake called from behind me. When he caught up, he put his hands on his knees and panted. "I am not as fast or have as long of a stride as you…cut me some slack." He shook his head. "Now I know how Shannon feels…"

I chuckled and pulled my scarf down. "Yeah, she has to run to keep up with me. You probably have to do the same."

"Yeah, pretty much." He tried to fix his messy, white hair. "I want to find something to cheer Aymie up. Want to do some looting?"

I laughed, slightly surprised. "Never thought you would be the type to ask that. You know we really shouldn't…"

"We'll leave them a note," he insisted, "that way it won't be stealing. With everything we've sacrificed for people, I don't think they'll mind if we took a thing or two. I'm hoping not anyway… We loot needs, why not wants?"

I thought about it for a moment and finally gave in. "Okay, fine. I needed to get something for Shannon anyway. But if the owners are there, we trade like we usually do."

Blake smiled and led me down the street to the remains of some large shops. We made a few stops before we came across a high class jewelry and clothing store. "Definitely this one," Blake said as he kicked the double glass doors in.

I turned on my flashlight and looked around. I whistled at the sight. "Man, this place must've been incredible."

"Definitely for the higher class," Blake observed. He picked a fur coat up off the ground. "I'm going to see if I can find Aymie a nice head wrap. She keeps getting insecure because her bandana falls off easily." He paused and his eyes stared into the distance. "She's so beautiful," he added as if in a trance, "I don't know why she should care."

"Unfortunately girls are crazy insecure," I told him, walking over decapitated mannequins. "I think that's a nice gift for her. I approve."

"Good. I always need your approval first, don't I?" he replied, smirking. "What are you going to find for Shannon?"

"I'm thinking of some nice jewelry or something," I told him. I kept the details to myself. "She isn't really the fancy type, but maybe if I find something up her alley."

"Sounds good to me. Something Celtic or Italian looking should do it," he joked. Saying nothing else, he went to the back of the massive store to find something for my sister.

Going over to the jewelry section, I looked in the cases. Someone had already raided them. The glass was cracked and almost everything was gone. Carefully, I removed the debris to find a few jewels left underneath. Nothing was what I wanted.

While I was searching the third case, I spotted something out of the corner of my eye. It wasn't a shiny jewel. It was two dark eyes peering out of a pile of clothing to my left. I looked closer to see if it was just another body.

The eyes blinked.

I jumped and whipped out my pistol. "Blake!" I shouted. "Someone's here."

I kept my attention locked on the eyes that looked back at me through the dusty clothing. They didn't move. When Blake rushed to my side, he pulled his gun out and aimed. The eyes turned to stare at the white haired one. They processed Blake for a moment. Then, the person began to move the clothing away, but was too weak. Carefully, I went to help them.

Underneath the clothing was a middle aged man dressed in a tattered suit and tie. His black skin was covered in cuts, and his hair was matted and caked in blood. His right arm looked dislocated and he appeared to be in a lot of pain. He looked up at me with such hatred. "Kill me," he spat through gritted teeth. You took everything from me, now take my life."

Kneeling down, I stared back at his face. "We are not Xenophonians. We are here to help you."

He didn't believe me and studied my figure. "You wear the same uniforms and were about to steal my jewelry."

"I was going to leave a note," I protested. Hesitantly, I touched the man's arm. "Does it hurt?"

He shook his head. "I lost feeling in it a week ago." His eyes darted from me to Blake and back again. "If you aren't Xenophon, who are you?"

"RRPR," Blake stated. "My name is Bain and this is S. Hodgins. We are so sorry about what happened…we got here too late."

The man scoffed. "You think? I'm the only one left on this block." He thought for a moment. "Well, you're here now and haven't killed me yet. Who am I to judge? You probably have troubles of your own."

"Yes, we do," I stated firmly. "Our entire base was destroyed, along with the rest of our team and whatever survivors we rescued."

The black man's face fell. "I'm sorry…please, don't be offended by what I say."

"You've been hiding here for over a week, we understand," Blake replied sympathetically. "Let us help you. We will take you back with us. Hopefully fix that arm of yours."

"Thank you, I appreciate it." The man placed his good hand on his chest. "Call me Prince."

"Nice to meet you, Prince," I said. I put my gun back in its holster and helped him to his feet. When he was steady, Blake wrapped the man's arm in a sling to keep it from moving before Aymie could look at it.

Prince hissed at the pain, but was able to compose himself. "Thank you," he said on an exhale.

"That's what we're here for," Blake said. "Now I know this probably isn't the most appropriate question to ask at this moment," he held up a pink head wrap he found for my sister, "How much for this?"

Prince laughed. "Keep it, Bain. Consider it me paying you back. Although, it seems a bit small for your head of white hair."

"For my girlfriend," Blake told him. "She has alopecia."

"Oh, sorry to hear that," Prince said, clicking his tongue. He turned to me. "I'm guessing you weren't taking that jewelry for yourself?" I shook my head. With a sigh, he jerked his chin towards the broken glass cases.

I was ecstatic. "Thank you, man. You have no idea how much this means to me."

"Don't mention it, but at least let me help you pick something out. It is my job after all." He wobbled over behind the counter. With his good hand, he fixed his suit and jokingly acted as if he was helping a customer of royalty. For a person on the brink of death, he sure knew how to keep up appearances. "Now, what do you have in mind, my good fellow?"

With a smile, I explained to him what I was thinking. After a few moments of moving the trashed cases, we found the perfect one. It looked Celtic and was expensive. "She's going to love this," Prince stated as he put it in a small velvet box.

Blake patted my back. "She sure will."

Taking the gift, I shoved it in my pocket and we led Prince back to the hotel. Thankfully, we found food in the abandoned shops nearby. It was stale, but better than nothing.

# SHANE: XVIII

It was dark when we returned and we found the girls sitting in the lobby with the walkie-talkie and Mark's laptop. They cleaned up a bit, clearing a path for us to walk without tripping and killing ourselves.

"You boys were gone a while," Aymie said, jumping up to greet us. She gave Blake a kiss and me a hug. When she pulled away, she saw Prince clutching his arm behind me. "Oh my goodness! Who is this?" she asked, surprised.

"This is Prince," Blake explained. "The one survivor we found today."

"Most likely the only survivor," Prince told her.

"Please, come in and let's clean you up." She took him by the good arm and led him to the couches where Shannon was working diligently. Blake and I went over and sat down on couches opposite each other. I reclined next to Shannon while Blake sat with Aymie and helped her bandage Prince.

Peeking over Shannon's shoulder, I tried to see what she was doing. She had the walkie-talkie hooked up to the computer. Her eyes locked on the screen. I held a stale piece of bread out to her. She didn't notice. I cleared my throat. "Shannon?"

It took her a few minutes, but she finally responded. "What?" She took her eye off the computer and finally noticed the bread in my hand. She sighed and graciously took it. "Thank you, Shane."

"You're welcome," I mumbled. After a few minutes of being ignored, I stood up and went to stand in the open doorway of the hotel. I wanted attention, she didn't give it to me, so I needed to get away. She didn't notice I left. I looked over my shoulder and saw her still hunched over, working away.

*Now I know how she felt when I never spent time with her at WHYP.* I thought back to the days where I would run around and hang with other girls. Leaning against the doorway, I closed my eyes and began to regret every moment I didn't spend with her when our lives were normal…well, semi-normal.

I stood there thinking for a while until I felt a tap on my arm. "Shane?"

I turned to see Shannon. Her blue eyes filled with sadness. Her freckled face covered in dirt. I rubbed my hand through her short, curly brown hair and said, "Hey, what's wrong?"

"It's more like what's wrong with you?" she asked. "Are you okay?"

"I don't know," I replied, honestly. "Everything that's happening has been hard to comprehend."

"You're lying," she replied, crossing her arms.

I rolled my eyes. "How can you tell?"

"You used the word 'comprehend'," she said with a smile.

"You caught me." I rubbed the back of my neck and confessed, "I've been worried about you, Shannon. All that happened…your sisters, our friends…everything. I hear you up at night, screaming and crying yet you don't come to me for help. Why?"

She bit her lip and looked away. "I'm sorry, Shane…I need to be strong. I can't let you see me like this."

I put my strong hands on her shoulders and looked into her eyes. "I am supposed to protect you. I'm supposed to be there for you, but you don't let me in." I shook her gently. "Please, Shannon. I care about you more than you'll ever know. Please, let me prove it to you." I stroked her face and tried to lean in and kiss her for the first time, but she pushed me away. My heart broke as she pressed her fragile fingers to my lips. In all those years, I never shared a real kiss with her.

She smiled and explained herself: "You don't need to show me that way. Don't be upset. I like to help you practice patience," she smirked. More seriously, she added, "You've sacrificed more for me than you'll ever know. That is proof enough." She reached behind her and unclasped her necklace. The Celtic knot key and eight silver hoops dangled from the leather cord as she held it up. The metal glistened bright in the moonlight. "I'm sorry I haven't been the best girlfriend. Now, it's my turn to make it up. This is a promise that I will be more trusting and do anything for you." She stood on her tiptoes and put the necklace around my neck.

When she pulled away, I grabbed the key and rubbed it between my thumb and forefinger. I wanted to ask why, but no words would come out.

Rubbing my cheek, she explained its meaning: "In the Hollinger family, a girl's key is meant for one person. It unlocks the keep safe box we hold so dear, but it means so much more," she looked into my eyes, "I kept myself pure for you and forever will I remain yours."

My face turned bright red and I couldn't believe what I was hearing. That was *way* better than a first kiss. I laughed softly until it became hearty. I grabbed the Celtic key necklace and rubbed it again. I couldn't believe myself, but I actually began crying. I was the happiest man in the world. Despite the destruction, sorrow, and horrible things around, she made my life. I wiped my tears away and snatched Shannon off the ground, pulling her close to me as her legs dangled. I buried my face in her shoulder and cried. I felt her wrap her arms around me.

I held her until Aymie yelled to us: "Shane, Shannon! We got a response."

I didn't want to let her go, but that was great news, too. Slowly, I put Shannon down. She looked up and giggled. "You sure are an emotional one," she teased as she wiped the tears off my face. Taking me by the hand, she led us back to where the others were. "What did they say?" she asked my sister.

A smile spread across Aymie's face. "There are WHYP members nearby."

"Wait, WHYP? Not RRPR?" Shannon asked, confused.

"Yes," Aymie said, "We have to hurry, though. Apparently another OX attack is coming."

"Can we trust this? What if it's a trap?" I asked, quickly packing our things.

"We have no choice," Blake told me. "We have to try." Obeying, we all got ready. We disposed of any evidence that we were in the hotel in case we were being followed. We loaded our weapons, grabbed our bags, and tiptoed out into the night. We formed a circle around Prince to protect him as we made our way down the dark, eerie streets.

I felt like we were being followed, but every time I turned to check there was nothing there. "We should go faster," I advised.

We picked up our pace. The transmission came from the location of Joint Base Lewis-McChord, so that's where we were headed. I gripped my pistol until my knuckles were white as we approached the huge complex.

The military grounds were enormous. People could be hiding anywhere. The beautiful brick buildings had been destroyed and trash littered the ground. Old aircrafts and military vehicles had been defiled and turned to scrap heaps. We walked for a while and still didn't find anything. We went to the air force section of the base and stood on the runway, looking around.

"This is a little suspicious," Prince whispered.

Blake looked at the remains of an airplane that failed to take off. "Maybe we misread it?"

"No, they have to be here," Shannon said in her electronic voice which startled Prince.

"Geez, girl. What was that?!" he exclaimed a bit too loudly.

She tapped her mask a few times and the voice copier returned to normal. "Sorry, this thing keeps malfunctioning. I use it to help me breathe and get into places that need voice recognition. Anyway, we couldn't have misread it. They have to be here."

Before we could say anything, the runway lights flashed on, blinding us. Shielding our eyes, we tried to recoup as fast as we could, but we heard footsteps closing in. My vision was still out of focus and I couldn't tell who they were. We four RRPR members dropped into stances and faced outwards, guns pointed and ready to fight.

"Whoa, hold your fire!" a familiar voice said.

When I regained my sight, I was able to make out the faces. I almost dropped my gun when I saw the two leaders. "Thyme? Nic?" I said with a gasp.

The two Royal Veteran Combatants smiled. "Yes, we are alive!" Nic exclaimed, raising his hairy arms into the air.

"But…we watched you get shot. Repeatedly," Shannon said, slowly taking off her mask.

He waved his big hand. "You often forget I'm not human. I'm a

Mutant."

"But, Thyme? How are you here?" Aymie asked.

Thyme smiled. He looked much older than we last saw him. His dark eyes were sharp and his black face started to wrinkle. "It's been almost ten years, I know," he said. "We are alive and still thriving. The WHYP mansion was destroyed, but we merged with an old friend of ours. She was one of the original Royal Veteran Umbrellas, Virginia Michaelson." He chuckled. "We thought she settled down to have a family after she left us. Turns out Mr. Wyght sent her on a mission across the country to build another home with the help of the American military."

"Our military isn't dead?" Blake marveled.

"Then where have they been?!" Prince exclaimed. "Our homes have been destroyed, people slaughtered and taken."

"The military follows the order of the government," Thyme reminded him, wagging his finger. "They have been restricted and basically fighting themselves. Thankfully, we have the good ones on our side. Remember, we are all human." He motioned for us to follow him.

We were led down the long, bright runway and up to the old museum. Once inside, Thyme brought us to a room with pale walls. It was filled with posters, wax figures, and war information.

"Wait here," Thyme instructed as he, Nic, and two other soldiers went to different exhibits. Thyme rubbed his hand over the poster before him. "Wars will end," he looked longingly at the faces of the marines, "truth will triumph, and deaths will be avenged. *Semper Fidelis*."

One of Thyme's men raised his hand above a wax air force soldier. "Aim high," he rested his hand on its hat, "that others may live."

"*Non sibi sed patriae*," a third spoke aloud as he rubbed his hand along a model of an old navy ship.

Nic lifted his hairy arm. "This we'll defend," he said finally as he patted the largest army mural.

When they finished, they all pressed a part of their exhibit simultaneously and we heard the sound of mechanical gears. In front of me, a large stone memorial of fallen soldiers shook and moved away, revealing a hidden staircase to somewhere below the museum. In silence, we followed Thyme, Nic, and the other soldiers down the many *many* flights of steps.

Finally, we reached the bottom. Exiting the stairway, we came out into what looked like a large concrete city. Construction lights dangled from the hundred foot high ceilings. Buildings that served as homes and shops stood erect before us. Hundreds of men and women scurried about their work, most of them dressed in black uniforms like our own.

We weren't alone.

Nic turned around and held his long arms outstretched. "Aymie, Blake, Shane, Shannon, and…you other person." He cleared his throat and exclaimed, "Welcome to our base and home for survivors.

"Welcome to the Underground."

# CHAPTER 53
## Shane: XIX

I can't believe we've come to the end of the story and just in time. We'll be at our destination in half an hour! Man, time flies when you're having fun. Okay, okay! I'll get on with it. Sheesh…

"No. Way," I said in disbelief as Nic led us through the Underground. I tried to take in the many sights at once. It was a hidden city. Pipes and wires ran along the cold concrete walls, leading to other sections of the Underground and the base above. We walked through an open plaza of the city.

We passed a working bronze fountain that marked the center of the circle of wooden huts and shops. They had everything. Food, clothing stores, entertainment shops, everything. Civilians and soldiers went about their day, not even noticing we were walking past. They lived as if life was normal.

"How big is this place?" I asked, taking a deep breath. The air wasn't the best and it smelled of dirt and must, but no one dared complain.

Thyme slung his rifle over his shoulder. "The entire base of JBLM housed more than 25,000 soldiers and civilian workers," he explained. "This is the same size."

"Does OX know about this place?" Aymie asked as little kids brushed past her while playing tag.

"Not yet, let's keep it that way," Thyme told her.

"But Nic, how did you get here? Who survived? Who is with you?" Shannon asked desperately.

Nic smiled and turned to her. "Patience, Shannon. You know that better than anyone." She crossed her arms and kept quiet.

Finally, we made it to the first tunnel at the back of the main plaza. An open roofed box car was waiting for us on the tracks. It was old, rusted, and wooden. No electricity ran to it.

Hopping aboard, I asked the obvious question: "So, how does it go?"

"You're lucky you have me here," Nic said, chuckling, "otherwise you would have to do it the hard way. We're working on fixing it though. This whole place needs upgrades." He hopped over the back rail of the cart to the platform where the pump lever was. "Might want to hang on tight." Taking his advice, we gripped the rail and braced ourselves. With Nic's Mutant Gorilla strength, it was a breeze for him. With one hand, he pumped the box car and we were on our way in no time.

As we zipped down the long tunnel, I tried to get a feel of our new home. There were many tracks branching off down different tunnels. Thankfully, there were signs above each so we wouldn't get lost. I tried to read them, but we were going too quick.

Nic forcefully pulled the brake and we screeched to a halt. Prince would've toppled overboard if Thyme hadn't grabbed him by the collar. We stopped next to a platform with a large, metal door in the center.

"Don't worry, we won't have to move by box car as much as the civilians," Nic informed. "RRPR is all in one place."

"Wait, so I have to travel like that all the time?" Prince objected. He pulled away from Thyme and motioned to his broken arm.

"Well, you could always join our team," Thyme suggested, going over to the door. He flicked open a security pad, entered the password, and scanned his retinas. The door rumbled and slid aside.

Behind it was a large open room with finished wooden floors. The walls were red and large oil paintings of *all* the Royal Veterans from WHYP hung on them. Some showed signs of damage and wear. Thyme and the others salvaged and restored as much as they could. I walked around and looked at the many familiar faces.

I reached the Agricola Branch. There were many paintings but I only cared about one: Marian. I looked up and saw her smiling face above me. Her light eyes looked out with such kindness.

*I found her Marian*, I thought to myself. *I will give Marlene back her past.* As I was staring, Shannon came over and tapped my arm. She looked up at me with compassion. She knew what was going on in my head.

"A few of these pictures will be moved soon," Thyme said aloud as we admired the paintings. "Unfortunately, most to the 'Hall of the Fallen'." We paused for a moment to remember all the deceased Royals and Royal Veterans.

"Don't worry, Shane, that's not where your picture is," Nic announced, trying to make the mood lighter. "The RRPR Royal Veteran paintings are on our main battleship."

"We have a battleship?" Blake said, amazed.

"Like one that goes on water?" I asked. "Do we have to ride on it while it's in the water? Do you have to go into the water to get to it?"

"We sure do have a battle ship," Nic said with a grin. "It's incredible. We have more than five. Yes, Shane you need to swim two miles to get to it," he added sarcastically, "and then when you are on it, it is in the water." He chuckled. "You'll be fine. You don't need to get wet. Anyway, we are going to need them when we go get Mark."

I froze and stopped thinking about the horrors of H2O. "Wait, what did you say?"

"Oh yeah, forgot to mention," Nic replied, rubbing his reddish Mohawk. "Mark sent out a message this morning saying that things are heating up and he has proof that Nikita needs to be destroyed. He should send out the next message after your guys' birthday."

I couldn't believe my ears…frankly, no one could. "Mark can come home?!" Aymie exclaimed, trying to contain her excitement.

"That's what we need to talk about," Thyme told her. He motioned to the door to his right, which opened as if waiting for his cue. Coming through were many familiar faces. I couldn't believe it. So many survived.

Shannon was the happiest of all. Tears streamed down her face as she counted all six of her sisters who lined up in a row. A few had casts and the youngest—eleven-year-old Rachel—was still in her leg brace from her injury 5 years ago. Johanna was alive too as was Sonny and Myles. They were unharmed, but Sonny's hair was shorter now and uneven as if PH slashed his ponytail off with his sword. Finally, the last to come out of the room were the original surviving Royal Veterans from WHYP, Director Wyght, and Papa E.

Shannon ran up to her sisters and embraced them. She sobbed and kissed their heads individually. When she pulled away, I went over to hug them. Before I could do anything, Rebecca tackled me, then Agnes, then Carol-Ann… then Rachel…then Peggy…then Lucy… Despite their broken bones, they still managed to try and break mine as I was crushed beneath the six teenage girls. It didn't help my broken ribs, but I sucked it up for them.

"Serves you right for leaving and scaring us like that," Johanna joked as she leaned over me. She saw Shannon's Celtic necklace flopping around my neck as I tried to get up from the dog pile. She pointed to it and tried to speak, but nothing came out. Her mind seemed blown, and she turned to her best friend for answers. With tears in her eyes, Shannon smiled and said she would explain later.

Calming down, Shannon finally said, "I don't understand. There was no chance of survival in that battle…how did you escape?"

"You should have more trust, Shannon," Johanna said, punching her in the arm. "You must have not observed Joshua Wolfrum in the sea of OX soldiers."

"He helped you all escape?" Blake asked.

"Not on his own," Director Wyght said, coming out of the crowd. "He kept PH distracted and sabotaged his weapons. It was his Royal Veteran Umbrella predecessor who got the rest of us out." He waved his hand and motioned for an individual to step forward.

Emerging from the crowd was a beautiful middle aged woman with smooth pale skin. Her golden hair was pulled back into a French braid and she wore a white t-shirt and black combat pants that were held up by a blue utility belt. Her brown eyes were soft and kind. "Welcome, Blake, Aymie, Shane, and Shannon. We have been expecting you." Her voice was melodic and sweet. "My name is Virginia Michaelson; one of the first Royal Veteran Umbrellas. I am glad you received our transmission."

"We're happy you sent it," Blake said. "We would've been wandering around Tacoma for days."

"Frankly, I'm happy it took a few hours to reach you." She looked at Prince. "I am so sorry we missed you in our searches. We could've sworn we found everyone."

"Wait, it was you who came into the city the second time?" Prince asked, amazed.

She nodded. "All those you saw taken away are now safe. Some only resisted because they were afraid, but we never brought anyone against their will."

"I appreciate that, ma'am," Prince said.

"Is that who this guy is?" Director Wyght asked, pointing to our new friend.

"Yes, we saved him when we were searching a store," Blake explained.

The Director nodded approvingly. "I'm glad you went window shopping then. Now, let's go over our plan for when Mark sends us the next message." The RRPR members followed the Director and Virginia through a few hallways and into the conference room, leaving the original WHYP Royal Veterans with Shannon's sisters and Prince.

Now, I am not going to tell you all about the plan, because we just lived through that. Isn't it weird to think that what I'm telling you right now happened at the *exact* same time you were getting Mark out of custody? Crazy, right?!

Okay, so before I close the story with us coming to your rescue, I'll talk about what happened when Mark sent out his final unexpected message…the message that only *one* person was supposed to respond to.

Believe it or not, it was Aymie, Mark, and my birthday when the transmission was received: June 23rd. We had all turned twenty-five, but it meant that another year had passed without Mark. This time, we knew he would be our late present.

For me, it was the greatest birthday of my life.

Despite the upcoming battle between us and Sonny's horrid "father" Nikita, my friends were still able to throw my sister and me a nice party. It was the evening after all the battle preparations had been made and our ships were set. Now, we waited for Mark's command. Apparently, the ships could make it there in less than a day. Despite their size, they moved fast; one of the great technological advances of Powell Enterprises.

That night, our friends surprised us with cake, gifts, and decorations in the Underground's officer dining hall. It resembled the one at WHYP. Going in, we were greeted by our closest friends. They kept the party exclusive to Royals to avoid having to ration dessert to hundreds of soldiers.

We sat down around the wooden tables and talked for hours. We told everyone about our two month long journey without them, and they shared with us how Virginia and her group saved them.

"They had to destroy our entire base," Nic told us solemnly. "Everything was lost…including many lives. Unfortunately, it was a necessary sacrifice. If PH got his hands on our information, we would all be dead."

Myles nodded and wiped cake off his soft face. "PH escaped, but Joshua Wolfrum has a good handle on him. PH seems to trust him a great deal. We'll see what happens. He is going to start communicating with us more frequently." He turned to my girlfriend and pointed his fork towards her. "I hope you still don't mind writing him letters."

"Like love letters?" Carol-Ann teased, not noticing Agnes stealing her dessert from under her nose.

Shannon rolled her eyes. "That wasn't even clever, Carol-Ann. And no, I don't mind at all."

"Good," the blond teen responded. "If it gets to be too much, we can have someone write letters back to him with you. Now," he pushed his plate away and stood up. "I think it's time for gifts."

"What could you have possibly gotten us?" Aymie asked as she held Carol-Ann back from slapping Agnes for stealing her cake.

"Nothing too spectacular, but we hope you like it," Myles said with a grin. He went to grab Aymie's gift. It wasn't wrapped, but it didn't need to be. It was a large, beautiful wooden frame with a picture collage that Blake had put together. Carefully, Myles brought it over and handed it to my sister.

Looking it over, Aymie began to tear up. She gingerly rubbed her fingers over the glass and experienced nostalgia. She looked at all our younger faces and remembered the good times we had at WHYP. Right in the center was a picture of Aymie, Mark, and I after we performed for an outside gig with our old band, *Left Lane Only*. We looked so happy. She stroked Mark's face and began crying. Her tears dripped onto the frame like gentle rain against a window.

"We'll see him soon," I whispered as I wrapped my arm around her. "We'll be a family again."

She sniffled and nodded. With puffy eyes, she looked up and thanked everyone. "I can't even tell you how much I love this. I will treasure it forever."

"Glad you like it," Myles exclaimed. "It was Blake's idea. Oh, and he got you this lovely thing too!" He happily gave my sister a little bag.

She took out the pink head wrap Blake got from Prince's place. She giggled, slipped it on, and tied the knot at the base of her neck. "Thank you, Blake. Thank you everyone."

"You're welcome, but we're not done yet," Myles said with a grin. Walking back over, he went to get my gift. "Now this one isn't new, but I think it's just as good." Slowly, he lifted up something I knew all too well: my guitar. I was amazed. My sticker covered instrument looked just as it did before RRPR was destroyed.

"Dude, how did you?!" I exclaimed as I jumped up.

He held out my guitar and said, "The moment I heard PH was coming, this was the first thing I grabbed."

I gently took the instrument from my friend. Putting the strap over my shoulder, I wrapped my fingers around its neck and began to pluck the strings. Still in tune. I couldn't help but smile as I played one of our band's—*Left Lane Only*'s—original songs. It meant the world to have it back… the happy memories of my life with Chuck and Monika and the Regal Circus played like a movie over in my head.

"Thank you so much, Myles," I beamed, finishing the melody. "I can't believe you did that for me."

He looked at me with his blue eyes and smiled. "I gave it to you the first day we met when you brought me back to my parents at the fair. It holds many memories." I gave my best friend a hug and sat down to play and sing.

"I missed you singing so much!" Rebecca squealed after I did a few solo songs.

"I could listen to your crooner-like voice all day," Carol-Ann added. She put her elbows on the table and rested her chin on her fists. Her eyes were lost as if she was in a trance.

"Let's not let it get to his head again," Shannon said, laughing. "Although, I do agree." I always loved it when she complimented me. Seeing her smile made my heart pound. Not to mention I was extra nervous that night…

"Oh, and there is one more gift," Myles said, interrupting. He jumped up from his seat one last time and ran to the head of the table. He pulled out a handkerchief cushioning a gift inside. With a smirk, Myles slowly peeled it away, revealing two pieces of wood that were all too familiar to my sister and me: Mark's favorite drumsticks.

Seeing the pair, Aymie and I couldn't help but get emotional thinking of all the great times we shared together, playing as siblings.

"We're going to bring these to the battleship for Mark," Myles said quietly. "Maybe you can all play for us again."

"Most definitely," Aymie said. Her fingers danced along an imaginary piano.

"We'll get a piano again someday," Blake said, wrapping his arm around her. "Shannon, were they able to save your viola?"

"Yeah, I was able to pack some of my stuff into the trucks before

PH attacked." She patted the backpack she had next to her. "They have my viola, my keep safe box, and my notes on my brother and parents."

"Awesome, we're all set," Nic said, standing up. "Now, unfortunately I think we have to bring this party to a close. We plan to depart for the Isles tomorrow morning so we can take our time getting there."

"I'd rather get there and kill Nikita now," Sonny grumbled as he stood up.

Carol-Ann latched onto his arm. She missed hanging around him. "Can we come too?" she asked, looking up at him with her blue eyes.

"Sorry, but it's too dangerous for you girls," Sonny said, rubbing her reddish-blonde hair. "You and your other sisters will stay here."

"But, I want to see Mark," Rachel cried, struggling to get up with her brace.

"Look what happened last time you disobeyed," the second oldest—Peggy—reminded. "We can be Mark's welcoming party."

"Well, what are we waiting for!" Agnes yelled. "Let's go decorate the hall!" With that, she ran off with Carol-Ann and Rachel hobbled not too far behind.

"Please make sure they don't break anything," Shannon told Peggy and Lucy.

"Shouldn't they make sure Lucy doesn't break anything?" Myles joked. Lucy pretended to throw a punch at him, causing him to flinch. She and Peggy laughed and went to watch their sisters.

After everything was cleaned up, we said our goodnights and headed towards the bedrooms. I slung my guitar over my shoulder and ran to catch Shannon, which wasn't hard. She had a short stride. "Hey, Shannon," I quietly called. I wanted to spend time with her before curfew.

Turning around, she saw me and smiled. "Hi, birthday boy. What're you doing?"

"Do you want to take a walk with me?" I fiddled with the key around my neck. "I heard there is a secret way to get to the surface."

"I thought you'd never ask," she replied, gripping the straps of her backpack. I quietly led her out the Hall of Royals and to the open tunnel that led back to the main plaza.

Rather than taking the box car, we walked along the train tracks until we came across an old rusted door that supposedly led to an ordinary maintenance room. However, behind the old shelves of supplies was a secret door to the surface. It was well protected and could only be accessed by a Royal Veteran with the highest clearance, which I had. I granted us access and the shelves moved aside, revealing an old service elevator that we rode to the surface.

We stepped out into the cool summer night. The stars were shining, and the wind blew gently against our faces. Together, we walked hand in hand. We went along the paths of the base and made our way up to the top of a high hill, silently looking out at the valleys below.

We watched the stars and the moon. This time, Shannon observed out of admiration. She wasn't screaming at the sky. She was at peace. Her blue eyes sparkled in the light of the heavens. Her curly brown hair blew in the wind, wrapping her bangs around her freckled cheeks.

After staring at her for a few moments, I brought my attention back to the view. The sight was breathtaking…but it reminded me of the day I lost my Uncle Chuck and Aunt Monika to Gerrior and Masdit. The day I developed Aquaphobia. The day my life changed.

Shannon could tell something was going through my head. "Are you okay?"

"This place…" I slowly began, "It reminds me of when I was six. When… you know."

She took my hand. "We don't have to stay up here. I don't want you to be upset."

"No, no, it's fine," I told her. "In fact, despite how horrible it was, I couldn't be more grateful." I slipped my guitar off my back and leaned it against a tree. I grabbed both her hands and looked into her eyes. "If it wasn't for those horrible events, I would have never been brought to you and your family. Without you, I probably would be a lost soul right now. You gave me a Faith, a purpose, and you brought me to my family. You saved all of us and do whatever you can to help us without asking anything in return." I took a shaky breath. "Despite all my mistakes and faults, you've always managed to forgive me ever since we met. That day you and your sisters tied me to a chair when I was thirteen and you were eleven."

She giggled. "That was a great day," she said with a sigh. "We had so much fun dragging you in and trying to wrap those ropes around you."

"I can imagine," I said, smiling. "I'm so happy you tied me up that day. The moment I saw you…I didn't know what to think. I felt something, but never knew what it was. Now, I do." I stroked the freckles on her face. "You gave me everything Shannon. Your time, your talents," I tapped the key around my neck, "yourself." Trembling, I put my hands behind my neck, took off my dog tag, and slid it over her head. "Now it's my turn."

She looked down and rubbed the "*H*" etched in the silver. Smiling, she looked up at me and whispered, "Shane, I don't know what to say."

What was in her eyes was like something I'd never seen before. My heart pounded even harder and my hands were clammy. "You don't have to say anything, yet," I told her, talking a step back. I shakily reached into my pocket and pulled out the velvet box that I had gotten from Prince back in the city. Bending down on one knee, I slowly opened it and presented it to her, saying the words that would change our lives forever:

"Shannon Hollinger, will you marry me?"

She gasped and clasped her hand over her mouth. She teared up and couldn't believe it. Inside the little box was a beautiful diamond ring with a Celtic band. She looked at it and back at me. She lost it.

Sobbing, she was able to make out one word: "Yes."

My heart raced as she dropped down to the floor to meet me eye level. "Yes, yes, yes," she repeated, wiping the unending tears from her face. She flung her arms around my neck and cried.

I'm not going to lie, I cried too as I held her. After a long while, she pulled away. Taking her hand, I slipped the ring on her thin finger. She admired the ring and tried to compliment it, but no words would come out.

Finally, I pulled her to her feet and put my fingers between hers. I stared into her beautiful eyes. I could only think of one thing to say: "Shannon, I love you."

Sniffling, she nodded and said, "I love you too, Shane."

Hearing those words for the first time from her made my heart almost pop out of my chest…like it did every time I was with her. Not knowing how to make it stop, I wrapped my arms around her thighs and lifted her up so her head was slightly above mine.

She put one arm around my neck and the other above my heart as she did the first time she kissed my cheek. Feeling the humping in my chest, she laughed and said, "Your heart races almost as fast as you can run."

"It races only after you, my dear" I told her.

She giggled. "That was so cheesy."

"Well, I tried," I whispered. With one hand, I touched her face and pulled it to mine. Closing my eyes, I sweetly pressed my lips to hers.

Finally, we shared our first true kiss in the starlight.

[Okay, okay, stop screaming, girls! Yes, Shannon and I are engaged. I have to admit, Alison, it was very romantic. Yes, Sami, we are very excited. Yes, Yared, I told you I cried… No, I'm not a baby, Lucas. You'll understand someday.

[Thank you, Mark. Having your approval and blessing means everything… You know you're going to be my best man, right? Of course! No, Myles doesn't mind.

[Okay, okay, I'll get on with it, Shannon. I know we only have a few minutes left before we get there; she wants me to finish up. Really she just wants me to tell you how she left me a few hours after we got engaged…]

Shannon and I sat on that hill for hours. I played my guitar and we sang together. I didn't want that night to end. Unfortunately, our happy night ended on a sour note.

Johanna came barreling up the hill yelling, "Shannon! Shane! Where the heck are you?!"

"Up here, Johanna!" Shannon called. "Don't yell so loud!"

"Don't be a hypocrite, then!" Johanna replied sarcastically as she reached the top of the hill. With her hands on her knees, she panted and looked up at us. "I hope I'm not interrupting anything important."

"No, the important stuff is over." Shannon wiggled her decorated finger.

It took Johanna a second to understand, but when she did, she started freaking out and screaming, making more noise than before. She hopped up and down and hugged Shannon. Through her yelling and crying I could make out her saying, "Finally! That only took forever! Gosh, Shane. For the fastest runner out there you sure are slow."

"Hey, hey, we've all been busy," I replied in defense. "Besides, I don't see you giving your heart key necklace to Nic anytime soon."

She steadied her breathing and calmed down. "Oh shut up," she said, waving her hand. She gave the two of us a hug. "Oh goodness, I can't believe it!" She pulled away and turned to Shannon, "Did you give him your box yet?"

"When we get back inside I will," she said, elbowing me. "You'll get to see my horrid handwriting from over the years. I won't tell you anymore until you see for yourself."

"Yes, because I have good news and bad news," Johanna interrupted, sounding more serious. "Let's get back and let Director tell you."

We hastily made our way down the cliff, back to the service elevator, and to the conference room. We found everyone sitting at their designated spots at the table.

Once we were settled, Director Wyght explained, "Good news is, Mark contacted us."

"Okay, but what's the bad news?" Aymie asked, slightly worried.

"Mark contacted us," he repeated. "He says he needs help. Our ships are ready, but he doesn't want us to cause a scene yet. Someone needs to leave early tomorrow by jet to do a solo mission."

"I'll do it," I volunteered immediately. "Anything to get my brother back."

The Director shook his head. "Sorry, Shane. Your broken

ribs aren't fully healed. If you take another blow before absolutely necessary, they might never be the same."

"I'm completely fine," I told him. "It's been two months."

"Yeah, but you have too much pride and didn't rest," Sonny retorted. "Aymie and Blake told us you took more hits when you tried to escape OX scouts."

"We need you well, Shane," the Director added. "I'm sorry."

I was disappointed, but understood. I was just worried about who would try and take my place. Unfortunately, it was the last person I wanted to volunteer.

"Let me go instead," Shannon insisted. "Myles and I have gone over all the information that Mark sent us about the Isles. I know the place the best."

"Absolutely not," the Director commanded. "Your knowledge is far too valuable, not to mention you have the dormant poison in your lungs."

"That's why I have my mask," she protested.

"That doesn't matter!" the Director snapped. "You and Shane will remain here and that is final."

"He's right, Shannon," Sonny said softly. "Nikita is ruthless. If you are caught, he'll kill you. I don't think that's how you want to spend the night of your engagement." He smiled and pointed to the ring on her finger. All the Royals gasped.

The moment it clicked in Aymie's brain she began squealing. "I'm going to have a sister!" She jumped up, ran over to Shannon, and hugged her. Even though Shannon was disappointed with the Director's decision, she was still happy and embraced Aymie.

"Now I *really* won't let you two leave," Director Wyght said with a smile. "I am sending Myles. He knows the Isles like Shannon. Plus Nikita has never met him so he won't be recognized. This will be his first official mission."

Myles pumped his fist into the air, but I protested. "Sir, you can't be serious."

Offended, Myles gave me a dirty look. "I'm nineteen now, Shane," he objected. "I can handle myself."

"Yeah, against everything but Lucy," Nic joked.

"She is probably tougher than Nikita though," Sonny replied.

"Enough!" the Director hollered. "My decision is final. Myles, go prepare. Everyone else get to bed." As he was leaving, he turned back and looked at Shannon and me. "Congrats, you two. I'm happy you finally got the guts to ask her, Shane." He winked and went out of the room.

"Seriously? Does everyone think I was afraid?" I asked, frustrated. One by one, they all agreed with the Director.

"Sorry, Shane, he's right," Nic said, patting me on the back. "We're all happy for you guys though."

"Thank you, we're happy too," I said. I wrapped my arm around my fiancé who seemed lost in thought.

"Well, I'm heading to bed," Myles announced. "Big mission tomorrow morning! See you all at the Isles." With that, he left. Slowly, people began to disperse, leaving Shannon and me there alone.

"You okay, Shannon?" I asked once Johanna left.

She sighed. "Mostly just disappointed about the mission, but let's not talk about that. I really am the happiest I've ever been," she grabbed her backpack off the floor. Unzipping it, she pulled out a small wooden box with a lock. "I think it's time for me to give this to you."

My eyes lit up as I looked at the little box. I reached for it, but she pulled it away. "Nope! I have one more thing to put in it," she told me, holding out her hand. I took the necklace off and placed it on her smooth palm. "Close your eyes. You can't see it while I'm here." I obeyed and put my hands on my face. I heard the box open, her scribbling something, and the light crinkle of paper.

Once I heard the box shut, I opened my eyes. "Can I look inside, now?"

She shook her head. "Nope. Wait until tomorrow morning. You'll need the whole day to go through it all."

I stroked her face and chuckled. "Well, I've waited this long. I have the box now." I leaned towards her and tried to kiss her lips, but she pushed me away.

With a smile, she explained before I could get upset. "I told you,

I like to make you practice patience. I also like to tease you."

"Ugh, fine," I told her. "But once we are married, I am kissing you whenever I want."

She laughed and pressed her nose against mine. I felt her breath on my face and was tempted to steal a kiss. She really loved to tease me. "Deal," she whispered with a smirk. Standing up, she put the key back around my neck and handed me the box. She patted my face and said, "Good night, Shane. I love you."

Those were my favorite words. "Love you too; see you in the morning." With that, we both went to our own rooms, and I got ready for bed.

Lying down, I wasn't sure I'd be able to sleep. I was so excited because I finally was going to spend forever with the girl of my dreams. Also, my brother was finally coming back.

Yet, I had a nervous feeling on top of it all. I was worried that my best friend was going on a dangerous mission for the first time. Despite all these thoughts, I was able to slip into a deep sleep.

The next morning, I woke up early and got dressed in my black combat uniform. I wanted to see Myles off before he left. As I was grabbing my jacket off my desk chair, I saw Shannon's box sitting neatly on the table. Curious, I decided to just see what was inside, not planning on going through it yet. Taking off my necklace, I unlocked it and lifted the lid.

Inside was not what I was expecting.

On the very top of a pile of letters was Shannon's engagement ring. Shakily, I pulled it out along with a note. I slowly read the simple message: *See you at the Isles.*

I dropped the ring back into the box, busted through my door, and rushed down the hall. "Stanley! Stanley!" I called the whole way down. I searched the entire RRPR wing of the Underground. I couldn't find them. I made my way to the surface where the jets were and found all the Royals and the Director.

"Stanley!" I yelled.

"Shane! Where is Shannon?" he bellowed.

Skidding to a stop in front of him, I panted and said, "She's at the

Isles."

He gritted his teeth and spat, "That little…" He clenched his fists. "One of our pilots dropped someone off last night, but they won't say who. She disobeyed a direct order."

"We have to go help her!" I cried. "What if she gets caught like Sonny said?"

"Don't worry, we are leaving right now," the Director said, trying to calm me down. "Go get your things. This plane is going to take us to the battle ships. We leave the moment we board."

I rushed back into the Underground, grabbed my bag, and raced back to the top. In no time, the Director, we seven Royals, and over a thousand soldiers boarded the planes to get to the battle ships. Finally, we were airborne and on our way to help Shannon and Mark. We had no idea what to expect but that didn't matter. Whether it was life or death, joy or pain, we didn't care.

We left the Mainland with one purpose: to save our friends and destroy the evil of the Isles.

# EPILOGUE
## Mark: XVII

And you know the rest from there. Shannon came to us on the Forbidden Island; RRPR came and blew up Mr. Bamber's private plane; we were taken to their ships; and so forth.

So, that's our story! From the beginning of our lives until now. Wow, we just told you guys twenty-five years' worth of stories in two weeks. It only took that long because of stops, layovers, and whatever.

I can't believe how much I missed, Shane and Aymie. I'm glad we were able to talk about all this. Frankly, I think this helped the three of us as well. Not to mention our new Isle friends now know the "tale for another time".

I hope you are all satisfied with knowing our past and the origins of RRPR. I also pray you still trust me. I know that my beginning was troublesome, but look where I am now. You all helped me get there. For that, I thank you.

Whoa, look at this, guys. We are here. I'm so excited to see this place and everyone again. I keep imagining how everyone's changed. It's crazy just to see how you guys have grown, Shane.

Geez, Nic, easy on the brakes! Are you okay, Donnie? You went flying there.

Watch your step getting out of the truck. I said watch your step, Aaron. I didn't say fall on your face. Lucas, Axel, stop laughing.

Wow, this base is incredible. I've never seen anything like it. Despite the rubble and destruction, this place still is amazing. The grass isn't greener over here, but it will have to do. The Order of Xenophon still doesn't know anything? Good. Let's keep it that way.

So, what do you guys plan to do with our stories? I know they are written down now. Keep them with yours? Sounds good to me.

What's that, Shannon? You want to send all of them to Joshua Wolfrum? The Alexus' stories from the Isles too? That's cool with me, how about you guys? It's a go, Shannon. Send them away. Who is going to help you write the letters?

Whoa, Yared, really? You want to write *letters*? Hey, I didn't mean it as an insult, I'm just wondering. I didn't think cold-hearted Seers did that sort of thing. Relax; it was a joke, man. All right, Shannon, looks like Yared is your pen-pal partner.

Man, the walk to this museum took forever. You want me to say one of the passwords, Shane? I'd be honored.

"This we'll defend."

That was incredibly complicated. I'm not saying that's a bad thing! Okay, fine, I'll shut up and go down the stairs. Geez, there are a lot of stairs.

Finally, at the bottom. Wow…I don't even know what to say. This place…it's amazing. I could stand here and admire it all day, but we have work to do.

Aaron, have you been recording me this whole time? Was it still writing on paper? Well, I guess you could call that the epilogue to our story…I hope when we look back on it we don't find it boring because it just seems like me talking to myself. Okay, I'll give it a dramatic ending. Maybe that will make it better.

*Ahem*, well, without further ado. Alison, Sami, Aaron, Axel, Lucas, Yared, Ethan, and Donnie. I, Mark Timothy Hodgins, would personally like to welcome you to RRPR's official base and civilian safe haven.

Welcome, my Isle members, to the Underground.

# THE END OF BOOK 2 OF
# *THE TERRA TESTIMONIES*

# DON'T MISS

## BOOK 3

# THE UNDERGROUND

# Mr. Popularity's
## List of Friends

Geez, guys, do we really have to call this that? You all need to learn to grow up and let this go. Yeah, yeah, I'm sorry.

Oh, this is Shane by the way (if you couldn't tell).

Anyway, this section of our testimonies is meant to help you if you forget who someone is. We only have descriptions for the nine main Royals the Isle Members first met. However, there is a list of some other people you've encountered in our long tale.

The Royals are separated by Branch. Their ages are not stated but rather how old they are in relation to the triplets. So if you want to know the specific number you will have to do some math. Sorry about that.

The rest are in alphabetical order (except for the Hollinger girls). Remember, not everyone you heard about will be in here. Shannon said something about them being "unnecessary", "spoilers", or whatever. So if you're annoyed that you can't find someone don't blame me.

# THE ISLES
## ROYALS OF RRPR

## COMBATANTS

**CO-DIRECTOR AND ROYAL VETERAN**: Nicolas Gabriel Eerkens

A brawny, hairy man with violet eyes and a red Mohawk. With Gorilla DNA rushing through his veins, he is the strongest and bravest of all the Combatants. Even though he loses his temper, he only wants to protect others. *CODENAME: Kong*

**ROYAL STRATEGIST**: Shannon Veronica Hollinger

The oldest of the seven Hollinger girls. She has curly brown hair, blue eyes, and freckles on her pale face. She is a remarkable detective and a hard fighter. Don't let her short height fool you. *CODENAME: Detective*

**ROYAL FIGHTER**: Sonny Louis Wilcox (aka Erik Patya)

The adopted son of Nikita Patya and an OX traitor. He's an ex-assassin with a reserved and bitter nature, but he can enjoy himself when he feels like it. He has red eyes and long slick black hair that's usually tied back. The scars on his arms are reminders why he needs to get revenge on Patya and OX. They must pay for the pain they inflicted upon him. *CODENAME: Mars*

## POLYMATHS

**ROYAL VETERAN**: Aymie Margaret Hodgins

A tall, slender young woman with striking gray eyes. Her alopecia doesn't take away from her beautiful persona and caring heart. She is a skilled seamstress, has a photographic memory, and is a classical pianist. *CODENAME: Princess*

# LIST OF FRIENDS
## DRONES

**ROYAL VETERAN:** Myles Powell Junior

Myles is six years younger than the triplets but the smartest individual in all of RRPR. This blond, blue-eyed prodigy is the heir to Powell Enterprises. Anything he thinks of, he can build. He loves his best friend, Shane, and will do anything for his colleagues. *CODENAME: Einstein*

## NERDS

**ROYAL VETERAN:** Mark Timothy Hodgins

The greatest hacker and thief in the world. (He's also a pretty good drummer). He is tall and lanky with blue eyes and long brown hair shaved to one side. The three earrings on his right ear are reminders of his beginnings with Fallout in Brooklyn, NY. He means well but feels like everyone has something against him. *CODENAME: Bandit*

## AGRICOLA

**ROYAL VETERAN:** Shane Thomas Hodgins

The fastest human alive and a skilled acrobat. He is tall, strong, and handsome. He has perfect thick brown hair and green eyes. His crooner singing and guitar skills also get him a lot of attention (which he loves). Even though he's full of himself, he still cares for his family and friends and would sacrifice anything for them. *CODENAME: Zippy*

# THE ISLES
## UMBRELLAS

<u>ROYAL VETERAN</u>: Johanna Cecelia Watterson

RRPR's Psychologist and Shannon's best friend. She works with Papa E in counseling and takes care of the little Hollinger girls. She is tall and has green eyes and long, thick, golden hair. She has a quick witted, sarcastic nature and loves to have fun. *CODENAME: Doc*

<u>THE WEAPON</u>: Blake Aleksander Bain

Aymie's childhood best friend and photographer at WHYP/RRPR. He has short, soft white hair and bright blue eyes because of his rare condition of Waardenburg Syndrome. God granted him the gift of having precognitive dreams. He sees events before they happen. He has a timid nature but will stand up in the face of danger. *CODENAME: REM*

## HOLLINGER GIRLS

### NAME - YEARS YOUNGER THAN THE TRIPLETS

Shannon – Two years
Margaret (Peggy) – Six years
Lucy – Seven years
Carol-Ann – Ten years
Rebecca – Eleven years
Agnes – Twelve years
Rachel – Thirteen years

# LIST OF FRIENDS
## <u>EVERYONE ELSE</u>

Alexandrea McCracken – *A Drone and one of Aymie's friends*

Best, Marian – *Royal Veteran Agricola of WHYP*

Big Daddy (Victor) – *Mark's foster father and the leader of Fallout*

Brand – *Mark's partner from Fallout*

Clive Foxwood – *A Nerd and one of Mark's friends*

Couch, Mason – *Big Daddy's right hand man and a powerful drug lord and cook. Creator of Couch's Concoction*

Derek Rocks – *A Nerd and one of Mark's friends*

Dylan Cheatle – *An Umbrella and one of Aymie's friends. Works in the kitchen with Blake*

Flicks, Gregory – *Royal Veteran Drone of WHYP*

Janelle Arends – *Aymie's best friend from the orphanage*

Jordan – *Mutant Slow loris and Mark's friend from Fallout*

Myles Powell Senior – *Co Founder of WHYP and owner of Powell Enterprises*

Papa E (Father Edgar) – *Chaplain of WHYP*

Roxanne Pontiff – *A Combatant and one of Aymie's friends*

Stanley Wyght – *Founder/Director of WHYP and RRPR*

Theo – *Mutant Shrew and Mark's friend from Fallout*

Thyme, Justin – *Royal Veteran Combatant of WHYP*

Vandewater, Guy – *Royal Veteran Nerd of WHYP*

Wolfrum, Joshua – *Royal Umbrella of WHYP and man on the inside*

Zander Grath – *A Combatant and one of Aymie's friends (he's obsessed with her)*

Zarra, Adeline – *Royal Veteran Polymath of WHYP*

# ABOUT THE AUTHOR

## Sara Francis

Ever since she could remember, Sara Francis was always a story teller. At first, she told them through music as a song writer. In her early teenage years, Sara Francis felt called to tell stories through work as a writer and media communicator for an online magazine. From there, everything fell into place.

Now, Sara Francis has a BS in Media Communications, is the author of several books, and is a speaker. Throughout it all, there is always a story she is trying to convey. Whether she tells them through her writings, art, or music, her stories always have a deep, truth filled meaning behind them. Every word she writes, everything she designs, every song she performs means something more and connects with the world we live in today. Through her work, she hopes to inspire people and encourage them to seek what is true.

Sara Francis is determined to light a torch in the darkness with the desire that people will do the same and make the world bright again.

# THE ISLES

# MORE INFORMATION

- » Visit Sara Francis' site for her other books, updates, services, study guides, and more: **www.sara-francis.com**
- » Want to read more? Visit Sara Francis' blog for writing advice, author interviews, and short stories of the characters in The Terra Testimonies: **www.sara-francis.com/blog**
- » Follow Sara Francis on social media:
    - » Facebook:@sarafrancisauthor
    - » Twitter: @sfrancis_author
    - » Instagram: @sarafrancis_author
    - » Visit the author's site to subscribe to her YouTube channel!
- » Any questions or would like to book Sara Francis for an event or workshop? Contact us at **info@sara-francis.com**

***Author Request:*** If you enjoyed the book, please be sure to tell your friends, share on social media, or leave a review on Amazon, Lulu, Goodreads, or any book review site!